Mask of vengeance

Timothy O'Brien

Brighton Publishing LLC
435 N. Harris Drive
Mesa, AZ 85203

Mask of Vengeance

Timothy O'Brien

Brighton Publishing LLC
435 N. Harris Drive
Mesa, AZ 85203
www.BrightonPublishing.com

Printed in the United States of America

ISBN 13: 978-1-62183-332-1

ISBN 10: 1-621833-321

First Edition

Cover design: Tom Rodriguez

Dedication

Dedicated to James Gilson

A good friend who left us way too soon

and will always be missed.

To David Tobin,

Though you may not remember me, I was your student back in 1999. I had learned quite a bit and that knowledge led me down the road to becoming an author. I would like to thank you for giving me the tools I needed to accomplish my dreams and achieve this novel. So thank you, thank you very much.

Your former student,

Timothy O'Brien

Prologue

November rain falls hard on Benton City, New Jersey. The time is close to midnight.

Vincent Angelo Scorpione sits silently in his favorite red leather chair in his living room. A fire crackles in the fireplace before him. He is surrounded by furnishings of Italian vine-embossed leather couches, fine Persian rugs laid across polished hardwood floors, and many original paintings by both classic and modern artists displayed on the walls. Four-foot tall mahogany wood paneling leads up to maroon Victorian-style wallpaper. The fireplace is of black marble, the mouth of which is four feet tall and four feet wide. A crystal glass of thirty-year-old Scotch rests in Vincent's hand as he calmly watches the rain pour down the outside of his wide plate-glass window, warping the view of the outside world in long, flowing streams.

In the public eye, Vincent is an all-around nice guy: charitable, friendly, lovable. He owns a large and successful distribution company, attends church every Sunday, makes regular donations to several well-known charities, and even supports the local youth outreach programs.

But beneath what you see, past the smiling face, the laughter, and the impeccable credentials, lies something much darker: Vincent Scorpione is also a crime lord. His company is a front for gun trafficking and the dealing of illegal narcotics of all types. His connections to youth outreach programs keep him in contact with the local gangs, creating buyers for his products. The few hundred thousand dollars in pocket change he tosses toward charities preserves his positive public image.

Cruel and remorseless, Vincent has killed many in his sixty-five years.

However, he will soon pay for his wrongdoing. Not through the court system, where his dirty lawyers can move for dismissal any incriminating evidence because of improper handling at the crime scene. Nor at the hands of a cop with an inflated and distorted sense of justice who is willing to go above the law. Tonight, Vincent's punishment will come from a most unexpected source.

Resting on the rooftop of the mansion next door lies an assassin watching from the shadows through a pair of binoculars. For the past few days she's been observing Vincent, carefully noting where he's likely to be and when. She has found that he's very predictable: you could practically set the time by his routine.

The tarp propped up around her keeps her dry and able to concentrate on her task. She notices her breath billowing in tiny clouds as the temperature outside continues to drop. She sets down the binoculars and rubs her hands for warmth. The thin gloves she's wearing hardly keep away the cold.

Beside her is a Dragunov SVD sniper rifle equipped with a heat vision scope. She's been waiting patiently for quite some time. Even though Vincent has been home for over an hour now, she won't shoot just yet. He's sitting in such a way that only his right side is visible through the living room window. She waits for the prime shot: the heart.

The clock above Vincent's fireplace strikes 11:45 p.m., its chimes echoing throughout the room. Apparently finally ready for bed, Vincent slowly gets up from his chair and finishes what's left of his drink. He walks over to the window to take one last look into the night.

Checking through her binoculars again, she thinks, *There it is—the perfect shot!*

She takes up her rifle and props the gun barrel on a wooden block for stability. As she takes aim through the infrared scope, she notes that his body heat is obscured by the cold rain running down the window. She reaches into the pouch hanging from her waist and pulls out a remote detonator device. Knowing that the glass would interfere with the bullet's trajectory and that the weather would affect visibility, she placed tiny charges on the window before Vincent came home.

She flips the switch on the remote and hits the button, exploding the glass into tiny shards. As Vincent stumbles back in shock, she lines up the crosshairs over his heart. Her finger wraps around the trigger. She takes a deep breath and holds it in.

Time slows in the precious few seconds that follow. The rain comes to a halt and the wind stills. Exhaling, she pulls the trigger, and the rifle discharges the round from its shell. The bullet spins through the air, crashing through crystal orbs of water along its path, until it finally pierces the heart of its target.

With a gasp, Vincent clutches his chest. A cold weakness spreads through his body, and he collapses to the floor. A brief moment passes, and the life finally disappears from his eyes.

"I finally got you, bastard." She laughs aloud in a strange warped voice. Then, smoking rifle in hand, she pulls the tarp aside and stands up. The thick storm clouds clear away, and a full moon shines down, finally driving away the shadows and exposing her it's bright light. She wears a dark gray bodysuit that emphasizes every curve of her figure. A white Japanese kitsune fox mask covers her face. Her ponytail of brown hair is tied by a long red ribbon that flutters in the wind. Two brown eyes are all that can be seen through the eye openings in the mask. She wears black gloves and tactical boots that appear grooved and textured in a unique dragon scale style. Numerous pouches hang from her belt.

She places the rifle in a leather carrying bag, zips it up, and secures the strap across her chest and over her shoulder. Then she sprints off into the night, jumping from rooftop to rooftop until she disappears into the distance. Never once does she realize she was being watched.

Across the street, gazing through binoculars from his bedroom window stands a seventeen-year-old boy named Patrick O'Hara. He feels terror run through him as he holds the magnified lenses to his eyes, his vision fixed on the spot where the assassin disappeared from his sight. Once the shock wears off, he comes back to his senses and dials 9-1-1.

Minutes later, five police cars, two fire trucks, and an ambulance pull up at the Scorpione estate. An hour later, crime scene tape stretches across the entrance, and at any moment the boy expects to see his neighbor's body, covered by a black bag, wheeled out on a stretcher, just like on TV.

Patrick gives his statement to the local police as his parents stand by him. The officer thanks him for the information and the initial call and asks him to stick around for the detective, who might need to ask him a few more questions.

Shivering in the cold, Patrick sees again the image of the assassin. That sleek female form garbed in black and gray almost shimmering in the silver light of the moon. That sight stayed with him, and it made him feel nervous. He wonders whether the assassin noticed him. And if so, would she come back for him?

Chapter One

A shiny black Ford Crown Victoria pulled up to the curb in front of the Scorpione house. Inside the car was Detective James "Jimmy" Ziminski. In the army, Jimmy's comrades had nicknamed him "Jimmy Zims." That was over twenty years ago, during the Gulf War. Now he was a homicide detective for the Benton City Police Department. Benton City born and bred, Jimmy knew this town like a cleric knows whiskey: every nook and cranny, every dark shadow the general public never saw.

An open tan overcoat covered his charcoal suit, which was pressed without a wrinkle. He wore a crisp white shirt with the top button undone. A spotless red tie hung loosely from the collar. His black leather shoes were polished to perfection. On his left wrist, a silver wristwatch showed the time: 12:30 a.m. on the dot.

Jimmy took a second to look at the mansion through his passenger-side window. *The Scorpiones,* he thought with certain uneasiness. Jimmy didn't particularly like getting this assignment, as they may have been responsible for the loss of someone close to him—an allegation he still struggled to prove.

Letting out a sigh as he thought of that person, he ran his fingers through his short, blond hair, slightly graying on the sides. He reached into his overcoat and took out a photograph of himself and his ex-partner Tommy. Both men were smiling, and Jimmy was resting his arm on Tommy's shoulder as they stood in front of the Crown Victoria. The picture commemorated the day they'd both been promoted to Homicide. That was four years ago.

Just over a year ago now, Tommy had been recruited for an undercover job. His experience in Spec Ops in the army had made him a prime candidate. The job itself was classified, and Tommy couldn't give any details to Jimmy or even to his own family. Two months later, he'd been found dead.

Tommy had become Jimmy's best friend. More than that, he was like a brother. The department had tried to assign other partners after Tommy's death, but none of them had worked out. It was only with Tommy that Jimmy had shared a special rapport. After a while Jimmy had decided it was better to just work on his own.

Jimmy slid the photo back into his pocket and put on his game face. He was all alone now and couldn't afford to show any chinks in his armor. His fellow cops could sense uneasiness like a pack of hungry wolves sniffing out fresh meat. In the world of law enforcement, a good rep meant everything. One big screw-up and it was an automatic demotion. The hell if Jimmy was going to let that happen.

He got out of the car and walked over to one of the officers standing by. "Wilkins." Jimmy looked over the scene. "What've we got?"

"Detective. We have one eyewitness named Patrick O'Hara. A teenager who lives across the street."

"Is that him over there?" Jimmy motioned to the wavy-haired boy standing next to the ambulance.

Wilkins nodded. "And those are his parents behind him. Michael and Andrea O'Hara. I told them to stick around in case you needed to ask more questions."

"Okay, anything else?"

"Yes, the plate glass window of the living room was shattered and the local residents reported hearing a loud explosion. Vincent Scorpione was found dead on the floor by the fireplace with one entry wound in his chest. One gunshot was reported, just after the explosion."

That was a long shot, Jimmy thought. He surveyed the size of the property. *A sniper rifle? We could be dealing with a pro here.* "That's it?"

"That's all we have for now, sir. Forensics is still going over the living room."

Jimmy looked at the boy again. "Don't let him go anywhere. Tell him I'll be there in a minute. I'm just gonna have a look around first."

"You got it."

Jimmy crossed the large front courtyard and went around the side of the house to look at the shattered living room window. As he put on a pair of latex gloves, he noticed several things: Most of the glass lay inside the living room, pulverized to tiny shards, suggesting that multiple explosives had likely been placed on the outside of the window. Since the window molding had been destroyed as well, the explosives had probably been positioned evenly along the edges of the glass. Plate glass was pretty tough. Someone didn't want the window interfering with the bullet's path.

Forensic specialists were taking pictures of Vincent's body and dusting the furniture for prints. Jimmy walked up the wooden ramp placed there by the other officers and through

Would plate glass shatter into tiny shards?

the large opening where the window used to be. Once inside, Jimmy crossed the room and stood over the body. He narrowed his eyes in contempt as he stared at the former crime boss.

Vincent Scorpione, Jimmy said to himself, *I can't say I'm sorry to see you dead. I'm sure a lot of people feel the same way.* The entry wound was through the chest, just like Wilkins had said. Vincent had fallen directly away from the window, meaning he must have been looking outside when it happened.

Jimmy looked toward the back wall opposite the window and walked closer. There in the hardwood floor at the foot of the wall was a small oval-shaped hole. It looked fresh and, judging by the size of the hole, was made by a typical sniper round. Jimmy gave a shout and waved over one of the forensics team.

"Johnson, someone needs to extract this bullet and tell me what the caliber is."

"No problem, detective. I'll get someone right on it."

As Johnson walked away, Jimmy went to the window. Vincent was about 5'9", and the height of the bullet wound in his chest would be about four and half feet from the floor. The bullet's trajectory seemed to have been angled downward. His eyes focused on the neighboring house. Jimmy took out his radio and keyed the mic. "Ziminski calling Officer Wilkins, come in."

A second later Wilkins's voice came over the radio. "This is Wilkins—go ahead."

"Ask one of the firemen if they can grab a twenty-foot ladder and meet me at the mansion facing the broken window. Let the residents know our investigation may have to extend onto their property. Their cooperation would be appreciated."

Minutes later, Jimmy was on the roof next door holding a flashlight. He found a green tarp, a wooden block, and a basic metal tent framework. That area of the roof had almost no angle to it at all. The wooden block was lying close to the roof's edge, and the tarp and framework looked as if they'd been flung to the side. The assassin must have been lying down right there, keeping dry from the rain. He noticed a notch in the block, indicating that the killer must have kept his aim steady by resting the rifle barrel along the indentation in the wood. With that kind of setup, he could have been lying here for hours.

The light of the flashlight lit up a shiny object in front of the wood block. Kneeling down for a closer look, Jimmy saw that it was a shell casing. The assassin had left the shell behind. A pro would have been tidier than this. Maybe they were dealing with an amateur.

Then he saw something else catching the light a few feet away. At first glance, it looked like a syringe without a needle. He picked it up to take a closer look. He had seen this sort of thing in the military. It was a cartridge for an injector gun, similar to the type the army used for immunizations. He turned it around and saw a small group of numbers, probably a serial number.

Jimmy keyed his radio again. "Ziminski to Wilkins, come in."

"Go ahead."

"Found more evidence on the neighbor's roof. South side facing the living room. You can add this location to the forensic team's to-do list."

"Roger that."

It was time to talk to the witness. Jimmy climbed down from the roof, crossed the front yard, and found Pat waiting patiently with his parents. Despite wearing jackets, they all looked cold. After all, they'd been standing around in the midnight air for a while. After Jimmy got the parents' permission to question Patrick, he turned to the boy. "Don't worry Patrick, this will only take a minute." He pulled out a note pad and pen as he began. "All right, how old are you?"

"Um, seventeen, sir," Pat said shakily.

Noticing the teen's edginess, Jimmy took a more reassuring tone. "There's no need to be nervous. This is a routine questioning. Just try to relax and answer to the best of your ability, okay?"

Patrick took a deep breath and let it out, which seemed to calm him a little. "I think I'm okay now."

"Let's start from the beginning. About what time did you become aware of the incident?"

"Let's see—I remember hearing a loud boom. It woke me from a dead sleep. I looked at my clock and it said 11:46 pm."

"Okay, and what happened next?"

"I got out of bed and looked outside. There was some smoke coming from Mr. Scorpione's window across the street. Then I heard a loud gunshot. That's when I saw something strange on the roof of the house next door. So I grabbed my binoculars from my desk drawer and took a closer look."

"And what did you see on the rooftop?"

"There was some sort of tent with someone inside it. I couldn't tell at first because the tent covered her, but it was a girl."

"A girl?" Jimmy couldn't hide his surprise.

"Yeah, and then she threw the tent off her and stood up. That's when the moon came out and it got brighter. I was able to see her clearly then."

"Was this girl holding a weapon? A rifle, maybe?"

"She was holding a sniper rifle, yes. You know, the kind you see in the movies."

"What kind? Could you describe it?"

"Um, let me think—it looked like a... what was it? Dragi? Dragon? Dragunov! That's it! It was a Dragunov SVD. It was just like the one Daniel Henney used in that superhero movie. I could tell because the Dragunovs have an AK look with a long barrel and a square hole in the butt stock."

"You're absolutely sure?"

Patrick nodded.

"All right, about this girl—could you describe her?"

"In the light I could make out a few details. She was wearing some kind of weird white mask. She was also wearing a dark black and gray body suit. She had a long ponytail. Let's see, what else. Oh, there was a belt around her waist with lots of pockets."

"You said a mask? What did it look like?"

"It was shaped like an animal face. Like a cat or a fox maybe."

"Okay, can you tell me what happened next, after she stood up?"

"She packed up the rifle in a long bag and threw it over her shoulder and took off that way." Patrick pointed northward. "She was jumping from house to house."

"You mean she ran along the roof, got down and climbed up onto the next house and so on?"

"No, I mean she really jumped from house to house. Like, she jumped really far and really fast."

Jimmy let out a laugh. "Son, I think that's impossible. Those houses are pretty far apart."

"Tell her that! I saw it with my own eyes, I swear. It didn't seem human."

"Okay, I believe you. Can you tell me anything else that would help?"

"That's about it. That's all I saw."

"I see. Well, I think we're just about done here. Thank you for answering my questions, Patrick. You've been very helpful." Jimmy looked to the parents as he reached into his pocket. "Mr. and Mrs. O'Hara, thank you very much for your cooperation. Here's my card. That's my office number at the police station; my cell phone number is on the back. If you or Patrick remember anything else—anything at all—call me day or night. And if you can make yourselves available in case we need to ask further questions, that would be great."

Patrick's father slid the card in his pocket. "Sure, no problem."

Jimmy gave a nonchalant wave, got into his car, and drove away.

Chapter Two

Patrick was able to get back to sleep after an hour of tossing and turning, his thoughts going over the ruckus across the street. The next morning, he awoke to see a few police cars still at the Scorpione estate. He looked over at his clock. It was half past six, time to get up for school. The eastern horizon glowed, the coming dawn casting reds and purples on the underbellies of passing clouds.

Exhausted, he dragged himself out of bed and shuffled into the bathroom, where he brushed his teeth and took a shower. The whole time he couldn't get the image of the assassin out of his head. The vision of her holding up that rifle in wicked victory—it burned in his mind like a brand.

Patrick attended Kingsley Academy, a private school that concentrated on preparing students for the business world. Most of the student body was comprised of children from wealthy families; Patrick was no exception. The rest attended through grants and scholarships. Kingsley had proudly held a ninety-nine percent graduation rate for the past twenty years, making it one of the finest institutions in the country.

Patrick went to school that morning in a sort of daze, the incident from the previous night still weighing heavy on his thoughts. He sat through his boring first-period English class, not paying much attention to the teacher, who spoke in a monotone.

Who was she? He wondered as he rested his chin on his palm and gazed out the second-floor window to the city outside. *Who was under that mask?* He didn't realize that he'd said it out loud.

"Did you say something, O'Hara?" Mr. Todd called from the front of the room.

That snapped Patrick out of his thoughts, and he immediately sat upright in his chair. "It was nothing, sir. Nothing at all."

He heard a few laughs around him. A girl in the back said in a low voice, "God, what a spaz!" The guy in sunglasses beside him whispered in a London accent, "Oy, stop drawing attention this way, O'Hara. I'm trying to get some sleep over here."

"That's good, O'Hara," Mr. Todd said. "Since you're not preoccupied, you can open up to page 105 and start reading from the top paragraph."

"Yes, sir." Patrick groaned, taking his book in hand. The laughter continued as he flipped through to the correct page.

Lunch was no different. Patrick was so lost in thought that he wasn't paying attention to his classmates sitting at the lunch table. The punk rocker with the red Mohawk sitting next to Patrick was Vic West. Sitting across from Vic was Mike Davison, the cool guy from Bayswater, London wearing shades and a leather jacket. Next to Mike was Ayu Hamaguchi, the cute girl from Tokyo.

Ayu opened her lunch bag and took out a silver thermos. After twisting the top off, she held it out to Vic and said, "Would you like some barley tea, Vic? It's very healthy for you."

Vic looked at the thermos suspiciously. "What's in barley tea? I might not like it."

Mike jumped in. "What do you mean, 'what's in barley tea?' It's barley—thus, the name of the tea. Otherwise it would be called 'something else' tea. You got it now, Vicky-boy?"

"Shut up, I knew that!" Vic shot back.

"Next you'll be asking what's in orange juice," Mike said.

"Ah, orengii juusu wa ichiban desu!" Ayu added.

"Yeah, what she said," Mike concurred.

"Hey, I don't speak French, okay?" Vic said. "I know what's in orange juice. It's got the fruit in it, right?"

"It has a fruit in it. Can you tell me what that fruit is?"

"No, wait, don't tell me." Vic thought hard. "It's named after a color, right?"

Mike just shook his head with a sigh. "I think the chemicals you put in your hair are finally soaking into your brain."

"Hey, do you realize how hard it is to get it this shade of red?" Vic said. "I had to dye it five times."

Mike smiled. "Yeah, mate, that's why it looks orange now."

"N-no it doesn't. Does it?" Vic got up and ran toward the bathroom. "Gotta find a mirror. I'll be back!"

Ayu turned to Mike and whispered, "Vic is very gullible, huh?"

Mike laughed. "Gullible is an understatement, sweetheart. Once I told him they were serving brownies in the basement. It took him three hours to figure out our school doesn't have a basement."

Ayu let out a giggle.

Mike then looked at Pat, who was staring at nothing in particular. "Oy, space-case! What's got you shootin' past Saturn?"

"Huh?"

"Jeez, man! You were spacing out in class too." Mike leaned forward. "You still thinking about that killer chick you saw last night?"

Pat let out a sigh. "Yeah. Sorry I'm out of it today, Mike."

"Forget about her, man. She's probably halfway 'round the world by now. You've seen the films. Assassins don't stick around after they hit their mark. What do you think, they're gonna hang out and see what's playing at the cinema? Check out the sights? BANG, and they're gone, mate. That's all there is to it."

"I don't know, man." Pat said. "She might not be finished yet. Maybe it's not over."

Mike turned to Ayu. "What do you think, Ayu? Think we should get Irish boy here a hobby? Get his mind off of things?"

Ayu lit up with excitement. "I have some manga you can borrow! Do you like manga?"

Pat waved his hand. "No, I'm good. Thanks."

Ayu made a sad face.

"Don't worry, Ayu." Mike patted her on the shoulder. "I'm sure there's someone in this school who likes those Japanese comics."

Ayu held out a book to Mike. "Are you sure you don't want to read—"

"Yes, I'm sure, sweetheart," Mike interrupted.

Yes, just another day at lunch, thought Pat.

Stephanie Sebastiano was a typical introvert who kept mostly to herself. She had few friends, but she considered the ones she did have to be very close. She hadn't been very popular with the students since she'd first come to this school a year ago.

Stephanie stood outside the gates, hugging her book bag to her chest in silence. Her soft brown eyes were cast to the ground, her mind miles away. Most of the students passing by paid her no attention, since she tended to be nearly invisible. The ones who did notice made snickering comments amongst their friends. She heard someone say, "She's so weird."

Stephanie lowered her head. She was aware of the cruel comments and kept telling herself she didn't care, but the words still hurt. She wished she could be more open and social. Whenever she tried to speak her mind, she either froze up or spoke too quietly to be heard. She couldn't help how she was, and she hated that about herself.

"Hi, Steph," a familiar voice called.

Stephanie raised her eyes to the boy with wavy brown hair before her.

"Hi Pat," she replied happily, running her fingers through her dark brown hair. "What's up?"

As they started to walk, Patrick immediately felt the need to tell Stephanie about what had happened the night before.

"You won't believe what I saw last night." Patrick pointed toward the east end of the city. "You know Mr. Scorpione who lives across the street from me?"

"Well, I've never really met him." Stephanie's voice became quieter. "Did something happen?"

Pat looked around for any eavesdroppers before continuing. "He was killed last night."

She raised a hand to her mouth in surprise. "Oh my God! That's terrible."

"Yeah, a big boom at his house woke me from a dead sleep, and then there was a gunshot. I called the cops right after."

"Wait, what happened?"

"Someone exploded Mr. Scorpione's living room window, and then they shot him. When I called the cops I told them to hurry, and they came pretty fast too."

"Benton seems like such a quiet city. It's scary to think things like that are happening right in your neighborhood, you know?"

"Yeah, you're right. Did I say I saw who did it?"

She stopped him by grabbing his arm. "You did?" She said loudly as a look of worry had rushed over her.

Patrick was thrown off by the sudden change in her. Stephanie never raised her voice. "Yeah, that's what I told the cops when I called them. Why? What's wrong?"

The tone of her voice was one thing he noticed was unusual. Another was the anxiety and concern in those soft brown eyes that stared desperately into his. And finally, how tightly she held his arm gave him an idea just how afraid she was for him.

"Who was it?" she asked, "and did they see you?"

"It was a girl, but she wore a mask. I have no idea who she was, and besides that, she took off pretty quick. I don't think she saw me."

Stephanie turned away and let out a sigh of what seemed to be relief. "Oh, thank God. I was so afraid you'd been seen—that you'd be in danger."

"Don't worry, I'm sure she didn't see me. You okay, Steph? You're not acting like your usual self."

"It's nothing." She brought her eyes back to him as her shyness took hold once more. "I'm—I was just concerned for you, that's all."

A brief, awkward silence fell over their conversation as they continued down the sidewalk. Patrick was offset by her sudden burst of emotion moments before. At the same time, he felt flattered she was genuinely concerned for him and that thought gave him a small smile he didn't allow her to see.

"I wonder who it is." Patrick glanced at the students passing by. "It might be someone at our school. Or even someone we know."

Stephanie tapped her fingers against the book bag in her arms. "Our school or someone we know? You really think so?"

"Oh, you should've seen her, Steph." Pat couldn't help a sense of excitement as he thought about the assassin again. "The way she moved—like Cat Woman from *Batman* or Ninja Master from that movie last year."

Stephanie let out a giggle as her nervousness seemed to disappear. "There you go again, Pat. Your mind's running away from you. Well, I hope they find whoever did it."

"I caught the news on my smart phone between classes. The police chief, I think his name was Stonebreaker, said the killer must be good at what she does, but he didn't say much of anything else about the case. I don't think they have many leads or clues yet. Otherwise he would've said, 'We're very close to finding the killer,' or 'The investigation is making good progress,' or something like that. Did I mention I was the one who called the police?"

She let out a laugh. "Only three times so far, but who's counting?"

"Heh! I guess you're right."

Stephanie became quiet as they continued their walk down one of the main roads. Patrick tried to pick up the conversation again. "So, Steph, what are you doing later on?"

"Going to gymnastics practice and then to see my sister right after, like usual."

They reached the street where they usually parted ways, and he said, "If you want to hang out, call my cell, okay?"

"Sure thing."

"Oh, and I hope your sister is doing better."

Sadness briefly touched her expression. She looked away and said quietly, "As good as can be expected."

Chapter Three

In fifteen minutes, Stephanie was at her gymnastics class a few blocks away. She changed, stepped into the gym, and set down her bag by the wall near the doorway. She was doing her stretches when her classmate Lisa Smith walked past. Lisa had started at the Academy around the same time as Stephanie. Although Lisa came from poverty, she was able to attend school at the Academy through a government scholarship because of her high grades and extraordinary athletic ability. Lately, however, her grades and attendance had been slipping. As long as Stephanie had known Lisa, she had never smiled. She always had a serious, even standoffish demeanor.

Lisa's long dark hair was pulled back in a ponytail. Her brown eyes showed intensity.

"Hi, Lisa," Stephanie called to her.

Lisa tossed back an indifferent "Hey." She stopped near Stephanie, sat on the floor, and began her stretches. Her body was lithe and fit.

Stephanie talked while she stretched. "I didn't see you in class today."

"Yeah. So?"

"You didn't skip again, did you?"

"So what if I did, Stephanie? I missed the part where that's any of your business. I don't poke around in your personal life, do I?"

"Jeez, you don't have to bite my head off."

Lisa let out a sigh. "You're right. I'm sorry, I'm just a little on edge today."

Stephanie noticed a mark on Lisa's shoulder. "Is that another bruise? Are you okay?"

"Y-yeah, it's nothing." Lisa covered it with her hand. "I just tripped and hit it on a table at home. Look, let's just drop it, okay?"

"Okay. I find it funny—even though you skip school, you never miss a gymnastics class."

Lisa stood up, flexed her arm, and gave her bicep a pat. "You know me—can't let these muscles weaken. I gotta keep 'em toned or my performance will start hurting."

"I guess you're not the best in the class for nothing. You've definitely got dedication."

Lisa raised an eyebrow. "Come on, we both know you're better. I've seen you do incredible moves—moves even I have trouble with."

Stephanie hopped to her feet and gave Lisa a modest smile. "I'm not that great, but thanks. Now that dedication I was talking about—if you applied that to school, you might get better grades."

Lisa looked away with an uneasy expression. "Yeah, it's just this, um, part-time job I got. I work late and skip school sometimes just to catch up on sleep, that's all. You understand, right?"

"I guess, but it's not like you can't nap in study hall. That old room could put anyone to sleep."

Lisa shrugged. "Whatever."

Stephanie moved closer and continued in a quiet voice, "You heard about what happened to Vincent Scorpione last night, right?"

At the mention of the name, Lisa's whole mood darkened. "I say the old man deserved to die."

"What?" Stephanie was shocked at her comment.

A cold and merciless tone flowed in Lisa's voice. "Everyone knows what he was, even if the D.A. couldn't prove it."

Out of concern, Stephanie reached out to touch Lisa's arm. "Still, I wouldn't say he deserved to die like—"

Lisa grabbed Stephanie's hand. "He flooded the streets with drugs!" she said, the volume of her voice rising. "My little brother Jake died overdosing on heroin he got from Vincent's pushers."

Stephanie stared at her own hand in Lisa's, remembering the sad news of Jake's death several weeks ago. Lisa released her hand and said, "How about the local gangs? Where do you think they get their guns from, huh? My friends Bobby and Josh were shot in the city last year. Vincent might as well have pulled the trigger himself."

Stephanie shook her head.

"Vincent spread nothing but poison and death," Lisa continued. "I'll never see Jake, Bobby, or Josh ever again, all because of him. So don't you tell me he didn't deserve to die the way he did."

Stephanie spoke in a weak voice. "I—I'm sorry. I didn't know you really felt that way. But I still think killing is wrong."

Seeing Stephanie's reaction, Lisa seemed to calm down a bit. "No, I'm sorry. I overreacted... again. It's just that I miss Jake so much." Tears formed in her eyes. "Damn it! I miss my brother."

As Lisa cried, Stephanie moved in and hugged her until she finally stopped.

Guenther A. Borgestedt Psychological Institute was well known throughout the country. When it came to treating the mentally ill, it had prestigious credentials. It was home to resident 2151980, better known to her family as Jennifer Lynn Sebastiano. She'd been institutionalized at the institute since she'd suffered a psychological break over a year ago.

She'd been a normal teenage girl whose ever-attentive father had showered her with love and affection her whole life. He'd sheltered her from all the bad and given her nothing but good, not to mention everything she ever wanted. He was her whole world, and she was his sunshine. She couldn't imagine living without him. She was daddy's girl.

But she had wakened one dark morning to be told that as she slept her father had been gunned down by angry mobsters and left to die alone on the concrete floor of a dark, dank warehouse on the waterfront. He'd been ripped from her life, leaving only a gaping, bleeding hole—and he was never coming back. Jennifer had dropped into a pit of darkness in her soul, with no way out.

After the mental break, Jennifer's twin, Stephanie, had been very worried for her. Their mother had admitted Jennifer to the institute so that she could receive the best care possible. The family had been praying for a fast recovery, but right now that seemed unlikely. She had made little, if any, progress.

Jennifer's white room was furnished with only a white bed, a white night table, and a simple chair she never used, which also happened to be white. The fluorescent light in the ceiling hummed constantly and flickered now and then. Jennifer was constantly watched through a camera mounted on the ceiling in the corner of her room. Meals were brought to her three times a day. If she needed to use the bathroom, she was escorted by a female orderly and then brought directly back to her room. Exercise lasted an hour a day, also under close observation.

She was so closely monitored this way for a reason: When she'd first arrived at the Institute, she'd tried to kill herself three times, each time by a clever means and all within the span of a month. A final attempt three months ago had marked the fourth time. With no other means available, she had taken a metal spoon from one of her meals and hidden it. Over the course of a week, she'd sharpened the handle on the brass leg of her bed frame until it was like a razor. Luckily, one of the orderlies happened to check on her at the very moment she pulled it across her throat. Otherwise, she would surely have died. The resulting scar striped the left side of her neck.

Now Jennifer sat motionless on the floor, arms folded over bent knees, staring blankly across the white tile floor. She had no TV, radio, or anything else that might stir her already sensitive mind. Her only sources of entertainment were her own thoughts, which caused her to quietly laugh to herself now and then.

Suddenly the silence was broken. The familiar sound of a certain set of shoes coming down the hallway drew her attention. The door unlocked and opened. There in the doorway, with a sweet smile, was her sister Stephanie. Jennifer's face lit up with joy. She yelled happily, jumped up, and threw her arms around her sister.

"Stephie, Stephie, Stephie!" She hopped up and down as she held her sister tight. Finally she paused, looked up at the camera, and moved her mouth to Stephanie's ear. "He died, didn't he?"

Stephanie's eyes widened in surprise as she grabbed her sister by the shoulders. "W-what! Jennifer, what are you talking about?"

"Vincent Scorpione. He's dead, isn't he?" Jennifer asked plainly.

Stephanie lowered her eyes and gave a nod. "Yes, he's dead. But how did you know about that?"

"The ravens told me."

"What ravens? What are you talking about?"

"The tow of the flow of the row. With black wings the words he sings ring and make the church bells ding and reach the ears of the son of the king." Jennifer broke away from her sister's grip and twirled around the room. "And the ravens dance. They dance circles around all these things!" She laughed and danced merrily round and round. Her eyes were far away as her body seemed to move to an unheard melody.

Stephanie caught her sister in her arms and carefully sat her down on the bed. "Now calm down, Jennifer. You don't know what you're talking about. You're just overexcited, that's all." She held Jennifer close and stroked her hair while she rocked her back and forth. This always helped her twin relax.

Finally Jennifer laid her head on Stephanie's chest. "Stephie," Jennifer said, closing her eyes, "I miss Daddy."

Tears welled in Stephanie's eyes at the mention of their father. She closed her eyes, shedding tears that mingled with her sister's. She held Jennifer closer, and they cried together. "I miss him too, Jenny," she said.

She rested her head on her sister's, and they sat in silence. After a while, Jennifer was calm enough to fall asleep in her arms. Stephanie laid her down on the bed, pulled up the covers, and gave her a kiss on the forehead. She tapped a few times on the door, and an orderly let her out.

Patrick sat at his desk in his room with the lights out, staring out the window to where he'd seen the assassin across the street. The street lamps outside faintly illuminated his room. He'd been sitting like this for a while. His mind was whirling with the possibilities of the murderous girl's identity and her whereabouts. Would she strike again, or was she done? Was she hiding out nearby, or was she long gone?

A yell came up the stairs, snapping him from his thoughts. "Patrick!" his mother called. "Telephone for you. It's Joey Scorpione."

Pat hopped up from his chair, ran downstairs, and made his way to the living room, where the telephone receiver was turned up on the table, waiting for him.

"Joey, you didn't make it to school today," he said. "I know what happened. How are you holding up?"

"Bad." Joseph let out a cold sigh that disturbed Patrick. "Real bad."

"Yeah, I can understand," Patrick said in a somber tone. "I'm really sorry about your grandfather."

"The cops were at our house all day, askin' questions. I—I can't believe it. I just saw him a couple hours before it happened. We were out with the whole family at Uncle Tony's restaurant."

"Wow, that's rough."

"Hey, Pat, what's with your cell? I called, but you didn't answer."

"Sorry, must've left it on silent again."

"No prob. Anyway, word is you saw it happen. Who was it?" Joseph asked eagerly. "What did she look like?"

"Calm down, Joey, I couldn't see much. From what I could tell she might've been our age, maybe a little older. She might even be from around here or go to our school."

"Let me tell you something." The anger in Joey's voice grew. "I'm gonna find that girl. And when I do, I'm gonna kill her for what she did."

"Joey, think about what you're saying. Do you really want to do that?"

"Yes." Joey's words were heated. "She's gonna pay!"

"Maybe you should get some counseling or something. It would help you deal—"

Joey's angry voice cut Pat off. "I don't need counseling, and I don't need help."

Pat moved the phone away as the receiver clicked loudly in his ear. He sighed and set the phone back on the hook. He looked outside at the now-empty Scorpione mansion across the street.

"What's happening around here?" he asked himself.

Chapter Four

Stephanie tossed and turned in her sleep, horrible dreams mixing with painful memories in a nightmarish cocktail. She awoke with a gasp, and realized tears were in her eyes. She'd been crying in her sleep again. Wiping her wet cheeks, she turned on the light and slipped out of bed. From the dresser she picked up a framed picture of herself in her father's arms with Jenny hugging them both. She and her sister were only nine at the time. It was a warm spring day in New York's Central Park, and they were celebrating their birthday. Just holding that picture in her hands made the warm, happy memories flow once more. In those days, merely being together with her mom, dad, and sister was all the happiness she had needed. Life was so good then.

She smiled as she ran her fingers along the image of her father. Then, slowly, her smile disappeared. She gently set down the picture frame, opened her dresser drawer, and pulled out a newspaper clipping. The headline read,

Killed in the Line of Duty

Wiping another tear from her eye, she read the article.

Detective Thomas Sebastiano of the Benton City Police Department was found dead this morning in building four of the warehouse district. When asked to comment on the highly decorated officer's untimely demise, Police Chief Edward

Stonebreaker said Sebastiano "was a good friend and a vital part of the Department." Stonebreaker also said, "Sebastiano's killers will be brought to justice no matter what." However, Stonebreaker refused to comment on the rumors circulating in his department suggesting that at the time of Sebastiano's death, he had been involved in an undercover operation with the purpose of discovering the head of a local crime syndicate and that he was murdered before he could reveal the identities of the men involved in the organization, especially that of the main boss...

Dropping her head, she gritted her teeth and threw the clipping to the floor. "Vincent," she muttered.

At the Benton City Police Department, Jimmy sat in his office going over reports and his personal notes. A cold cup of coffee sat in front of him. He'd been at it for several hours. Finally he dropped the papers on the desk and leaned back in his chair. He took a deep breath as he tried to rub the tiredness from his eyes. Glancing over at the wall clock, he realized it was 3:15 a.m.

"Damn, it's that late already?" He took a sip of his coffee, only to spit it back into the cup. "Blech! When did this get cold?" He set it down and looked over at the coffee pot, which was empty. He probably shouldn't make any more; he needed to sleep sometime this week.

He took out the forensic files and read through the key parts.

The serial number hadn't turned up anything on the injector cartridge. However, Patrick O'Hara had provided a good lead: The bullet turned out to be a 7.62x54mmR, which indeed matched the round of a Dragunov SVD sniper rifle. The shell casing found on the roof also confirmed it. He had checked the local gun stores. No one had bought that type of rifle or ammunition within the past six months, meaning the killer had either brought it with her from out of state or had made a special order with the gun dealers on the streets.

He thought about the mask O'Hara had mentioned. Could it be Japanese?

Jimmy glanced over at his phone.

His friend, Lin Misaki, might still be awake. She usually worked late into the night at the newspaper she wrote for. Sometimes she even fell asleep at her desk. It was worth a try.

On the main news floor of the *New York Watchman*, one of the most successful newspapers in New York City, all was dark save for one lit monitor, its screen saver on. At the desk, a Japanese woman sat with her head down, fast asleep. One hand rested near the keyboard of her computer, holding a pair of thin-rimmed glasses with round lenses. The other hand provided a place to rest her head on the wooden desk. The headphones covering her ears were connected to an MP3 player, which was playing Japanese love songs on a loop.

Lin Misaki had been born in Tokyo, but her parents had moved with her to New York when she was eight, so they could take advantage of several business opportunities. When she graduated high school at eighteen, her parents moved back to Tokyo.

Lin, however, remained in America, where she studied journalism at Columbia University, and then earned her master's at NYU. Soon after, she began applying to newspapers for a job. Many turned her down, but one newspaper saw enough in her work to give her a chance.

Almost twenty years and two Pulitzer Prizes later, here she was, senior investigative reporter for the *Watchman.*

Her desk phone rang, waking her from a dead sleep. Her head jerked up. She blindly reached out and picked up the phone as she pulled her headphones off.

"Lin?" The voice on the other end said.

"Jimmy?" She groaned sleepily as she brushed her hair out of her eyes. She opened them just enough to look at her watch. "It's three-twenty in the morning."

"Yeah, and you're still at work, aren't you?"

Lin opened her eyes a bit more and looked around. "Oh—you're right."

"You're starting to get predictable."

Lin put on her glasses and stretched her arms. "Hey now, it's called dedication to the job. Something you and I are both cursed with apparently."

Jimmy snorted in agreement.

"What can I do for you so early in the morning?"

"I'm working a murder case. Vincent Scorpione was killed."

"Someone killed Vincent? We all know he was well-liked," she said sarcastically. "Do we know who did it?"

Jimmy took a few moments to divulge many details of the case while Lin took notes. One thing in particular piqued Lin's interest. "You said this girl wore a mask. What kind was it?"

"Patrick O'Hara described it as a white mask shaped like a cat's or fox's face."

"Fox? Hm..." She thought for a moment. "Sounds like it could be a kitsune kamen."

"Wait. A kita whatta?"

"Kitsune kamen," she said with a laugh. "It means fox mask. In Japan, children usually wear them at summer festivals. However, according to legend it was also used long ago by ninja to hide their identities from enemies and rival clans."

"So what are you saying—I might have a Yakuza running around Benton?"

"Jimmy, Yakuza are thugs with big back tattoos and bad attitudes, and they carry swords they don't know how to use. They're not stealthy by any means. In fact, they're rather loud."

"Oh, no. Please don't tell me—"

"Yup, you may have a ninja problem."

"Great, now I have one of the turtles running around my city."

"Don't take it so lightly, Jimmy," Lin cautioned. "If this is a real ninja you're dealing with, you have to be careful."

"You aren't kidding, are you? You're saying ninjas really exist?"

"Of course. Centuries ago in Japan, ninja clans were employed by the shogun to eliminate undesirables or gather information. According to my trustworthy sources, a number of those clans still exist today. All I can say is, Vincent must have pissed off some powerful people in Japan to invite that kind of retribution."

"This is getting really complicated. Couldn't it just be some amateur or fanatic who watches too many TV shows?"

"Doubtful. From what Patrick described, 'leaping from house to house' doesn't sound like the capability of a normal human being. The body would have to be trained to beyond peak ability and maybe even artificially enhanced to perform at that level. That might explain the injector cartridge you found on the roof. What was that serial number, by the way?"

Jimmy found the report and read it off. "I cross-referenced it with several pharmaceutical companies and came up with nil."

"Tell you what—I'll do some digging on my end and let you know if I find anything."

"Much appreciated. I owe you one."

"You still owe me from last time," she said with a chuckle, "but if you let me write the story, we'll call it square. What do you say?"

"You've got yourself a deal."

Lin let out a yawn. "I'd better head home and get some sleep. I'd suggest you do the same, but I won't waste my breath. I know how you are when it comes to an important case."

"Actually, I think I'll close up for the night and start fresh tomorrow." Jimmy massaged the tenseness from the back of his neck. "Some sleep should help the wheels turn a little better."

"I remember back in college when we'd pull all-nighters four days in a row and it wouldn't phase us. We must be getting old."

"Well, we're only forty, but if it makes you feel better, in dog years we're way past retirement."

Lin smiled as she let out a modest giggle.

Ducking and weaving with more skill than a boxer, Pat maneuvered through the crowded hallways to his first class. Every day he told himself he'd take the long way around to avoid the traffic, but he always ended up resorting to this route. He wondered if it was laziness on his part or just his fear of being late and inviting Mrs. Sherman's wrath. The last person who was late not only got the first, second, and third degree, but she also made him stand out in the hallway for twenty minutes holding a big sign over his head that said I'M TARDY. *That ain't gonna be me,* Pat told himself.

Joey Scorpione came out of nowhere and joined him, giving Pat's shoulder a nudge.

"Joey!" Pat was surprised to see him so soon. "What's happening? You doing any better after—"

"I'm good, man." Joey smiled, although it didn't look genuine. "Don't worry about me."

Maybe he really is coping, Pat thought. *But so fast?*

Joey pulled him closer and said in a low voice, "It's that little witch assassin who's got something to be worried about."

Pat let out a disheartened sigh. Nothing had changed.

Joey clenched his fist. "I'll find her soon. That's a promise."

"How do you know she's even still in this state? She might have skipped town a long time ago."

"Whoa, whoa, whoa!" Joey stopped him. "Yesterday, you were all, 'Maybe she's a teen like us who goes to our school,' and now you're like, 'She's long gone'? What's the deal, man?"

"Maybe you should just let it go. I mean, look what it's doing to you."

"No one's lettin' anything go, okay? She's gonna get what's comin' to her and that's a promise, you got that?"

"Why don't you just leave it to the police? I'm sure they'll find her eventually."

"The cops?" Joey laughed. "You kidding? They couldn't find their way out of a one-room apartment. No, I'm gonna find her. Besides, if things get too tough, I can always ask the family for help."

"I still don't think you should get involved with this," Pat said, trying to be as tactful as possible. "I mean, your family doesn't exactly follow the straight and narrow."

Joey grabbed Pat by the shoulder and pushed him up against a locker. "Hey! No one was able to connect my family to that drug deal or the kid who died from an overdose—Jake whatever-the-hell-his name was. My family wouldn't be involved in something like that. I know they wouldn't!" Joey pushed a little harder. "What my family is good at is getting things done. Got me?"

"All right!" Pat held his hands up in surrender. "Just take it easy."

Suddenly someone grabbed Joey's hand and swiftly put him in an arm lock so painful it brought him to his knees. He looked up to see a very pissed-off Japanese girl with a long ponytail. She leaned down and spoke into his ear. "If you ask me, your granddaddy got exactly what he deserved." Twisting his arm harder, she made him grunt in pain. "I hope the rest of your gangster family follows him soon!" Then she released him and stormed off down the hallway.

That's when Pat noticed the red ribbon wrapped around her ponytail. "Hey, wait a minute," he called out as she disappeared. "That's—" But she was gone.

"Damn!" Joey grabbed his arm as he stood up. "What the hell was up with that?"

"Kira Shirou is definitely captain of the karate team for a reason." Pat said. "You know she's got a grudge against your family after Vincent forced her father to sell his distribution company to him for half its net worth."

"Grandpa said Kenichi Shirou agreed to the terms. It's not his fault her father got screwed on the deal. And why take it out on me? I wasn't even there." Joey felt his hand. "Damn, that girl's got a kung fu grip. Anyway, sorry about that—I get a little wired sometimes."

"I know." Pat straightened his shirt, trying to ignore the curious eyes around them. "Don't worry about it."

"Um, Pat?" Stephanie appeared beside him with a look of concern. "Is everything okay?"

Before Pat could say a word, Joey jumped in. "Yeah, everything's fine. Just got a little worked up, that's all." He gave Pat a slap on the back. "No harm done, right, Pat?"

"Yeah, everything's fine, Steph," Pat reassured her. Then he looked to Joey.

"Listen, I'd better get going." Joey rubbed his arm as the pain subsided. "Catch up with you later."

Stephanie raised an eyebrow as Joey turned on his heel and seemed to power-walk down the hallway. "Is he always that energetic?"

Pat let out a breath of exhaustion. "Honestly? Sometimes he's more than I can handle, but I think he'll be fine. He's still pretty bent out of shape about his grandfather."

"I see," Stephanie said. "It really is tough losing someone you love. Believe me, I know."

Pat and Stephanie started down the hall together. Shyness may have been Stephanie's weakness, but with Pat she seemed able to relax and be a little more open. It was as if he gave her the confidence she needed to make her feel stronger.

"Joseph seems a little more agitated than usual," Stephanie said. "Is it just his grandfather's death, or is something else going on as well?"

"Well, it seems he's hell-bent on finding the girl who did it." He glanced back to make sure Joey was gone and continued in a whisper, "He wants to kill her."

"K-kill?" Stephanie said nervously. "Don't you think he should get some help?"

Pat rubbed the back of his head. "That might do more harm than good. Joey doesn't like being told what to do, let alone being told what to think. I'm sure he'll come around from it eventually. Just give him some time."

Stephanie tightened her grip on her books, her voice becoming uneasy. "Y-yeah, that's all he needs. Just a little time."

"Listen, I know Joey can be a hothead sometimes, but I don't think he would actually kill anyone."

She looked up at him quickly. "Are you sure? Do you know him that well?"

Pat considered her worries for a moment before answering. "You know what? I'm not sure. This is a new side of him I've never seen before. Sure, he's talked about beatin' the crap out of people, but never killing them."

She just shook her head. "Think about it—what if he goes into a paranoid rage and kills the first girl he thinks is the assassin?"

Pat stopped in front of his classroom. "Then I guess we'll have to keep a close eye on him from now on, won't we?"

With a slight nod, she gave him a tender smile and a wave, and walked away. As she left, Pat couldn't shake the feeling that she was still troubled.

Chapter Five

Pat sat at the lunch table staring at his hot food while mulling over Joey's situation. Across from him, Mike and Vic were engaged in another enlightening conversation, while Ayu, sitting to his left, quietly read her Japanese manga comics.

"So let me get this straight." Vic's eyes widened as if he couldn't believe what he'd just heard. "You're telling me that a snail is not an insect?"

"Vic, how many times do we have to go over this? Insects are enclosed in an exoskeleton shell composed of chitin," Mike recited. "Though snails do have a shell, they are not insects. Got it?"

"But wait, caterpillars are soft, right? They got no exie-skeleton thingy. Plus they change into butterflies, which are insects. So why can't snails be insects too?"

Mike shook his head. "How did you even get into this school?"

Vic shrugged. "My dad donated the school's new science wing, so they waived most of the requirements for me."

Mike rolled his eyes. "Well, that explains a lot."

Vic gave a nod. "Yeah, Dad says having less stress over the requirements will help me come out of my shell."

"But if you did come out of your shell," Mike said with a mischievous smile, "would you still be an insect or would you turn into a mollusk?"

"An insect—no, wait—what was that other thing you said?"

Pat shook his head, and Ayu giggled behind her book as she listened to the boys' banter. He wondered if she understood their humor; she seemed to be having a good time.

Mike looked over at Pat and waved to grab his attention. "Irish-boy, what's got you down today? Same story: killer girls looking for real estate?"

Pat hesitated. He didn't want word of Joey's situation getting around. He forced a laugh. "Heh, yeah. You never know. She could still be around."

"Move on, man. Guys our age should be thinking of the three Gs: girls, games, and good food. I give you credit for thinking of girls, though—psycho-killer girls, but girls nonetheless."

Ayu jumped in. "If that interests you, Pat, I have a manga about ninja girls. You might like it."

Pat shook his head. "Thanks, but I'm good."

Ayu made a sad face, and a thought occurred to Pat. What if Kira was the assassin? She had some skillful moves, not to mention a lot of strength for a girl her size.

"Hey, space-case." Mike interrupted Pat's thoughts. "Did you just zip past *Voyager 1* this time?"

"No, I'm cool," Pat said. "Just thinkin' about the usual."

"Why don't you get a hobby, like working on cars or motorcycles?" Mike suggested. "You know, something to get your mind off things and clear your head."

Vic chimed in, "I got it! I'll let you borrow my punk rock CDs. Vomit Boy, Rotten Dog Food, Sidewalk Lunch. Those bands always help me clear my head."

Mike laughed. "Yeah, the problem is they clear your head of everything."

"Thanks, Vic," Pat said, "but I think I'll pass."

Vic gave a shrug.

Maybe I should keep an eye on Kira too, Pat thought. *Maybe she's... her.*

After school, when Stephanie went to visit her sister, she brought a book with her. It was called *Wishful Thinking,* a part of Jennifer's favorite teen novel series: *The Young and the Hopeful.* The story was set in a Brooklyn high school and centered on romance and teen problems. Jennifer had started reading the books when she was fourteen and had been hooked ever since.

Due to Jennifer's long stretch of calm behavior, the institute had approved Stephanie's reading the books to her sister, but nothing more. When Stephanie read, Jennifer hung on every word, perhaps because now more than ever, the stories illustrated the life she could be living had things been a little different.

Stephanie opened the door to her sister's room and saw Jennifer sitting on her bed holding a Rubik's cube. Two of the sides, red and yellow, were finished. The door closed behind her as Stephanie sat down next to her sister.

"Hi, Jenny." Stephanie placed a comforting hand on her shoulder. "How are things today?"

"You know, no matter how hard I try, I can never finish all six sides," Jennifer said as she dropped the cube next to her on the bed.

"I brought the next book in your favorite series." Stephanie held up the book to her. "Would you like me to read it to you?"

"I'd rather read it by myself." Jennifer folded her arms and turned her head in a pout.

"Now, Jenny, you know the rules. You're not allowed to keep anything like this. I'm only able to read it to you."

Jennifer sat up straight. "Yeah, yeah, all right, I want to hear it."

Stephanie opened up to the first page and began reading as her sister leaned back against the wall. But before she had read a full paragraph, Jennifer interrupted her.

"Stephie?"

"Yes?" Stephanie closed the book but kept her finger in the page.

"Do you think the soul leaves the body right before or just after death?"

"What?" Stephanie was shocked. "Why would you ask me that?"

"Everyone dies. Is it really a weird question?"

"I guess I don't feel comfortable discussing this."

Stephanie opened to the page she'd been reading and bent her head to continue, but Jennifer grabbed the book and tossed it to the floor. "Daddy died, right? Did his soul leave his body before he felt the pain, or—"

"Jennifer, that's enough!" Stephanie raised her voice as she got up from the bed. "I won't hear any more of this." She picked up the book, walked over to the door, and gave a few quick knocks. The door opened, and Stephanie turned back to her sister. "I'm sorry I raised my voice. I know you miss him—so do I. I'll see you tomorrow, Jenny."

Jennifer looked away, her mouth in a grim line, brows furrowed. She didn't say a word.

After Stephanie left, Jennifer sat on her bed, alone again. She had never intended to upset her sister. In her mind she was simply asking a question.

"I'm sorry, Stephie," Jennifer said quietly. "I didn't mean to make you yell."

A young Japanese woman wearing a white lab coat and holding a file folder in her hands met Stephanie in the hallway.

"Doctor Tachibana," Stephanie greeted her. "It's good to see you again."

"Now, Stephanie," the woman said with a pleasant smile, "I told you, you can call me Mei."

"Sorry. I forgot, Mei. Pronounced like the month of May, right?"

"Yes, you remembered."

"Jennifer's weekly psych evaluation is today, right?"

Mei glanced at Jennifer's door. "Yes, it is. She's due in my office in about an hour. Since you visit her almost daily, perhaps you could tell me your sense of how she's doing?"

Stephanie let out an uneasy sigh. "She was very active yesterday and maybe even a little manic. She did another one of her rhyming rants."

"That's becoming more and more frequent, you would say?"

"Yes. She did it a couple of times last week, after your last evaluation. Today she asked a disturbing question—whether the soul leaves the body before or after death."

"I see." Mei lowered her head in thought for a moment. "We'll have to take that into consideration when we review her medication levels."

Stephanie noticed a jagged scar on Mei's right forearm, which was half covered by the sleeve of her lab coat.

"That looks like a nasty scar, Mei. If you don't mind my asking, how did you get it?"

"Oh, this?" Mei pulled up her sleeve. "It happened a long time ago. My family owns a summer home in Okayama, Japan. When I was a little girl I wandered too far into the woods and was attacked by a wild boar. He charged me, cut my arm with his tusk, circled around, and charged me again. I thought I was done for." A reminiscent smile came over her. "Then, like a bolt of lightning, my father appeared with his sword and cut the boar clean in half in the blink of an eye. He saved my life."

"Wow, that's amazing. Is your father a sword master?"

"Yes, he is. He says sword practice helps calm his mind so he can run his company efficiently." Mei glanced at Jennifer's door again. "Well, I'd better get back to work. Maybe I'll see you again soon?"

Stephanie nodded, and they parted. As one of the orderlies escorted Stephanie out, she remembered the first time she had met Mei. A little over two months earlier, Mei had contacted Stephanie's mother, Linda, concerning Jennifer's case. Mei said she might be able to help Jennifer with a new experimental treatment. Linda had agreed to hear her out and invited her to come to the house so they could talk in person. Within three days, Mei was sitting in their living room, discussing the details of the treatment with Linda and Stephanie.

"Mrs. Sebastiano," Mei had said, handing her business card to Linda with both hands, as was the Japanese custom, "as head of the Psychological Research Division of Tachibana Corporation in Japan, I have personally developed a treatment I believe can help your daughter's condition."

Linda studied the business card for a moment, and then looked up at her visitor. "Doctor Tachibana, how did you learn about my daughter?"

"Please, call me Mei, like the month of May. The Borgestedt Institute came to us for insight on your daughter's condition. Naturally, we took an interest. In the past two years we've treated seventeen patients with symptoms similar to Jennifer's. Eight have returned to being productive members of society, and the remaining nine continue to show great improvement."

"And you're absolutely sure you can help my daughter?"

"Some patients we have treated have shown more violent symptoms than your daughter's," Mei said reassuringly, "but that hasn't stood in the way of complete success."

"And how will this work?" Stephanie chimed in.

"To begin, my company will contact the institute, and we will work together in administering treatment."

"Will my daughter receive medications as part of these treatments?" Linda asked.

"Medications are a part of our daily treatment, along with meditation and relaxation exercises. This, along with weekly therapy and evaluation sessions, can help us better treat her and put her on the path to leading a normal life again."

Linda shook her head and sighed. "I would love to accept your help, but I don't think I can afford a specialist of your caliber right now."

"Rest assured, this treatment will come at no additional cost to you. We will be working directly with the institute."

Linda glanced down at the business card again and then at Stephanie. Stephanie gave her a reassuring smile and a nod of approval. Linda looked back at Mei. "All right, I'll accept your offer."

But it had already been two months since they'd begun the treatment. How much longer would it be until Jenny was well again?

Across town, Joey, in the back seat of his family's Mercedes S-Class sedan, was arriving at the front steps of his family's large estate. The driver got out, opened Joey's door, and carried his backpack for him.

Joey's after-school activities usually ran pretty late. He was the leader of the debate team, made up of two dozen students. Those meetings could last into the early evening, depending on the subject of discussion.

Joey's home schedule afterward consisted of rigorous exercise and training. Daily, upon coming home, he would grab a bottle of purified water from the fridge and a protein bar from the pantry. Then he would go up to his room, do fifteen minutes on the jump rope and twenty minutes on his punching bag, and perform four sets of eighty crunches with one-minute breaks between each set. Once he finished, he would eat his protein bar, chug the whole bottle of water, and head for the shower covered in sweat.

Today, after an especially hard workout, Joey grabbed a towel and threw it over his shoulder. As he walked down the long second-floor hallway connecting the east and west wings, he passed a framed photo of his grandfather at a much younger age. In the black-and-white photo, Vincent was sitting on a courtyard bench with his wife and two young sons. Joey's grandmother, Edith, had passed away several years before Joey was born. Joey had never known her, but from what his grandfather had told him, he knew she was one of the sweetest women ever. Sitting between Vincent and Edith was Joey's uncle Anthony, the older son, and his own father Jonathan, the younger. Both were no more than children at the time.

Joey remembered the good times he'd spent with his grandfather. When he was a kid, Vincent often took him to the zoo, the movies, and the park. When he was older, they had gone to local boxing matches together, and Joey soon formed a love of boxing. Just the idea of it—settling the struggle for dominance with a pair of gloves in a ring—fascinated him.

Before long, Joey had started dreaming of becoming a professional boxer someday. He wanted more than anything to be like the great Kenny "The Killer" Leary. At the age of eight, Joey had had the pleasure of seeing Leary's last fight ever. At retirement, Leary had completed his career with a total of eighty-five wins to one loss, and that sole loss was due to a technicality.

When Joey had told his grandfather about his dream, Vincent simply smiled and told him that if that was what Joey wanted, then he'd be in his corner the whole way, cheering him on.

Joey had wanted his grandfather to see him make it to the prizefighting ring, to see him become a great fighter. Now that would never happen. And he blamed it all on a girl whose name and face he didn't know. Remembering this inescapable fact, he slammed his fist into the wall beside the photo.

"Damn that witch! She's gonna pay for what she did," he cried. "I swear to you, Grandpa, I'll find her."

Not too far away was someone who was equally upset over Vincent's death: his son, Anthony "Tony" Scorpione. Since he was the oldest son, Tony would inherit the family business.

In a darkened room somewhere in the downtown district, Tony stood at the head of a polished mahogany table, surrounded by twelve shady-looking people in sharp dress who were talking amongst themselves. Growing impatient, Tony stood and slammed his fist down on the table, causing the glass of Scotch in front of him to bounce. The room fell silent. All eyes were on him.

"Listen up, all of ya!" Tony barked. "I want this girl found, you understand? I want her name, I want her family's names, and I want her friends' names. I want you to hunt this tramp down and bring her to me, so I can take care of this personally. Understood?"

Without a moment's hesitation, all the men stood up and said in unison, "You got it, boss."

Tony sat down and grabbed his glass of Scotch. "All right, now all of ya get outta here."

The men nodded and walked out the door of the conference room, except for one of them. A man in an expensive Italian suit walked up to Tony, placed his hand on his shoulder, and said, "Dad's death will be avenged, Tony. I swear this to you as your brother."

"Thank you, Johnny." Tony patted his brother's back gratefully. "You've never let me down."

"This'll be over soon, I assure you," Johnny said. He gave Tony's shoulder a squeeze and walked out.

Alone in the room, Tony sipped his Scotch. Enjoying the warm feeling of the potent liquor flowing down his throat, he started to relax. He looked up, as if seeing beyond the old faded ceiling tiles. "Don't you worry, Pop." Tony pulled a gun from inside his coat. "I'll get her for you. ' A life for a life'—isn't that what you always used to say?"

He took a moment to look at the gun. The dim lights subtly reflected off the black gunmetal of the M1911 Colt semi-automatic pistol. It was an effective gun, but not entirely common in that area among the crime elements. He set it on the table next to his glass, now almost drained of Scotch. His father had given the gun to him as a gift on his eighteenth birthday. As he'd handed Tony the pistol, he'd told him, "Tony, in this life, you can't rely on charm and charisma alone to get you through social situations. Sometimes, you need a little extra enthusiasm. Got me?"

At that moment, Tony had begun to understand the family business and his role within it.

He looked down at the gun one more time. "I'll get her, Pop." Tony swallowed the remaining Scotch in one gulp. "I swear to you."

Chapter Six

Stephanie walked steadily down the hallway, trying to make it to her first class on time despite the heavy traffic. She held her books firmly across her chest, like a shield for protection. Halfway there, three freshman boys, all with devious smiles and dark intentions in their eyes, stopped her and backed her against the lockers. She tried to keep her head down and avoid eye contact. She knew who they were: Tyler, Connor, and Brad. Tyler fancied himself the leader of this little pack of rejects, leaving, of course, Connor and Brad as his lackeys.

The three were nothing but trouble, and this wasn't the first time Stephanie had dealt with them. It seemed to be the weekly ritual of these miscreants to give her as much grief as possible.

"Please," Stephanie said, trying to move between them, "I have to get to class."

But the boys huddled up close, cutting off her escape.

"Don't you mean to your padded room, Stephanie?" Tyler jeered.

"Yeah," Connor said, "when are you gonna join your sister in the asylum?"

"If you want," Brad chimed in, "I can put you in a straightjacket. It would be a lot of fun."

Tyler leaned over her, ran his fingers through her hair, and stroked her cheek. That gesture sparked something inside her. It was small at first, but as she felt his filthy fingers move along her skin and his horrid breath hit her face, it grew. Stephanie began to shake as she finally realized what this feeling was: anger. It was all she could do to hold it inside, but she feared it wouldn't be long before she hit the breaking point.

"Well, what's it gonna be, Stephanie?" Tyler laughed. "I could keep you locked up in my room, hehehe!"

The sound of their laughter drove her closer and closer to the edge.

"Aww, poor little Stephanie," Connor mocked. "You gonna cry now?"

That was it. She couldn't hold back any longer. Clenching her fists, she looked up at them with fiery eyes and was about to open her mouth to curse them with all the pent-up fury erupting in her heart, when she heard someone else's angry voice instead.

"Hey! What the hell's going on?"

From out of nowhere, Joey grabbed Tyler and threw him up against the locker beside Stephanie. Joey pressed his forearm hard across the side of the other boy's jaw as he held him firmly in place.

"W-what's wrong, Joey?" Tyler said, his voice almost muffled by Joey's arm. "We were just having some fun. What do you care about her? She's just some geek."

Joey gave Tyler a hard right knee to the stomach and let him drop. As Tyler coughed and hacked on the floor, Joey placed his hand gently on Stephanie's shoulder, then turned, and pointed a finger at the three of them. "This girl is with me.

If I catch any of you so much as looking at her, you're all gonna have a really bad day. You got me?"

The boys nodded nervously.

"Then show some respect and apologize to the lady," Joey demanded.

"I—I'm really sorry," Brad said. "We apologize for making you upset."

Conner was next. "Yeah, um, sorry for giving you a hard time and disrespecting your sister."

Tyler shakily rose to his feet and joined his friends. "I'm really sorry for making you uncomfortable, and I didn't mean to harass you," he said in a tone of remorse as he held his midsection. "With all due respect, we hope your sister is doing much better."

Stephanie gave a silent nod before looking up at Joey.

"All right, all of you," Joey said, "now get the hell out of here."

The boys responded by making like cockroaches and disappearing as quickly as possible. Joey turned to Stephanie with a look of concern. "You all right?"

She simply nodded, still upset.

He put both hands on her shoulders in a comforting gesture.

"How long has this been goin' on?"

She responded sheepishly, her head lowered. "About a month."

"A month?" Joey looked down the hallway to where the three idiots had disappeared. "Well, they sure as hell won't be doing it anymore." He looked back at her and spoke more softly. "I'm glad I happened to be walking by when I did. It's okay now. You don't have to worry about them anymore."

"Thank you," she said sincerely. "Thank you so much. I don't know what I would have done if you hadn't shown up."

"Hey, don't worry about it." He gave her a charming smile. "You got any problems, anything at all, you let me know. I'll take care of it, all right?"

She returned a grateful smile. "Okay."

"All right." Joey loosened his neck nonchalantly. "Well, I'm gonna head off to class. I'll see you later, all right, Stephanie?"

"Okay, Joseph. See you later. And thanks again."

"Hey, call me Joey." He cracked a smile and gave her a wave as he moved in the other direction, melting into the crowd as Stephanie gathered her things and continued on to her own class.

Because he was possibly one of the most popular guys in the entire school, Joey's influence stretched from one end of the building to the other. From the teaching staff to the debate club members to the football team, he knew everyone. Now that was status—and he wasn't afraid to flaunt it like a superstar.

However, there was another reason he was so famous (or notorious, depending on your perspective): he had a massive temper. Even the tiniest thing could set him off. That was why everyone took his threats seriously. Once he lost it, people stayed out of his way like they'd avoid a runaway freight train. On top of that, out of all the rivals he'd fought to reach the top of the high school totem pole, he'd never lost a single fistfight, leaving all of his opponents lying at his feet. Joey showed no mercy and was vindictive when it came to protecting his friends.

As he passed through the crowd, he caught sight of someone he'd been looking for—a shifty-eyed boy in a baseball cap with a scruffy teen goatee. Joey called out to him from across the hall. "Billy Thomkins! You've been talkin' trash about my buddy Shawn."

Once Billy saw who was yelling at him, he immediately turned tail and ran. Joey went after him. "Hey, get back here! The more you run, the worse your beating's gonna be. Be smart."

Stephanie sat in Economics class, her mind beginning to wander. When this happened, she usually daydreamed about her favorite mystery novels or fantasized about walking through sunny fields on a warm spring day. But as she fantasized this time, other visions slowly crept into her mind.

At first the differences were subtle. The warm spring breeze caressing the tall grasses grew ice cold. The blue sky above became an ominous darkening gray. Suddenly the entire landscape changed, and in her mind's eye, she found herself inside a dimly lit warehouse. Water covered the concrete floor at her feet, and the smell of old mildew and fresh gunfire hung in the air. On the catwalks above her, shady-looking men were holstering their pistols. In front of her was Vincent, smiling in a satisfied way while looking at something on the floor between them.

No, she thought, *I don't like this.* She looked down. There on the cold, wet concrete was her father—lying in a pool of his own blood. The shock of the vision caused her to jump in her chair with a gasp. Several books fell from her desk to the floor, gaining the attention of the teacher.

"Miss Sebastiano, is something wrong?"

"No, Mr. Bernardo." Stephanie quickly regained her senses. "Nothing's wrong. I'm sorry." She leaned over, gathered her books, and placed them back on her desk.

Mr. Bernardo gave her a look and continued with his lecture on American economics. Stephanie tuned him out as her concerns again moved toward the internal. *I saw it again,* she thought nervously. *Why do I keep seeing it?* Her worries were interrupted by the bell ringing over the intercom system, signaling the end of the class period. She picked up her books one by one and placed them in her bag, feeling a sense of uneasiness as memories of the vision continued to haunt her.

Why must I see it over and over again? She wondered.

Across town at the institute, Jennifer sat motionless on the floor of her room. Hunched over, her arms around her knees, she hung her head. Her eyes were hidden behind her long bangs. Out of nowhere, a smile flitted across her face and she laughed quietly to herself, finding something amusing in her own thoughts.

"Blade shining in the fire's light… a killing stroke… the wall turns red… his portrait defiled… the shadow disappears."

Later that night, a white delivery truck drove through the city. The shipping manifest lying on the passenger seat listed the cargo as twelve boxes of stuffed animals going to a small toy shop on the east end of town. Strangely, it was a quarter past eleven, and the delivery was being made to a shop that had closed at half past nine. Not only that, but the suspension was riding pretty low for a newer truck carrying only teddy bears and fuzzy giraffes.

The driver was a short, stocky man with a scruffy beard. He wore a dirty, red, hooded sweatshirt and faded jeans. He had a teardrop tattoo under his left eye and flame tattoos on his forearms showing from under his sleeves. The man looked well built, like he could wrestle a rhino to the ground.

He took a sip from his coffee and placed the cup back in its holder on the dashboard. Allowing himself a deep yawn, he reached over and searched through the local radio stations, but found nothing he liked. As he was driving through an intersection, he was startled by a loud thump, as if something had fallen on top of the truck. The force was so strong it shook the whole vehicle. He immediately slammed on the brakes and pulled over to the side of the road. He put the truck in park, let out a few curse words, and got out. He took a walk around the vehicle looking for anything wrong. Nothing appeared to be damaged, and there was no one else around.

Stepping back a few feet, he got a view of the top of the truck. He couldn't see anything. He looked down the street to where he suspected the truck had been hit. The pavement was clear, and nothing looked unusual. He scratched his head, dumbfounded. "What the hell hit the truck?"

As he looked down, he noticed something strange. At his feet, he saw two shadows instead of just his own, both cast from the same street light. He let out a "Huh?" as he quickly turned around. He saw only a fist, and then all went black.

Standing silently over the unconscious driver was the assassin, rubbing the knuckles of her right hand. The glossy finish of her white fox mask shone in the dim light of the street lamp. She set a hand on her hip in a pretentious pose.

"My friend, you sure picked the wrong night to make a delivery."

She knelt down, unhooked the ring of keys from his belt, opened the passenger-side door, and grabbed the manifest from the seat. Then she walked around to the back rollup door, where she started sifting through the keys on the ring. Finally, she held up a single key, inserted it into the padlock, and turned. It opened with a click. She tossed the lock aside, lifted up the door, and hopped in. She glanced at the manifest, then at the cargo, and flung the sheet of paper away.

"Stuffed animals aren't packed in heavy wooden crates," she said to the night. "But I can sure guess what is." She grabbed the crowbar hanging from the hook beside her and used it to tear open a box.

"I knew it," she said as soon as she saw its contents. Inside were twenty AK-47 rifles with illegal thirty-round magazines. She quickly tore open another box and found thirty MAC-10s. In box after box there were M-16 assault rifles, P90 submachine guns, Uzis, TEC-9s, and more—enough weapons in that one truck to arm a small army and start a small war, and they were all going to the east side, where the gang presence was strongest. And who would benefit most from providing them with all this artillery?

"The Scorpiones." Her tone was disdainful. "They're still selling guns, which means someone is still running the family. My guess would be the oldest son, Antonio." She reached into a pouch hanging from her belt and took out a small bomb with a timer preset to ten seconds. *This will put a nice dent in their income*, she thought. She placed it between the crates, flipped the switch, and got clear. Ten seconds counted down, and with a boom loud enough to shatter the windows of a nearby building, the entire truck was reduced to scrap.

The masked bomber ran down the street at a speed that would have put an Olympic runner to shame. The long ribbon tying her ponytail rippled in the wind as her feet pounded the pavement sending debris flying into the air. She stopped several blocks away and took a moment to look at her wrist, which was wrapped with a digital readout that showed the level of a certain serum in her bloodstream. It was down to twenty percent. She reached into the side pocket on her belt and took out a compact injector gun to give herself a booster shot.

She hitched up the fabric from her forearm, pressed the gun to her skin, and pulled the trigger. She immediately felt the effects of the serum now coursing through her veins. Her body felt like a violent thunderstorm, a raging hurricane: powerful and unstoppable. Her blood was on fire.

"Yes!" She let out a laugh despite herself. "Now that's more like it."

Looking up to the rooftops, she crouched low to the pavement. Then she jumped, seemingly with no effort at all, toward the second-story level of the building in front of her. She ricocheted off the brick surface there and hurtled toward the roof ledge of the building across the street, where she caught a grip with one hand. A quick kick off the wall, a back flip over the ledge, and her feet landed on the rooftop.

Suddenly her earpiece began to beep quickly, followed by a voice. "This is Den Mother. Status report."

The assassin touched her earpiece and responded, "I read you. Information was accurate. The shipment has been intercepted and the arms eliminated."

"Excellent. Return to base immediately."

"Copy that. Out."

The assassin took a deep breath as she crouched low on the rooftop. For a moment she was completely still. Then she shot up like a bullet from a gun, a leap so powerful it cracked that area of the concrete roof. With agility and strength unimaginable, she bounded from ledge to ledge, roof to roof, across the city.

The assassin's shadowy figure appeared as a lightning-fast blur to the observing eye, but to her the world had slowed to a crawl. Far below, cars and buses rolled sluggishly down the avenues and people appeared almost as statues. Jets and helicopters seemed frozen in the sky as she glided effortlessly through the air from one building to the next.

This was true freedom. No one could catch her. They couldn't even stop her. She grinned under her mask. All she had to do was complete her missions, and she was given all this power.

Like a violent wind, she finally disappeared on the dark night's horizon.

Chapter Seven

Early the next morning, Pat rubbed the sleep from his eyes as he walked into his bathroom. After he showered and brushed his teeth, he was ready to tackle the new day. When he went downstairs, his parents were already seated at the breakfast table. The morning news was just starting on the small flat-screen TV on the counter.

"Morning Mom, Dad."

"Morning, son," his father said, lowering his newspaper to give Pat a nod. "Do you know what happened last night?"

"What do you mean?" Pat slid two slices of whole-grain bread into the toaster, more focused on the emptiness in his stomach than the morning news.

"It's all over the news, sweetie." His mom pointed to the TV. "Just watch."

Pat remained silent as the announcer continued his story.

At this time it still isn't clear whether Vincent Scorpione's killer was involved in the incident. Repeating our top story, this is the information we have so far: Last night at around 11:15 p.m. on Cooper Avenue and Sixth, a delivery truck, which was allegedly carrying several boxes of stuffed animals, was intercepted and the driver knocked unconscious. Soon after, the truck exploded. Due to the condition of the wreckage, local authorities were unable to match its cargo with the shipping manifest, which was found several blocks away.

There have been several reported but as yet unconfirmed sightings of the mysterious killer of Vincent Scorpione in that area of the city during the time of the explosion. However it still isn't clear whether Scorpione's killer was involved. We'll have more on this story as it develops. This has been Richard Conrad with Channel 3 Morning News.

The slices of toast popped up as Pat slowly scratched his head in thought. He guessed the assassin wasn't gone after all. "Wow," he said aloud as he spread some butter on his toast. "But hold on a second—why go to all the trouble of blowing up a delivery truck filled with stuffed animals?"

"It does seem a little strange," his father said, his head buried in the newspaper again.

"Today is your Spanish test, right, Pat?" his mother said. "Is this one going to be tougher than the last?"

Pat sat down at the table and took a bite of his toast. "Yeah, Mrs. Lopez has a real big one waiting for us."

"I hope you've been studying." His mother wagged her finger at him. "I don't want to see another C on your report card, mister."

"Yes, I've been studying, Mom. And it was only that one time I got the C."

"That's because you didn't apply yourself enough," she said. "I know you're smarter than that, Patrick. You have a lot of potential. A little motivation can go a long way."

"I know, I know," Pat groaned. "I'm doing the best I can."

His mother looked at her watch. "I have to be at the Institute in half an hour." She grabbed her coat from one of the chairs at the table. "All right, you two, I'll be home late. Dinner's in the fridge, just heat it up in the microwave." She lowered her husband's paper to give him a kiss, and left.

Pat took another bite of toast. "Hey, Dad, aren't you supposed to be at the office by now?"

"I took a half day today. I have a doctor's appointment at nine, so I'll be at work around noon." His father folded the paper and set it on the table. "So, have you thought about which college you want to go to yet?"

"C-college?" Pat stumbled over the word. "Uh, well, not really. Isn't it a little early for that?"

His father raised an eyebrow. "It's never too early. The sooner, the better. Why, your mother and I both graduated high school early and were immediately accepted into Harvard."

Pat knew all too well that his father's master's degree in journalism had led him to his current position as editor-in-chief of the *Watchman,* just as his mother's doctorate in medicine had helped her become the director of the Thompson Medical Research Institute. Pat couldn't help but feel a little intimidated by his parents' accomplishments.

"That's the thing, Dad," Pat said. "You and Mom are a lot to live up to. I don't know if I can do as well as you two did."

His father leaned forward in his chair and laid his hand on his son's shoulder. "Listen to me: you can achieve anything, so long as you put your mind to it. With a solid will, nothing is impossible. Remember that."

Pat thought about it for a moment. Maybe his father was right, and the only thing holding him back was self-doubt. Just in case, he gave his dad a lopsided grin. "Right—thanks, Dad."

His father gave Pat's shoulder a loving pat, and then looked at his watch. "I'd better get going. Traffic is going to be brutal. You'd better get going, too. You don't want to be late for school."

His father took one last sip of his coffee and hurried toward the door. Pat grabbed his coat and book bag and ran out the door behind him.

It was sunny out and not too cold, a pretty decent day for mid-November. As Pat walked to school, passing by the many stately homes in his neighborhood, his thoughts turned to Stephanie. He was worried about her. He knew that she hadn't been right since her father's death, but lately she'd been acting more and more distant, even for her. He thought about the way she stared into space, as if she were separate from the reality surrounding her. He saw it almost every day now. She hadn't been interested in hanging out on the weekends lately, and it had been weeks since they'd even gone out for coffee. He hoped nothing was wrong.

Twenty minutes later, Pat passed through the school entrance, where he ran into Joey. They exchanged greetings and started walking. "So how's the moving been going?" Pat asked.

"We're all finished. It's kind of cool living across the street from you." His tone turned sad. "Besides, Grandpa would've wanted it that way, and it seemed wrong to leave the house empty, you know?" But his smile quickly returned. "Hey, why don't you and Stephanie stop by the house sometime? My dad would love to see you guys again."

"Sure, man, that sounds great." Pat looked up and down the hall. "By the way, I've been looking for Steph. Have you seen her around? She's been acting a little strange lately."

"I saw her yesterday. Three idiot lower classmen have been giving her problems." Joey grinned as he clenched his fist. "But I took care of 'em. They won't be bothering her anymore."

Pat felt his worries lessen slightly. "Maybe that's what it was. Thank you helping her out, Joey, I really appreciate that."

"Hey! A friend of yours is a friend of mine, right? Besides, I really like Stephanie. She's a nice girl, and I hate to see her treated like that." Joey hooked his arm around Pat's neck, pulled him in close, and said quietly, "So when ya gonna make your move, man?"

"What move?"

"Yeah, man, you've known her for a while now. You two seem pretty close. Come on—tell me you've at least asked her out on a date."

"I, uh..." Pat stumbled over his words. Then he quickly diverted Joey's attention down the hall. "Hey, wait—there she is." Less than twenty steps away was a certain girl looking downward, shyly holding her books across her chest as she walked along. "Hey, Steph!" Pat waved his hand above the crowd. "Over here."

Stephanie looked up, and when she saw Pat's smiling face, her spirits seemed to brighten. Carefully maneuvering through the traffic, she joined them. "Hi, Pat, Joseph." She brushed her bangs to one side and gave them a pleased smile.

"Stephanie, I keep tellin' you." Joey shook his head and gave her a fake frown. "Just call me Joey."

"Right." Stephanie let out short laugh. "Sorry, Joey."

"So where are you heading to now?" Pat asked.

"World History," she said. "Big test today. Oh, joy."

"Anyway…" Pat glanced over at Joey, who gave him the go-for-it nod. "Did you want to hang out tonight, Steph? We could go see a movie or something."

"Sure, that sounds like fun. Joey, do you want to come along, too?"

"Me? No, sorry, there's stuff I gotta do," Joey said quickly. "And my dad needs to talk to me about something. So maybe next time, huh?" The bell rang, prompting everyone around them to hurry to their classes. "Hey, I'll catch you guys later." Joey gave Pat a sly thumbs-up behind Stephanie's back before he ran to class.

"So what time did you want to get together tonight?" Pat asked as they hurried to class together.

"How about seven?"

"Sounds perfect. How about we meet at the theater on Fourth Street?"

She agreed, and the two quickly ran to their separate classes. Pat was sure no one could tell by looking at him, but his heart was racing a mile a minute.

I did it! I can't believe I actually asked her out, he thought. *This is awesome!*

Stephanie sat down at her desk. *Did he just do what I think he did?* She wondered. She felt herself smiling and wondered if anybody noticed.

When she'd first come to this school, she had tried so hard to make friends. She would greet people and introduce herself the best she could, but most of the students simply turned their backs and ignored her. Others laughed and made cruel comments about her plain hair and minimal makeup. Her shy demeanor and lack of eye contact were also targets for attack. Her old school had never been like that. There, everyone got along and no one judged, but here? Here was a different story.

For a while Stephanie had given up. To hell with these people and their cruel attitudes. It was bad enough that she had difficulties in social situations, but this school had more upturned noses than a rhinoplasty clinic. So she decided, since they obviously didn't need her, she didn't need them either. What did it matter if she didn't have friends? She had come to this school to learn, and that was it.

That had been her mode of thinking, until one day, one little chance encounter had changed her whole world. A month into her first semester, she was hurrying down the hall, late for class, not looking where she was going. She accidently bumped into a boy and dropped all her books. Assuming he would just keep on walking and ignore her like everyone else, she got down and gathered her books. But then she was shocked to hear three words: "Are you okay?"

She looked up, astonished at this boy with wavy brown hair and blue eyes. He was actually on the floor with her picking up her books and handing them to her with a smile.

After they got up, she lowered her head and said quietly, "Thank you."

"Don't worry about it," he said. "By the way, I'm Patrick O'Hara. Don't think I've seen you around. Are you new here?" He had held out his hand to shake, but she had hesitated, staring at it for a moment as if not knowing what to do. Then she had slowly reached out.

"I'm—I'm Stephanie Sebastiano. Nice to meet you, Patrick. I just started here a month ago."

"Cool, Stephanie." The bell rang over the intercom. "Listen, I gotta go or I'll be late for class, but I'll see you around, okay?"

And he did. After that, they saw each other almost every day and quickly became good friends.

Remembering that chance encounter kept a warm smile on her face throughout class, causing much curiosity and speculation among her peers—who noticed.

In a darkened room somewhere in the downtown district, Tony Scorpione sat on a cushy leather sofa and smoked a fine cigar. His lowered eyebrows and deep frown reflected his sour mood. Before long the doors at the other end of the room opened. Two of his men hauled in the delivery truck driver and dropped him at Tony's feet.

The driver was covered in bruises, and blood dripped from his lip onto the floor. He was shaking uncontrollably. He slowly raised his head, and Tony glared at him, took in a big puff of his cigar, leaned close, and blew the smoke into the driver's face, causing him to cough.

"Rocco." Tony shook his head. "Rocco, Rocco, Rocco. I hire you for a simple job; just one simple job. Do you remember what you told me when I asked you if you could do it?"

Rocco lowered his head. "Please, boss. I—"

Tony's furious voice rang through the room. "You told me it was no problem."

"Boss, it wasn't my fault," Rocco continued with caution. "It was that girl. She—"

"Shut up!" Tony stood and began to circle the man on the floor. "I hired you for one reason and one reason only. You were the toughest man in Sing Sing. Anyone who ever got in your way, you crushed 'em. Hell, you pulverized 'em."

"Yeah, but…"

"Shut up!" Tony regained his composure and bent close to Rocco again. "So tell me, why did you have a problem with one little lady who likes Halloween?"

"She snuck up on me and—"

"I already know that. You got beat up by a girl, right? But that's not what concerns me right now. Can that tiny little brain of yours venture a guess as to what does?"

"Uh, your guns?"

"Bingo!" Tony grinned maliciously. "Absolutely right, Rocky-boy. How about another one? Guess how much that shipment cost me."

"I, um, I don't know, Boss."

Tony's grin disappeared. He came close to Rocco's ear, as if to whisper. "I'll tell you how much: one hundred and fifty thousand dollars, that's how much." Tony grabbed him by the shirt and raised the man to his feet. "That was the mother lode. I was going to make a fortune selling those guns on the street, and then BOOM! All of 'em went up in smoke. Why? Because some two-bit moron with a cheeseburger for a brain let his clock get cleaned out by a girl who plays dress-up."

Tony slapped the man across the face and threw him to the floor. Rocco got up on his knees, pleading, "Please, Boss, give me another chance and I'll never let you down again."

"You don't know how right you are, Rocky-boy." Tony pulled out his gun and shot Rocco between the eyes. By the time he hit the floor, he was already dead. Tony holstered his gun and then motioned to his men. "Clean up this filth. He's bleedin' all over my new carpet."

Chapter Eight

After school, Stephanie visited her sister as usual. As soon as Jennifer saw Stephanie walk through her door, she was overcome with excitement. "Stephie!" She threw her arms around her sister, giving her a bear hug.

Stephanie hugged her sister back. "How are you doing today?"

"I'm as happy as a bee in a honey jar," Jennifer replied in a singing voice.

They both sat down on the bed, and Stephanie brought out her book. "Let's see, where did we leave off?" She flipped through the pages. "Here we are." She began to read, but Jennifer interrupted her before she got through the first page.

"Stephie?" she said, softly.

"Yes?"

Jennifer clasped Stephanie's hand. "Don't worry. Things will get better. I promise."

Stephanie looked at her sister curiously for a moment, but then she smiled. "I know they will."

A half hour and a chapter later, Stephanie left. Once Jennifer was alone again, she frowned. "Oh, my dear sister. Unfortunately, things will get worse before they get better."

At the Scorpione estate, Johnny stood at the foot of the stairs and called, "Joey! Come here, I gotta talk to you for a minute."

A few moments later, Joey appeared at the top of the stairs with a towel around his neck. "Yeah, Dad?"

"You done workin' out?"

Joey bounded down the stairs. "Yeah, what's up?"

"Your birthday's coming up in a week. Seventeen, my boy. That's quite an age. So, what do you want?" Johnny put his arm around his son's shoulders. "A big party? I can make it happen. You can invite all your friends. Anything you want—just name it."

"A party sounds awesome, Dad!"

"You got it." Johnny and his son walked into the living room. "We'll hold it in the ballroom. It's big enough, right? You can have a live band and everything." Johnny's tone suddenly became somber. "You know, that's where your granddad held all his parties."

"Yeah, I remember Grandpa's parties. They were really something."

"All right, I'll set everything up. Don't you worry about a thing, son." Johnny gave his boy a friendly thump on the back. "Go hop in the shower. I got some calls I gotta make."

"Thanks, Dad," Joey called out as he ran back up the stairs. "Thanks a lot!"

"Forget about it!" his dad cheerfully shot back.

Johnny walked back toward the library, singing a Dean Martin song to himself. He'd never shared with his son the true nature of the family business. It was better that way. He preferred to wait until the boy came of age before he divulged all of the family's secrets to him. As far as Joey knew, his grandfather had established a highly successful distribution company in the 1960s and kept a lot of hired muscle around to protect his interests. But that was all he knew.

The doorbell rang, and Johnny checked the security camera feed before opening the door. The grainy feed showed a girl, and she looked harmless. He opened the door to find Stephanie Sebastiano standing on his doorstep, holding a notebook.

"Hello Stephanie." Johnny gave her a welcoming smile. "What a surprise! So, what brings you to our neck of the woods, eh?"

"Hi Mr. Scorpione. I was visiting my sister at the institute, and when I left, I realized I still had Joey's notebook that he loaned me." She held the notebook out to him, "Could you please give this back to him?"

"Sure thing. I'll see that he gets it." As Johnny reached out to take the notebook, Stephanie seemed to freeze, and she narrowed her eyes. Johnny noticed the look on her face. "You all right, kid?"

"Uh, yeah, I'm fine." Her voice sounded shaky.

"Hey, did you wanna come inside? I'm sure Joey would love to see ya. He should be down in a couple of minutes."

"Uh no, that's okay." She slowly stepped back. "I really have to get going anyway."

"All right then," he said, "take it easy, Stephanie, and don't be stranger, you got that?"

Stephanie walked across the grounds toward the main gate, and she could feel herself trembling. When Mr. Scorpione had reached out for Joey's notebook, his Italian suit jacket had opened up just enough to reveal his holstered Colt .45 revolver.

That gun, she thought. *I've seen a gun like it before...in my dream.*

The traffic down Fourth Street was hectic that evening, as usual for the entertainment district around that time. In front of the local theater, Pat and Stephanie met up amidst the moving crowds. The foot traffic was almost as bad as it was in the hallways at Kingsley between classes.

From Stephanie's faraway demeanor, Pat could tell something wasn't right. "You okay, Steph?"

"Me? Oh, I'm fine." She glanced at the movie posters, as if seeking to change the subject. "So, what movie are we seeing?"

"Well, I was looking at that one called *Alone,* with Kate Beckerman." Patrick pointed to a poster showing a brunette holding a gun in front of a background of a desert sunset and a pursuing helicopter. "It looks really good. Have you heard of it?"

"Nope." She stepped closer to the poster. "What's it about?"

"This woman is looking for her husband who's an FBI agent. He got kidnapped by a terrorist group and she's searching the world for him."

"Well… it sounds interesting." She smiled, but she sounded a little unsure.

Pat pointed to the posters down the wall. "If that doesn't sound good, we could always see *Freddy Loses His Car* or *Jackie Shanahan versus the Leprechauns,* or we could even see *Planet of the Monkeys.* I heard that one has a funny banana-throwing scene."

"Okay, you've sold me." She let out a giggle. "Let's see *Alone."*

Two hours later, Stephanie left the theater with Pat, talking lightheartedly about the movie they'd just seen.

"I couldn't believe that ending," Pat said, sounding full of enthusiasm. "Who would've thought the conspiracy went all the way up to the head of the FBI? The action scenes were so cool, too. How about you? What were your favorite parts?"

"I really liked seeing the girl save the guy for a change. Plus, I liked the scenes of Paris. I really want to go there someday. It looks so romantic."

"Paris, huh?" Patrick paused for a second. "How about we go there together?"

Stephanie couldn't believe what she was hearing. "Really? You'd really go there with me?"

"Sure," he said. "It's better than going alone, right?"

"No, that's not it. I mean, you being there would be..." She felt herself blushing. "With you it would just be—special."

Pat didn't reply, and her stomach twisted into a knot. She immediately regretted what she had just said, certain that it would make the atmosphere awkward. Then Pat gently touched her shoulder. "If that's what you think, then we'll definitely go."

Hearing those words from him not only brought Stephanie a feeling of relief, but hopeful anticipation as well. "Seriously?"

"Yeah. In fact, let's make it a promise, Steph."

Her smile matched his. "Yes, it's definitely a promise."

Stephanie and Patrick walked up the polished gray marble steps that led up to cherry wood double doors at the front entrance of Stephanie's stately home. A crystal-encased light shone above them. A cool breeze, seemingly coming from nowhere, moved Stephanie's silky hair.

It was at that moment that Pat saw a beauty in her he hadn't noticed before. Her soft brown eyes sparkled in the light. The fair skin of her cheeks, smooth and without blemish, glowed in the cold air. Her lips, naturally red without a hint of lipstick, made magic in her smile. He could no longer perceive her as just a friend. Pat had finally recognized her as an elegant young woman. And with that realization, Pat felt an internal crisis rising within him. This was it, the end of the date, the part where the guy was supposed to say goodnight in a romantic way. But what could he say? He didn't want to quote some movie line; that would sound lame. What to do?

"Pat?" Stephanie's voice shook him from his thoughts.

"Huh?"

"You got so quiet all of a sudden. Are you okay?"

"Me?" He put on a brave face. "No, I'm fine."

"Well, I had a great time tonight. Thank you so much for treating me."

"I—I had a great time too." Again, Pat felt awkward as they stood together in the silence of the night. Then he forced himself to say something, anything. "Did you want to get together again tomorrow?"

"Sure," she said eagerly. "I'd like that."

They gazed into each other's eyes, and Pat agonized over whether to close the distance between them. After a moment, Stephanie stepped toward the door and said, "Well, I'd better head in. Thanks again, Pat. Goodnight."

"Yeah. Goodnight, Steph."

After she went inside, Pat started for home. A smile came over him as a thought crossed his mind. *Paris with me would be special, huh?*

Inside her house, Stephanie leaned her back against the door. "Patrick…" she said with a sigh, and she couldn't help smiling to herself. " It's a promise then."

She was about to move toward the staircase when suddenly her head began to swim. The dizziness was so strong that she lowered herself to her knees for fear of losing her balance. For a moment, she thought she saw several white feathers float by, but she wasn't sure if they were real or not. As she held her head in an attempt to steady the vertigo, a vision came into her mind's eye. The here and now was swept away, and she found herself in another place.

Along the main street of the business district stood an antique shop she'd never seen before. It was after hours and the front door was locked, but inside an old man up on a ladder was diligently cleaning the shelves of his shop, being extremely careful, as most of his collection was fragile.

One item on a shelf toward the back of the shop seemed to stand out. It was a mirror, Japanese in design, circular, and about seven inches in diameter. Two skillfully crafted silver dragons formed the molding. Red silk tassels hung from their tails. Despite its obvious age, the mirror's reflection still shone clear as crystal, and the silver sparkled as if polished to a flawless finish.

The old man got down from the shelves and took a moment to rub his back. Somehow Stephanie knew that there had been no customers all day long and that he had taken that time to clean the dust from his entire collection. He sat down behind the counter, took a sip from his coffee cup, and lit a cigarette. He leaned forward, resting his elbows on the glass counter, took a long drag, and slowly exhaled, enjoying the peaceful quiet.

The old man appeared to be startled when he heard a loud noise. In Stephanie's vision, three armed men kicked the front door in and burst into the shop. They pulled the helpless owner over the counter and threw him to the floor. One who appeared to be the leader pulled out his revolver and pointed it at the old man's head, shouting, "Give me all your money now!" The leader didn't appear to be angry; in fact, he had a strange smile that looked familiar to Stephanie. Then she recognized him—it was Vincent Scorpione. But he was so young.

The old man pleaded with the robbers. "Listen to me, all I have is $40 in the cash register. Please take it and go."

Vincent let out a laugh. "Forty bucks ain't good enough, gramps." Vincent's eye caught the mirror on the shelf. "Hey, how about this thing?" He hopped over the counter and grabbed the mirror from its display. "This's gotta be worth a lot of money, right?"

"No, don't!" the old man yelled. "A foreign buyer is coming tomorrow to pick it up. The money he's offering will help me pay all my debts. Take anything else, I beg you!"

"Oh man, now it's mine for sure." Vincent smiled greedily as he looked at his reflection. "Put this one in the van, boys, and grab anything else that'll land us some cash."

"Please, give it back." The old man grabbed Vincent's jacket. "That mirror is the only hope I have left."

That's when Vincent lost his temper. "Get the hell off of me!" he yelled as he smacked the old man away. He pulled back the hammer on his revolver and shot one round into the old man's chest, right through his heart.

Seeing the old man drop dead at Vincent's feet, the other two men panicked. They quickly grabbed whatever they could carry and ran out of the shop.

Vincent stood staring at the old man's lifeless body as if in shock. If Stephanie didn't know any better, she would swear it was the first time Vincent had killed anyone. For a brief moment, he looked as if he would vomit. The tiniest bit of horror was in his eyes. Then a strange calm seemed to sweep over him, followed by astonishment. That's when he probably realized how easy it was. Just pull the trigger, and bang! They're gone.

"Vinnie!" one of his men called from outside. "Come on, the cops will be here any minute." Seeing that Vincent was acting stunned, the man ran over and grabbed him by the arm. "Let's go."

Vincent nodded and seemed to snap out of his trance. He stuffed the mirror inside his jacket, ran out of the shop, and jumped into the black van waiting outside. They burned rubber down the road, turned sharply around a corner and disappeared.

Suddenly, everything faded, and Stephanie found herself curled up on the hardwood floor of her house.

"Why?" she said softly, feeling tears welling up in her eyes. "Why do I keep seeing these things? What does it all mean?"

Chapter Nine

It was nearing 8:30 p.m., and a deep chill filled the air as the temperature dropped. Dark storm clouds gathered on the horizon, waiting for the chance to cover the city in cold, unforgiving rain.

Jimmy crossed the police parking lot and got into his Crown Victoria. He clicked on the dome light and turned down the volume on the police band radio as he started reviewing files on the local gangs. Who would have the money and the guts to hire a specialist to kill Vincent Scorpione, the biggest crime boss in New Jersey? He flipped a page in his file. The Latin Royals?

Word had it that Vincent had sold them out to the Black Pythons. They had attacked the Royals' headquarters and almost killed their leader, Roberto Dominguez. Good motive, but Roberto lacked the capital to hire a skilled assassin.

Jimmy flipped to the next page.

Then there were the Black Pythons. Two months after the Royals incident, Vincent had allegedly tipped off the ATF that the Pythons were involved in gunrunning. The Pythons got shut down and sent to jail, while Vincent cornered the market in arms deals. The Pythons' leader, Orlando "4-O" Johnson, entered a plea deal. After naming all his buyers, he got only four years.

Jimmy brought out Orlando's file.

Orlando had been released from prison just three weeks earlier. He had motive, but not the finances. The ATF had seized his assets because it was all illegal gun money.

Jimmy let out a sigh as he closed the file folder and dropped it onto the passenger seat. He started the car and put it in gear. Time to get some info.

At a little after 9:00 p.m., Jimmy pulled up to a street corner on the lower end of town by the docks. He was dressed in plainclothes and driving an old beat-up Buick Skylark. The area was a typical blooming garden of prostitution and narcotics. Women in satin and lace pranced along the sidewalks, while their pimps kept close watch from the shadows. In the alleys, pale, slender pushers in cheap clothes and gold chains advertised their highly addictive merchandise to those who walked by.

One of these pushers was Mikey Jenkins, Jimmy's informant. About 5'5", a little heavyset, and not very intimidating, Mikey made his living the best way he knew how: selling drugs. He carried everything from Ecstasy to LSD to hashish.

A few years ago when Jimmy worked Vice, he'd busted Mikey for trafficking five pounds of marijuana between New York City and Benton. Mikey was looking at five years, so he entered a plea deal. He gave up the names of all his suppliers and got only twelve months in the state penitentiary.

Now Mikey kept his ear to the ground. So long as he continued to give Jimmy information, Jimmy agreed to look the other way, as long as Mikey kept his business away from school yards. In police work, this arrangement could sometimes be viewed as a necessary evil. Besides, "word on the street" was almost always reliable.

"Mikey," Jimmy said as he walked up to him, "how's it going?"

Mikey gave him a crooked smile. "How are ya?"

Jimmy quickly looked around before continuing in a quiet voice. "I need some of your special stash. Can you hook me up?"

Mikey gave a nod. "Follow me."

They walked into a nearby bar, went all the way to the back, and sat down where it was dark and secluded.

"You hear about the explosion last night on Cooper Avenue, Mikey?"

"Yeah, that was Tony Scorpione's shipment. Rifles, pistols, SMGs, you name it. He hired a guy named Rocco to deliver the goods. Rocco spent some time in Sing Sing; he was a real tough bastard. Anyway, he pulls over, gets out, and that assassin girl comes out of nowhere. Bam! She knocks him out cold. I'm talkin' Mike Tyson here. He never saw it comin'. Then she blows up the guns and takes off like a bat outta hell. I mean fast! The Flash would run out of breath trying to catch up to this girl."

"Why would she destroy the guns and leave the driver alive?"

"Beats the hell outta me, but that driver wasn't livin' for long. They dragged Rocco back to Tony, and he shot him in the head."

"How much did Tony lose?"

"A hundred fifty grand."

Jimmy let out a breath of amazement. "Tony must have been heated. So when's his next shipment?"

"Soon—middle of next week sometime. That's all I know right now."

"Thanks for the info. So…how's business been going?"

"Ain't been the same since I got away from the schools."

Jimmy gave him a glare.

"Hey, relax, I'm kidding. Besides, all I got out of those kids was chump change anyway. I don't miss it."

Jimmy got up. "When will you have more info on the shipment?"

Mikey thought about it for a second. "What's today? Friday? Talk to me on Monday. I'll have more for you then."

"Sounds good. Take it easy, Mikey." Jimmy stopped and turned back. "By the way, who saw the whole thing go down with Tony's shipment?'

"It was, um—" Mikey took a moment to think. "What was her name again? Oh yeah, Terri from the Street Cats."

"Terri Vasquez?"

"Yeah…" Mikey seemed surprised. "You know her?"

"We had a couple run-ins, mostly because of that gang she rolls with. Where does she hang out these days?"

"Toro's Matador. It's a Latin bar a couple blocks down the road. If she ain't at the bar orderin' drinks, she's at the pool tables hustling for money."

Jimmy let out a laugh. "Some things never change. Take it easy, pal."

"See ya around."

Jimmy left the bar and got back into his car. He sat there thinking. It didn't make sense. Why would the assassin be targeting Tony's gun shipments? It was a pretty bold move. Was it to spite him? To call him out?

In his restaurant, Don Marco's, Tony was finishing a baked mostaccioli dinner. After one last bite, he set down his fork, wiped his mouth on a napkin, and tossed it onto the table. A young brunette waitress walked over and smiled at him sweetly.

"Will that be all, Mr. Scorpione? Can I get you a coffee or maybe some cannoli?"

"No, Lisa, I think I'll call it a night." He looked at his men. "Boys, this is Lisa Smith. I recently hired her to work evenings."

They each gave a nod. "It's a pleasure, young lady."

"Lisa," Tony continued, "I'm very sorry to hear about your brother Jake. I can't imagine what you and your mother must be going through. You know, your mother… she was so pretty."

At the mention of Jake's name Lisa twitched almost imperceptibly in the dim light. However, it was when he spoke of her mother that she almost broke her sunny façade.

"I greatly appreciate that, Mr. Scorpione." Lisa seemed to be trying to maintain her composure. "I also want to thank you for letting me work here. I really need the money."

"Forget about it," he said with a sly smile. "I'm always willing to help out a kid in need." He wrapped his arm around her waist, pulled her close, and spoke quietly. "Have you considered my little business proposition? There's a lot of money in it for you. Just need you to run some packages to my friends."

"I don't know, Mr. Scorpione." She swallowed hard. "I don't feel right about it."

Tony grabbed her by the arm. "Hey! I did you a favor, all right? I gave you a good-paying job. I'm not even gonna mention how much you make in tips. The least you can do is this one little thing for me, understand?"

"Please, Mr. Scorpione." She tried to free herself from his grip. "You're hurting me."

Then Tony noticed the curious stares of his customers. He let go, pointed his finger at her, and whispered, "Don't you ever disrespect me. I don't care how many people are watching, I will slap you senseless, you get me? Now go on break. Sheila can cover for you."

Lisa, clearly upset, ran for the back room and disappeared.

"All right, boys." Tony got up and grabbed his coat from the chair next to him. "Let's head to Frankie's bar. He owes me a couple drinks. Bobby, bring the car around."

A few minutes later they were standing outside in front of the restaurant. The overcast clouds above reflected the soft amber glow of the city. A hard, icy wind hit the back of Tony's neck, causing a shiver to roll over him.

"Where the hell is Bobby?" He looked at his gold watch. "I told him to bring the car around five minutes ago."

"You want I should check on him, Boss?" one of his men said.

"Yeah, tell him to get his ass out here. It's freezing!"

Tony pulled out his cell phone, but before he could dial the first number he heard a ruckus behind him. First it sounded like a butcher chopping meat, then like sacks of potatoes hitting the ground.

He turned and dropped his phone in horror. Two of his men lay on the sidewalk. Both were cut clean in half at the waist. Tony froze in shock. "Holy Mary, mother of God," he breathed.

Then Bobby's severed head landed at Tony's feet, and he jumped back in fright. Tony looked up. There on the edge of the restaurant roof was the assassin, staring back at him, bloody sword in hand.

Tony began to quiver. He called out for the rest of his men. "Donnie! Nicky! Help!" The assassin looked mockingly toward the entrance of the restaurant, and then slowly shook her head at Tony. Sweat formed on Tony's brow, and a cold chill ran down his back. "What—what now?" he asked nervously.

The assassin pointed to her sword and then to Tony.

Tony's hands trembled as he pulled out his 1911 Colt. He took shaky aim and started firing. But each shot was deflected by the unnatural speed of her reflexes. The bullets bounced off the surface of her blade as it moved almost faster than the eye could see.

"Forget this, I ain't dyin'!" Tony turned and ran. He could hear nothing but his heartbeat banging like a sledgehammer in his ears. His leg muscles burned as his expensive leather shoes clacked on the pavement in quick succession. This was more running than he'd done in years. He glanced behind him: the assassin bounded from light post to light post with ease.

Tony saw an abandoned apartment building on his left and quickly ducked inside. He slammed the door shut, found a small chair, and jammed it against the door knob. He knew it wouldn't stop her for long. After all, she had taken down three of his strongest men in under five minutes. Tony bent over, coughing and hacking as he tried to catch his breath. His mind was spinning. Terror and paranoia had firmly taken hold. Nothing seemed real and everything was trying to kill him.

A few minutes passed. All was silent as he stood there in the darkness alone. He felt calm slowly return, and he was able to breathe deeply once more. Only the light from outside illuminated the main hallway where he stood. Dirt and garbage covered the floors, and graffiti decorated the walls. Tony listened carefully. When he could hear nothing other than the wind hitting the building, his confidence returned.

"Heh!" He let out a laugh. "Guess she gave up, huh? Yeah, nobody gets the better of Antonio Scorpione." Then a sudden knock at the entrance door almost made him jump out of his skin. "Ya ain't gettin' in," he called out nervously. He felt the terror return. "Give it up."

Another knock came, as mild and simple as the first.

"What's the matter?" Tony asked as he edged closer to the door. "Can't get in?"

A whisper came to his right ear. "I'm already here."

With a loud scream, Tony backed up quickly, tripped, and fell to the floor. He looked up to see the assassin standing over him. She cocked her head to one side as she pressed her blood-stained blade to his throat. In his mind he imagined a wicked smile curling from ear to ear behind the mask. The mask itself was cold, emotionless—like the face of death. Its dark eyes stared silently, a stare that was ominous and patient, yet merciless and foreboding.

She raised the blade in the air, ready to deliver the killing stroke. But then her attention was drawn to a beep from the mechanism around her wrist. She looked at the readout, which Tony could see, even in his panic, read, "15%."

While she was distracted, Tony took the opportunity to scramble to his feet and run for it. He dashed up the staircase, one floor, two floors—it didn't matter to him, he just needed to get as far away from her as possible.

On the fourth floor he found an open apartment and ran inside. Panting and gasping, he slammed the door behind him and locked the deadbolt. Once he had caught his breath, he put his ear to the door and listened.

A long moment passed. Then he heard the faint sound of steady footsteps coming up the staircase. The footsteps were slow and calm, as if they were mocking him, telling him that hiding was useless. The steps grew louder and more oppressive with each flight. The closer they came, the more intensely the terror gripped him. Tony backed up against the wall and raised his gun to the door. Then he realized the magazine was empty. He dropped out the magazine and slid in a replacement with a click. His hands trembled, and sweat poured down his face. The shadows around him seemed to move closer, reaching out to him in his mad paranoia.

The footsteps finally stopped just outside the door. The knob twisted once. Tony tiptoed closer and hid in the corner on the hinge side of the door. His heart was beating hard. The knob twisted again. Then there was silence. For a second, Tony wondered if his pursuer might have moved on, but he didn't hear more footsteps, so he couldn't be sure.

Suddenly the door exploded into the room, pieces of wood flying everywhere. The shock drained the blood from Tony's face. Cautiously, he looked over to see a black tactical boot hanging in midair just inside the doorway. The assassin lowered her foot and stepped inside.

Tony didn't move, he didn't even breathe. He was right behind her, and he had a decision to make: he could turn tail, get the hell out of there, and pray she didn't catch him before he could escape; he could hope she didn't hear the slide on his gun click, aim, and shoot her in the back; or he could stand stock-still in the dark corner and hope she didn't notice him before she left.

Tony aimed his gun and slowly pulled back on the slide to charge the barrel. *Just a little more,* he thought, *and I can shoot her.* But the click of the slide drew her attention. In a split second, she knocked the gun from Tony's hand with a roundhouse kick. Then she grabbed him by the coat and hoisted him up, his feet dangling above the floor. With little effort she threw him across the room. He hit the wall hard, breaking wood and plaster on impact. He shook his head, trying to get rid of the daze swirling in his brain. He had to get back on his feet.

He looked up to see her standing over him once more. She glanced at the readout on her wrist. Tony could see that it now read "9%."

"Hmm," her warped voice said quietly, "just enough left to get the job done." She reached into her belt, took out a pair of slender metal gauntlets tipped with razor-sharp claws, and put them on. "Tony Scorpione, I'm going to enjoy ripping you apart, piece by piece."

Is this it? Tony thought as he edged away from her, holding one hand in front of his face. *Is this how it ends?*

Then a crash came from downstairs, followed by loud voices. "Police! We got a disturbance call. Come out right now!"

The assassin turned her head for a second, which was just long enough for Tony to draw his spare .32 caliber revolver from inside his coat and fire a bullet right into her midsection. She fell to the floor with a scream. Tony stood up slowly, leaning his back against the wall for balance. As she clutched her stomach, he lined up his sights on her forehead.

"Heh! Guess I ain't gonna die tonight after all, huh?" His feeling of triumph was short-lived; without warning, he felt a sharp pain in his chest, followed by the stinging feeling of cold. He looked down. A long blade was sticking out of his chest, and his blood was pouring onto the floor from the fresh wound. A steel katana blade had pierced his heart from the wall behind him.

With the last of his strength he grabbed the blade with both hands. It retracted back into the wall, allowing him to fall to the floor. The life drained from his body in seconds.

Chapter Ten

With great pain, the assassin sat up and looked at Tony. Another masked figure emerged from the room behind the wall. She wore the same outfit and mask as the first assassin.

"Damn you, Wolf!" the first girl called out. "He was mine. After what he did, I deserved to kill him."

The second assassin tapped a button on her wrist computer, and the design on her mask changed from a kitsune fox to an okami wolf.

"Oh yeah?" Wolf said. "What were you gonna do, Fox? Bleed all over him?"

"Ugh!" Fox groaned through the pain. "I could… ah… I could've done something."

"Why didn't you dodge the bullet?" Wolf said. "You took the serum, right? You should be good for another half hour at least."

"I only had the booster shot with me." Fox groaned again. "I didn't think it would take this long."

"What did you think was going to happen? Of course he was going to run." Wolf knelt down next to Fox, took out a flashlight, and shone it on her wound. Then she stripped off the dead man's jacket, ripped off a sleeve, and held it firmly against the wound. "This isn't good. Looks like a gut wound. I don't think it will kill you, but we still gotta get you some help." Wolf pressed the com button on her wrist computer. "Wolf to Den Mother, come in."

"This is Den Mother. Go ahead, Wolf."

"I've silenced the target, but he shot Fox first. She needs help. Plus the police are in the building checking the lower floors."

"Wolf, I want you to answer me very carefully. Where exactly is the wound?"

"I'm pretty sure it's in her stomach."

"Is the wound on the right or left side of her abdomen?"

"The right."

"What color is the blood?"

"It's dark in here, but it looks like it's almost black."

"Wolf, the bullet's in her liver, which means she's in big trouble. How fast is she bleeding?"

"Real fast, like a stuck pig. Oh God, there's so much coming out, I can't stop it."

"That's what I was afraid of. The liver is filled with arteries. The bullet probably hit one of the larger ones."

"We can just bring her back to headquarters. You're good with this stuff, right? You can fix her up."

"She's already out of time. She'll bleed out in a matter of minutes, especially with the serum still in her system."

"What!" Fox listened in on her own earpiece. "You mean I'm going to die?"

The voice on her earpiece was cold, calm. "If I recall correctly, Fox, it was you who said you didn't care if you died, as long as Tony died first."

"Yeah, but—" Tears began to fall behind Fox's mask. Her voice was shaky. "I didn't think I would really die."

"Wolf, take her equipment and get out of there."

"What? We can't just leave her here, damn it! We have to do something."

"Please, please help me…" Fox's voice was becoming weaker and weaker. She grabbed at Wolf's arm. "Don't leave me."

Wolf took Fox's hand and held it tight.

"Listen to me," Den Mother said, "I understand how you feel, but there is nothing more we can do for her. I'm sorry, but you need to move. Now."

Fox could no longer speak. She was starting to drift away. There was no light, no sound, just cold and numbness moving over her body. She closed her eyes, willing herself to live.

Wolf felt for the pulse in Fox's wrist, but it was becoming fainter and fainter. She checked the pulse in Fox's neck. Barely there. A few seconds passed, and then there was nothing.

"She gone," Wolf said. She took Fox's hands and folded them over her stomach—a sign of respect. But a noise at the doorway made her turn, and she found herself looking into the beam of a flashlight. Two uniformed officers stood just inside the door.

"Police—hold it right there!" one shouted. "Put your hands where we can see them."

With a single gesture, Wolf threw two unusual knives. They flashed through the air and hit the officers necks with deadly force. The men dropped their flashlights as they fell to the floor, their throats bleeding profusely.

Wolf placed her hand over the dead assassin's. "I always teased you, but you were still my friend. You didn't deserve to go like this, but we knew the risks when we signed up, didn't we. I just thought we'd make it out together. Goodbye, Fox."

Wolf quickly took Fox's gauntlets, utility belts, and wrist computer. Then she pressed her com button. "Wolf to Den Mother—returning to base."

"Roger that."

Wolf opened a window. She took one last look back at her friend and disappeared into the night.

Around the corner from where he had left Mikey, Detective Jimmy Ziminski walked out of a convenience mart with a tall cup of coffee in his hand. He hopped in the Skylark and was about to head over to Toro's Matador when his cell phone rang. He looked at the number on the ID. It was Dispatch. *This can't be good,* he thought. He opened the phone. "Ziminski."

"Been listening to your radio, detective?"

"It's in the other car, Ashley. I'm undercover right now. Why? What's up?"

"Two officers are down at the abandoned apartments at 1496 Robinson Street. The uniforms on scene say they found your assassin dead when they got there."

"The assassin? Wait—that's down the street from Tony Scorpione's restaurant."

"That would explain why Tony is dead as well."

"Tony too?"

"That's what I said."

"All right, Ashley. Tell them I'm on my way."

"Will do, detective."

Jimmy drove a couple of blocks over, parked the Skylark, and got back into his Crown Vic. The car started up with a roar. He flipped on the lights and sirens and put the pedal to the floor. *This could be it,* he told himself. *This could be our lucky break.*

He arrived on scene in less than five minutes. In the past, he had busted a lot of criminals hiding out in these old apartments, so he was familiar with the building. It had been officially condemned a year before, but the city hadn't gotten around to tearing it down. The apartments had probably been impressive when they were first built in the 1930s, but now this pile of rotting plaster, flaking paint, and termite-ridden floorboards was awaiting the loving caress of a wrecking ball.

All the windows were dark. Needless to say, there was no power, so Jimmy took out his flashlight and stepped inside. Lieutenant Freddy Williams led him to the stairs, and they started their climb. Williams, a tall, heavyset man with gray hair, was a twenty-five-year veteran of the force and had known Jimmy since he was just a rookie. And even though Jimmy now outranked him as a detective, he still had the utmost respect for Freddy.

As they climbed the steps, Freddy stopped on the second-floor landing to take a breather, and Jimmy stopped with him. "So how you been, kid?" Freddy asked.

"Oh, I can't complain. This assassin business has been keeping me pretty busy. You?"

"Same stuff, different day. Police work don't change: Bad people do bad things and we catch 'em."

"Amen to that, Freddy. So, how's your granddaughter Amy doing?"

"She just turned eight last month."

"She's still taking those piano lessons?"

"Yes, indeed. That little girl is a dynamo. She learns so fast and her playing is phenomenal, a regular Beethoven. My daughter is still a teller at the Federal Loan and Reserve on Main Street. Oh, let me tell you, Jimmy, it makes me so mad—Vanessa works nine hours a day, five days a week at the bank, while her worthless husband sits at home on the couch and watches TV."

"Lou still hasn't found a job?"

"Nope, and I don't think he's lifted a finger to try. Sometimes I just want to slap that bum. How about you, kid? When are you gonna find someone? You're getting to that age, you know—when opportunities start to disappear." Freddy gave him a wink and started up the stairs again.

"Come on, Freddy. You know I'm married to my work. I gotta give a hundred and ten percent or else the Scorpiones will win."

The sounds of their footsteps echoed up the empty stairwell. Tiny creatures could be heard scurrying about in the darkness beyond.

Freddy's breath was coming in gasps as they climbed further. "Even so—once you find that one—that perfect one—you'll wonder how you ever lived—without 'er."

Jimmy took a quiet, somber tone. "How's your wife doing?"

"It doesn't look good. The leukemia is spreading. The doctors are doing their best with the chemo, but… they're saying Lucy may not have much time left."

"I'm sorry, man. She's in my prayers."

"Thanks, I really appreciate that." Freddy and Jimmy had reached the landing on the fourth floor, and Freddy turned down a long hallway. Jimmy followed. "Thirty-two years I've been married to the most wonderful woman in the world. I have two daughters, an idiot son-in-law, and a granddaughter who's smart as a whip. I feel so fortunate for all I've been blessed with. And it all started thirty-three years ago in front of that flower shop in Brooklyn when I asked Lucy if she wanted to grab a coffee with me." Freddy took a moment to let out a reminiscent sigh. Then he looked back at Jimmy.

"Just remember, too much work ain't good for you. You need a balance in your life. Otherwise, before you know it, you'll be an old man with a pile of papers on his desk and nothing to go home to. Just find that special girl." Freddy turned to look at Jimmy over his shoulder. "She might even be someone you already know."

An image of Lin smiling at her desk flashed in Jimmy's mind.

"Wait, what was that?" Freddy asked.

"What was what?"

"I saw that smile. You were thinking of someone just now, weren't you?"

Wiping the smile off his face, Jimmy decided to avoid the subject. "Thanks, Freddy." Jimmy moved ahead of him. "I appreciate the thought, and I'll keep it mind."

"Hey, c'mon!" Freddy's smile grew wider. "You just gonna cut me off like that?"

Jimmy didn't reply; they had arrived at the open door to the apartment on the fourth floor. A few officers were inside looking around with flashlights. Another officer was setting up a series of car batteries and floodlights, and just as Jimmy and Freddy stepped inside, he flipped the switch and lit up the place nice and bright.

Jimmy scanned the room while Freddy stepped aside to speak with the officers who had arrived ahead of them. The scene was horrific: on the floor of the living room were four dead bodies. Two fellow cops near the door, Tony Scorpione against the far wall, and a small figure wearing a mask right in the middle. An officer was taking photos of the scene for the case file. No one had covered the faces of the deceased or even closed their eyes. He had seen death before, but two of their own—Jimmy shook his head and set his feelings aside for the moment.

The body in front of Jimmy, in the middle of the room, was the one he assumed was the assassin—wearing a mask and lying in a puddle of blood. He spotted the source of all that blood: a single bullet wound to the midsection just under the right wrist. Oddly, the hands were folded across the stomach. From there, the body appeared to be a female.

"Hey, Freddy!" Jimmy waved him over. "Come here a second, would ya?"

Freddy walked over. "What's up?"

"Have these bodies been moved in any way?"

Freddy quickly spoke with the other officers, and they all shook their heads. "The bodies are just as we found 'em."

"All right, if Robbie is done taking pictures, let's get four officers and have them search the rest of the building—see if they can find anything. I'm gonna get started here."

"You got it." Freddy turned to the others. "All right, boys, let's clear the room. Search this building top to bottom."

Once everyone had left, Jimmy got down to business. Body number two rested against the far wall. Jimmy had already recognized him as none other than Tony Scorpione, confirming Ashley's warning earlier. Jimmy started with Tony. He squatted next to the body, careful not to let his clothing trail in the pools of blood, and took a good look at the man while he put on a pair of latex gloves. "Tony, Tony, Tony, so quick to follow in your father's footsteps," he muttered.

He took a voice recorder from his coat pocket and pushed the record button. "Friday, November twentieth, nine-sixteen p.m. Address one-four-nine-six Robinson Street, apartment four-zero-five. Subject One identified as Antonio Scorpione. Deep puncture wound to the chest through the heart, resulting in massive blood loss. It looks to be a stab wound." Jimmy used one gloved finger to move the dead man's torn clothing aside so he could examine the wound more closely. "This is interesting: the flesh around the wound is protruding outward, which means he was probably impaled from behind by a long, sharp blade." He looked above the body. "I see a blood smear on the wall leading up to a small, elongated hole the same shape as the wound. So he may have been stabbed by something that came through the wall behind him, like a blade, or maybe a sword."

Jimmy noted the pistol lying next to Tony. Then he looked at the assassin. "Wait a minute. A wound like this to the heart would kill in seconds. So if the assassin got him through the wall…"

Jimmy turned on his flashlight and walked around into the next room, checking the wall behind Tony. He peered through the small hole there. "I'm inside the bedroom on the other side of the wall. If the assassin stood here and got Tony through the heart, that's a sure kill. She wouldn't be in a hurry to get to the other room. Even so, with that wound, Tony wouldn't be alive long enough to hold up a gun, let alone aim and fire."

Jimmy walked back around to Tony. "So Tony had to shoot her before he received the wound, which means she wasn't working alone. That would explain the assassin's folded hands. Someone was saying goodbye."

Just then Freddy stuck his head back into the room. "You doin' okay here, Jimmy?" he asked.

"Yeah, no worries."

Freddy went back to his search, and Jimmy walked over to where the assassin lay. "Let's see what your story is, shall we?" Jimmy squatted next to her, again taking care to avoid the copious amount of drying blood. "Subject Two is a deceased female, wearing what appears to be a white mask, possibly Asian in style, resembling an animal like a fox. Subject is also wearing a dark gray, tight-fitting body suit made from an unusual looking fabric, possibly military grade. Age and identity are yet unknown, but subject appears to be a teenager. Hands are folded across the abdomen, most likely placed that way postmortem. Bullet wound on the right side of the abdomen, probably courtesy of Mr. Scorpione, and judging from the severe blood loss, it went through the liver. I saw a lot of good men die that way in the Persian Gulf."

Jimmy stopped recording for a moment and heaved a sigh. This just wasn't right. It was one thing for soldiers to die on the battlefield fighting for America's freedom, but this? A young girl dying in a filthy abandoned building while trying to kill some scumbag gangster?

Jimmy resumed recording. "I'm removing the mask now." With his gloved hand he eased it off and set it aside, marveling at what lay beneath. Her face looked like an angel's; one glance gave him the impression of pure innocence and virtue, a girl completely incapable of anything remotely terrible. Her expression was one of sadness and pain. Dried tears on her cheeks formed tiny rivers of sorrow.

Not what you'd expect from a cold-blooded killer, he thought. *She's only a teenager.*

The lieutenant entered the room and came to stand next to him. When he saw her face, Freddy exclaimed, "Hey, I know that girl."

Jimmy paused his recorder again. "Who is she?"

"That's Lisa Smith, Jake Smith's older sister. She was brought in about a week ago for shoplifting at the mall."

"You're absolutely sure?"

"Positive. I could never forget her face. She slapped three officers on her way to processing. Sure was a moody one. Her mother bailed her out that same night."

"Yeah, Jake's sister. Now I remember. Gabe over in Vice was talking about his recent case. He suspected the Scorpiones were supplying drugs to the streets, so he got in contact with a young dealer named Jacob Smith. Gabe was in the process of tracking down Jacob's supplier, but then the kid overdosed on heroin. What was the mother's name—Sharon?"

"Yeah, Sharon Smith." Freddy nodded. "I had to call her after I brought Lisa in."

"Thanks." Jimmy clicked the recorder back on. "Subject two was identified by Lieutenant Fredrick Williams as Lisa Smith. Mother's name is Sharon Smith."

Jimmy moved on to the two deceased officers. He took a deep breath before beginning. He had known these men; not well, but he had known them to be good, honest, hardworking cops. "The bodies of officers Samuel Rodriguez and Richard Wilkins were found just inside the doorway of the apartment. Both have strange-looking knives in their throats." Jimmy took out two evidence bags. "Removing the first knife from Officer Rodriguez." He looked at it carefully. "The knife appears to be made of iron, is approximately seven inches in length, shaped like a spike with a leather-wrapped handle and a small ring at the end. Now removing second identical knife from Officer Wilkins."

Jimmy placed the knives in separate bags and sealed them. "The knives apparently severed the left jugular vein of each officer, causing fatal blood loss."

Jimmy stood and started examining the pieces of wood strewn across the floor. "Interesting. It appears the door of the apartment was broken to pieces. Wooden fragments are spread throughout the room. It would seem that an explosive was used, except none of the pieces of wood shows burn marks of any kind." Jimmy flipped over a piece and found an odd mark. "There's a deep boot imprint in one of the larger pieces. Likely made by the right foot." He held the print next to the dead girl's right boot. "Imprint matches the tread on Lisa Smith's boots. So what happened here? She couldn't have just kicked the door in herself. The amount of strength that would take—it just doesn't make sense."

Jimmy glanced back at the hole in the wall and then at Freddy. He stopped the recorder. "Freddy, I think we've probably got another assassin on our hands."

"What makes you say that?"

"The gun sitting next to Tony, the gunshot wound in Lisa's abdomen, and the hole in the wall. It all points to one scenario: Tony kills Lisa, and then Tony is killed from behind by someone else. There's another killer out there. I'm sure of it."

Freddy scratched his head. He seemed about to say something, but he hesitated.

"What's on your mind, Freddy?"

"I don't know, Jimmy. Maybe these assassins, they've been doing some good, you know? I mean, Vincent and Tony, they weren't the best people in the world."

"Even so, that would make the assassins vigilantes. I don't tolerate vigilantes in my city. Yeah, Vincent and Tony were the scum of the earth, but they still deserved a fair trial for their crimes. Like it or not, that's the way the system works. If not for that system, there'd be chaos in the streets. Come on, Freddy. You used to hammer that stuff into my head daily."

"You're right. You know, I've been on this force for twenty-five years and I've been trying to catch Vincent red-handed for fifteen of 'em. Guess when you spend that long chasing after a criminal, you sometimes forget he still has rights."

"Don't worry about it. Happens to the best of us." Jimmy put away his recorder. "I'm all set here. Go ahead and send in forensics and the coroner. Oh, and, Freddy—keep Lisa's involvement quiet until the mother can officially identify her."

On his way out of the building, Jimmy called dispatch on his cell phone and asked to be sent Sharon Smith's address and phone number. This was the part of the job he hated the most. He got into his car and opened his laptop, which was hooked into the police server. Jimmy opened the new message flashing on his screen: 365 Bellview Street, Apartment 2. Phone number (551) 555-3251. He dialed the number and listened as it rang, still uncertain what to say.

After three rings he finally heard a voice on the other end. He identified himself.

"Police?" Sharon Smith said. "Have you brought my daughter in for shoplifting again? I'm so fed up with her. Keep her there, and I'll pick her up in the morning."

"Ma'am, we believe we've found your daughter Lisa. I would like you to please come down to the station and identify her."

"Identify? What are you… oh, God, no!" Sharon began to sob and scream. "Please, God, not my baby!"

"I'm very sorry, ma'am."

Jimmy heard a click on the other end of the line, and he closed his cell and dropped it onto the passenger seat. He took in a deep breath and let out a long sigh as he put his hand to his head. "Damn. It never gets easier, does it?"

Would police do notification of death by phone?

Chapter Eleven

Jimmy paced back and forth inside the entrance of the police station. The clock behind the desk officer seemed to tick slowly as it inched toward 11:00 p.m.

Through the doors, Jimmy saw an old Buick Estate station wagon pull up outside. A small woman, wearing a tan canvas coat and carrying a leather purse, stepped out. She walked into the station with loud, impatient steps and looked right at Jimmy. Her body was shaking, and she spoke nervously. "I'm Sharon Smith, and I want to know what's happened to my daughter. Where is she?"

"Ms. Smith, I'm Detective James Ziminski. I need to ask you to prepare yourself. I know this isn't easy—"

"Stop." Sharon held up her hand. "Please—just take me to my daughter."

"Fair enough." Jimmy gave a nod and gestured to the door leading into the main police floor. "Please follow me."

Jimmy led her down a flight of stairs to the basement morgue. At the end of the room, under a bright light, lay a covered body on a gurney. When she saw it, Sharon stood in the doorway, frozen. Jimmy laid a gentle hand on her shoulder to help give her strength. Slowly, she moved forward and walked up to the gurney.

Jimmy carefully pulled back the white sheet from the face. As soon as Sharon saw her, she gasped, then collapsed to her knees and broke down into tears. Jimmy got down next to her and put an arm around her shoulders.

"It's her," she wailed. "That's my baby."

Jimmy waited a few minutes until she'd calmed down before he helped her to her feet and gave her a tissue. "Ms. Smith, when you're ready, I'd like to ask you a few questions."

She nodded silently and dried her eyes. Jimmy took her back to his office, sat her down, and got her a cup of coffee. Then he went behind his desk, pulled out his case files, and laid them out in front of him.

"Ms. Smith, we found your daughter in an abandoned apartment building on Robinson Street. We believe Lisa died from severe blood loss from a gunshot wound."

She gasped and put her hand to her mouth.

"Of course, an autopsy will have to be performed to determine the exact cause of death. Now before I go into further detail, I must ask if your daughter was involved in any way with Tony Scorpione?"

Sharon's eyes grew wide. She lowered her head for a moment.

"Ms. Smith?"

She wouldn't meet his gaze. "Why do you ask?"

"I ask because Tony Scorpione's body was found with a hole in his chest just a few feet from your daughter. On top of that, there were three sliced-up—" (he almost said *piles of meat* but thought better of it) "bodies that were once Tony's henchmen found lying outside his restaurant. Now I'll ask you again: did your daughter have any involvement with Tony Scorpione?"

"It—" Sharon started off shakily. "It all started seventeen years ago. I used to work as a waitress at Tony's restaurant. He seemed so nice and was really kind to me. I quit high school at fifteen, and I really needed the money. My mother was a useless drunk, and my father left us long before that. Tony was the only one willing to help me out. He always said I was pretty… that I was so pretty."

"Yes, go on. Take your time."

She stared past him, lost in her memories. "One night he brought me into his office. Three of his men were in there, and they locked the door behind me." Tears formed in her eyes and trickled down her cheeks. "He, um—he beat me and—and he raped me. He said if I ever told the police, he would kill me. I was so scared."

"I can't even imagine what you must have gone through," Jimmy said.

She dabbed at her eyes with the tissue. "A few weeks later, I found out I was pregnant. It was Tony's. I never told him. I just quit and found another job at the cardboard factory downtown. I never wanted to have anything to do with Tony again, so I kept as far away from him as possible. I had the baby and raised her on my own. That baby was Lisa."

"My God, she was his daughter?" Jimmy exclaimed. "And he never even knew?"

"No. But Lisa did. I finally told her about six months ago. She was curious about her father, kept asking questions. I couldn't hide it anymore. She deserved to know the truth, so I told her everything."

That would have given Lisa motive, Jimmy thought. Kill the man who raped her mother. But she ended up being killed first.

"Tell me," Sharon pleaded, "what the hell was my daughter doing there?"

"That's still under investigation, but when we found her, she matched the description of the assassin who murdered Vincent Scorpione."

"That's impossible! There's no way she could have done that."

"In my line of work, I've found that given enough motivation, anyone is capable of doing anything. Your daughter definitely had motivation, didn't she? She wanted revenge on the man who did something unforgivable to her mother."

"But she—she couldn't have."

"Let me ask you this: What was her reaction when you told her the truth?"

Sharon looked away in silence.

"She was angry, wasn't she? More than that, she was furious. And I think, deep in her heart, she wanted revenge."

She shook her head, her mouth set in a grim line. "I still don't believe it."

"One of my officer's spoke to a girl named Sheila who works at Don Marco's. She said Lisa had been working at Tony's restaurant for at least two weeks as a waitress, just like you were. My guess is she wanted to get close to him for one reason and one reason only." He didn't want to, but he had to press her for the truth. "Now you're going to sit there and tell me you had no idea what was going on?"

"I knew something was going on, all right!" Sharon shot back. "She was always out late, even on school nights. I figured she was just out with friends. But she did talk a lot about how much she hated Tony, how much she hated the whole Scorpione family. She said many times that she wanted to kill him."

"Did it ever occur to you that she would actually go through with it?"

"No, she was an angry teenager so I figured it was normal."

"From what I've seen in this case so far, it's anything but normal."

Sharon covered her face as the tears started to come again. That was when Jimmy felt his conscience tell him to put it in reverse. "Look, I'm sorry, Ms. Smith. You've already suffered a great loss. Your son Jacob, to die at fifteen—that's a tragedy. And now, to lose Lisa as well…" Jimmy helped her up and led her to the door. "The last thing you need right now is to be badgered by my questions. You should go home and get some rest. Here's my card; I'll be in touch."

Sharon gave a nod and was about to leave when she turned back. "There was one other thing."

"What's that?"

"Lisa said she met someone from out of town. Said this person was the answer to all her prayers, but she wouldn't tell me anything more than that."

"How long ago was this?"

"Two or three weeks ago."

"Thank you very much for your help." He shook her hand and held the door open for her. "You've given us a lot of valuable information."

"Promise me you'll find whoever did this to my baby. Find the person who led her down this path."

"I promise that I'll do everything in my power to see that whoever is responsible will be brought to justice, ma'am."

Sharon left his office quietly, closing the door behind her. Jimmy sat back at his desk, picked up his phone, and dialed the crime lab.

"Patty? It's Jimmy Ziminski. Any luck on that empty injector cartridge we found at the Scorpione crime scene?"

"The cartridge? Yeah, we found something all right. It contained a fluid with traces of high-grade amphetamines and anabolic steroids. But that's not all."

"What else?"

"Well, there were some strange enzymes in the fluid that I've never seen before. It may take some time before I can identify exactly what we're looking at here."

"Thanks, Patty. Keep me posted."

Steroids would explain the deep footprint and the broken door. But he'd never seen steroids that could allow a person to jump so far in a single bound. That was where it stopped making sense. Lisa was toned, but not really muscular. Steroids take time to build mass and strength. The results aren't instantaneous. Was it the enzymes? Could they have been the unknown factor?

Jimmy's phone rang. It was Lin.

"I found something on that serial number you gave me," she told him. "I traced the numbers back to a pharmaceutical company in Sendai, Japan. It's called Kaifuku. As I dug further, I found out they don't currently have any registered employees, but they're still producing product. I think it's a puppet company for something else. That's all I've got so far."

Jimmy grinned; he could always count on Lin's resourcefulness. "I'm not going to ask you how you came across that information."

"Mum's the word. I'll let you know when I find out more."

"Thanks Lin. I owe you—that is—"

"Go ahead, you can say it. I'll just add this favor to the rest of them."

Jimmy hung up the phone and leaned back in his chair. *This case just keeps getting better and better,* he thought. It looked like another late night.

He glanced over at his coffee pot, which was empty. First things first. He needed more coffee.

Chapter Twelve

The nightmare was always the same. Stephanie found herself outside a warehouse on the waterfront. The night was dark. A cold wind moved her hair and caressed her face with icy fingers, sending shivers down the back of her neck. A single white feather tumbled through the air, floating aimlessly before disappearing from her sight.

Stephanie looked toward the end of the warehouse and saw an exit door wide open, a dim light coming from inside. As she drew closer, she heard voices, but they were so faint she couldn't make them out. Curious, she stepped inside.

Now sheltered from the cold wind, she could feel the warmth of the suspended blower heaters above her. Large wooden crates were stacked up against the walls and spread randomly across the vast concrete floor. As she began to walk farther into the warehouse, she could hear the voices more clearly. There, standing in a well-lit area on the far side, were several well-dressed people.

Once she was close enough to see them, she recognized one of the men. It was Vincent Scorpione, with several of his guards on either side of him. Vincent was dressed in a fine Italian suit and held a silver briefcase. Many other men, armed with pistols and semi-automatic rifles, could be seen throughout the warehouse, patrolling the building.

Even as Stephanie walked right by them, no one seemed to notice her. It was as if she were completely invisible.

Then another man came in through the open doorway. He held a case of his own and was dressed in a gray suit and black tie. He calmly walked past the many crates and headed toward the lights. He finally emerged from the shadows and stood before Vincent with a confident look about him.

Stephanie let out a gasp as she recognized this man. "Dad?" But her father couldn't hear her. She stuck to the shadows as if by instinct, even though she knew no one could sec her. She looked on silently as her father, Tommy Sebastiano, began to talk with Vincent Scorpione.

"So…" Vincent took out a cigar and lighter from his inside coat pocket. He lit the cigar and took a long puff before letting the pungent smoke out into the cool warehouse air. His eyes zeroed in on the briefcase in Tommy's hand. "Did you get me what I asked for?"

"I sure did, Mr. Scorpione." Her father opened the case; inside were eight walnut-sized diamonds that sparkled brilliantly in the light. Tommy gave Vincent an easy smile. "Eight chunks of ice, just like we agreed."

Vincent stepped closer, held a jeweler's loupe to his eye, and inspected the merchandise. He took his time, looking carefully at each one. Once he was satisfied, he put the loupe away and grinned widely at Stephanie's father. "Tommy, you've never let me down."

Stephanie seemed able to hear and see as if she were her father, to see from his perspective. *How odd,* she thought. *It's like this is happening to me. But I'm just watching.*

Vincent went on. "Gotta admit I had my doubts you could pull this off. But as always, you didn't disappoint." Vincent turned to his men. "Boys, take the ice and keep it cool, will ya?"

One of Vincent's men closed the case and took it from Tommy's hands before moving back among Vincent's other muscle. Then Vincent held up his own silver case. "Now, just like we agreed, a million in cash." Vincent opened the case and displayed neatly stacked bundles of large-denomination bills. Tommy pulled out a black light and inspected the money for any marked bills. Satisfied, he gave Vincent a nod of approval.

Vincent closed the silver case and started to pass it to Tommy, but before he could complete the action, one of his men burst into the warehouse. "Boss," the man yelled, "he's a cop, he's a cop!"

Vincent threw the case behind him. One of his men caught it in midair and ran outside with it. The other men pulled out their guns and took aim. Tommy ducked for cover behind a large wooden crate, keeping low as a barrage of gunfire pounded the crate. The gunfire stopped, and after a short silence Vincent's furious voice filled the warehouse.

"You're a damn blue-boy, Tommy! I let you into my business, my dealings, and even my home. How do you think I look now, eh? I let a pig stroll right into my organization."

Tommy pulled out his .45 caliber pistol, ran out from cover, and took out five of Vincent's men before jumping behind another crate. More gunfire erupted as more men came from everywhere carrying Uzis and Tec-9s, demolishing Tommy's cover. A bullet grazed Tommy's shoulder before he could find better cover behind a metal support beam.

"Nowhere to run now, Tommy," Vincent called out. "I got this place locked down."

Tommy called out, "The only one getting locked down is you, Vincent—for twenty-five to life."

"How 'bout I give you the death penalty, huh, Tommy? How's that sound?"

Tommy looked around and saw a wrench. He grabbed it and threw it as hard as he could against the far wall. The loud clang drew the men's attention, giving Tommy the perfect opportunity to take out several others. More men appeared on the catwalks above, opening fire with automatic rifles. Tommy shot another man in the shoulder, and then his magazine was empty. With no spare magazines on him, Tommy laid the gun at his feet before running for more cover. He ducked behind a circuit breaker box as bullets rained down on him from the catwalks. Thinking fast, he opened the box and cut the power.

Darkness filled the warehouse for a few short seconds before emergency lights came on. Vincent, fully armed and ready to kill, went to the circuit breaker box, followed closely by one of his men, but Tommy was nowhere in sight.

"You're sure the exits are locked down?" Vincent snarled.

"Yes, boss, everything's airtight."

"Then find him!" Vincent noticed a puddle of blood on the floor. "He can't be far. Losin' that much blood, he's gonna get dizzy soon. He'll mess up and that's when we'll nail him."

The man nodded, and the rest continued their search.

Tommy had heard everything. Sliding down to the floor, he rested his back against the wall on the opposite side of the warehouse. He pulled a bandana from his back pocket and pressed it tight to his shoulder to slow the bleeding. Then he studied his surroundings the best he could in the dim glow of the emergency lights. Heavy warehouse lights were hanging down from the ceiling, suspended by heavy cables. There were gas-fueled heating fans, metal catwalks secured by metal cables bolted to the ceiling, two forklifts parked to his right, a locked shipping office to his left, a dead man with a gun in his hand in the far corner, and a full gas can sitting in front of him. He felt in his pocket and pulled out a lighter. He could hear Vincent and his men talking as they continued to search the building. Vincent's impatience and anger seemed to grow with each passing minute.

"Anyone found him yet?"

"No, boss."

"Well, move your asses," Vincent barked. "He's in here somewhere, damn it!"

A sudden explosion went off on the catwalk above them, setting off the sprinkler systems. Within moments Vincent and his men were drenched, and an inch of water covered the floor.

"What the hell just happened?" Vincent yelled. "Someone answer me now!"

"Damn, do you ever shut up?" Tommy stepped out from behind the power box. "My ears are starting to hurt."

Vincent yelled to his men, "Shoot him! Shoot him now!"

The men took aim and pulled their triggers, but nothing happened. Confused, they shook their guns and tried again. Nothing.

"Don't bother," Tommy said. "Once the firing pins get soaked, those guns are useless."

The sprinklers finally stopped. Vincent threw his gun down in a fit, and the rest of the men followed suit. Tommy reached inside his jacket and pulled out the gun he'd taken from one of the dead men. He leveled it at Vincent, and with his other hand he took out his badge. "This gun is nice and dry, however. Vincent Scorpione, you're under arrest for the trafficking of and intent to distribute the illegal narcotics stored in these crates. And I might as well add, attempted murder of a police officer." Tommy kept Vincent in his sights. "I'm taking you in."

Tommy approached Vincent cautiously. Scowling, Vincent raised his hands. Then, he smiled as the barrel of a gun pressed against Tommy's back.

"I kept this gun dry as well, Tommy-boy," a voice said from behind him. "Nothing personal. It's just business."

"Don't do it!" Stephanie yelled, running to her father as fast as she could, but her legs wouldn't move right. It was like she was moving in slow motion. "Please, don't shoot him!"

A single gunshot echoed through the warehouse.

"Daddy!" Stephanie cried out, her heart seeming to wrench to a stop. She felt tears burn in her eyes.

Tommy fell forward as his daughter reached out to catch him. But her arms grasped nothing as she passed right through him like an apparition. She fell to her knees beside her father. Tommy lay dead on the cold wet concrete beside her.

For a long time she stayed there, as if frozen. When she finally looked up at the man who had murdered her father, she realized that time itself was standing still. An eerie silence filled the room. The man standing over her was in shadow, wearing a long, dark coat. The metal of the gun he held reflected the dim light ever so slightly. A still pillar of smoke floated up from the barrel.

Ever since she'd first had this nightmare, she's searched through books and magazines trying to find that gun. Finally, she ran across it. It was a Colt .45 revolver, pretty much the Cadillac of revolvers, known for its power and reliability. The coat the murderer wore was the Battocello brand, made from fine Italian leather. His shiny black leather shoes were Sperazza, also imported, his black leather gloves branded with the insignia of Ruffina on the wrist.

But the nightmare was always the same. She could see all this detail, but she was never able to see the murderer's face, ever. "It can't end this way. It just can't..." Stephanie said weakly.

The nightmare had always ended the same way—until now. "No!" Anger grew inside her, strengthening her resolve. "I won't let it." Stephanie rose to her feet. She felt waves of force pushing against her, like powerful gales of wind trying to hold her back. But she fought them. She moved forward, pushing with all her might. "A little farther," she said, struggling, "and I can see his face."

The wind pushed harder, now like a brick wall smashing against her. But she didn't give up, her resolve growing with each blast. "Come on, damn it! Just... a little... more." And inch by inch she came closer and closer, until finally she could make out the murderer's face in the dim light. Her eyes grew wide with shock as she recognized him.

She awoke and sat up in her bed, breathing heavily. A long moment passed before the shock finally wore off. Then she uttered, "Jonathan Scorpione."

The weekend passed quickly, and the halls of Kingsley Academy bustled once more with life. Floors that lay silent over the weekend now echoed loudly with the pounding feet of Monday morning.

Stephanie walked through the first-floor hallway, keeping pace with the normal traffic. She was trying to remember if she had a quiz coming up in her English class, when she felt a hand touch her shoulder from behind.

The air filled with swirling white feathers. Once they cleared away, she found herself in a different place. It was a kitchen. Though it was morning, the world outside the window was still dark. A dim light above the stove lit the area. On the floor was a puddle of water coming from the bottom of the fridge. Apparently the cooling unit had failed during the night, allowing the ice in the freezer to melt.

Then in walked Pat, his eyes still half-closed from sleepiness. He took one step into the puddle and slipped backwards, landing flat on his back.

The vision ended, and Stephanie was back in the hallway of the school. She turned around and saw Pat standing there.

"Hey, Steph." His expression was switching back and forth between a casual smile and a grimace of pain as he rubbed his back.

"You okay?"

"Oh, this? Yeah, this morning I—"

Stephanie finished his sentence for him. "Walked into the kitchen, slipped on some water, and hurt your back, right?"

"I… yeah." Pat looked shocked. "How'd you know?"

"I, um… I didn't." She looked away. "It was just a lucky guess."

"Well, that was one heck of a lucky guess."

What had just happened? Stephanie tried to hide her distress. Had she really just seen what had happened to Pat this morning? She turned back and stared at him.

"What's wrong?" Pat asked. "Is there something on my face?"

She reached out and touched his shoulder. Nothing happened. She pulled her hand back and looked at it. She touched him again—still nothing.

"What? What is it, Steph?"

She dropped her hand to her side and quickly said, "Oh, it was nothing. There was just some lint on your shirt, that's all. I got it for you."

"Thanks." He looked perplexed. "Guess I didn't see it."

"No problem." She smiled. "So what's going on in your classes today?"

They started walking together as Pat talked about the lessons coming up. Stephanie, however, was preoccupied with her own thoughts. Whatever had happened, it wasn't working now. What was happening to her? Could she really see into the past?

She looked over at Pat, who was still rubbing his sore back. She placed a gentle hand on his lower back.

"I really hope your back feels better soon." She let out a little laugh. "But I'm sure it would have been pretty funny to actually see it happen this morning."

"Hey! It wasn't funny to me." They shared a laugh together as they walked down the hallway.

This was nice, she thought. Just being with him like this. It felt so nice.

Chapter Thirteen

A few minutes later, Stephanie walked into her first-period classroom. The room's front wall held a classic black board and a new white dry erase board as the school was still in the process of updating their classrooms. She looked around and noticed that not only were the ordinary students there, but most of the more interesting ones were also in attendance.

Of those interesting students, the first was Billy Mason, the football jock. As usual, he sat in the back corner surrounded by his buddies, trying to look cool while twirling a football on his fingers. His father, Jack, owned one of the best football teams in the NFL; they'd won the Super Bowl last season. An egomaniac, Billy often taunted those he viewed as less popular. He did this partly because he enjoyed it and partly for the amusement of his fellow jocks and the mindless sycophants who surrounded him. He was well hated among the Intellectual, Loner, and Low Self-Esteem sub-groups of the Kingsley Academy student body.

Next was Stacy Stevens, the blonde-haired, ponytailed cheerleader sitting a few rows to the left, who couldn't help but stare at Billy with dreamy eyes. Her mother, Talia, owned a nationwide chain of department stores. Billy was the only guy in school who mattered to Stacy. The blown-up Xeroxed copies of his yearbook photos, framed with red hearts and pasted all over the inside of her locker, proved that. Stacy had asked him out a hundred times and each time got the cold shoulder, but she still hoped someday he'd come around.

Four chairs up from her was Kira Shirou, captain of the Karate team. Her father, Kenichi, owned a large Japanese conglomerate that produced everything from cars to DVD players. Unfortunately—due, allegedly, to Vincent Scorpione's scheming—he'd had to sell all his distribution and delivery resources for half their net worth. Kenichi had sent his daughter Kira to an American school so that she might become a company leader who could better connect with the Western world.

Usually Kira exuded strength and confidence; she never let anything bring her down. Today, however, Kira seemed depressed about something. She was also shaking slightly, as if she were shivering in a cold breeze. It was a brisk, overcast day, and surely even students with such strong constitutions could get down from time to time. But despite the cold weather outside, it was quite warm inside the classroom. The fact that she was shivering in such a toasty room was a bit strange to Stephanie.

Then there was Trish Helmsworth, the super smart bookworm sitting next to the windows. Her mother, Tara, owned a large publishing company that had gone international last year, clearing well over a billion dollars. Emotionally reserved and a girl of few words, Trish was talented at avoiding lengthy conversation. She was almost always seen with her nose buried in a book.

And lastly, the class wouldn't have been complete without Chris Kensington, the teacher's pet, who sat right up front. His father, Anthony, was chairman of one of the largest car companies in America. A heavyset boy, Chris showed up to class five minutes early every day, usually carrying on an intellectual conversation with the teacher, Emma Roberts, by the time everyone else arrived. Always willing to answer every single question the teacher tossed out, Chris had become an annoyance and irritation to most of his classmates.

Stephanie sat down in front of Trish and noticed the empty chair to her right. She let out a sigh. She wished Lisa would at least make an effort to come to class more than once a week. Then Stephanie turned to Trish, who was reading quietly. A blue barrette over Trisha's left ear held back her dark, shoulder-length hair. The lenses of her silver-rimmed glasses reflected the words of the pages she read. The dark gray cardigan over her uniform kept the chill from the windows at bay.

"Hey Trish," Stephanie said, "we're having a quiz on Friday, right? I was wondering if you could tell me which chapters it covers."

Without letting her eyes leave the book propped in her hand, Trish simply pointed to the upper right-hand corner of the whiteboard at the front of the room. Stephanie zeroed in on Mrs. Roberts' note handwritten there in dry erase marker, which read, "Quiz will cover chaps 4–5. Study!"

"Oh, I see. Thanks." Stephanie looked closer at the cover of the book Trish was reading. "So, you're reading Yeats, huh?"

"Yes," Trish answered in an emotionless voice.

"He's a poet, right?"

"Yes."

"Is he any good?"

"Very good."

"What's your favorite poem he wrote?"

Trish immediately quoted Yeats's poem "Aedh Wishes for the Cloths of Heaven," an inspirational work that moved Stephanie spiritually and intellectually as she heard it. "Wow, that's pretty deep," she commented. "I had no idea you read that kind of poetry."

Trish shrugged and put the book of poetry in her bag. Then she took out another book, *Hyperion,* a sci-fi novel by Dan Simmons. She opened to the first page and started reading to herself.

"Well," Stephanie said, feeling that yet another conversation between them, if she could call it that, had come to a quick end, "good talking to you."

Trish didn't look up. "Mm-hmm."

Most of the class had sat down by the time Mrs. Emma Roberts entered the room. A tall woman with green eyes and red hair, Emma was a strong presence in the classroom, with her no-nonsense personality and strict teaching style. Stephanie wondered if Emma had arrived a minute late to avoid talking to Chris Kensington. Maybe he annoyed her too.

The expression on her face was more somber than usual. "All right, class, listen up!" Everyone stopped talking at the sound of her voice. "I'm afraid I have some sad news."

Several students started whispering in the back, but Mrs. Roberts grabbed the yardstick resting against the wall behind her and whacked it on her desk with a loud crack. "Quiet! Quiet, please!" She took a deep breath and let it out in an audible sigh. "Lisa Smith, your classmate and a dear friend to some of you, was found dead Friday night."

Stephanie felt a sharp pain in her heart at the news. She jumped to her feet, knocking most of her books to the floor. "What? How did it happen?"

"Whoa!" Billy the jock said. "The shy girl speaks." He and his friends started laughing, but once they saw Mrs. Roberts grab the yardstick again, they all shut up at the same time.

"Her body was found in an abandoned apartment building on Robinson. The police aren't releasing any further information." She turned her attention to Stephanie, who was becoming more and more distraught. "I'm so sorry, Stephanie. I know she was your friend."

A lump formed in Stephanie's throat; tears welled in her eyes. "I—I need to go." She went to the front of the classroom, and Mrs. Roberts handed her a hall pass.

"Go," she said kindly. "Take as long as you need, sweetie."

Stephanie took the pass gratefully and quickly exited the classroom. She hurried to the girls' restroom, ran into the last stall, and locked it. Then she let out the breath she hadn't realized she was holding, and it came out as a sob.

Lisa was one of the few friends she had. Now she was gone, just like that. It was as if a big knife had come and cut Lisa right out of Stephanie's life. She felt so much pain and angst in her heart that her tears flowed in streams. She used a wad of toilet tissue to dab the tears from her eyes, wondering how it could have happened. She had just seen Lisa at practice last Friday. She beat her hand on the stall door. "Why? Why Lisa? What happened?"

Several minutes passed before Stephanie finally calmed down. She took a minute to splash water on her face at the sink, washing away her tears, before leaving the restroom. As she walked down the hallway, her mind was still on Lisa and how she might have died, what she might have experienced, and how she might have felt under what had to be horrific circumstances.

Then, slowly at first but quickly growing more intense, Stephanie felt a strong headache coming on. Vertigo began to set in as the pain became more than she could bear. Her balance was starting to go, so she knelt on the floor. For a moment, she thought she saw a white dove flit by. Then the hallway disappeared from her vision; blue lockers, and gray tile floors dissolved away into floating white feathers. The dank smell of mold and rotten wood filled the air. The air itself became bitterly cold. She could feel dusty floorboards underneath her, decayed and giving way under her fingertips.

Abruptly the feathers disappeared, and she found herself in a dark room, lit only by the light from outside a cracked window. Stephanie strained to see in the dimness. *Is this an apartment?* She asked herself, bewildered. *Wait—could this be the abandoned apartment building on Robinson?*

Then bright lamps appeared and police officers filled the room. On the floor before her was a slight figure wearing a mask, and across the room was the body of Tony Scorpione. Stephanie got to her feet and stood over the masked figure. The officers milling around didn't seem to notice her; they just went about their business as if she wasn't there. It was just like her dream of the warehouse—she was a phantom.

She looked all around her, not understanding what she was seeing. Where was Lisa? In walked a blond male detective wearing a tan overcoat. She recognized him right away. It was Stephanie's uncle Jimmy. He squatted down next to the body and began to examine it. She heard Jimmy speak into his tape recorder, giving details regarding the assassin's wound, her possible age, and so on. Then he said, "I'm removing the mask now."

Stephanie came closer. Had the police found out who the assassin was?

When Jimmy pulled off the mask and set it aside, Stephanie gasped and covered her mouth in shock. "Oh, God! Lisa?" She shook her head, unbelieving. "No, it can't be."

Stephanie felt a strong tug on her arm. Something was pulling her away from the scene. Suddenly she was in the school hallway again, curled up on the tile floor. A single white feather landed gently on the floor next to her, but quickly disappeared. She looked up and realized she was surrounded by teachers. The school nurse was holding her by the arm, a worried look on her face.

"Stephanie, answer me!" The nurse continued to shake her arm. "Can you hear me?"

Stephanie blinked hard, trying to relieve the dizziness in her vision. She sat up slowly. "What… what happened?"

"Oh, thank goodness." The nurse let out a long sigh of relief. "A student saw you lying on the floor in a daze. We've been trying to shake you out of it for almost ten minutes now."

"Thanks. Sorry. I'm okay." Stephanie wanted to tell the concerned faces above her what she had experienced, but she decided not to. She didn't think they'd believe her. She would just keep that freaky stuff to herself for now.

One of the male teachers reached down with a smile and grabbed Stephanie's hand, while the nurse took her other hand, and she stood up between them, a bit shaky. "I felt a little dizzy. I think I might have passed out. I, um, skipped breakfast today. Maybe that's why." It was a lie, just a cover story to lead the nurse to a false conclusion.

"Well, I still think you should come to my office and rest for a while." The nurse motioned for Stephanie to come with her.

As she followed the nurse, Stephanie was still haunted by her vision. How could Lisa have been the assassin? Had she really killed Tony Scorpione? That must have been why the police were keeping so quiet about the circumstances surrounding her death.

Oh, Lisa! She thought. *You died in such a cold, dark place. You should have talked to me. We could have prevented this. But you just shut me out again.*

Once inside the nurse's office, Stephanie sat down on the narrow bed against the wall. The faint smell of rubbing alcohol hung in the air. The fluorescent bulbs in the ceiling tiles seemed too bright compared to the ambient light from the cloudy skies outside. The nurse shone a light in Stephanie's eyes and asked if she still felt dizzy or was experiencing any tingling in her hands or feet.

"No, I—I feel fine," Stephanie said. "I had a little headache but it's gone now."

"Even so, I don't want you leaving that bed until at least lunchtime, got it?"

"Okay." Stephanie nodded.

The nurse sat down at her desk, and Stephanie stretched out on the bed and turned to face the windows. This power or ability she had—she didn't know what it was, but it was starting to scare her. Was this how it was going to be? It was going to just hit her out of nowhere and then, boom, she was on the floor? Could she even control this—whatever it was?

As she stared out at the tall, leafless trees gently swaying in the wind outside the second-floor window, she felt the tender embrace of sleep beginning to take hold. Her eyelids grew heavier. She could hear the muffled sounds of the wind hitting the windows, the tap of the keyboard as the nurse filled out her daily activity report, the faraway voices of teachers instructing their classes, muffled by closed doors.

The next moment, Stephanie found herself in another place. A warm, salty breeze caressed her face. The hot sun hung high overhead in the clear blue sky. Waves gently rolled up on the shore. The feeling of warm sand under her bare feet felt strange at first, but then it triggered something: reminiscence. She knew this place. The sun, the breeze, the waves, the white sand, even the boardwalk off in the distance: it was Wildwood Beach, the place her parents had taken her and her sister when they were young.

Stephanie was eight years old again, wearing her favorite pink swimsuit on that hot July day so long ago. She felt the grape Popsicle slowly dripping down her hand as it melted. When she saw her father and sister building a sand castle, she smiled and laughed. "Yeah, a sand castle!" she shouted. "I wanna help, I wanna help!"

They waved her over, and she trotted giddily through the sand and sat down next to them, starting to form her side of the castle. A few feet away, her mother relaxed on her beach towel, working on her tan as classic rock tunes played on the small radio beside her.

It was such sweet nostalgia. To relive those wonderful days brought a much-needed calm to her soul.

Suddenly, Stephanie found herself standing in line at a baseball stadium snack bar. She remembered this place very well. It was Yankee Stadium. Her father had taken Stephanie and her twin sister there to see a Yankees game for their tenth birthday. The savory smells of hot dogs, cheese nachos, and hot pretzels wafted through the air, though they mingled with the unpleasant odors of cigarettes, cheap cologne, sweat, and the chemical stench of hairspray.

The line was long, but it was moving steadily. She stood up on her tippy toes to see her ultimate goal over the counter: the hot pretzels. She loved them with a side of nacho cheese, and to top them off, an ice-cold Coke. The crisp $10 bill in her hand was more than enough to cover it.

When it was finally Stephanie's turn to order, the pleasant-faced woman behind the counter gave her a big smile and said, "What can I get you, young lady?"

Then something strange happened—Stephanie froze up. She realized she had never purchased anything before. She had no idea what to do. The lady winced, though she was waiting patiently, but Stephanie couldn't speak. She turned around and began to run away when her sister Jennifer stopped her.

"What's wrong, Stephie?" Jennifer looked over at the counter and back at her sister; Stephanie felt herself shaking with fear. "It's all right. Just go up to the lady and tell her what you want. Here, I'll show you. Uncle Jimmy explained this to me a little while ago."

Jennifer took her sister's hand and they both got back in line. When they eventually got back up to the counter, Jennifer turned to her sister. "What do you want?"

Stephanie whispered in her sister's ear. Jennifer nodded. "That sounds good." She called to the woman behind the counter, "Hello, ma'am, we need two hot pretzels with nacho cheese and two ice-cold Cokes, please." Jennifer took the $10 bill from her sister's hand and slapped it down on the counter.

The woman gave a nod. "You got it, little ladies."

Jennifer turned back to Stephanie and said, "You see? It's that simple. Think you can do it by yourself next time?"

Stephanie gave her a tiny smile and a nod.

The stadium scene dissolved. Now Stephanie was in her first year of middle school. Twelve years old and terrified, she was being held against a locker by a tall, mean-looking girl two grades ahead of her. Stephanie covered her face to hide the tears flowing down her cheeks. Her knees were shaking, her whole body trembling. She couldn't breathe.

The girl's name was Tabitha Beasley. She had short brown hair, piercing green eyes, and braces. Her reputation was that of a typical bully: preying upon the weak and helpless for her own amusement.

"Give me your lunch money now, pipsqueak!" Tabitha demanded. "Do it, or else I'll give you something to really cry about!"

From between her fingers, Stephanie saw a shoe kick out and strike Tabitha behind the knee, knocking her off balance. Then she was pushed to the floor.

"Hey!" a loud voice sounded. "Leave my sister alone!"

Stephanie moved her hands away from her face to see that Jennifer had come to her rescue.

Tabitha stood up and glared at Jennifer. "Why you—!" Enraged, she wound up and threw a punch right at Jennifer's face, but Jennifer was quick. She easily dodged the attack and countered with a hard fist to Tabitha's solar plexus. Tabitha dropped to the floor, holding her stomach.

"There's more where that came from if you don't get lost right now!" Jennifer said, standing over Tabitha with her hands on her hips.

Tabitha got up and started her retreat. "This ain't over, you little twin tramps," she yelled. "I'll get you!"

"Oh, yeah?" Jennifer boasted. "Bring it on, Ugly, 'cause I got two fists and a hell of a right kick."

Once the girl was gone, Jennifer ran to her sister to comfort her. "Stephie, you okay?"

A mix of fear and relief made Stephanie cry into her sister's embrace.

"Don't worry," Jennifer reassured her, "it's all over. You know you really should stand up for yourself. If you don't, people will walk all over you. It's a good thing I'm here, huh?"

Stephanie nodded as she rested her cheek on her sister's shoulder.

Now it was two years later, and Stephanie was sitting on a bench beside ten other girls in a crowded school gymnasium. It was the local gymnastics championships, and Stephanie was up next to perform. She could already feel it: the freeze-up. Anxiety was beginning to close its grip on her.

Then she felt a friendly pat on her shoulder. It was Jennifer. "Hey, what's up, sis? You okay?"

"I don't know, Jenny." Stephanie began to fidget in her nervousness. "I don't know if I can do this."

"What are you talking about? We've practiced these moves together over and over again. We've got them down solid."

"Yeah, but..." Stephanie lowered her head. "...I've never performed in front of so many people before. There's gotta be like three hundred people here."

"Nah, more like five hundred."

"That's not helping, Jenny."

"Oh, right. Sorry about that."

"What if I mess up out there? What am I supposed to do then?"

"Don't worry about it. Most of these people you'll never meet, let alone ever see again. So who cares what they think? Stop worrying so much. Just go out there and do your best, that's what I say. Here, watch me." Jennifer waved to the coach to get her attention. "Hey, Coach Webster! Can I go next? My sister needs a little more time."

"All right, Jenny," the coach agreed. "You're up."

Coach Webster took up the microphone and announced, "Next up on the bars is Jennifer Sebastiano, who will be demonstrating the swing forward to tucked roll backwards to low bar, Stalder release with counter movement to high bar, and will dismount with an underswing front tuck salto with a half turn."

As Jennifer ran out to the bars, Stephanie felt a pang of guilt. Her sister had to always cover for her whenever she froze up. But that was just one more reason she loved her so much. She was always there for her no matter what, just as sisters should be. Stephanie felt so lucky to have such a caring sister. But she also felt envy. She envied Jennifer for her personality: such cool confidence, courage, and pride, all traits Stephanie felt she lacked.

Oh, Jenny, Stephanie thought as she watched her sister perform, *I wish I could face the crowd as easily as you. You hold your head high and show a big smile without fear. You take life head-on with no regrets. You truly are blessed, my sister. Though we're twins, I sometimes feel we couldn't be more different.*

Jennifer performed each move with the exact grace and ease she and her sister had practiced. Then came the dismount and landing. And as Jennifer raised her arms and showed her bright smile, the crowd let out a big cheer. The four observing judges showed their decisions: Two tens, one nine, and one nine-point-five. Jennifer gave a bow, received her coach's congratulatory hug with grace, and ran back to Stephanie.

"Wow, that was great!" Stephanie said as she hugged her sister.

"All right, Stephie, you go out there and show them what you can do. I believe in you."

"But I don't—"

"Okay, listen." Jennifer laid her hands on Stephanie's shoulders. "Just imagine the crowd isn't even there. Imagine we're all alone practicing together. Okay? Think you can do that?"

"Yeah, I think I can."

The coach walked up to them. "You ready, Stephanie?"

Stephanie nodded.

"Okay, then, you're up!" The coach walked back to her station and took up the microphone again. "Next up is Stephanie Sebastiano, who will be demonstrating the clear-hip Hecht with half turn, swing forward with half turn to handstand on low bar and will dismount with underswing with half turn to salto backwards tucked with full turn."

"All right, Stephie." Jenny rubbed her sister's shoulders enthusiastically. "Now take a deep breath and remember: there's no crowd. It's just you and me. Got it?"

Stephanie closed her eyes, took a deep breath, and slowly let it out. She smiled at her sister with a nod, and then ran out to the bars. *No crowd, just Jenny and me,* she thought. *I can do this.* She leapt up onto the bars and began her moves. She felt a clarity and flow come over her. With each grab of the bar and each swing, she could feel her confidence in her abilities grow stronger. Then finally the dismount and landing. She raised her arms up high and gave her brightest smile, just as she had practiced.

At first the crowd was silent. Then the entire building erupted with cheers and applause. The four judges seemed to find their decision an easy one; each raised a ten in the air. Stephanie gave her bow and ran back into her sister's arms.

"I did it!" she crowed, jumping up and down. "I can't believe I did it!"

"You were incredible out there, Stephie, absolutely amazing! I knew you could do it. Didn't I tell you? Once you forget about the crowd, the moves just flow, don't they?"

"Thank you so much! What would I do without you?"

"Hey, that's what sisters are for. We hold each other up and support one another." Jenny grinned, took her sister's hand, and led her toward the locker room vending machine. "Come on. We got ten minutes till the next round starts. Gatorade's on me!"

Chapter Fourteen

In the school nurse's office, Stephanie appeared to be sleeping. The nurse glanced over at her, satisfied that a rest would be the best thing for her.

But in Stephanie's mind, the past had become her reality. She was living it all over again.

The inevitable day came. The sisters were sixteen. Their mother's scream woke both Stephanie and Jennifer out of a dead sleep. They jumped from their beds, ran into the living room to see what the matter was, and found their mother weeping uncontrollably on the floor. The phone receiver had dropped out of her hand.

While Stephanie comforted her mother, Jennifer picked up the phone. "Hello? Uncle Jimmy? What's going on? Mom's crying and—what did you say? Oh, no... when? Oh my God!" Jennifer had begun to cry. She hung up the phone, got down on the floor with her sister and mother, and hugged them.

"Stephie," she sobbed, "that was Uncle Jimmy. He said that Dad is—he said Dad died."

Shock took Stephanie's breath away and threatened to stop her heart from beating. She looked away for a moment and said, "My dream... no, it can't be. How's that possible?"

"What did you say?" Jennifer asked.

Stephanie just shook her head.

After that, it was as if a dark cloud formed over their house. Almost the whole day, no one said a single word. Their mother sat in the kitchen motionless, staring out the sliding doors to the back courtyard. Stephanie was holed up in her room, curled up on her bed hugging her pillow to her chest, paying no attention to the sit-com on her small flat screen TV. Jennifer lay silent on the living room sofa, her legs stretched out over the edge. Her eyes were fixed on the shiny set of car keys dangling from her fingers over her face.

Jennifer and Stephanie had earned their driver's licenses just a month before. "It's a privilege granting freedom to travel wherever one chooses," her father had once told her. Well, that was a freedom Jennifer was in dire need of. All she wanted was to get away from this silent hell of a reality and go someplace, anyplace but here.

She hopped off the sofa and headed toward the garage. She raised the garage door and pulled off the car cover to reveal a 1967 Chevy Camaro SS, jet black with white racing stripes. It was their father's baby, his pride and joy. When they were kids, he would drive Stephanie and Jennifer all over town in that car. And sometimes he would take them down the long country roads of eastern Pennsylvania.

As she ran her hand along the smooth, flawless, mirror-like finish on the hood, Jennifer remembered fondly those long drives. How her father would open up the throttle all the way. The sound of the engine roaring loud like a lion—so exciting. That invigorating feeling of the acceleration pushing them back in their seats. They would go so fast it felt as if the tires had left the asphalt and they were flying. Flying so fast, no worries or troubles could ever catch them.

Stephanie had learned to drive in their mother's Ford Taurus, a front-wheel-drive vehicle with a good safety rating. But Jennifer? It was this one, this raw power on wheels, this furious lion—this was the car Jennifer knew best. Every single detail from bumper to bumper was familiar to her. How it ran, drove, and handled. The newly rebuilt 350-cubic-inch engine, producing 325 horsepower; a gas pedal that was a little sensitive; dual exhaust pipes, chrome; racing suspension, good for cornering; four-speed manual transmission that slipped between third and fourth gears, so you had to double-clutch it; original steering wheel with leather racing grips—a wheel that vibrated past 70 mph so you had to hold it firm; and to top it off, an all-black leather interior.

It wasn't her father's idea for Jennifer to learn to drive in this car. She'd had to beg him for three whole weeks before he finally broke down and said, "Okay, okay! But if you scratch it, you're going to drive your mother's car for the rest of your life."

Now Dad was gone. Gone! Jennifer got into the front seat of the Camaro and closed the door with that familiar metal slam. She took a deep breath, inhaling the pleasant scent of old leather mixed with her father's cologne. She turned the key in the ignition; the engine started up with a furious growl. The song playing on the tape deck was loud and rockin': Led Zeppelin's "Whole Lotta Love," her father's favorite song.

Jennifer revved the engine a couple of times—that was the roar she remembered. How she had missed it.

She saw her mother appear at the side door of the garage, looking to see what was going on. When she saw Jennifer in the driver's seat, she grabbed for the driver's side door and frantically tried to open it to stop her daughter, but she was too late. Jennifer released the parking brake, dropped it into first, and slammed on the gas. The car howled as she peeled down the driveway and took off into the residential street, headed for the main road.

After dodging traffic and running stop signs and red lights, she entered the highway and opened the throttle all the way. *Finally!* She exulted. *This is freedom.*

She made it seven miles down the highway before she noticed the flashing police lights in her rearview mirror. God knows she couldn't hear the siren over the engine and the music. She geared down, pulled over to the side of the road, and shut the car off. Although she'd never been stopped before, she dutifully rolled down the window. She heard footsteps coming alongside the car; when they finally came to a stop, Jennifer didn't even have to look to see who it was—she already knew.

"Hey, Uncle Jimmy."

Jimmy Ziminski placed both hands on the door, leaned into the open window, and stared at Jennifer disapprovingly. Then he let out a deep sigh as he ran his hands through his hair in frustrated irritation. He seemed about to yell, but he held himself back. He said in a calm voice, "You know, you're lucky your mother called me. When she told me what you were doing, I couldn't believe it. Do you realize how many favors I had to call in just to keep the traffic cops off your ass?" Then his voice got louder. "A big black Camaro screaming down Main Street is pretty hard to miss, young lady. What were you thinking?"

"I'm sorry, Uncle Jimmy. I—"

"Sorry for what? Sorry for scaring the living daylights out of your poor mother and sister? Are you sorry for that? Or are you sorry for cutting off five cars while you tore up Main Street? No, wait, I've got it: You're sorry for running two red lights and three stop signs. How about that?"

"Uncle Jimmy—"

"What would your father think, God rest his soul, if he saw you right now? I think he'd be ashamed." Jimmy closed his eyes, raised his hands in the air, and clenched his fists, seemingly at the peak of his anger. Then he took a deep breath, relaxed his hands as he slowly let it out, and took a more reasonable tone. "Listen, Jenny, I've known you since you were in diapers. This ain't like you. Talk to me. Help me understand."

"I miss him," Jennifer said softly, her voice catching in her throat. "I miss him so much."

"I know, Jenny. I miss him too. He was the best damn cop I've ever known, and he was an even better friend." Jimmy laid a hand on her shoulder. "Go on home, kid."

"Thanks, Uncle Jimmy. Thank you so much."

"Don't worry about it," he said as she started the car. He raised his voice over the roar of the engine. "And you better go the speed limit all the way home or so help me, I'll lock you up myself."

Jenny nodded, swallowed hard, and gave him a grim-faced wave as she pulled away.

She made her way toward home down the long city roads, obeying the traffic laws just as Jimmy had demanded. Heavy clouds had since moved in overhead. It looked like it would rain soon. She stopped at an intersection, put the car in neutral, and waited patiently for the red light to change. While she waited, she searched through the radio stations for something good. She stopped on a classic rock station once she heard one of her favorite songs, "Bad Moon Rising." She turned up the volume, started nodding her head to the beat, and sang along with the lyrics.

The light turned green. She shifted into first and started moving forward. Then Jennifer saw something out of the corner of her eye and looked to her left. It was the front end of a pickup truck coming right at her at full speed.

There was no time. There was no warning. There was only a loud crash, and then…

Nothing.

Jennifer woke up in a hospital bed with a pounding headache. She looked to her right and saw her mother and her sister asleep where they sat together on a couch near the window. They seemed to be sleeping uneasily. Stephanie was covered by a blanket. Mom had a worried look on her face as she snored softly, rosary beads wrapped around her hand, holding a Bible on her lap as if she had fallen asleep while praying.

Jennifer looked out the window. It was nighttime. On the other side of the river, the New York City skyline sparkled and shone in the distance. The dark clouds from earlier had moved on. Now the skies were clear as a full moon slowly crept up over the countless skyscrapers. Jennifer's eyes were fixed there for a few moments as she reflected on what had happened today.

A bad moon rising, she thought. *Huh.*

The pain in her head seemed to pulse with the beating of her heart. It hurt so much, she almost couldn't think clearly. She lifted a hand to her head and felt bandages there. "Ooooooh," she groaned through the throbbing pain.

"How are you feeling, kid?"

She rolled her head to the left and saw Jimmy standing there, wearing a concerned look.

"It feels like someone's remodeling the inside of my head with a sledgehammer. What happened?"

"A guy ran a red light and hit you pretty hard. Don't worry, we got him. He'd just left a bar and was driving with four shots of whiskey and a beer in him." Jimmy pulled up a chair next to the bed. "You have a few cuts and bruises, and Doc said you might have a concussion, but you'll be just fine."

"How's the car?" Jennifer asked.

"Pretty smashed up. It'll probably take a lot of time and money to fix it."

"Oh, no." Jenny let out a depressed sigh. The last thing she remembered before the accident was the pickup's front grill coming right at her. In her mind, she pictured the Camaro all wrecked. She figured the damages included a bent frame and two broken axles at the very least.

Jimmy let out a laugh. "Now that's funny."

"What is?" She couldn't imagine what he could be laughing at.

"You're more concerned about the fate of the Camaro than yourself."

"It's not just any car." Her tone became somber. "It's Dad's car."

"Don't worry, Jenny." He laid a reassuring hand on her shoulder. "It'll drive again—just not anytime soon."

"Ugh." She groaned as another sharp pain hit her head. "What time is it?"

Jimmy glanced at his watch. "Quarter past eleven. You've been out for over eight hours. By the way, the doctor said there shouldn't be any lasting damage, but he thinks you need to stay here a couple of days for observation."

"That shouldn't be a problem, Uncle Jimmy. Right now I'm pretty tired." She rolled away from him and faced the window. Then she said under her breath, "I'm just tired… of everything."

"Well, you get some rest then, Jenny. I'll be around in the morning to check on you."

"Thanks, Uncle Jimmy."

Jimmy walked out of the room and left Jennifer to her own thoughts. She stared out at the bright, silvery moon. She felt different. Not just because of her injuries, but there was something else. Something was wrong. Her spirit felt heavier. Maybe even her nerve was gone, like her inner strength had disappeared.

What was this feeling of hopelessness? What was there left to live for? Dad was gone—and now the Camaro was done. Because of her head injury, her balance could be messed up, so she guessed she could be kissing gymnastics goodbye as well. She had nothing now.

There was just no point to anything anymore, was there?

Two days later, Jenny was released from the hospital. Aside from a black eye and bruises on her left temple and cheek, the doctors felt she was fit enough to go home, although he recommended she take it easy for a week. Unbeknownst to them, however, the state of her mind wasn't healthy.

Her dad's funeral was the same day she came home. It rained hard all day long. Everyone was dressed in their best. Jimmy stepped up to the podium and gave an inspiring speech about what a great police officer Tommy had been and cited his long, distinguished record of service with the department. Stephanie and their mother couldn't hold back their tears and wept quietly. A priest stood over the coffin and gave the final prayer. Once he had finished, four officers raised their rifles into the air and fired three shots in unison.

The whole time, Jennifer felt unaffected. Whether it was numbness from the shock of her father's death or because she was still in a bad way from her accident, no one was certain at the time. Her speech became monotone and unemotional, her movements clumsy, sluggish, as if she was always exhausted, regardless of the amount of sleep she'd had. She refused to make eye contact with anyone. It was as if she'd built a wall around herself and wouldn't let anyone in.

The day after their dad's funeral, Jennifer stopped talking altogether. Stephanie and their mother tried to cajole her into speaking, to say something, anything, but their efforts were useless.

Two days after the funeral, Jennifer wouldn't leave the house. She just wandered around aimlessly like a haunting wraith. She went from room to room, remaining for a few moments in each one, then moving on to the next. She didn't eat or drink much at all.

On the third day, she stayed in her room, not putting forth the effort to even leave her own bed. She just sat there motionless, staring at the wall for hours on end. At that point, Linda had had enough. She picked up the phone and called Jennifer's doctor. While Linda was on the phone in the den, setting up an appointment, Jennifer got out of bed. She walked through the kitchen and left through the back door, wearing nothing but her pajamas.

Stephanie noticed Jennifer leaving. She had no idea where her sister was going, but she had a bad feeling. But by the time Stephanie got outside, she couldn't see where her sister had gone. Jennifer wasn't in the back yard, nor was she in the garage where the wrecked Camaro sat. Stephanie ran out to the front yard and looked up and down the street. She spotted Jennifer walking down the sidewalk and turning the corner at the next block.

"Jennifer, wait up!" she called out, taking off at a jog. As Stephanie started to catch up with her, Jennifer began to run. Trying to keep up, Stephanie followed her for a few blocks until Jennifer paused at a busy road. Jennifer looked up and down the road as if in a daze. Then she started walking. She didn't wait for the green light, didn't watch for the Walk signal, didn't even slow down as she walked right into oncoming traffic.

"Jennifer!" Stephanie cried out as several cars swerved out of the way and honked their horns. She was still half a block behind her sister. She strained herself to the max, pumping her legs as hard as she could, praying she'd reach Jennifer before she got hurt.

Jennifer stopped abruptly when a pickup truck sped toward her. She turned and faced the truck, stretching out her arms as if beckoning to it. The truck kept coming, and Stephanie ran faster than she'd ever run before. Her legs were on fire, brimstone burned in her chest, but she pushed herself harder and harder. "Please, God," Stephanie prayed aloud, "please let me save her."

She reached her sister and pushed her out of the way with only a second to spare. Jennifer landed safely on the grass near the sidewalk. Stephanie, however, wasn't so lucky. The edge of the bumper caught her and tumbled her end over end, and she landed at the curb a battered mess. At the hospital later on, she was found to have three broken ribs, a dislocated shoulder, and numerous scrapes and bruises.

At the moment of impact, the pickup driver's attention was drawn back to the road, and he slammed on his brakes. He got out of the truck and immediately called 9-1-1 on his cell phone. Despite the amount of pain she was in, Stephanie was glad to see that her sister was all right. If she had been a second later, Jennifer surely would have died.

Shortly after, Jennifer was admitted to the Borgestedt Institute at their doctor's recommendation. When she fought the orderlies, she was more like a wild animal than a teen-aged girl, ripping and clawing, punching and biting them with everything she had, much to the horror of her bewildered mother and sister. One orderly received a bad cut above the eye from her right hook. Another suffered a broken jaw from her uppercut. And one lucky one walked away with only scratches across his face. Eventually they were able to bring Jennifer under control through the use of drugs and restraints.

After a week of intense psychoanalysis, the specialists at the institute diagnosed Jennifer with major depressive disorder with strong thoughts of suicide. She was determined to take her own life, no matter what she had to do. On top of that, she suffered a complete mental breakdown after her first night there.

It was officially the worst week of Stephanie's and Jennifer's lives. Their father's death, Jennifer's accident and suicide attempt, Stephanie's close call, and Jennifer's admittance to the institute—it all added up to a horrific few days. And it had all started with a single gunshot in a cold, dark warehouse.

Chapter Fifteen

Stephanie woke up in the nurse's office. The weather outside hadn't changed, and the nurse was filling out paperwork at her desk. The clock on the wall showed 12:45 in the afternoon. She had been sleeping for quite a while.

Stephanie let out a sob that sounded more like a sigh, remembering all the things she'd just dreamed. Good things, bad things, sad and terrible alike. She hadn't thought about those things in a long time.

She'd often wondered what had been going through her sister's head the day of her accident. What had she experienced and how had it felt? In light of that, was Stephanie really seeing into the past again, or was it just a theoretical scenario created by her own mind? It was so difficult for her to be sure.

The sounds of Stephanie stirring on the bed drew the nurse's attention. "Ah, so you're awake." She came over and took a close look at her patient. "How are you feeling—any better?"

Stephanie gave a nod. "Yes, much better."

"Feeling any headaches or dizziness?"

Stephanie shook her head.

The nurse felt Stephanie's forehead for a moment. "You don't feel warm. It's definitely not a fever." She sat down at her desk and leaned back in the chair. "As far as I can tell, what you experienced was just low blood sugar from skipping breakfast. Now that you've gotten some rest, you should probably head to lunch and eat something nutritious. And I know this will sound like a cliché, but eat breakfast every day from now on. It's the most important meal of the day."

They both got up, and the nurse escorted her out. "All right then. Have a good afternoon, and take care of yourself."

"Thanks, I will."

Out in the hallway, Stephanie found Patrick sitting next to the door, waiting for her.

"Pat?" she said, surprised. "How long have you been out here?"

"Oh, not long. I sort of just got here."

She knew it was a lie. She noticed his notebooks and text books for English class lying on the floor next to the doorway. His English class had ended four periods ago. Most likely he was too embarrassed to admit he'd been sitting there the whole time she was inside. And that thoughtfulness on his part brought a grateful smile to her face.

"I see," she said, helping him up off the floor. "So you heard about what happened?"

"Yeah, just a little while ago. I wanted to see how you were doing."

"I was feeling real dizzy and I had a bad headache, but I'm much better now. The nurse said it was just low blood sugar from skipping breakfast."

Well, that was the official explanation, she thought. But she wasn't sure he would believe the truth. She still wasn't sure she believed it herself. All of this weirdness was happening so fast.

Pat heaved a sigh of relief. "I was worried it might be something serious. I'm glad you're okay."

Stephanie felt her cheeks become flushed. He was really worried about her? That kind of made her happy.

"Hey," he said, placing a hand on her arm, "my lunch period is starting right now. You probably haven't eaten yet. Want to grab a bite together?"

"Sure." She smiled again. "That sounds great."

Stephanie continued the rest of the school day without any further incidents. However, she was more anxious now than ever before, fearing another episode could come on at any moment.

Figuring her normal routine could help distract her from whatever was going on in her head, she went to gymnastics practice. Before warm-ups, the instructor held a little memorial service for Lisa. She had all the girls form a circle and share their experiences and thoughts regarding their teammate. Many of the girls shed tears and told happy or funny stories. It seemed to give the other girls some much-needed closure, but Stephanie was still haunted by her vision of the abandoned apartment.

After gymnastics, Stephanie went on to the institute to spend some time with her sister. She brought the *Wishful Thinking* book with her, hoping it would brighten Jennifer's mood. The orderlies unlocked the room, and Stephanie stepped inside. Jennifer was sitting on the floor in the corner, rocking slowly back and forth. She was saying things that didn't make sense, at least not to anyone but herself.

"Shining blade, red, so red now, but still shining in the fire," Jennifer rambled. "On the water, big explosion, ka-boom! Guns, so many guns. Uncle Jimmy, tell them to stop shooting. Mask of the devil, menacing, menacing! Plans within plans. Mirror, princess's mirror. Clouds, so white, so soft, passing by underneath."

Stephanie helped her sister stand up and led her over to her bed. "How are you doing today?" she asked.

Jennifer looked at her sister suddenly, as if she had noticed her just that second. "Oh—Stephie, it's you. I guess I'm back here now."

"Yes, you've always been here, Jenny."

"No, I was away." Jennifer's hands were fidgeting. "Not here, not now. But now I'm back."

"Well, okay." Her sister's strange statements puzzled Stephanie. "I brought your favorite book. I figured we could pick up where we left off."

Jennifer nodded. "Yeah, yeah, I'd like that. Good story. Very good story so far. But still much to come. Lots of things to come."

"Yeah," Stephanie said uneasily as she opened to the bookmarked page. "I'm sure the story gets better from here too."

Stephanie started to read as Jennifer sat cross-legged on the bed and leaned back against the wall to get more comfortable. But once again, she barely got started before Jennifer interrupted.

"Stephie?"

"Yes?"

"On your way home, watch out for David Woodward. He might hurt you."

Stephanie was taken aback by her sister's words. "Oh? Um, okay. I'll definitely watch out for him then."

She continued her reading.

An hour and a half later, Stephanie said goodnight to her sister and left the room. That's when she saw Mei Tachibana waiting patiently. Mei smiled kindly.

"How do you feel Jennifer is doing today?"

Stephanie lowered her voice since they were standing right outside Jennifer's door. "Well, her mood seemed strange. She was rambling about a few things that didn't make sense. She almost seemed to be in a trance. Then when she snapped out of it, she talked about being far away and that she was back in the now, whatever that meant."

"Hmm…" Mei thought for a moment before continuing. "A warped perception of time. Feelings of going back and forth, unable to determine which time is real time. That could be a symptom of another disorder entirely."

Stephanie immediately thought of her own visions. "Could it?"

"Yes. This has been showing up in her sessions as well. I'll have to go over all the data in order to determine a proper diagnosis."

"Okay, please keep us posted—Mom and I have been praying for her get better."

"I promise Jennifer will be better," Mei reassured her. "I will do my utmost to make sure of that."

"Thank you. You really are a blessing."

Mei bobbed her head in a kind of bow. "I help people. It's what I do."

As Mei walked off towards her office, Stephanie looked at her sister through the small, reinforced glass window in the door.

Please, God, she prayed, *help my sister get better. Heal her mind so she can come home. We miss her so much.*

Stephanie started on her way home. As she walked along, she wondered about what her sister had said to her. Her talking had seemed a little stranger than usual. And what was all that about David Woodward or whatever? Who was that? Was it just more nonsense?

Oh, Jennifer, she thought. *It seems our roles have become reversed. You were always the one looking after me. Now I'm the one looking after you.*

Deep in thought as she started to cross the street, she failed to see a box truck heading right for her. The driver slammed on his brakes and laid on the horn, shaking her from her thoughts in time to see the front grill of the truck mere feet away from her and closing fast.

Then a strong arm wrapped around her and pulled her safely out of the way. The truck finally came to a stop twenty feet down the road. Stephanie looked up and saw a tall police officer holding her.

"You okay, Miss?" he asked in a deep voice. Speechless, all Stephanie could do was nod. He released his grip on her and said, "Good thing I happened to be walking by. You need to look where you're going from now on."

"Yeah, I will," Stephanie said, a little shaken. "I wasn't paying attention, Officer. Thank you so much."

"It's why I'm here. I'm just glad you're safe."

The driver of the truck had gotten out and was running up the road. "I'm so sorry," he called out. He looked from Stephanie to the policeman and back to Stephanie, his face white as a sheet. "Are you okay, young lady? You just walked right out in front of me. I didn't have enough time to brake."

"I'm fine," Stephanie said. "Don't worry about it."

The officer stepped aside with the truck driver to ask him a few routine questions. While he was checking the driver's ID, Stephanie noticed the side of the box truck. There, in big blue letters, was a sign that read,

David Woodward and Sons

Carpentry at its best!

Her heart dropped and her eyes grew wide. She read the name out loud. "David Woodward."

"Yeah, that's me," the driver said, tucking his license back in his wallet. "If you need any woodwork done in your house, Woodward is the name to call."

Jennifer knew! She thought in amazement. *But... how?*

Chapter Sixteen

Jimmy walked into his office with a fresh cup of coffee from a beanery up the street. His own coffee supply had run out earlier that morning. That was when he had decided to head back home, take a shower, and catch up on some sleep. He had rolled back into headquarters at about one in the afternoon to continue his work.

Now, as he set his coffee on the desk, Jimmy glanced at the time: just past 5:00. The sun was setting, pouring its light through the window and illuminating the city map on the wall in a deep red-orange. Red tacks were pinned on the map at three locations: the Scorpione estate, the location of the delivery van explosion, and the abandoned apartments on Robinson.

Monday night already, he thought. He sat in his comfortable chair, deciding he'd better pick up the pace if he was going to crack this thing. He was burning the candle at both ends, but that hadn't stopped him before. When his phone rang, he picked it up and heard his superior's voice on the other end.

"What can I do for you, Chief?"

"How goes the case?" Stonebreaker asked.

"I'm making progress. It's just another murder case. I'll find who's responsible soon enough."

"That's where you're wrong, Jimmy. This isn't just any case. It's Vincent Scorpione's murder we're talking about. We can't afford to make any mistakes. Understood?"

"Don't worry, sir, I'll have this case solved faster than a fat kid can unwrap a chocolate bar—and without the mess."

"That's the spirit. I knew I promoted you for a reason. Carry on."

Jimmy hung up the phone and picked up Tony's murder file, reading through it one more time. Evidence found at the crime scene had finally come through from forensics. Two guns were found: one M1911 Colt semi-automatic on the floor just inside the apartment doorway, and one .32 caliber Smith & Wesson revolver lying next to Tony's body. A boot print on the reconstructed door was a female size eight, which matched Lisa's size.

But here was the interesting part: four strands of long hair were found, and they didn't belong to Lisa or Tony. Analysis showed the hair was fresh and not left over from a former tenant. The hair had been determined to be Asian. This definitely narrowed down their suspects, but not by much. If the assassin was another female and a resident of the city, she could be any one of hundreds of Japanese, Chinese, Vietnamese, Thai, or Filipino women living in the greater Benton area.

But what if she was a visitor from out of town? A DNA test would take about two weeks. And even then, he could hope for a match only if she had a criminal record and her DNA was already in the International Police Database. Jimmy dropped the file on his desk with a sigh. This case kept getting better and better.

His eyes drifted to the empty desk covered in dust on the other end of the room. These cases had seemed so much easier when he and Tommy had worked them together. The department knew it was the Scorpiones who had killed Tommy, beyond a shadow of a doubt, but all the evidence and files on the case had disappeared, leaving them with nothing. Only the police had access to the evidence and file rooms. That was how Jimmy had known that Vincent had someone on the inside. He still had his suspects, but nothing solid. God, he couldn't believe it had already been a year since Tommy died.

He rubbed his temples, then picked up his phone and dialed the coroner's office downstairs. It rang three times before a man picked up on the other end. "Morgue, Dominic Rodriguez speaking."

"Hey Dom, it's Jimmy. You finish that autopsy report on Lisa Smith yet?"

"Yeah, just a couple minutes ago. A copy should be headed up toward your desk as we speak."

"Good, good. So give me the highlights. What've we got?"

"I found some pretty unusual things."

"Tell me about it." Jimmy let out a short laugh. "It's been a pretty unusual case so far."

"First off, I did some blood work and found a strange compound in her bloodstream. I double-checked with Patty in the crime lab, and it's an exact match to the stuff you found in the syringe at the Vincent Scorpione crime scene."

"Yeah, Patty mentioned it was a mixture of amphetamines, steroids, and a strange enzyme she'd never seen before."

"She's still calling universities around the country trying to find a match." Dom paused briefly. Jimmy could hear pages rustling. "I also found two more things during the autopsy. First thing was her muscles."

"What about them?"

"Almost every major muscle in her body had significant micro tears in the tissue itself."

"That's definitely something."

"It gets better. Out of curiosity, I did some x-rays and found the second thing."

"Which is?"

"Her bones. Nearly all of them had thousands of hairline fractures. Both femurs, radii, ulnas, and humeri—'

"English, Dom."

"Sorry. Um, yeah, bones in the arms and legs showed tons of them, mostly around the elbow, shoulder, and knee joints. I found several more throughout her lumbar vertebrae, the bones of her hands, her feet. I've never seen anything like this before."

"Do you think the strange substance in the syringe could be the cause? We have reason to believe these assassins are shooting themselves up with this stuff."

"I don't know for sure, but if that's true, whatever this stuff is, it made her body work so hard it was literally ripping itself apart. I mean, come on! Veteran professional wrestlers in their fifties or over-the-hill football players don't even show this kind of damage."

"A performance enhancer with these types of effects can't possibly be available in this country. A witness said he saw our assassin jumping from one house to another. We're talking Scorpione's neighborhood. So that's at least a hundred feet between houses. This isn't watered-down stuff made in a meth-head's basement."

"Then what are you thinking?"

"It's gotta be something cutting edge, maybe even engineered. And if so, this kind of research would need a large financial backing. Is it a black project by a pharmaceutical company maybe? There are a lot of big companies with deep pockets. Who could even pursue this kind of research? Could it be foreign interests? Russia? China? Japan? Or it could even be made right here in the good old U.S. of A."

"I can practically hear the wheels turning in your head over the phone. I'll let you get back to work, Jimmy."

"Thanks. Oh, and one more thing."

"What is it?"

"If a person were taking this compound we found in the syringe, what would be the side effects or warning signs to look for? Any guesses?"

"Well, we know one of the components is an anabolic steroid. With that you're probably looking at increased aggression, irritability, and overall moodiness. As for amphetamines, during the 'come down' phase, the body goes through weakness and the shakes. Possibly cold sweats, disorientation. Why? Are you thinking of checking out the local schools?"

"It's a thought, but looking for a moody, irritable, aggressive teenager—needle in a haystack is an understatement."

Just as Jimmy hung up the phone, a knock came at his open door. He looked up to see a rookie officer holding a file.

"Pete, come on in." Jimmy waved him into the room. "Is that the file from Dominic?"

"Yes, sir. He just handed it to me a few minutes ago."

"Thanks." Jimmy took the file and laid it on his desk.

"Well, if that's all," Pete turned to leave. "I'd better get back to work."

Then something occurred to Jimmy, and he stopped Pete before he could reach the door.

"Hold on a second. How're things working for you so far?" Jimmy motioned to the seat in front of his desk. "Why don't you sit down a minute?"

Pete eased into the chair. "Well, I'm still getting some experience, but I'm sure I could get a lot more without being cooped up in the file room sorting reports or the evidence room cataloging all day."

"How long have you been working those rooms? About a year, hasn't it been?"

"Yes, sir, a little over a year now. To tell you the truth, when I graduated from the police academy, I never pictured myself being placed in Evidence and Filing right off the bat."

"Don't let it get you down," Jimmy said with a grin. "After all, I got started in the evidence room."

"Wow! Seriously?"

"It's no lie. I worked Evidence for fourteen months before I got to work the patrols. Anyway, what I wanted to ask you is this: Since you've been working those rooms, have you ever noticed anything unusual? Any strange comings and goings from the other officers over the past year?"

"No, not really." Pete thought about it for a moment. "Actually, when I first started, there were quite a few times I saw one officer going through the files late in the evening. He would even take a few files with him when he left. Being new I thought it was just normal. But knowing what I know now, it was against procedure."

"So he never signed the files out."

"No, sir."

"Did he even write his name on the sign-in sheet?"

"Not that I remember, no. I asked him about it once or twice, but he said not to worry about it and that he did it all the time."

"Do you remember his name?"

"Let me think. It was, um, Robert Hawes. I'm pretty sure he works in—"

Jimmy jumped in. "Internal Affairs, right?"

"That's right."

"I suppose that would make sense," Jimmy said to himself.

"What would, sir?"

"Nothing, nothing. Just thinking out loud. I probably shouldn't keep you any longer. Tell you what—I'll talk to the chief and see if he can find you a spot on the patrols."

"That would be great! I'd really appreciate that." Pete left Jimmy's office with a spring in his step, seeming in far greater spirits than when he'd come in.

Jimmy closed his office door and looked outside at the fading twilight on the horizon, pondering. *Bobby Hawes in Internal Affairs,* he thought. *Of course, it would make sense, wouldn't it?* Working late hours after the chief had left for the day. If he'd been seen fishing through the file room, not signing in or out, and taking files with him, who was to say he hadn't done the same in the evidence room? Jimmy thought maybe he was finally narrowing down his suspects. Bobby Hawes could be on the Scorpione take.

Johnny Scorpione stood in his living room, staring out the plate glass window into the darkening evening skies. As the light faded, the street lamps started coming on. The windows of the houses up and down the street glowed. The stars began to come out across the heavens, twinkling gently like tiny diamonds.

One of his men entered the room from the main hallway. Johnny could tell who it was by the sound of his leather shoes on the hardwood floor. The man's name was Donnie Cappella, and he had just recently joined the employ of the Scorpiones. Donnie hesitated as Johnny continued to look out the window, not acknowledging his presence. Finally he spoke in a quiet and careful tone. "Uh, Boss? How ya doin'?"

A long moment passed before Johnny finally turned to him. He slowly folded his arms and looked at Donnie with a serious expression. "My entire family is being hunted down. My father was murdered in this very room, right where I'm standing. I just buried my only brother who died in a dirt-hole of an abandoned apartment building. I fear for the life of my son, who may be the next target of this assassin. And now the burden of leading the family business falls on me. Keeping all that in mind, Donnie, how do you think I'm doing?"

"Um…not so good, Boss?"

"Not so good," Johnny repeated calmly, with a dry laugh. "Sounds about right. So tell me, why'd you come in here?"

"Why? Oh, yeah—our man at the police department came through with some real good info. Turns out there were two assassins. There was the one your brother shot, Lisa Smith. And then there's the one who killed him. The one who got away."

"I see. No other leads yet?"

"None yet, Boss."

Johnny decided to change the subject. "Okay, then. So how's our next delivery?"

"It's already on the water and should be in on Wednesday night at Pier 15. Name of the ship is *Demetrius.*"

"What time?"

"Eleven p.m."

"What's on the manifest?"

Donnie pulled out a piece of paper with scribbled notes on it and read it out loud. "Two hundred each of AKs, Uzis, Tec-nines, and Mac-tens. Two magazines for each weapon. Three thousand rounds of 7.62mm rifle ammunition. Six thousand rounds of 9mm submachine gun ammunition. And it should all be in a container marked with serial number 89425G."

"Good. That dealer we found in Romania really came through for us. This is the mother lode, Donnie. Rally together twenty-five of our finest men and get them to Pier 15 on Wednesday night to guard that delivery."

"Twenty-five guys? That's almost all of 'em."

Johnny narrowed his eyes and glared at him, saying nothing.

"R-right, Boss." Donnie apparently understood what Johnny left unsaid. "Twenty-five guys. You got it."

"Anybody so much as sees a shadow move, I want hot lead flying. Kill the assassin on sight. Got me?"

"Got you loud and clear. Also, we think we've found the rat that's been leaking info about our organization. He's being dealt with as we speak. Down by the docks."

"Do you think he's talked about the shipment yet?"

"It's possible, but there's no way to be sure until we shake him down."

"Just to be safe, I want to move the delivery up three hours to eight o'clock. Get in contact with the boat and let them know."

"You got it."

"Good, now get out."

Once Donnie was gone, Johnny turned his eyes once more to the view outside. His mood darkened as he carefully scanned the deepening shadows along the edges of the estate. Dad was gone, and now Tony. What type of threat was he dealing with here? Who had his family (or his family's business) screwed over to earn this kind of retribution? This enemy was killing off his family and destroying their business. They sent an assassin who showed up out of nowhere and then disappeared without a trace.

How was he supposed to fight that?

He furrowed his brow and narrowed his eyes in discontent. He had never pictured himself as a leader; he was a go-to guy. It was what he was good at. Anything that needed to be done, he did it. That was who he was. Not… this. But Tony wasn't Dad when it came to leading the family either. Tony was too hot tempered, too impulsive. He didn't think. What this family needed was brains to wisely run things. That was what Johnny could bring to the table. But could he really live up to his father's legacy? Did he really have what it took?

Johnny sat down in front of the fireplace to warm up a bit from being so close to the cold window. He eased back into the comfort of the soft leather cushions of his father's old chair and leaned his head back with a sigh.

I miss my Diana, he thought. After she'd died giving birth to Joey, he'd felt lost. She always knew the right thing to say. She'd given him strength, wisdom, inspiration. *What would you say now, Diana? What advice would you give to pull me through this storm?*

Lying on the roof above Johnny was the wolf assassin with her finger to her earpiece. She had placed a microphone in Johnny's living room by the fireplace several days ago.

"So, eight o'clock it is, Mr. Scorpione," she muttered, gazing out toward the business district. "Tonight, however, I have something special planned."

Chapter Seventeen

In a dark alley by the docks, Mikey Jenkins lit a cigarette, briefly illuminating the filthy, wet gloom surrounding him. Two large rats scurried by his feet, heading toward the dumpsters several yards away. A stray cat knocked over a garbage can trying to catch one of them. The low roar of the club and entertainment district several blocks to the west could still be heard from where he was. The breeze was cold, and Mikey turned up the collar on his jacket.

Suddenly he felt a hand touch his shoulder, and he jumped. He turned quickly to see Jimmy Ziminski smiling back at him. Mikey was so deep in thought, he'd almost forgotten Jimmy was supposed to stop by sometime tonight to get more information.

"You seem a little edgier than usual," the detective said. "Sure you're not taking too much of your own poison?"

"No, I'm cool. Just too quiet out here, is all."

"Any new word on that shipment?"

"Yeah, word says it's goin' down Wednesday night at eleven o'clock, Pier 15." Mikey rubbed his hands together, blew on them, regretting he'd forgotten his gloves tonight.

"How big of a shipment are we talking about?"

"Big—real big. Lots of guns and lots of ammo. Should be the biggest shipment yet."

"All right, so Wednesday night. Hey, you sure you're doing okay, Mikey? You don't look so great."

"No, I'm good." What Mikey was, was nervous, and with good reason, but he wouldn't say that to a cop. "Was up all day and drinkin' too much coffee."

"Coffee, huh? Right." The detective gave a short, sharp laugh. "Hey, I really appreciate the info, Mikey. It's gonna be a great help."

Mikey shrugged. "One more Scorpione in jail suits me just fine. Glad I can do my part."

Jimmy walked away, and Mikey saw him get into his car parked up the street and drive off. Mikey was about to leave as well when two large men in dark coats and leather gloves blocked one end of the alley. It was what he'd feared since he started meeting with the cops. Mikey quickly turned to go out the other way only to see two more men blocking that end as well. Panicking, he tried the doors along the walls, but they were all locked.

The four men closed in, grabbed him, and pushed him against the wall. Mikey struggled hard, but it was useless to waste his energy in their iron grips.

"How's it goin', Mikey?" the largest of the men said, the one with the scar over his eye. "Business good?"

"Well, you know." Mikey breathed hard, tried to calm himself and smile nonchalantly. "Business is business, right?"

"Mr. Scorpione gave you a very simple task. You sell the goods, and we give you your cut."

"Yeah, yeah. That's what I've been doin'. Selling the merchandise. Nothin' wrong with that, right?"

"We hear you've been selling something else," Scar said. "That would be information—to cops."

"W-what are ya talking about? I ain't been talking to no cops, I don't even know no cops. They don't know me and—"

"Shut up!" Scar got in Mikey's face. "We wanna know who you been talking to. What's his name?"

Mikey was terrified. He knew if he didn't talk, his life would be over. For a moment, he wanted to tell them it was Det. Ziminski, just to save his own skin. But then something happened inside him, something that gave him courage, conviction. For once in his rotten life, he wanted to do something right.

"No," Mikey said plainly.

"What?" Scar said, as if the word were foreign to him.

"I ain't telling you nothin'. I'm done with you Scorpione bastards. You're going down."

"Well, if you ain't gonna talk, there's only one way this is gonna end." Scar reached into his coat and took out a black Beretta with an extended barrel. He took a step back, leveling the weapon at Mikey's chest. The other men pulled out their guns and did the same, and Mikey squeezed his eyes closed, preparing for the inevitable, and wondering how many "Our Fathers" he'd have time to say.

Good luck, Jimmy, he thought.

Then, just as Mikey was sure his time was up, he heard slicing noises cutting through the air, followed by the sound of something heavy hitting the ground. Then another, and another, until finally he opened his eyes to see all four men lying dead at his feet. A piece of paper lay on one of the bodies. Shaking, Mikey picked it up and read:

Lay low for a while and leave the Scorpiones to me.

-A Friend

At the bottom of the page was a small ink brush drawing of a wolf. Mikey shoved the paper into his back pocket. He looked to the sky, folded his hands in prayer and said, "Thank you, God, thank you so much. And whoever this friend is, God bless 'em!"

Then Mikey ran off into the night.

Jimmy walked into Toro's Matador bar. There were five pool tables on his left, a long cherry wood bar on his right, and several tables and chairs in between. A professional wrestling match was showing on the big screen TV at the other end of the bar. Several smaller screens scattered throughout the bar showed hockey, football, and basketball games. The smell of beer, hard liquor, and Latin food filled the air.

The detective found a seat at the bar and watched the wrestling match for a minute before beckoning the bartender. The man wiped down the bar in front of him and gave him a welcoming smile.

"How's it going, friend?"

"Not too bad," Jimmy replied. "So who's wrestling right now?"

"The big guy in blue is Leviathan and the little guy in the green Lucha Libre mask is Emilio Vega. Vega is who I'm rootin' for. He's got some sweet wrestling moves for a little guy, and he's fast. Maybe too fast for Leviathan. He's gonna be in trouble if he can't work around Vega's speed."

"Nice. Hope Vega wins then. I always root for the little guy." Jimmy looked up and down the bar. "You seen Terri around?"

The bar tender gave him a curious look. "Terri…?"

"Terri Vasquez."

"Yeah, she's right over there. Number five." The bartender pointed to the last pool table by the back wall. "She's been workin' that same table all night."

Jimmy looked over and saw a Latina in her mid-twenties with a long ponytail. She was holding—and counting—a thick stack of bills.

"Yup, that'd be her all right," Jimmy said with a laugh.

"Can I get you a drink, friend?"

"Club soda with lime."

"Oh, a badge, huh?"

"How'd you know?

"Anyone who comes through my door askin' about Terri and doesn't order alcohol is either a saint or a detective, and I don't see no halo around your head."

"Heh, good call."

The bartender brought the drink and set it in front of him, and Jimmy reached for his wallet. "What do I owe you?"

"It's on the house. Keep those streets safe, eh?"

Jimmy lifted his glass. "Salud. I appreciate it." He took a sip and made his way toward table five. As soon as Terri saw him, she jammed the stack of money into her back pocket and gave him a big smile.

"Detective Ziminski, nice to see you. Still drinkin' club soda?"

"Still hustling money, Terri?"

"Listen, I was just holding it for someone else. I—"

"Relax, that's not what I'm here for. I just want to ask you a few questions about that truck explosion you saw last week. All I want to know is what you saw that night, and you can go back to your business."

Jimmy waved her over to a spot at the bar. She gave a smirk, trotted across the room, and sat down on the stool next to him. After spinning around once, she slapped her hands down on the bar and called out to the bartender. "Julio, I'll have a shot of Patron Silver." The bartender poured the drink; she drank it, set the shot glass down, and turned to Jimmy. "That's much better. Okay, that night I was standing on the corner of Cooper and Sixth Avenue waiting for my friend Tatyana. We were gonna go clubbin' that night. Then I saw this big delivery truck drive by. I didn't pay it no mind until I saw this girl in a white mask jump down from a five-story building and land right on top of it. Boom! The truck came to a hard stop, and the girl jumped into the shadows. When the driver came out, she just appeared behind him like magic, and bam! Knocked him out cold. I was like, 'Ay dios mio!' I got so scared I hid behind a car."

"What did she do next?"

"I peeked out and saw her take his keys. She opened the back of the truck and got inside for about a minute, then she split right before the whole thing blew up. It was definitely the assassin. I read the description in the newspaper, and it was definitely her. But, well..." She thought for a moment. "There were a couple things that were even weirder."

"Like what?"

"Her mask. When I first saw it, it was like a fox. But then as she was running away it changed and looked like a wolf or something. Then it went back to a fox."

"A wolf?" That could be the second assassin.

"Yeah, it was like an Asian type of wolf mask."

"Anything else you remember?"

"Well, there was another thing: her hair."

"Her hair?"

"Yeah, if there's one thing I know, it's hair. Her hair was long, black, and flowing like silk. And I've only seen that kind of hair on my Asian girlfriends."

"You're sure?"

"Oh, I'm positive. Didn't I mention I'm a hairdresser now?"

"I guess I've been out of the loop, Terri." Asian hair… the hair they'd found in the abandoned apartment was Asian. He could now be more certain of the ethnicity of the second assassin. "Do you remember which direction she headed?"

"I think it was north. She must have been in a hurry—she was running faster than my brother when the rent is due."

"Anything else?"

"No, that's all I remember."

"All right, Terri. Thanks for the info, and try to keep on the straight and narrow, okay?"

She gave him a mock salute. "You know me, detective."

"That's what I'm talking about," Jimmy said with a laugh.

On his way out the door, he ran right into Mikey, who was wide-eyed and out of breath. "Jimmy!" Mikey gasped, breathing like he'd just run a marathon. Then he lowered his voice to a whisper. "Ya gotta help me, please. There were four guys from the Scorpiones and they were gonna kill me. I thought I was a goner, but then somebody murdered 'em and I found this note and—"

"Whoa, whoa!" Jimmy took him by the shoulders. "Calm down a minute and catch your breath, will ya?" The detective led him back inside the bar to a quiet table in the back.

"Here, take a seat." Jimmy pulled out a chair for him. "Now tell me what this is all about."

Mikey sank into the chair, glancing around and over his shoulder like he was sure someone was still after him. He told Jimmy everything that had happened, and Jimmy took notes. He was more than interested, especially when it came to Mikey's employers.

"You never told me you worked for the Scorpiones." Jimmy's voice became heated. "That's something you should have told me right from the get-go."

"Well, you know—I worked for them part-time here and there, but I guess they considered it fulltime."

"It's still an important detail," Jimmy said, rolling his eyes.

"I know, I know. I'm sorry. But I never expected to get in this deep."

"Have you spoken to him, the new head of the family? Can you tell me who he is?"

"It's son number two, Johnny Scorpione. Side note—he's a lot easier to deal with than his late brother, Tony."

"I thought so. He's the only one left. Mikey, I'm taking you into protective custody, but on one condition."

"What's that?"

"When we finally catch Johnny Scorpione, you'll take the stand and testify against him."

Mikey considered his options, which weren't many. Then he gave a nod. "Sure, Jimmy. As long as I'm protected, I give you my word I'll take the stand."

Jimmy and Mikey left the bar, got into Jimmy's unmarked police car, and headed downtown to the police station. All the while, something just didn't seem right to Jimmy. If Mikey was right and the assassin had killed Johnny's henchmen, that didn't make sense. Why would this assassin kill Tony and then save Mikey, who was working for the family? An assassin with a sense of justice? That was something he'd never heard of.

Among the many businesses based on Main Street was the Scorpione Distribution Company. Theirs was a five-story brick building with several wide cement steps out front leading to double glass doors. Inside were the administration offices where they stored all their business records and files.

A stiff breeze had crept in from the east, bringing bitter cold with it. The street was quiet, save for the sounds of old newspapers rolling across the asphalt and the electric hum of the street lamps. A window flew open on the alley side of the Scorpione building, and the assassin hopped out. She walked casually to the middle of the street, with slow swaggering steps, and then took out a remote detonator from a pocket on her waist belt. When she flipped the switch at one end, the red button on the other end lit up.

She crouched low, then with a powerful leap, shot a half mile straight up into the air. In her wake she left only a plume of dust and a crack in the pavement. As she reached the apex of her mid-air flight, she pressed the button. Down below, the Scorpione offices erupted in a fiery explosion. The windows of the surrounding buildings shattered, and glass and mortar rained onto the streets below. The assassin, landing a few blocks away, had a perfect view of the destruction. A mountain of black smoke rose from the flaming rubble, darkening the sky above. The surrounding streets were like flowing rivers of broken glass, and the light of the flames set the surrounding buildings aglow.

Within moments, the assassin heard police and fire sirens in the distance. Admiring her handiwork, she put away the detonator, folded her arms, and casually leaned against a tall brick chimney to her right. She gave a short laugh. "All you hold dear shall turn to dust in your hands, Jonathan Scorpione. I'll make sure of it."

Then she turned and disappeared into the night.

Jimmy walked Mikey into the downtown police station, where Lt. Freddy Williams met them. Jimmy and Freddy exchanged nods, then Jimmy motioned to Mikey.

"This is Mikey Jenkins, my informant. He worked for the Scorpiones and can give us the inside scoop on their organization. They got wise and tried to kill him earlier tonight. He needs to be protected."

"No problem," Freddy said with a nod.

Jimmy needed a minute with Freddy—alone. "Mikey, go clean up in the men's room, it's right there." He pointed to a door down the hall, and once Mikey had left them, he moved closer to Freddy and spoke confidentially. "I have reason to believe the Scorpiones have a mole in our department. I don't have anything solid, but just be wary. Also, contact the FBI. I know they've been trying to get the Scorpiones for tax evasion. Mikey's been inside. He could be their ticket to taking the Scorpiones down. In the meantime, keep Mikey safe and away from the other officers."

"You got it."

Mikey came out of the men's room, and Freddy laid a hand on his shoulder and steered him down the hall. "I'm Lieutenant Williams, and I'll be taking care of you. Now listen closely: while you're here, keep your head down and don't talk to no one. If any officers start demanding information, tell them they need to talk directly to me, Lieutenant Williams. Got it?"

"Y-yes. Thanks, Lieutenant." Mikey sounded like he was still shaken up from his earlier encounter.

"Don't be so nervous, kid." Freddy clapped him on the back. "You're in good hands now."

As Jimmy watched them walk away, his cell phone rang. He looked at the caller ID, and then answered the call. "Yeah, go ahead, Ashley."

"Scorpione Distribution on Main Street just went up in smoke. Big explosion; knocked the windows out for two city blocks. Think it's your assassin again?"

"I'd bet my paycheck on it. Thanks for the heads-up."

Jimmy put away his phone and turned toward the door. He guessed he'd better head out to the campfire. It might just be an arson, but if the assassin was involved, he could tie it into his investigation.

"Hey Jimmy, hold on."

Jimmy turned to see Phil Taylor, the department's communications technician, holding out a sheet of paper. "Here's something you may be interested in."

Jimmy took it, studied it. "Looks like a bunch of radio frequencies and times they were received."

"Yeah. The ones that are underlined are encrypted transmissions I've been receiving since last week. They're on an old emergency frequency. Since we updated the system last year, we almost never use it. I wouldn't have noticed it if not for the encryption. This department doesn't use an encryption this advanced."

"What does this have to do with my investigation?"

"Look closer at the dates and times." Phil stood with his arms crossed over his chest, waiting. And then Jimmy got it.

"My God! They match up with the assassin attacks."

"Right."

"Wait a minute—you mean to tell me she's using our own system to communicate?"

Phil nodded. "Yep. She must have hacked our network and piggybacked the system."

Jimmy noticed the transmission time all the way at the bottom of the page. The last encrypted transmission had come in just a few minutes ago. The explosion on Main Street—they could pin this one on the assassin too. "Is there a way we can triangulate the signal and find the source?"

"I can probably set up a monitor on all the cell phone towers in the area. After that, finding the source won't be a problem."

"All right, get on it. Let me know the next time you receive that frequency, and leave a copy of that printout on my desk."

Phil turned to go back to Communications while Jimmy headed out the door. There had to be someone heading up the assassins, and tracing this frequency could lead him right to them. The delivery truck, the distribution offices—it seemed this latest assassin was only interested in destroying Scorpione business interests. If that was the case, it was a sure bet she'd want to hit the next gun shipment on Wednesday night.

And that's when they would track her down.

"All of our records—everything is gone?" Johnny paced the floor of his living room, his fists clenched. "Are you telling me there weren't any backups off-site?"

"We were working on upgrading the system, Boss, but it wasn't done yet." Donnie stood by the door, ready to exit quickly should the boss come unglued.

"Damn! If it was that ninja girl, she hit us exactly where it hurts. The IRS is already breathing down our necks. Our tax records were in that building, and now it's all up in smoke? This is going to be a legal nightmare. Donnie, call our lawyer and get him on this ASAP."

"But we had that whole place rigged with motion sensors and whatnot." Donnie chewed his lip, thinking hard. "How'd she get in?"

Johnny came up close to him and spoke slowly and clearly. "Donnie. She's a ninja. It's what they do. Any other semi-intelligent questions?"

Donnie just shrugged and shook his head.

"All right, this girl wants to play hardball, let's play hardball. I want you to call in the mercenaries."

"The mercenaries? Wait, you mean those mercenaries? But—they're nuts."

"And that may be exactly what we need right now. Besides, I know they've been itchin' for a good fight. They keep complaining the Middle East doesn't challenge 'em anymore. Well, I've got a challenge for 'em. I want them at Pier 15 on Wednesday night with the rest of the men. Tell them there's a $100,000 bonus on top of their usual fee if they can bring me the assassin alive."

"You sure about this, Boss?"

"Drugs don't bring in the revenue they used to. Nowadays, it's guns that bring in the big money. We lose this shipment and we lose the confidence of our clients. They'll start buying from someone else, and then what will we have? Scraps, that's what. I ain't surviving on scraps again, Donnie. I will not do it."

"What do you mean?"

"Twenty years ago, the family suffered a drought in business. The Feds were investigating our distribution company. Back then we were using the basement for cooking crystal meth. Then someone ratted us to the DEA. First they froze our bank accounts, and then they took all our assets. Our reputation was damaged, and we lost all our clients. After everything got settled, we had to slowly rebuild on nothing but scraps."

"But your family still made it back to the big time, right?"

"Yeah. Eventually. It took us seven years to get back to where we'd been." Johnny looked at his watch. "It's midnight already? Okay, call the mercenaries, tell them our offer, and let me know what they say."

"You got it, Boss."

Donnie left the room, and Johnny poured himself some scotch and stood by the fire. Taking a sip and savoring the flavor, he stared into the rolling flames.

She might be fast and skilled, but he'd see how she did against twenty-five of his best men, plus five former Delta Force soldiers.

Chapter Eighteen

Jennifer woke in the middle of the night. Her room was dark, silent. A tiny bit of light filtered in through the seven-inch window in her door. A chill hung in the air, and she pulled the covers up to her neck. The clock on her nightstand showed 4:05 in the morning. The clock ran on batteries because the orderlies feared she might use a cord to hurt herself.

All was calm as she stared off into the darkness of her room. She felt relief, and she sighed deeply, for things were calm in her mind as well. There were no racing thoughts or troubling visions, just calm.

Moments of mental clarity between bouts of dementia and mania could be a blessing. And for a patient such as Jennifer who suffered constant anguish, it was a blessing more precious than all the riches in the world. Often her head felt like it was splitting in two. The distinction between reality and fantasy would become more and more blurred. Many times she had asked herself, "Am I really here or am I somewhere else?"

During the day, just the hum of the fluorescent light above her head could be maddening. It could be loud, deafening almost. She'd complained about it many times, but the orderlies kept telling her it was just her imagination. They couldn't fool her—she knew it was loud and that they were just playing dumb. At times, it seemed the whole world was conspiring against her, that the doctors and the orderlies were coming up with little plots to keep her locked away in this small, white, padded prison.

So many questions plagued her mind. Was the medication actually helping her or just making her worse? Did they truly want her to get better, or did they just want to steal what she had in her head? Was this simple paranoia, or was she finally catching on to their schemes?

Then the noise would start in her head. The racing thoughts, flashing images—it all rushed in like a tidal wave. The walls around her became dirty, dripping with filth. Then they became white again, spotless. Back and forth, over and over again. She felt an urge for violence, to get free, to get away from this place of madness, because she wasn't crazy. She knew she wasn't. Everyone else was insane. Everyone except her. The need to get out—it was overwhelming, agonizing. Every moment in this place was utter torture.

Then there were times like now: quiet, peaceful, calm. The whole world was standing completely still and silent.

She reached in the darkness for the lamp on the night table and turned it on. It was a small plastic lamp that also ran on batteries. Its dim light illuminated a small area, creating deep shadows beyond the bed. She wanted to find her diary in the top drawer of the nightstand. Doctor Tachibana had said it would be healthy for Jennifer to write down her thoughts, expressing what she was feeling inside.

Jennifer had always liked Mei, ever since the doctor had first come to see her. She was always so caring and kind to Jennifer. She felt that Mei was truly trying to help her. To Jennifer, Mei was her rock in the storm.

Jennifer opened her diary and picked up a felt tip pen. She started to write about this beautiful relief from the storm that usually ravaged her mind. She couldn't remember the last time she'd felt this clear-headed. It had been at least a few weeks. As she continued to put her thoughts on paper, a loud caw echoed throughout the room. It frightened her so much that she dropped the pen and diary and looked around wildly for the source of the sound.

There, perched on the end of her bed, sat a raven.

Jennifer quickly moved back against the padded wall behind her. She felt the fear come over her once more because she knew what this meant. "No, not again. You're not real," she yelled at the bird. "You're not real!"

The raven cocked its head to the side and looked at Jennifer curiously. Another caw came from the far end of the room. There in the corner was another raven. More ravens appeared: on the floor, on her bed, on the nightstand. The room was soon filled with the twisted symphony of their calls. It was loud, too loud. Jennifer covered her ears, repeatedly yelling for them to stop.

Then they all took flight and began circling the room. Black feathers rained down on her, and soon everything became black as pitch. To her horror, the walls, the ceiling, and even the floor turned into hundreds of ravens.

Then they flew off in all directions, and her room was no more. Jennifer realized she was now somewhere else. It was a shipping yard by the harbor docks in the warehouse district. The night sky stretched overhead. The smells of putrid river water and smoke filled the air. She saw a large fire out on the water. Surrounding her were dozens of men in black suits. Guns drawn, they were trying to aim at a shadowy enemy that moved faster than they could see. Her uncle Jimmy appeared from behind, with an entire police force at his back.

One bullet flew. A dim figure was struck and fell to the ground. Jimmy yelled at his people to stop firing.

As Jennifer tried to get closer to the figure on the ground, the sounds of ravens returned. Her surroundings suddenly turned to millions of ravens bursting into the air and circling around her, as if she were in the eye of a hurricane. The screeching sounds of their calls were deafening. It seemed nothing else existed but this spinning whirlwind of flapping black wings.

Then everything changed again, and she found herself in a large, dimly lit living room. She was standing by a black marble fireplace, and she could feel the heat from the crackling yellow flames. The sweet scent of burning hickory hung in the air, as well as the smell of hard liquor and expensive cologne.

On top of the fireplace, next to a small silver clock, was a round antique mirror sitting on a pewter display stand. Two silver dragons circled its reflective surface. Even though she was gazing right into it, Jennifer couldn't see her reflection. She did, however, see the man sitting in a red leather chair behind her. She turned around and backed away toward the wall next to the fireplace. The details of his features were obscured, and she was unable to determine who he was.

The man took no notice of her. He just stared calmly into the fire while swirling a bit of scotch in his upraised crystal glass.

Then something caught her attention out of the corner of her eye. At the other end of the room, something shiny reflected the light of the fire. Jennifer turned just in time to see a shadowy figure, holding a long blade, rush toward the man. There was a quick flash from the blade as it moved. Then a spray of blood spattered across the wall beside the fireplace. Jennifer felt the blood hit her face, and she closed her eyes and screamed.

It was quiet once more. She opened her eyes and realized she was in her room again. She rubbed her face and looked at her hands: clean. Not a single spot of red. She looked over at the clock and raised an eyebrow at the time. It was three in the morning.

"But that can't be right." Jennifer picked up the clock and shook it. "It was just after four a little while ago."

Her door creaked open, and the light of the hallway flowed into her room. At first she was hesitant, listening carefully for any sign of life outside the doorway. All she could hear was the quiet hum of the outer lights. Jennifer put on her white shoes and tiptoed softly up to the open door. She peeked her head out, looking up and down the brightly lit corridor. Not a soul was in sight. The hallway itself was long, and the metal doors on either side seemed to go on forever in both directions. The gray tile floors were polished to perfection. The white walls were clean and spotless. Usually, when she was escorted from her room, she would catch the scent of sanitizer and other cleaning supplies from the janitor's closet just down the hall, but now the air was odorless.

Jennifer decided to leave the safety and confinement of her room and venture down the hallway to her left. As she walked, she could hear her footsteps echoing endlessly in both directions. She peered into the windows of the rooms she passed by and found them all empty.

Where is everyone? She thought, walking on. *Am I even in the Institute?*

She continued walking for what seemed like a long time. She noticed that the lights were slowly growing dimmer. A few even started to flicker. Smudges of dirt began to appear on the walls as she continued on, and small red stains appeared on the floor tiles. The metal doors started showing rust around the edges, becoming more and more corroded as she went farther. The red stains on the floor were becoming pools of blood, which she carefully avoided. Red and brown rust now covered the once clean metal doors. The lights continued to grow ever dimmer. The sounds of her footsteps changed from click-clack to splish-splash, because now there was an inch of blood covering the floor.

Curious, she stopped to look into one of the rooms. Through the small window, she could see a bare, rusted bed frame in the corner of the room and a pile of rotted wood that had once been a nightstand next to it. Claw marks covered the walls. Tiles were missing from the floor, and parts of the ceiling were falling down. Suddenly a man's grotesque face appeared in the window. Fright made Jennifer jump back and hit the wall behind her. His face was pasty white. He stared at her with reflective eyes that seemed to glow in the dim light. Apparently seeing the terror on Jennifer's face, the man grimaced, showing filthy black teeth.

Jennifer quickly moved away and started running down the hallway. Fear gripped her heart like a vice. Through the windows of the rooms she passed, she could see pale men and women with onyx eyes shedding long streams of black tears. Their bodies moved in strange and unnatural ways. Some were manic and ravenous, scraping at the walls with their sharp nails, trying to escape. Others seemed lost and unable to understand their surroundings, slowly walking in circles with vacant expressions.

Then they all noticed her at once and smiled welcoming smiles at her. They beckoned her with their gaunt, ashen hands to join them.

"No!" Jennifer yelled at them. "I'm not like you. I'm not crazy."

Faster and faster she ran down the hallway that now twisted with no end in sight. Every breath felt like fire in her lungs. The muscles in her legs seemed close to snapping. She didn't know how much longer she could keep it up. But even so, she had to keep going. She had to outrun this horrible madness closing in.

Then, off in the distance, she could see the end of the hallway and a light there. As she got closer, she could see a person in the light. Comfort and relief emanated from this person. Closer now, she recognized Mei. With a sweet smile on her face, Mei held out her arms as if to catch Jennifer in her embrace. Jennifer was so close. She reached out, ready to land securely in the arms of safety.

Without warning, a strong hand grabbed Jennifer by the arm and pulled her backward. She turned to see a woman wearing a horned mask covered in blood. The face of the mask reminded her of the devil himself. She was beyond horrified. It was all too much for her, and she just couldn't take it anymore. Jennifer closed her eyes tight and screamed at the top of her lungs. The ghastly, masked woman closed her grip on both arms now, shaking Jennifer back and forth.

A voice called out her name. "Jennifer! Jennifer!"

"No!" Jennifer screamed. "Get away from me."

"Jennifer, wake up. It's Mei. Wake up, Jenny."

She opened her eyes. She was on her bed again in the safety of her room, and Mei was holding her. Jennifer was unsure if this was real or another fantasy. She spoke softly. "Mei?"

"Oh, thank goodness," Mei said with relief. "It looks like you finally came out of it. You were having another episode, weren't you, dear?"

Jennifer hugged Mei tight. "You made it go away. You made it all go away. Thank you!"

"You're all right now," Mei said soothingly. "You're safe."

Jennifer glanced at the clock; it was now seven in the morning. Three hours of her life had been lost to a horrid living nightmare.

"Tell me, Jennifer," Mei said quietly. "Please tell me what you saw."

Jennifer tried to explain as best she could in rambling words. She finished with, "Then I came back. You brought me back here, Miss Mei. You saved me."

"That's right, Jenny," Mei said sweetly. "Everything is okay now."

Standing in the doorway was Mei's assistant, Saki Kitagawa. A reserved woman, both in personality and appearance, Saki was a diligent worker and always paid close attention to detail. She wore large, round glasses and put her long hair up in a neat, fashionable twist. A thick notebook in hand, Saki was carefully taking down every word for Jennifer's file, per Mei's orders.

Mei motioned to Saki to come closer. "Patient most likely suffered a psychotic episode, losing all touch with reality for a short period of time. Return to normalcy is followed by almost nonsensical ranting. We should probably double-check her medication doses. Also make sure there are no drug interactions going on."

Saki nodded as she took it all down.

"Mei," Jennifer said, "I'm not crazy. I really did see these things. They were real!"

"It's all right, Jenny," Mei comforted her. "I believe you. Now I'm just going to give you something to help you feel calmer, okay?"

Mei motioned to the nurse standing outside the doorway holding a silver tray of syringes and medicines. Once Mei had given her the shot of Thorazine, Jennifer could no longer focus. Her mind filled with fog. Lines became fuzzy and colors more brilliant. Miss Kitagawa's red blouse seemed to stand out the most. Jennifer stared at the blouse, amazed at that specific shade of red. Deep red… like the red mask she had seen. Then her attention was drawn to Mei's blue shirt under her white lab coat. It was such a deep blue, like the color of the sky or the ocean on a summer afternoon at the beach.

Soon Jennifer was lying comfortably in her bed, going through a book Mei had given her filled with the colorful artwork of the Chicago Art Museum.

Mei went out into the hallway with Saki, locking Jennifer's door behind them. She turned to her assistant. "We must continue to look for the proper doses of medication to bring those chemical levels in her brain back to normal. We should also continue monitoring her serotonin levels. Those are crucial. We're so close, Saki; I can feel it." Mei looked through the window to see Jennifer still quietly flipping through the book. "It may be taking longer than I anticipated, Jennifer," Mei said softly, "but I will cure you. Please be patient a little longer, okay?"

Chapter Nineteen

That Tuesday morning, the halls of Kingsley flowed with more student traffic than usual. It seemed as if not a single student was absent. Hundreds of elbows and shoulders brushed against one another. Countless soles clacked on the ceramic tiles beneath them.

Stephanie was standing by her locker quietly reviewing her calculus notes when she noticed Kira Shirou walking toward her. She put away her notebook and called out to her. "Kira, how are you?"

Kira took slow, wobbly steps as she moved carefully down the hallway toward Stephanie. Her knees seemed shaky; it looked like she was clinging to the wall to keep her balance. Finally seeming to realize that someone had called out to her, Kira stopped and looked over at Stephanie. She was very pale, and beads of sweat clung to her face and neck. Her breathing was heavy and labored. "Oh—it's you," she mumbled. "Did you need something?"

Stephanie was stunned by Kira's appearance. "Do *I* need something?" she said, deeply concerned. "What about you? You don't look well."

"I'm fine." Kira said, her weak voice growing louder with irritation. "Just leave me alone, okay?"

"You're not fine. Please, just let me take you to the nurse's office. She can help—"

"I said I'm fine, damn it!" Kira interrupted in an explosion of anger. She grabbed Stephanie by the shoulders, lifted her up from the floor with unnatural strength, and pressed her against the lockers. "Stay out of my business, understand? Or else I'll—ergh, ohhh!" Kira suddenly dropped Stephanie to the floor and leaned back against the wall, rubbing her arms as if she was in pain.

By this time a crowd had formed around the two girls. Stephanie was stunned and confused. She stood up, still determined to help. "Kira, please, you need help!"

But Kira just ignored her. With slow, weak steps, she started walking away. Then she swayed on her feet, her eyes rolled back, and she leaned against the locker again, sliding down until she collapsed to the floor.

Stephanie quickly moved to her side. "Kira? Kira!" She gently shook her. "Kira, wake up." Stephanie looked up at the boy standing closest to her in the crowd. "You! Go get the nurse and tell her Kira Shirou collapsed."

The boy seemed stunned. "Uh, I—"

"Don't stand there like an idiot, just do it—now!" The boy ran off toward the nurse's office while Stephanie sat down next to Kira and carefully cradled the girl's head on her lap. Several teachers soon appeared, wondering why their students were still standing in the hallway outside their classrooms. Stephanie briefly explained what happened and that the nurse should be on her way.

The following minute seemed an eternity, not knowing Kira's condition, whether she might live or die. Great relief came over her when she finally heard the school nurse's voice over the crowd.

"Move aside, I said, move aside! Let me through." The nurse knelt over Kira and placed her hand on her head. "She's burning up." She looked at Stephanie. "Jeez, what is it with you kids collapsing in the hallway? All right, tell me what happened, Stephanie."

"When I saw her five minutes ago, she looked really sick and pale. But when I said she should go see you, she got violent, and then she just collapsed."

The nurse listened to Kira's breathing and felt her wrist. Then she pulled out her cell phone and dialed 911. When she'd completed the call, she held Kira's hand in hers. "Come on, Kira. Stay with me."

The paramedics showed up in less than five minutes, which was nothing short of a miracle. In no time at all, Kira was breathing through an oxygen mask and secured to a gurney. Once she was loaded into the ambulance, she was on her way to Benton Mercy Hospital. Stephanie stood by the front windows of the school, watching the ambulance take Kira away. The crowd quickly shrank as the other students started heading back to their classes. Soon, the hallway was completely empty except for her.

As Stephanie pressed her hand against the cold glass window, her heart was heavy for Kira. She didn't like to see anyone get hurt, especially people she knew. The more she dwelt on the situation, the worse she felt. What was up with Kira? She'd never seen her like that, and she hoped she'd be okay. As for herself… what had got into her? The way she'd taken charge of the situation after Kira went down—that wasn't like her at all. Maybe she was changing in a good way. But aside from that, why did these things keep happening? First Lisa died, and now Kira was in trouble. She didn't know how much more she could take.

Stephanie felt a warm, gentle hand on her shoulder. A flash of Pat's face came to her mind. She turned and threw her arms around him.

"H-hey!" Patrick looked surprised at first, but then he held her as well. "How did you know it was me?"

"I always know when it's you, silly." She nuzzled her face into his shoulder as tears formed in her eyes.

"Come on..." Pat looked towards the security guard appearing at the end of the hallway. "Let's take this somewhere more private."

A few minutes later and the two were standing together in a quiet secluded corner of the school library, away from prying eyes.

Stephanie spoke softly as Pat listened.

"My friend Lisa Smith was killed recently. And now my classmate Kira Shirou is on her way to the hospital after collapsing. Why? Why do these things keep happening to the people around me, Pat?"

"It's okay." Pat held her ever closer. "I'm here."

"If I ever lost you, Pat..." Tears started to fall down her cheeks. "I don't know what I'd do." She hesitated for a moment, and then spoke more softly. "To be honest, you're the reason I'm here right now."

"What do you mean?"

"I've never told anyone this, but right before I met you, I was thinking of transferring to another school. The people here were becoming too much for me to deal with, so I just wanted to leave. Then—then I met you and everything changed." She gave him a tender smile. "Over the past year, spending time with you, it's made me feel like I can be a more open and confident person. That's all thanks to you."

Pat seemed at a loss for words. Then she heard him whisper in her ear, "Well, to be honest, I've been noticing you. Not just as a friend, but as something more." He moved back slowly so he could look at her, and he gently wiped the tears from her cheeks. "I just look into those soft brown eyes of yours and… well, I get this feeling of longing, like I want to be closer to you. But I wasn't sure how I could do that without jeopardizing our friendship."

"Asking me out on a date was a good start." She smiled. "Everything about that night was so perfect, I didn't want it to end."

"I didn't want it to end either."

She ran her fingers up his arms and over his chest. "I—I've wanted to be closer to you too."

"Really?"

Gazing into his eyes, she nodded.

Pat moved his arms around her waist and pulled her closer. Entranced and lost in each other's eyes, they steadily closed the distance lying between them. Stephanie's heart was racing, and she could feel the heat of his body against hers. Dreamy eyed, she tilted her head upward as he tilted his head down. He was so tall. Had he always been this tall?

They closed their eyes as their lips moved closer and closer. She could feel his nose graze the side of hers. So close, just a little further and… They were startled by a loud voice and heavy footsteps running up to them.

"Yo, Pat, Stephanie. Man are you guys hard to find. A buddy of mine saw you duck into the library. What are you two up to? Did you see that ambulance—whoa!"

They looked over to see Joey standing a few feet away, completely speechless at the sight of them standing so close together. The two quickly separated, and Stephanie felt her face grow warm with embarrassment. Pat was a little flushed as well.

Joey apologized immediately. "Wow, I am so sorry, I did not mean to interrupt." Joey started moving back toward the exit. "You guys just carry on. Make like I was never here." He disappeared hastily.

"Yeah, like that'll happen," they said in unison. They looked at each other and burst into lighthearted laughter. Their amusement died down and soon they were looking dreamily into each other's eyes once more.

Pat gave Stephanie's shoulder a loving rub. "I guess we'll have to pick this up later, huh?"

"I think we'll have to."

He ran his fingers down her arm and took her hand, giving it a gentle squeeze. She squeezed back, and then the two reluctantly parted and headed to their separate classes.

As she walked, Stephanie's cheeks were still warm, her heart still pounding. What was this feeling she was having? She felt so light, like she was walking on air. Everything seemed so fresh and new. Patrick… just being near him made her happy. Was this what it was like to be in love?

As Pat walked to his class, he couldn't stop thinking about what had just happened. He couldn't believe he'd been that close to her. He could still smell her perfume—sweet jasmine. She was so beautiful. He knew she could be shy, but when she opened up to him it was like her personality came out in a fireworks display. Steph was smart, kind, gentle, she loved to laugh, and she was such a wonderful person. He couldn't wait to see her again.

In Jimmy's office, the clock on the wall read 8:30 a.m. A tall coffee sat on his desk as he went through a filing box beside it labeled "Scorpione."

The large room outside his door held the Traffic and Safety divisions as well as Robbery and Auto Theft. Jimmy's division, Homicide, lay along the west wall. He could hear the morning noise of a dozen phones ringing and countless feet stomping. It was a typical Tuesday morning for the department. Incoming calls usually involved stolen cars, car accidents, robberies, burglaries, and pretty much anything else that wasn't Homicide or Vice. In fact, it was getting so loud, Jimmy had to get up and shut his door just so he could concentrate. Now that it was quiet once more, he could continue.

Quite a few files had been stored in the box, stacked up just short of full. Many of the documents were old. Some even dated back over twenty years ago. Most of the cases had either been dismissed or thrown out due to the usual Scorpione palm greasing and blackmail. The cases involving assault and battery? Tossed out for lack of credible witnesses. The cases involving murder? Dismissed for lack of evidence. The files went on and on.

Jimmy was hoping he would find something useful for his case, but so far there was nothing. *For a bunch of filthy animals, these Scorpiones kept their family name squeaky clean,* Jimmy thought as he dug through the files.

Then, at the very bottom, lying among paid-off parking and speeding tickets, Jimmy found a single report. The subject line read: "Breaking and Entering, Attempted Burglary." Jimmy started reading through the body of the report. It was dated about five years earlier on May 23. The person reporting the crime was Jonathan Scorpione.

At about 0100 in the morning at Vincent Scorpione's estate, two unknown assailants apparently entered the mansion through a broken window in the attic. They were described as wearing white masks and dark form-fitting clothing, and both appeared to be female. Age and ethnicity are unknown. The word "Ninja" was frequently used by Jonathan Scorpione to describe them. Apparently, they were attempting to steal an antique Japanese mirror when they were discovered by Jonathan, who had stopped by to check in on his father. Jonathan then took out his Colt .45 caliber revolver and fired two shots. One of the shots he believed mortally wounded one of the intruders. The other intruder dropped the mirror on the couch, grabbed her wounded partner, threw a smoke grenade, and fled the scene. The only evidence left behind was the spent grenade and a blood stain on the floor. The model of grenade, M-18, is common and can be found easily on the black market. The blood was tested and typed as B positive, but no further identity could be determined from the evidence gathered.

After reading the report, Jimmy moved all other files aside and laid it on his desk. If the ninjas in the report and the assassins terrorizing the city were from the same group, that meant a huge piece of the puzzle had just fallen into his lap. They may have been planning their attacks for a while now. If Jonathan Scorpione did in fact kill one of them, they might be after one thing and one thing only: revenge.

Jimmy glanced at the red tack on his map that had once been the offices of Scorpione Distribution. He needed to confirm this theory with Johnny. Now that Johnny's business had literally gone up in smoke, Jimmy couldn't imagine him being anyplace but at his estate right now. He might not get much out of him, but at least it was worth a try.

Jimmy took one last gulp of his coffee, grabbed his coat off the hanger by the door, and ran out of the office.

Chapter Twenty

Mei Tachibana was in her office going over her notes with Saki. The subtle scent of green tea from the cup on Mei's desk filled the air. It was a small office, no more than ten feet by twelve feet. Mei's desk was on one side while Saki's was on the other. The far wall was floor-to-ceiling shelves filled with books, with many volumes on anatomy, physiology, pharmacology, and psychology nestled here. Mei even had the *Diagnostic and Statistical Manual,* editions I through IV.

"I'm just not sure what it could be," Saki exclaimed, going over her notes. "Jennifer's serotonin levels are all normal. She responds fairly well to the Thorazine, but that should be viewed only as a temporary fix. The side effects are counter-productive, and she returns to her hallucinations and delusions as soon as it wears off."

Mei took a sip of her tea. "I agree. We can't keep shooting her up with Thorazine. It's like giving a hyperactive child Ritalin: it brings the subject under control, but it's by no means a cure. We need to create a treatment that will cure the problem itself. We've made little progress, and we're still far from determining the exact problem." Mei glanced through a few papers on her desk. "Her symptoms match up with several different disorders, but she can't possibly have all of them."

Saki flipped back several pages in her notes. "Well, we know her synaptic pathways were most likely damaged in the car crash, and her brain chemistry was also affected, resulting in a chemical imbalance. But many of the levels are still showing normal. Some are a little high and others slightly on the low side, but nothing drastic enough to cause the symptoms we're seeing."

Mei let out a sigh as she glanced at her silver watch. "It's eight forty-five already? These five-in-the-morning starts can be brutal. Do you want to take a break and grab something from the cafeteria?"

"Well, yes, I do, but—" Saki looked disturbed. "I don't like that guy Bobby who works the cash register. I've caught him staring at my butt, and he's always giving me those cheap pick-up lines. He acts like such a dope."

At the word "dope," something struck Mei. She grabbed the chart showing Jennifer's brain chemistry levels and carefully looked at the numbers. "That's it! Saki, you're a genius," Mei cried. She circled a set of numbers with her pen.

"What is it, Mei? What did I say?"

"Dopamine, Saki. I just remembered that too much or too little dopamine can cause either type one or type two schizophrenia. At first, I thought it may have been the serotonin because she displayed symptoms of anxiety, but this has to be the key." Mei showed her the numbers. "Look here—her dopamine is just high enough for her to show positive schizophrenic symptoms. According to a study done by Goldsmith, Shapiro, and Joyce in 1997, type one schizophrenics have excess dopamine levels in their limbic systems."

Saki nodded as she looked at the numbers herself. "You're right. Many of Jennifer's symptoms do match up with type one, and she does respond well to the antipsychotics."

"I think we've found it, Saki. Thorazine reduces Jennifer's symptoms, yes, but only because it blocks the dopamine receptors in her brain. My research department back in Tokyo has developed a compound called TZ328. It naturally reduces the amount of dopamine produced in the brain, just enough to fine-tune the levels with the proper dosage."

"How much has it been tested?" Saki asked.

"All two hundred clinical trials successfully lowered dopamine levels in the brain."

"Were there any side effects?"

"There were twenty-two subjects who experienced minor headaches and nausea, but those symptoms disappeared after a few days. The FDA has yet to approve the drug in the United States, but it's already being prescribed to mental patients in Japan, Germany, and the UK."

"Would you be able to bring it over here to the States though?"

Mei leaned back in her chair and folded her arms. "I'll have to go through some red tape. In order to treat a patient with an unapproved drug, I'll have to get a special permit from the FDA, which at the very least will take a few weeks on my own. Thankfully, my father has enough influence to turn a few weeks into a few hours. Just one phone call from him, and we'll be able to treat Jennifer by tomorrow."

"That's excellent news. Should we tell Jennifer now?"

"Yes, let's tell her the good news. She needs all the hope she can get."

Jimmy stood just outside the Scorpione estate, staring silently at the old brick mansion. Dry, gray leaves rolled by his feet as the branches of bare trees creaked and whined in the breeze. Even though the sun was shining through narrow cracks in the clouds, it was still bitterly cold. He wasn't sure if the uneasy chill he felt was from the brisk wind or just being so close to the estate. This was the home of the family who had killed his partner, after all. He knew it, he could feel it in his bones, but could he prove it? That was where he stood: close, yet so far away.

In his hand was a folder containing the break-in report. Jimmy expected mostly truth from Johnny, since the occurrence was most likely no fault of the family. What could Jimmy expect from this little meeting? Possibly a connection between the two assailants from five years ago and the assassins currently stalking the Scorpiones.

Jimmy took an uneasy step forward. Crossing the front courtyard, he glanced at the rooftop next door where the assassin had taken her shot at Vincent. Then he climbed the stone front steps and knocked on the large, dark paneled door.

A moment passed before the door opened. There was Johnny, staring right back at him with a look of surprise. Then his expression slowly changed to a devilish grin.

"Well, look who it is standing on my very doorstep," he said in a mocking tone. "You sure you have the right house, Detective Ziminski? I don't believe I've seen you since you questioned me regarding the unfortunate death of your partner."

"Has it been a year already, Johnny?"

"How's finding that evidence coming along? You know, the evidence allegedly connecting my family to Tommy Sebastiano's untimely demise?"

"As much as I would love to continue this pleasant remembrance of old times, Johnny, I have another matter I hope you can help me clear up."

Johnny stepped aside with a smile as he motioned Jimmy to enter. "Come in. I got nothin' to hide."

Jimmy followed him to the living room. "I'll try to make this brief."

"Don't worry, James," Johnny tossed over his shoulder. "I got nothing but time."

"So I heard." Jimmy stepped into the living room, where a fire crackled in the fireplace. "How is business, by the way?"

"My business is currently being carried away by dump trucks to the local landfill. No thanks to a certain annoying little explosives expert."

"Up in smoke, huh? Along with all your tax records, I'm sure. Is the IRS still breathing down your neck?"

"I have my lawyers taking care of matters as we speak."

"Of course you do."

Johnny sat down on the sofa by the big-screen television on the far end of the room. "Please, take a seat, Detective." Johnny gestured to the sofa across from him. "Tell me what I can help you with this fine day."

Jimmy handed him the file before sitting down himself. Johnny opened it and read the report. Then he set it on the coffee table between them.

"You want help with this? This is old news. I already told the police everything I know."

"I was hoping you could scan your memory for just a few more details."

"All right, ask away."

"In the report you were vague in your description of the suspects, resorting to 'they looked like ninjas,' 'white masks,' and 'tight outfits.' I was hoping you could give me more details on their appearance."

"It was five years ago, but I'll try."

"Let's start with the masks they were wearing." Jimmy took out his note pad and pen. "I need details."

Johnny leaned back on the couch, his hands locked behind his head. "Well, this room was pretty dim. Only the fire was going in here that night. As you know, I stopped by to check on Pops; he was already asleep at the time. Then I walked in here looking for the cigarette lighter I'd left behind the night before. That's when I caught sight of 'em right over there." Johnny pointed at the fireplace where the antique mirror still stood on display above the mantle. "They were trying to steal that mirror over there. They were wearing these weird masks like white animal faces. Pointy ears, long nose, painted-on whiskers, narrow slits for eyes. You know, that fancy Japanese crap."

Jimmy got up and walked over to the mirror. "So this is the thing they were trying to steal, huh? It might fetch a couple grand, but that certainly isn't worth all the trouble of taking it from a Scorpione."

"My father told me he found it in some antique gallery in New York years ago. Said the price he paid for it was practically a crime."

"Did he?" Jimmy pulled out his cell phone. "Mind if I snap a picture for my investigation?"

"Be my guest."

Jimmy took several photos from different angles, and then he sat back down across from Johnny. "Getting back to the description of the thieves—can you think of a specific animal the masks resembled?"

"Both of them were kind of the same, but they were different too, you know? One looked like a cat or a fox. The other looked more like a dog—no, a wolf. It was definitely a wolf."

"In the report, you mentioned they were carrying weapons. Can you be more specific?"

"They were both carrying these black ninja swords on their backs. The kind you see in old samurai movies. They never pulled 'em out, though." Johnny let out a laugh. "I never gave 'em the chance."

"Yeah, so I read. How about what they were wearing. What kind of outfits did they have on?"

"They were wearing these dark gray suits that fit tight like spandex, but the weave was different. It had a weird shine to it, like it was made of something other than fabric. The thing that stood out the most was their hands. They had silver claws, but it was more than that, some sort of metal gloves, like—"

"Like what?" Jimmy asked. "Gauntlets?"

"Yeah, sort of like that, but they weren't bulky like medieval armor. They were more, I don't know, slender to fit their little hands."

"I see. What else do you remember?"

"They had on black boots—almost like what your SWAT team wears, but more form-fitting. They also had these black belts around their waists with a boatload of pockets in 'em."

Jimmy kept writing, jotting it all down in his notes.

"What's this all about?" Johnny leaned forward, resting his elbows on his knees. "Why're you askin' me about a crime I stopped five years ago?"

"The description you just gave closely matches witness accounts of the assassin who destroyed a delivery truck on Cooper and Sixth several days ago. And the assassin who killed your father."

A look of shock came over Johnny's face. "No lie?"

"It's no surprise you never made the connection," Jimmy continued. "You haven't seen these recent assassins yourself. And your 'employees,' I would assume, haven't gotten a close enough look to give an accurate description. Well, not the ones still alive anyway. Besides, the description in the newspaper was fairly vague. 'Dark clothing, white mask, and long ponytail' doesn't give much information at all."

Sweat formed on Johnny's brow. "Tell me—what do you think they want?"

"Oh, I think you know what they want. You shot one of them, didn't you? Maybe even killed her? They're back, Johnny, and I don't think they're planning anything pleasant for you."

Johnny stood up hastily, walked over to the window, and peered out. "I ain't afraid of nobody. Let 'em come. I'll be waiting." His words were tough and confident, but the shakiness in his voice betrayed his fear.

"They've been hunting your family down one by one." Jimmy stood, tucking his notebook and pen in his pocket. "You and your son are the only ones left. At the very least, think of Joseph's safety. We can take you both into protective custody. Just say the word, and I can make it happen."

"No!" Johnny shot back. "Scorpiones don't run away. A real man doesn't hide."

"Then you're a real foolish man. And soon you might be a real dead man. Come on, Johnny—let me help you. Give me something. Anything."

Johnny glared at him with cold eyes. "If there are no more questions, you're free to leave."

Jimmy was shocked. He didn't understand how a man could have so much foolish pride, especially when his own life was at stake. Or the life of his son. With a shrug, Jimmy laid his card on the coffee table. "You know where to reach me." He left without another word.

As he crossed the front courtyard toward his car parked on the street, Jimmy couldn't help but think, *Pride goeth before a fall, Johnny. I've done all I can. Now it's up to you. I may not like you, but I don't want to see you get killed either. This world has seen enough foolish sacrifice.*

Jimmy thought back to his days during the Gulf War and all the comrades he'd lost needlessly to that conflict. So many dead in the name of pride and glory: running into battle gung-ho and half-cocked, only to be cut down by enemy fire. Like his drill instructor had always said, "Bravery can be noble, but foolish bravery is just stupid."

As Jimmy checked the time on his watch, it occurred to him there was one special girl that he hasn't seen in quite a while. Figuring she would appreciate the visit, he hopped in his car and went.

Chapter Twenty-One

In class, Trish took notes in great detail as usual. Billy was twirling a football in his hands as usual. Stacy was preoccupied with Billy as usual. And Chris was brown-nosing as usual.

Trish noticed one thing, however, that was unusual: Stephanie's mood. As Trish had casually observed during her time in class with her, Stephanie typically gave her undivided attention to the lesson. She never missed a word and took excellent notes, just as Trish did.

But today, there was a different air about Stephanie. As she rested her chin on her palm, she seemed to be gazing dreamily at nothing in particular. A happy smile graced her features as she slowly traced a heart on her desk top with her finger.

Hm... Thought Trish. *Bet I know what's going on.*

The teacher had turned her back for no more than a few seconds, scratching on the blackboard with chalk, when Stephanie heard the whispered words in her ear. "You're in love," the voice said, and when she turned, shocked that she'd been discovered, she saw Trish settling back into the chair next to her. Stephanie quickly put a finger to her lips.

"Shhhh! Keep it down, Trish," she murmured, hoping no one else had heard. They all seemed to be paying attention to the teacher, surprisingly. "How did you know?"

"I read lots of romance novels. If you read enough of them, you know what to look for."

Stephanie raised an eyebrow. "Don't take this the wrong way, but if anyone needs a boyfriend, it's you."

Trish handed her a book, and Stephanie read the title.

"Romeo and Juliet?"

"It's a very good play. You should read it."

"I already have. I appreciate the thought, but I certainly hope my relationship doesn't end in tragedy."

"It's still very romantic. For two people to fall in love regardless of their family's quarrels is just so romantic."

"Yeah, but don't forget how it ended."

"It's still romantic."

Stephanie couldn't help but smile, admiring Trish's love of literature. Suddenly a piece of chalk ricocheted off Stephanie's desk. She looked to the front of the classroom and saw a scowling Miss Roberts, another piece of chalk ready in her hand. Everyone knew Miss Roberts' sense of aim was about as accurate as a black-ops sniper's. And they knew the first chalk was meant only as a warning.

"You two!" Miss Roberts yelled. "Eyes front, now."

"Yes, ma'am!" Stephanie and Trish said in unison, as they both faced forward at once.

Miss Roberts continued with her lecture, but as soon as her back was turned again, Trish leaned over and whispered, "Tell me the details later, okay?"

Stephanie nodded with the same dreamy smile she'd had before, retreating into her own thoughts as she gazed out the window. So many things were happening in her life. It was hard to keep track of what she felt and how she should react. She was worried and anxious about Kira's well-being, but at the same time she was overjoyed and excited at how close she and Patrick were becoming. Her visions of the past were disturbing and came on without warning, but with a little practice she thought she could control them.

She let out a sigh as she looked past the tall, bare trees and brick buildings of the academy and into the deep gray clouds of the horizon. Patrick… her mind kept coming back to him. She wondered what the future held for the two of them.

Sitting with his friends in the lunch room, Pat was leaning over the meatloaf, mashed potatoes, and string beans he'd procured from the chow line a few minutes before. Seemingly in a daze, he slowly mixed the potatoes and brown gravy with his fork. Even though he was sitting right next to Vic and across from Mike and Ayu, he was still far away.

Vic was explaining how coordinating his clothing with a certain day of the week had brought him good luck. "So it's like this: on Tuesdays, if I wear army boots, blue jeans, my black Ramones shirt with the hole in it, and my black leather vest, it'll bring me good luck."

"How do you figure that, Vicky-boy?" Mike asked in skepticism. "It might just be a coincidence."

"Well, last Tuesday, the first Tuesday of last month, and the second Tuesday of the month before, I wore the same outfit and get this: each of those days, I didn't trip in the science department hallway."

"I'm amazed you could remember what happened during all those days in one sitting," Mike said. "The reason you always trip in that hallway is because of the two short steps in the middle. And that's because when you wear your black jeans, you always wear them with those long chains that hang down. You raise your foot to take the first step, it gets caught in the chain, and boom, down you go. Those are the only steps in this school you actually use, because you always take the elevator to the second and third floors."

"Well, there are the steps outside the front entrance," Vic said in his defense.

"What are you talking about? You always walk up the handicap ramp."

"Oh, um, yeah." Vic scratched his head. "That's right."

"And the third thing, Vic—wearing a black shirt with a black leather vest is a fashion statement that would only make sense to you."

"Hey, just you wait. It'll be really popular this year."

"We all wear uniforms, dude. The only reason you get to wear something different is because your dad paid for the new science classrooms."

Ayu started giggling from behind her manga comics, although it was uncertain whether she was laughing at their conversation or at what she was reading.

Vic turned to Pat. "What do you think, Pat? Black shirt and black vest looks cool, right?"

A happy smile on his face, Pat continued twirling his gravy and potatoes, in his own world.

"Hey, he's spaced out again," Vic said. "Still thinking of that ninja girl?"

"No, no, no!" Mike signaled Vic to hold on as he stood up from his seat. "This is something different, Vicky-boy. This is definitely a different spaced-out look." He turned to Ayu. "Ayu, what do you think?"

Ayu lowered her book, took one look at Pat, and then nodded. "Yes. Very different spaced-out look today."

"That settles it," Mike declared, as he loosened his shoulders and straightened his tie. "This situation demands a closer investigation!"

Mike moved around to Pat's side of the table, while Vic and Ayu gathered around.

"Notice the blank stare as he repeatedly stirs his mashed potatoes," Mike pointed out, as Ayu and Vic silently nodded in agreement. "See the slight smile on his face as he thinks of something cool that just happened to him. And most important, people, notice the lack of response to my otherwise irritating observations." Mike folded his arms and stood tall. "There's only one conclusion, my friends, one conclusion that can be reached."

"And what's that?" Vic asked.

"I was getting to that, Vic. Now, as I was saying, only one conclusion can be reached." Mike pointed his finger at Pat in a dramatic way. "And it is this: Patrick O'Hara is in love."

"Huh?" Pat woke up from his daydream. "What's going on?"

"Don't deny it," Mike proclaimed. "The look is all over your face. You were thinking of a love interest just now, and that interest must be Stephanie. Oh, yes!"

"What?" Pat stuttered. "N-no, that's not it." But the truth was, Mike had hit it right.

"Come on, mate." Mike came close. "I see you two making eyes. I think you and Stephanie would make a great couple."

"You think so?" Pat asked quietly.

"Absolutely." Mike slapped him on the back. "Like Paris and Helen of Troy or Mark Antony and Cleopatra. Or Romeo and Juliet."

"Or Keitaro and Naru," Ayu chimed in.

"As good a romance as I'm sure that is, love," Mike said, "I'm not sure most people in thc States would get the reference." Ayu made a sad face as Mike patted her shoulder to comfort her.

"Hey, wait a minute," Pat said, "didn't Romeo and Juliet and Mark Antony and Cleopatra all end up dying?"

"Details, details." Mike waved his hand dismissively. "The point is, with a little nurturing, your tiny little love can grow into one of the greatest romances in history."

"History, huh? Cleopatra and Mark Antony, sure, but I don't think you can classify Romeo and Juliet as history, since it's a work of fiction."

"What did I tell you about details? Come on, think of the bigger picture. Think Scarlett O'Hara and Rhett Butler."

Pat rubbed his temples. "I think we're digressing a little here."

"You're right, Irish-boy." Mike sat back down across from him. "We just want you to know we're in your corner. If there's anything we can do to help your budding romance, let us know."

"Hah!" Pat let out a laugh. "If there is anything, I'll keep you informed. Thanks, guys."

Jimmy opened the front door to the Borgestedt Institute and walked up to the front desk. A middle-aged woman with narrow eyes, gray hair, and professional attire sat behind the desk. The sweet scent of lavender came from the vase of flowers beside her. The clock on the wall behind her had just hit 12:15 in the afternoon.

"Hello," Jimmy said as he wrote his name on the sign-in sheet in front of him. "I'm here to see Jennifer Sebastiano."

The woman stood up and turned the sheet toward her so she could read it. "Mr. James Ziminski?"

"Yes, that's me."

"Are you an immediate family member or acquaintance?"

"I'm a close friend of the family."

"I see." She picked up the phone next to her and made a call announcing the visitor. She listened for a moment before turning back to Jimmy. "I'm sorry, but Jennifer is in her one-hour exercise session right now. Would you be able to come back later?"

He really hated to make his next move, but he guessed there was no helping it. He pulled out his badge and ID and laid them on the desk. "I was hoping I could see her now if it's not too much trouble."

After inspecting the badge and ID, she turned around, whispered something urgently into the phone, and then hung up. "You can go right in, officer." She gave him directions.

Jimmy collected his credentials, and within five minutes, he was standing in front of the exercise center. To the left of the door, a long window stretched the length of the room. Looking inside, he saw that the room was fairly large and filled with expensive- looking exercise equipment. From bikes to bench presses to stair machines, they had it all. A young blonde woman in nurse's scrubs was sitting by the door looking over documents on a clipboard.

Jimmy smiled when he caught sight of Jennifer across the room on a treadmill, facing slightly away as she watched a video on the flat-screen television mounted on the wall above her. He gave a few quick taps on the door and entered. The blonde immediately stood up, reached out her hand, and shook his.

"Officer Ziminski? Hi, I'm Cindy Patterson. I'm one of the orderlies assigned to Jennifer. Mandy called my cell phone to let me know you were coming."

"It's nice to meet you, Cindy," Jimmy said politely. "It's been a while since I've seen Jennifer—a couple months actually. I figured since I was in the neighborhood, I'd check in on her."

"I didn't make the connection right away when Mandy said your name, but as soon as she mentioned the badge I knew you were the 'Uncle Jimmy' Jennifer talks about so often."

"Yup, that's me." Jimmy smiled. "So how's she doing?"

Cindy motioned for him to sit down as she did the same, then she spoke quietly. "Jennifer's had a few episodes here and there, but they've become less frequent over the past month and a half. Her doctor says her outlook is promising, but progress is still slow."

"I see. Who is her doctor, by the way?"

"Mei Tachibana. She's a specialist from Tokyo."

"May I speak with her if possible?"

"I'm afraid she's stepped out. She didn't mention when she'd be back."

"Does she have an assistant or secretary I could talk to?"

"Her assistant went with her."

"All right then." Jimmy looked at Jennifer, who was still facing away from him, striding along on the treadmill. "What's she watching right now?"

"A mild documentary on the animals of the African plains. We try to keep her away from newscasts or violent TV shows or pretty much anything that might upset her." She smiled. "However, I think seeing her Uncle Jimmy may brighten her spirits quite a bit." Cindy glanced at her watch and then called out, "Okay, Jennifer, you're all finished. I have a surprise for you. Someone special is here to see you."

"Really?" Jennifer said, stopping the treadmill and turning around. As soon as she saw Jimmy's smiling face, she hopped down and ran across the room, launching herself into Jimmy's arms.

"Uncle Jimmy!" she yelled as they hugged. "I missed you!"

"I missed you too, Jenny," Jimmy said. Then he moved back and looked at her warmly. "So how have you been, kiddo?"

They sat down together on a bench beside the weight racks.

"I've been good. I think physical activity keeps me clear for a while, so I'm seeing things pretty clear right now."

"Well, good, good. I understand your doctor's name is Mei. What can you tell me about her?"

"Miss Mei is a very nice person. She's been so good to me. I can tell she really wants to help me."

"Cindy tells me you're making progress. It sounds like Miss Mei is exactly the person you need to help you get better."

"Miss Mei told me not to get my hopes up yet, but she may have a new medicine that could help me."

"Is that right? What's it called?"

"She didn't tell me much about it, but they'll have to ship it all the way from Tokyo."

"Well, I hope it'll do the trick."

"Me too." Jenny smiled. "I trust Miss Mei. I know I can count on her."

"Then I guess I can count on her too. So tell me, how's your sister? Does she visit often?"

"Stephie is doing really good. She visits me every Monday through Friday without missing a single day. She reads to me and spends time with me."

"You're pretty lucky to have such a caring sister."

Jenny nodded merrily.

"What about your mother? How's she doing?

"Mom's good. She doesn't visit as much as Stephie, but she comes when she can. Every time, she tells me how much she loves and misses me." Jennifer's eyes suddenly became glassy, and she drifted off for a second.

"Jenny?" Jimmy said as he lightly touched her shoulder.

She grabbed his hand and clutched it tight. "Black night." Her words were dry, emotionless, almost as if she were in a trance. "So many guns, angry faces."

"Jennifer, are you okay?" Jimmy tried to free himself from her grasp so he could shake her out of it, but it was no use. "Come back, Jennifer."

Cindy saw what was happening and came over to try to help, but she couldn't separate them either.

"Moving like the wind," Jennifer continued her strange rant. "Ground soaked with blood. Painful heart. One bullet hits. Hold your fire! Fading away now. Pride and honor explode in a ball of flame."

"Jenny, what are you talking about?" Jimmy said. "I don't understand."

At that moment, Jennifer let go of his hand and fainted into Cindy's arms.

"What happened?" Jimmy cried. "Is she all right?"

"She seems to have passed out." Cindy cradled Jennifer in her arms. "I don't understand, though—I've never seen this happen to her before."

"Did she have some sort of episode?"

"I'm not sure and I have no idea why she fainted either. I'm sorry, but you'll have to continue your visit later."

"What can you do for her?"

"Don't worry." Cindy started to dial a number on her cell phone. "We'll take her to the infirmary and have her checked out. She's in good hands."

Jimmy knelt down, took Jennifer's hand, and prayed quietly.

Chapter Twenty-Two

Joey was walking down the hallway of the first-floor science section. *One more class to go and the day is done,* he thought. As he continued on, he couldn't help but think about the situation he'd interrupted involving Pat and Stephanie.

I'm such an idiot, he thought. *I should have realized what was happening with them, but I had to go and screw it up. They were good together, though.*

He was pretty sure he hadn't really messed anything up. Whatever—he would just apologize next time he saw them. His thoughts wandered to what they'd be serving for lunch tomorrow, then he stopped at the sight of four guys who were blocking his way. Each appeared fairly well built and pretty capable. The looks they were giving him were decidedly unfriendly, if not outright nasty.

"You must be the new transfer students," Joey said smugly, folding his arms. "Anything I can do to help you fine gentlemen?"

"You're Joey Scorpione, right? We hear you're the top dog around here," the first one said, cracking his knuckles.

"If we take you down, then we own this school," the second one said, rolling up his sleeves.

"So we're calling you out," the third one said, unbuttoning his uniform jacket.

The fourth and largest one, who seemed to be the leader, got right in Joey's face. "You ready to defend your title, pretty boy?' Cause we don't play nice."

"Well, if that's the way it's gotta be." Joey felt completely cool and relaxed. "Let's get right to it, shall we? Follow me."

Joey led them outside and all the way to the edge of the school property near a row of trees and shrubs, where the teachers and other students couldn't see them. The wind was cold, and dark clouds moved swiftly overhead. The horizon was almost black. Bad weather was on its way.

The four surrounded Joey on all sides, the hunger for violence blazing in their eyes like a pyre. Escape was not an option for Joey, but then again, retreat had never really been his style. He had too much pride for that. *A real man doesn't run away.* That's what his dad had taught him. *Fight your own battles and stand your ground.*

"All right, boys!" the leader yelled. "Let's squash this meatball." They ran at Joey all at once, fists raised high and ready to do damage. As they closed in, Joey simply braced himself and gave a short laugh.

Pat was sitting through his last class. All he could think about was seeing Stephanie after school. Next time they went out, maybe he should bring flowers for her. He wondered where they should eat. He couldn't just take her to some fast food place—that would be way too lame for a date. Maybe Chez Phillippe. That was a really nice restaurant. Did she like French food though? He'd have to ask her. Wait—did he like French food? He didn't think he'd ever had it before.

Back at the edge of the school property, the four guys who had challenged Joey were now lying face down on the ground and groaning in pain. Their faces were covered in cuts and bruises, their uniforms ripped and dirty. One had a broken jaw. Another had a dislocated shoulder. A third had at least one broken rib.

But despite their agony, it was the leader who had it the worst: his face was so swollen, he was almost unrecognizable. Both hands were broken, one kidney damaged, three ribs cracked. The cliché "a world of hurt" was an understatement compared to the pain this boy was feeling.

Joey, on the other hand, didn't have a scratch on him. He dusted off his hands as he stood over the groaning bunch. He gave them one look and shook his head with a quiet chuckle. "I guess I'm still the top dog, huh, guys?" he said smugly.

All they could do in response was groan louder.

"Joey Scorpione," he declared to the four. "Remember that name as long as you live. Got that?" They all nodded, and then Joey bent down and spoke quietly to them. "Now when the cops ask you who did this, you're gonna say you couldn't get a good look at the guy. Understand?"

They nodded again.

Joey stood up and started walking toward the school, but paused a moment and looked back. "Oh, and have nice day."

School had let out, and a light snow started to fall. The wind was bitter. The clouds above spread out like a dark blanket over the city.

Stephanie and Pat strolled on a sidewalk in the middle of town. Fine powdery flakes of snow gathered on the rough concrete walkway beneath their feet. No words had been exchanged between them since they'd left school. An air of awkwardness surrounded them. Neither could find the words to break the silence.

Pat glanced at her pretty hand swaying back and forth as she strode. Then he looked away. He was unsure whether or not to reach out and take it, but maybe now would be a good time to hold hands. They were an item now, right? Yeah, they should definitely hold hands. Okay, it was settled. He was going for it.

Then to his surprise, before he could reach out for hers, he felt her hand take his. He quickly looked over to see her sweet smile shining back at him.

"You know, I've been getting a little bolder lately," she said, giving his hand a squeeze. "I think I can blame you for that."

"Oh yeah?" Pat said, gently squeezing her hand back. "What makes you say that?"

"I'm not sure, but since I started spending time with you, day by day, I think my confidence has grown little by little. When Kira went down, I took charge for the first time in my life. I actually surprised myself. I was so concerned for Kira's well-being, I did it without even thinking about it."

Pat stopped her and looked into her eyes with his best smile. "You know, we never did finish our, um, conversation."

Stephanie's expression grew brighter and her blush deepened. "No, we didn't, did we?"

It was too late—Pat had already been drawn in by those soft brown eyes of hers. Slowly, they drew closer and closer, the promise of a kiss just inches away. They closed their eyes in anticipation. But they were shaken from their little world of romance by the abrupt sound of a car horn. They looked over and saw a black Ford Crown Victoria parked along the curb in front of them.

"Uncle Jimmy!" Stephanie called out when she saw him waving from the driver's seat.

Jimmy got out and went over to where they were. "Hey, Stephanie. How's it going?" He then looked to Pat. "Patrick O'Hara. It's good to see you again. Haven't seen you since that night outside the Scorpione estate. How are you?"

"Um, I'm doing good." Pat said stiffly. "It's good to see you as well, Detective Ziminski."

Jimmy then looked to Stephanie. "So…is young mister O'Hara your…boyfriend?"

A little embarrassed, Stephanie looked down sheepishly for a moment. Then she looked up at Pat and gained a confident smile.

"Yes." Stephanie said. "Yes, he is."

"Well, he certainly seems like a charming lad. I'm sure he'll take good care of you." Jimmy then laid a heavy hand on Pat's shoulder. "Because if he doesn't, he'll have me to answer to. Is that understood, young man?"

Pat took a hard gulp. "Yes, sir!"

"Good." Jimmy smiled. "Then we understand each other."

Jimmy looked to Stephanie. "I can give you a ride to wherever you're going if you want."

"Okay, sure." Stephanie nodded.

She turned to Pat. "Well, I'd better get going."

"Oh. All right." A slight tone of disappointment touched Pat's voice as he looked at the car and back at her. He was really looking forward to walking with her further. "You go ahead. I'll catch up with you later."

He moved to leave, but was stopped by Stephanie's hand catching hold of his. She came close, kissed his cheek, and whispered, "I'll see you soon, okay?"

Pat felt his spirits rise again.

Stephanie got into the car with Jimmy and reached across to give him a hug. "I've missed you so much, Uncle Jimmy. How have you been?"

"I've been good—nothing to complain about. This Scorpione case is keeping me busy. But first things first: tell me how long you've known Patrick."

Stephanie felt herself blushing. "Well, we've known each other for a year now. We started out as close friends. Then we, well, we realized we clicked together, you know? So now we're dating."

"Well, he seems like a good kid." Jimmy said, remembering back to the night he first met him. "Although, I never would've thought that young man I spoke to in the cold that night would end up being your boyfriend."

"I know you'll like him. He's always been a perfect gentleman to me."

"Good, that puts my mind at ease."

Jimmy put the car in drive, pulled away from the curb, and started down the road. Classic jazz played on the radio at low volume. The windshield wipers moved side to side, continuously clearing the powdery snow. Steady heat flowed from the vents in the dashboard, chasing away the chill air clinging to Stephanie.

"So on another note," Jimmy said, "I visited your sister today."

"Really?" Stephanie was pleased to know she wasn't the only one who cared enough to visit Jennifer. "Was she happy to see you?"

"You bet. As soon as she saw me, she hugged me as tight as she could. She told me you visit almost every day."

"Every chance I can. I know she's getting the best help available, but honestly, I worry about her. Being separated from her family in that big sterile place—I don't like it. Her only human contact most of the day is doctors and orderlies. That's why I visit so often, to give her something familiar to hold onto. To keep her tethered to the life she once had."

"A life she will have again," Jimmy said reassuringly. "I have faith she'll be back to her old self soon."

"I know, and so do I. It just hurts me to see her like that."

"She seemed healthy and well taken care of. Her mind seemed fairly clear. But then she had an episode. She started talking gibberish, strange things that didn't make sense."

"Oh, no." Stephanie lowered her head. "Not another one. She was doing so well, too."

"She said her doctor has a new medicine that might help her."

"That's great news. How soon will she start taking it?"

"She didn't say." Jimmy reached over to turn down the heat. "How's school? Is there anything new going on there?"

Stephanie remembered what had happened earlier that morning. "One of my classmates—something happened to her today. Her name is Kira Shirou. She came into school looking like death."

"What do you mean?"

"She usually looks great, really pulled together, but today she just didn't. She was pale, sweating, disoriented. When I tried to help her, she got really aggressive. Even violent. Then she did something impossible: she actually picked me up and held me up in the air."

"Hold on—how could a teenage girl be that strong?"

"I don't know, but right after that she collapsed, and she had to go to the hospital in an ambulance."

"Hmm… sweating, moodiness, aggression, and unnatural strength. What hospital did they take her to, do you remember?"

"I heard one of the paramedics say Benton Mercy. Why, what's up?"

"Just something I want to check out. You still go to that gymnastics place on Twenty-Seventh Street after school, right?"

Fifteen minutes later, after he'd dropped Stephanie off at gymnastics, Jimmy walked up the front steps of Benton Mercy Hospital and into the main lobby. In a large waiting area on his left, nearly two dozen people sat on cushioned chairs watching a talk show on the TV screen by the windows. Doctors and patients alike walked the halls with hurried steps. Every few seconds a doctor's name was announced over the speaker system, asking him or her to come to this department or that operating room.

Straight ahead was the main help desk, where two young-looking receptionists—one a brunette with Amy on her name tag and the other a redhead named Katie—busily moved back and forth between the filing cabinets and the desk computer. Jimmy walked up to the desk, smiled, and said, "Pretty busy today, huh?"

Amy let out a sigh. "Oh, you have no idea. It's been this way since morning."

"Looking around, you'd figure there's a city-wide emergency," Jimmy said, motioning to the activity around him.

Katie slapped a file down next to Amy. "It's like this every day. Is there something we can help you with, sir?"

"Yeah, sorry." Jimmy pulled out his notepad and glanced at the name Stephanie had given him. "I'm looking for a patient who was admitted here this morning. Kira Shirou. She would have come in via ambulance from Kingsley Academy."

"Okay." Amy sat down in front of the computer. "I'll need your name and a form of ID please."

Jimmy showed her his badge and ID.

"All right, thank you very much, Detective Ziminski." Amy started typing away at her keyboard. After a few seconds, the information popped up on her screen. "Let's see… you said the name was Kira Shirou?"

"Yes."

"According to my records, she's already been signed out," Amy said.

"That can't be right," Jimmy said, looking closely at the info. "According to a witness, Kira was in really bad shape. She even collapsed. You're telling me you just let someone take her out of here in that condition?"

"You're talking about the Japanese girl, right?" Katie said. "She walked out on her own."

"What?" Jimmy winced.

"Yeah, I was there when her aunt came in." Katie shrugged. "The girl made a miraculous recovery and was cleared by the hospital staff, and they both walked out."

Jimmy got his pen and pad ready. "Can I get the name of her aunt, please?"

Katie grabbed the sign-in clipboard from behind her and looked at it. "Let me see here. Her name was Hana Ishikawa, and she came in around noon. She had a valid driver's license, and Kira identified her as her aunt, so she was cleared to see the girl."

"She didn't happen to leave a number or address on the sign-in sheet, did she?" Jimmy asked.

"No, sorry," Amy said. "All we require is a valid ID."

"How about a basic description of this Hana Ishikawa?"

Katie thought hard. "Judging from the accent and obviously her name, she was Japanese. I would say she was in her mid-twenties, wearing a long, fur-lined, black leather coat, sunglasses, and a wide-rimmed, white satin hat with a black ribbon around it."

Jimmy looked up at the camera hanging from the ceiling about five feet above them. He probably couldn't hope to get anything reliable from security footage, considering the high camera angle and the large hat, but it wouldn't hurt to take a look. He let out a sigh as he ran his fingers through his hair. "Can I get her driver's license number?" He pointed to the camera above them. "And also, I'll need a copy of your security footage from today"

Within forty-five minutes, Jimmy was back in his office, sitting down at his desk with a steaming hot cup of coffee. He took out the DVD with the hospital footage on it and slid it into the disc drive. A list of several file names came up, each corresponding to an hour of the day. He opened the one for noon, and the video began. The time showing the hours, minutes, and seconds was displayed in the lower right corner of the screen.

The footage started at noon on the dot. As the minutes went by, a few people came up to the desk—a young woman holding an injured arm, an old woman rolling her husband in a wheelchair, a young man holding his head, and so on. Finally, at about 12:09 p.m., a woman matching the description he'd been given came up to the receptionist's desk, white hat and all. Jimmy was right—the angle of the camera and the large hat made facial identification almost impossible. The woman signed her name and showed her ID to the nurses, and they directed her down the hallway to her left. The woman nodded her head in gratitude and proceeded down the hallway.

All seemed normal until about 12:24 p.m., when several doctors and nurses ran by the desk, heading down the hallway in the direction the woman had gone. He fast-forwarded through the rest of that hour, seeing nothing out of the ordinary.

He accessed the next file. At about 1:04 p.m., the woman in the white hat emerged from the hallway. A Japanese teenager with a long ponytail, most likely Kira Shirou, was holding onto the woman's arm. The girl seemed in perfect health and even had a spring in her step as she walked. The woman signed all the necessary discharge paperwork for Kira at the desk.

Before they turned to leave, the mysterious woman paused for moment. She raised her head and looked directly at the camera. Forming a devilish smile, she tipped her hat to the camera. Then she took Kira gently by the arm, and they left.

Jimmy closed the video file and leaned back in his chair. *That was a little creepy*, he thought. He couldn't help but wonder if she was tipping her hat to hospital security or to him specifically. It was time to get some answers.

He started searching the Department of Motor Vehicles database for Kira's mysterious aunt. He ran a cross-check on the name and driver's license number and came up with nothing. He even tried several alternate spellings. Still nothing.

Jimmy rubbed his chin as he let out a snort of frustration. Whoever this woman was, she wasn't a resident of New Jersey or of any other state, for that matter. He sipped his coffee, picked up the phone, and dialed Lin Misaki, quickly bringing her up to speed on what he'd found so far on the Scorpione case.

"Today I got a possible lead with a girl named Kira Shirou who goes to Stephanie's school. According to Stephanie, she came into school today in really bad shape. From her description, Kira was showing the side-effects of amphetamines and steroids."

"What makes you think she's connected to your case?"

"Get this, Lin: before Kira collapsed, she demonstrated super-human strength. She picked Stephanie up and held her in the air."

"Now that's definitely something."

"They took Kira to the hospital this morning, but by the time I got there this afternoon, the nurses told me she'd already been signed out by her aunt a few hours before. They said Kira walked right out in perfect health. Kind of suspicious, don't ya think?"

"Suspicious is an understatement. Did you get her aunt's name?"

"Hana Ishikawa. The nurses said this woman had a valid driver's license, but I can't find her in the DMV database anywhere."

"I doubt you would. The woman who took Kira out of the hospital probably had a fake ID."

"What makes you say that?"

"Because Hana Ishikawa is the name of a famous Japanese pop singer, and she's been dead for more than eight years."

"So the elusive aunt is using a fake name. Damn it, these people are toying with us! In the hospital security footage, the woman actually looked up at the camera and smiled. Almost as if she knew I'd be watching the video later."

"What did she look like?"

"She was Japanese, wearing a large hat and sunglasses. The video quality isn't the best, so it's going to take some time to come up with an identification."

"Don't worry; you've found a big piece of the puzzle. You just have to figure out where it fits, that's all," Lin said. "I'd better get going. I have a story I have to turn in to the printers by five o'clock, and that was six minutes ago. If you need me, you know where to reach me."

"Thanks, Lin. What would I do without you?"

Lin gave a quick laugh, "Without me? Perish the thought."

Jimmy hung up and continued his search through the DMV database, bringing up Kira's file. She had a valid driver's license, and her address was 124 Cedar Street—same address as the Academy, in room 304 of the Academy dorms.

He called the Academy records office and gave his badge number to the woman who answered the phone, and she answered his questions. Kira lived alone in her dorm room, she explained, and her parents both lived in Japan.

Jimmy hung up the phone, still dissatisfied. "Come on, I need a break here," he said to himself, picking up his cup of coffee and taking a sip. It was cold. "I got to get moving on this case before the trail gets as cold as this coffee."

He removed the almost empty coffee pot and headed for the squad room to dump it out and get some fresh water.

An assassin sat on the ledge outside Jimmy's window. A Han'nya devil mask covered her face, red as blood. Two tiny horns sprang from the forehead; long fangs extended down from its wide grimace. A long, narrow, pointed nose led up to dark, glaring eyes. Protecting her hands were slender-clawed metal gauntlets, gleaming dimly as they reflected the street lights.

She paused to watch the sky, noting a break in the clouds on the western horizon. The sun had just set, and the sky was growing dimmer. The clouds reflected deep reds and purples. The wind had died down just a little, blowing mild gusts now and again. Some light, powdery snow had gathered along the edges of the buildings.

The assassin held a finger to her earpiece as she pressed a small listening device against the window glass. Then, once she'd determined no further information could be gathered, she wrapped up the device and packed it into her belt pocket.

"Keep investigating, James Ziminski," she said softly as she dug her claws into the hard brick and mortar of the outside wall and climbed toward the roof. "You see, when you track down a ninja, all you'll end up chasing is shadows."

Chapter Twenty-Three

The night was dark and quiet. The air was unusually still and bitter cold as heavy snow fell silently from the heavens. So thick was the snowfall, one could barely see twenty feet ahead. It was late, and traffic was practically nonexistent along the street running past the Borgestedt Institute.

The guard on duty, a stocky, gray-haired man in his late forties, was Institute Security Lieutenant Richard Parker. He sat at his desk in the main lobby, watching the feeds from the many cameras covering the property. Letting out a yawn, he happened to look at the screen showing the parking lot. *Same as usual,* he thought. *No activity whatsoever.*

Then he saw a silver BMW Z4 emerge from the obscurant snow and pull into the institute's parking lot. He took control of the camera and zoomed in as the car parked in the visitor's area. The door opened, and out stepped a tall woman with long, dark hair. She wore a black coat. Though young in appearance, she looked unnaturally pale, even in the dim lights of the parking lot. There was something unusual about her eyes. They reflected the light with a strange, almost mystical red hue on the color HD monitor.

The visitor took out a medium-sized box from the back seat and locked the car with the push of a button on her keychain. Her movements were smooth and graceful, almost catlike. As she walked toward the main entrance, she seemed to possess a regal confidence. She also seemed to possess a heightened awareness of her surroundings, as she appeared to react to gusts of wind before they happened.

Since it was after hours, she had to ring the buzzer next to the double glass doors. Parker pressed a button at his console and answered her over the intercom. "This is Security. How can I help you?"

"My name is Illyana Russovich." She spoke with a Russian accent, her soothing voice easy on the ears. "I have a package for Mei Tachibana. She should be expecting me."

"All right, just give me a moment while I check my records." Parker opened a black binder containing expected deliveries and looked down the list until he found her name. "Here we are. Please listen for the door to unlock and come right in, ma'am."

The door buzzed loudly, and the woman stepped inside. She walked casually through the lobby. Most of the area was dark, save for the lights above the Security desk.

As Illyana came into the light and placed the box on Parker's desk, every detail of her appearance became illuminated. She wore an ankle-length, black leather coat, with matching gloves and high-heeled boots. Her eyes were a light hazel green, enhanced by charcoal eyeliner and eye shadow. The fluorescent lights on the ceiling lit up the shimmering waves of her long, raven hair. Her flawless porcelain skin seemed to glow. The lipstick adorning her luscious lips was such a dark shade of red, it was almost black. And an easy smile completed her glamorous charm.

Amazed by her beauty, Parker sprang to his feet and greeted her warmly. "Good evening, Miss Russovich. I'm Security Lieutenant Richard Parker. Welcome to Guenther A. Borgestedt Institute."

"Why thank you, Officer Parker." She nodded in gratitude. "You are very kind."

"Mei Tachibana notified us you'd be coming. I apologize for the inconvenience, but before you can proceed I'll need to see a form of ID."

"It is no trouble. If you did not ask, you would not be doing your job, yes?" She offered him a smile that showed perfect white teeth. From her inside coat pocket, she took out her passport and laid it down before him. The passport was red leather, worn and faded. The guard opened it and looked at her information.

"That's unusual," Parker said.

"Yes?" She raised an eyebrow.

"Your photo—it's in black and white. You don't see that nowadays."

"That photo was taken at a post office in Moscow. At the time, their equipment was very dated, so it could not be helped."

"I see. What about your date of birth?" He squinted at the faded numbers. "I can barely read it."

"Now, now, Mr. Parker, it is not wise to pry when it comes to a woman's age." Illyana's smile showed warmth and even a hint of interest. The elbow she casually rested on the desk gave off an air of calm and relaxation. Her glaring eyes, however, sent a chill down Parker's spine. Then his mind became foggy. He couldn't focus. He shook his head in an attempt to clear away the haze, but to no avail.

He closed the passport and handed it back to her. "Everything, um, seems to be in order, Miss Russovich." With a shaky hand, he pointed down the hallway to his left. "If you head down that hall and make the first right, Miss Tachibana's office will be on the left."

She gave the slightest of nods. "Thank you." Then she took her box, walked down the hallway, and disappeared into the darkness.

What was up with that woman? Parker wondered as he sank down into his chair. *Those eyes—they were just plain creepy. Not only that, what about that passport? It looked ancient. And was that a hammer and sickle in the background of her photo? The USSR collapsed in 1991, but she didn't look a day over twenty-five.*

He rubbed his eyes, realizing now that he should have stopped her. Why hadn't he? He felt fine now, but at the time it was as if something had been clouding his judgment.

Saki sat across from Mei as they talked in their office over hot tea. The elegant piano melody of Erik Satie's *Gymnopedie No. 2* came from the speakers of a small CD player on Mei's desk. The old pipe heater beside them creaked and clacked as it slowly warmed up. The white steam from their tea cups formed rippling wisps that rose and disappeared into the cool air of the room.

"Have you calculated the correct dosage needed for Jennifer's treatment?" Mei asked as she went over her notes.

"I've run the numbers many times," Saki said. "Too little won't be effective, and too much would lead to negative side effects." She double-checked her printouts. "I believe 8.67cc's every eight hours should maintain a normal mental state free of negative or positive schizophrenic symptoms."

"Excellent." Mei closed her notes and placed them on the shelf above her desk. "We'll begin trials tomorrow—that is, of course, if we receive the drug tonight. It's getting late." She glanced at her watch. "Where is that expedited delivery? It should have arrived by now."

"Perhaps the package got caught up at the airport." Saki sipped her tea. "American security is very strict these days."

A woman's voice came from their doorway. "Actually, security was not a problem."

Saki was so startled by the voice, she dropped her tea cup. She closed her eyes, waiting for the inevitable crash on the floor, but to her surprise it never came. She opened her eyes to see the cup held in front of her by a leather-gloved hand.

"Illyana!" Mei said happily. "It's so good to see you."

"It is good to see you as well, Mei." Illyana placed the cup on Saki's desk before giving Mei a warm hug. "It has been so many weeks since I've seen you."

Saki's eyes were still wide with surprise. Seeing this, Mei said, "Saki, you remember my stepmother, I'm sure?"

"Of—of course." Saki stood and respectfully bowed to Illyana. "Please forgive me, ma'am. I had no idea the head mistress of House Tachibana would deliver the package herself."

"Oh, Saki!" Illyana shook her head. "You are still so very formal. You must try to relax every now and then, yes?"

"Yes, Jo-oh-sama." Saki stood rigidly. "Absolutely."

Illyana picked up the box she'd left by the doorway and placed it on Mei's desk. "Just as you requested: fifty vials of the medicine to help—what was her name—ah, yes, Jennifer."

"Thank you so much for taking the trouble to deliver this to us, Illyana," Mei said.

"Oh, it was no trouble at all." Illyana said with a smile. "Besides, it gives me a chance to see my wonderful Mei."

"How is my father doing?" Mei asked. "Is he still interested in buying out that German tech company?"

"The buyout of Schmitt & Snyder has been scheduled for the end of the month. And with that, your father is as busy as ever. Though he is cool and strict with his subordinates, he is still very much a teddy bear to me. Your father is the sweetest man I know."

"Yes, father shows that side only to the people closest to him," Mei said.

"Which reminds me," Illyana said, "your father sends his love and best of wishes on your endeavors here at the institute."

A smile came over Mei. "Send him my love as well, and make sure he keeps taking his herbal stress medicine."

Illyana let out a light-hearted laugh. "Tell me about it. With this buyout coming up, I must remind him every day." She looked at her silver-chained, onyx-faced watch. "Hmm, it's getting late. I must leave immediately if I hope to reach Tokyo by dawn." She hugged Mei again. "Take care of yourself, my little koshka. Saki, it is always a pleasure."

"Yes." Saki gave her a respectful nod. "Have a safe journey home, Jo-oh-sama."

Once Illyana was gone, Saki was finally able to relax. She plopped down in her chair and let out a long sigh of relief.

"What's wrong?" Mei picked up Saki's tea and handed it back to her. "Don't tell me you still get nervous around her."

Saki took a gulp from her cup before responding. "Jo-oh-sama is a wonderful person and is always kind to me whenever we meet. Yet, I can't help but be on edge when she's around. There's just something about her that makes me uneasy. You saw it yourself—the very sound of her voice made me drop my cup."

"Saki, you're stressed from working yourself so hard. I think your nerves are just frayed. Maybe I should give you tomorrow off and let you sleep in for once."

"Thank you, but I'll be fine." Saki showed Mei a tiny, reassuring smile. "Besides, you'll need me tomorrow for Jennifer's treatments."

"It's okay. We can always postpone."

"No, Jennifer needs this as soon as possible. She's been eagerly looking forward to the treatment since we told her about it. I'll just switch to chamomile tea to help me relax."

"All right, if you insist." Mei grabbed her gray wool coat and blue scarf from the hanger by the door. "I'm heading home for the night. Do you need help with anything before I go?"

"I just need to put away a few files, secure the medicine in the safe, and then lock the office. It shouldn't take me ten minutes."

Mei nodded as she slipped on her coat and wrapped the scarf snugly around her neck.

Once Mei was gone, Saki leaned back wearily in her chair. Her faraway gaze drifted to a framed photograph on her desk. It had been taken the day she'd graduated from Tokyo University after earning a master's degree in pharmacology. In the center of the photo, Saki stood in her blue graduation robe, holding her degree happily with both hands.

To Saki's right was her mother, Kotoko, smiling as she rested a loving hand on her daughter's shoulder. Kotoko's eyeglasses reflected the sunlight on that warm spring day, as did her slightly graying hair. To Saki's left was her father, Jin Kitagawa, a senior member of the Tachibana Corporation board of trustees. Jin was a slender man with a confident, positive outlook and a great sense of humor.

To Jin's left was Mei, smiling brightly. She was also in a graduation robe and holding her master's in psychology degree. To Mei's left was her father, Rikumaru, in a gray three-piece suit, a slight smile on his face as he rested his arm around his daughter's shoulders. Rikumaru's angular face wasn't very expressive, but still he did his best to smile for his daughter on that joyous day.

Saki could still remember the warm sun on her face as she held that rolled-up piece of paper in her hands. She had studied so hard for so long, and finally her dream had become reality. To be able to help people through medicine had been her goal since she was a teenager. However, she couldn't have reached that goal without the help and support of her longtime friend Mei.

The Kitagawas had walked side by side with the Tachibanas for many generations. Kotoko had been Rikumaru's assistant for over twenty-five years. Jin sat on the board as had his father before him. According to the Kitagawas, the reason for their close involvement with the Tachibanas could be traced back to mid-1860s Japan. It was a time when the military had absolute control over the country in the name of the Tokugawa Shogunate. The emperor himself was a mere figurehead without any real power. The Shinsengumi or "Newly Selected Corps," the Shogun's elite swordsmen group composed of some of the finest samurai who ever lived, scoured the countryside in search of the Imperialist rebels who wished to remove the shogun from power. The Imperialists were men and women who were loyal to the emperor and fought valiantly to return him to power.

In 1864, during the final years of the Shogunate, an Imperialist named Shoji Kitagawa lived in Kyoto with his family. The Imperialists had planned to take Kyoto and seize control of the Imperial Palace, but their plans were ultimately thwarted by the ever vigilant Shinsengumi. Shoji was waiting nervously with his family on that hot August night for orders to come down from the Imperialist ringleader, when a Shinsengumi brigade of five men broke down his door and invaded his home. They threatened to kill Shoji's family if he didn't give up the names of his fellow conspirators.

Shoji was frozen in terror and hesitated to answer. The leader of the brigade grew impatient. He drew his sword and raised it high, ready to cut down Shoji's wife. Still paralyzed with fear, Shoji could not speak. When the leader's sword finally came down, it was stopped suddenly by the sword of another Shinsengumi named Kotaro Tachibana. Kotaro was loyal to the corps and believed in the shogun's ideals. However, he could no longer take part in such vile acts. He knew there was no honor in the killing of innocent women and children—innocents he, as a Shinsengumi, had sworn to protect. And so Kotaro turned against his fellow brigade members and killed them.

Under cover of night, while the Imperialists and Shinsengumi forces battled at the front gates, Kotaro led the family safely out of the city through a secret passageway. After crossing a few miles of forest and fields, Kotaro decided they were now safe and that it was time to part ways with the family.

However, Shoji stopped Kotaro and swore to him an oath of loyalty for saving his family. Kotaro contemplated Shoji's oath for a long time, feeling himself unworthy of such service. Then Kotaro accepted, but on one condition: the Kitagawa would stand alongside the Tachibana as equals. Not as servants or slaves, but as advisors and comrades. And so, Kotaro confided in Shoji and told him the real reason he was in Kyoto. He was looking for something that had been stolen from his family's village long ago, a magical item that had given his clan great power. He had only rumors to go on, which had led him to Kyoto. Kotaro had joined the Shinsengumi so he could use his authority to aid him in his search, but he'd still come up with nothing.

Unquestioningly, Shoji agreed to help. And so, from that point on, there had never been a Tachibana without a Kitagawa to support them. And vice versa.

Saki began to sort through the day's files, but she soon found herself distracted and unable to focus. Urgent memories from her past refused to be ignored. She let out a long, drawn-out sigh as she reminisced about her time growing up in the Tachibana household. There was one memory in particular from Saki's childhood that haunted her to this day.

She couldn't have been more than seven years old at the time. It was a dark evening in the middle of a cold winter. Young little Saki had danced carefully down the hallways of the Tachibana mansion in her little pink kimono. The polished wooden floors were slippery with just her socks on, so she tried her best to maintain her balance.

As she wandered from one dark hallway to the next, she noticed a sliding door was open just a crack, shining a thin sliver of light onto the floor in front of her. Saki approached as quietly as she could, carefully tip-toeing to the door and peeking inside.

What she saw was Rikumaru Tachibana kneeling in the traditional Japanese way in the center of the room. Rikumaru had a strong frame and jet black hair pushed back from his angular face. His eyes were narrow, cold, and mean-looking. He calmly drank from his tea cup as Saki's mother, Kotoko, paced back and forth, reading him his business schedule for the following week. Dressed in professional attire, Kotoko straightened her large, round-framed glasses as she looked over the documents on her clipboard.

The fabric of Rikumaru's black silk kimono hissed as he moved to set down his tea. "Have the Aoyama clan demonstrated any willingness to negotiate after last week's incident?" His voice was deep and emanated authority.

Kotoko glanced through several documents. "Yes, they have, sir. They are still attempting to reestablish talks."

"I see. Keep stalling them. We need more time to investigate."

"Are you sure that is wise, sir?" Kotoko asked.

Rikumaru's only reply was silence.

"Very well then." Kotoko changed the subject. "There is the matter of the item you have been searching for in America. We may have found someone with information as to its whereabouts. One of our people will be contacting him within the next three days."

"That is excellent news." Rikumaru smiled slightly. "Keep me informed of your progress."

Then Kotoko knelt down beside Rikumaru and spoke softly. Saki couldn't quite make out what her mother was saying, so she placed her ear to the opening in the door.

"Sir..." Saki could barely hear her mother's whispers. "Rikumaru-sama... you mustn't blame yourself... an accident... wooden bridge was old... bound to give way sooner or later... Aoyama's daughter did the best she could to save Rei..."

"I was there, Kotoko!" Rikumaru whispered urgently. He lowered his head as grief took hold. "I should have been watching them more closely. Maybe I could have done something. Now my daughter Rei is gone."

"I know losing your wife in childbirth was hard. The triplets Mei, Mari, and Rei, were Lady Yuki's final gifts to you. Now… with Rei gone…"

Saki tried her best to listen harder. But then, she sensed a dark, heavy presence behind her, a presence so strong it sent chills down her spine. Slowly she turned and looked up, and saw a tall feminine figure standing over her. Dark shadows obscured the details except for the eyes. Those glowing red eyes filled Saki with horror such as she had never felt before.

The figure leaned down, moving her face terribly close to Saki's. She looked Saki in the eyes for a moment, as if studying her. Then the figure spoke in a low, inhuman voice. "Chto ty delaesh, devotshka?"

Saki let out a piercing scream, so loud it echoed through half the house.

"Saki!" Kotoko had immediately recognized her daughter's voice. "Saki, where are you?" Kotoko threw open the sliding door to see her daughter cowering alone on the floor with tears in her eyes. She took Saki in her arms and held her close. "What's wrong, Saki? Tell Mommy what happened."

"The lady!" Saki cried. "The dark lady! She wants to hurt me."

Kotoko looked up and down the hallway. They were completely alone, surrounded by silence. "There's no one here, sweetie," Kotoko assured her daughter, who was still shaking. "See?"

Saki looked around, and then she shook her head urgently. "No! She was here, Mommy. She was really tall, she had red eyes, and she said these weird words. I couldn't understand what she was saying."

Kotoko turned to Rikumaru, and they shared a look. It was as if they knew something but refused to speak of it aloud. Then Kotoko continued to comfort her daughter. "It's all right, my daughter. The dark lady is gone now." Kotoko walked with Saki down the hallway toward the well-lit common area. "Let's find Mei and Mari. You three can play together. How does that sound?"

Little Saki had rubbed the tears from her eyes and nodded.

Now, alone in her office, Saki gently swirled the cold tea in her cup. Her eyes traced the pale green liquid as it circled the bottom. The heater continued to click and clack beside her. All the lights were off except for her fluorescent desk lamp, which flickered now and again.

"What are you doing, little girl?" she said to herself, out loud. "In Russian, that's what you said to me in that dark hallway so long ago. I can't help but wonder: was there kindness behind those words or evil, Jo-oh-sama?"

Chapter Twenty-Four

Jimmy's office was quiet. Outside the window, the world was still dark. Resting on the desk, his head cushioned by his forearm, Jimmy snoozed away. After twenty straight hours of investigation, it felt like the best sleep he'd ever had.

Then his wonderful slumber was interrupted by a knock at the door. Jimmy awoke and straightened up in his chair. His eyes struggled to open in the brightness surrounding him. Someone had flipped on the bright overhead lights.

"Jimmy!" he heard a familiar voice call out.

Finally Jimmy's eyes focused on the heavyset lieutenant standing in his doorway.

"Freddy?" Jimmy stretched his arms and yawned. "What's going on?"

Freddy raised his hands in a "What the heck" gesture. "Me, what's going on? How about *you* what's going on?" Freddy closed the door behind him and sat down in front of Jimmy's desk. "It's Wednesday, five after six in the morning, and you got your head down on your desk. Don't tell me you slept here all night."

Jimmy rubbed the bridge of his nose. "Not the whole night. Just since one a.m."

"I've never seen a case get to you like this. Are you sure this is only about finding Vincent's killer?"

"Of course it is." Jimmy waved his hand dismissively. "What else would it be about?"

"I think it's about Tommy."

Jimmy averted his eyes and shook his head. "No, Freddy. It's not—"

"The hell it's not," Freddy interrupted. "You two were partners for years, cleaning up the streets every night. Don't tell me it doesn't make you angry, dealing with that mafia scum Johnny and knowing he might have put the bullet in Tommy himself. I'd be downright furious."

"I understand what you're saying." Jimmy's words sounded calm enough, but his fists were clenched and his body was starting to shake. "But we still haven't been able to prove—"

"Oh, don't give me that." Freddy stood up from his chair. "We all know the Scorpiones did it. Hell, they'd all be in jail right now if it weren't for the damn evidence disappearing. Don't you feel anything for Tommy's death, or did the army bleed all that emotion out of ya?"

Jimmy stood up quickly and slammed his hands on his desk. "Shut your damn mouth. You don't think I feel something every time I look those mooks in the eyes? Tommy lies in the cold ground while those bastards walk around scot-free. Every time I hear the Scorpione name I want to put a bullet in their heads. Now, thanks to these assassins, I know Tommy can rest a little easier with each Scorpione who goes down. My only concern is Johnny might be killed before I can get a confession out of him." Jimmy dropped back into his seat with an angry grunt, and a long, intense silence fell over the room, a silence finally broken by Freddy's voice.

"So there it is," Freddy began in a calm tone. "The mask finally cracks, and the real Jimmy finally shows through."

Jimmy didn't speak. He merely met Freddy's eyes with a hard gaze.

"So that's what it was," Freddy continued. "All that hatred and anger over Tommy's death… you buried it under a mound of detective work and cap-stoned it with a fake smile. You see, no one knows you like I do, kid. I took you and Tommy under my wing, remember? I trained you two. I knew the two of you like I knew my own children. No one gets over that kind of pain so quick. I know that pain, the pain of losing a brother to a mook with an itchy trigger finger. There's nothing like it. The darkness eating away at your soul, twisting in your gut like the blade of a knife. It took me years to keep it from eating me alive, but one thing I finally realized is you cannot get over it. There's just no way. That's how I knew you must've been hiding it all this time. And because I know you, I knew exactly how to break through that facade of yours. So don't think for a second you can hide who you really are from me."

Jimmy hung his head and sighed deep as he slowly raked his fingers through his hair. Then he looked up at Freddy and said simply, "Then I guess you know me too well, old man."

A smile came over Freddy's face. "Good. Now that we got that bull out of the way, we can get back to doing some police work. So what's the next move?"

Jimmy matched Freddy's smile. "I got a plan that might help us solve the evidence situation. But that comes later. First order of business: There's a party tonight, and Benton's finest are invited. I want as many police boots on those docks as possible. This is the mother lode for Johnny

Scorpione, the biggest gun shipment ever. The assassin won't be able to resist. It's her MO. Why else would she blow up the gun shipment going through town and destroy Johnny's distribution offices? It's because this assassin in particular wants to ruin Johnny's business—guns and drugs. These are his resources, his income. It's right in Sun Tzu's *The Art of War,* for crying out loud. If an enemy is well fortified, cut off his resources and eventually he'll starve and come out to face you."

"What are you talkin' about?" Freddy asked.

"Don't you see? That's what she's doing. She's calling him out. I'll bet Johnny's sending all his men to protect tonight's shipment. After she blows the shipment, she'll be met by Johnny's forces. She'll most likely be outnumbered and eventually killed. We can't let that happen. That's why we raid the Scorpione operation, arrest Johnny's men, and capture the assassin for questioning. If that fails and she gets away, I still have a backup plan."

"Like what?"

"She'll be communicating with the head assassin via radio frequency. That's how we'll track her."

"By triangulating that radio signal, right?"

"Exactly. Once the assassins start communicating, they'll lead us right to their base of operations."

"Let's pray nothing goes wrong," Freddy said, crossing his arms over his chest.

"Yeah, tell me about it. But this is the best plan we've got so far."

"How about the disappearing evidence? What's the plan there?"

Jimmy's smile grew wider. "That's where it gets good." He pulled up a chair and bent close to Freddy's ear, speaking quietly. No use giving information to eavesdroppers.

At eight in the morning the Borgestedt Institute was fairly busy. The usual nurses and orderlies walked the hallways, escorting patients from one place to the next. Outside, the sky was dark and overcast, as if the clouds were refusing to move on.

Jennifer sat in her room, on a corner of her bed, huddled against the wall. The little sleep she'd managed had been tormented by images of a red devil's face and long claws. She rocked herself back and forth, all the while trying desperately to ignore the long, drawn-out squawking noises filling the room.

A knock came at the door, shaking Jennifer from her torturous limbo. The door opened and in walked Mei, holding her clipboard. Saki followed close behind her, carrying disinfectant, a vial of medicine, and an empty syringe atop a plastic tray.

Mei seemed to immediately notice Jennifer's fear and anxiety, the way her body was locked in a defensive posture. "How are you feeling today, Jennifer?" Mei got down low and met Jennifer's downcast gaze. "Is everything all right?"

Jennifer looked at Mei, shivering as if she were freezing, despite the seventy-degree temperature in the room. "The wind, it's so cold," Jennifer muttered. "So cold coming off the river."

"What are you talking about?" Mei looked puzzled. "What wind?"

"Sorry, I—I can't be sure where I am right now. I'm not good, Miss Mei. I'm here, and then I'm in another place and time, and then I'm back again. And there's the woman with the bloody devil's mask." Jennifer raised her hands to her head as her eyes widened in terror. "She's invading my dreams. Those long silver claws will tear me to sheds."

Mei sat down on the bed beside her and gently rubbed Jennifer's shoulders to help calm her. "Shhh, it's all right. Those were just dreams. You're fine now. You see? You're in the here and now, with me."

Jennifer looked into Mei's kind eyes and slowly nodded her head. Mei could feel her shaking. "Now, I want you to take a few deep breaths and say to yourself, 'I am here and now.' Can you do that for me?"

Jennifer did as instructed and repeated the words.

"Good. Now breathe and say the words again."

Jennifer did so, and each time felt her anxiety grow smaller and smaller, until it was finally gone.

"There," Mei said. "Do you feel better now?"

"Yeah, I do. Thank you—I'm so glad you're here with me. I don't know what I'd do without you."

"It's all right," Mei assured her. "The terror of a nightmare stays with you until you learn to let it go. This image you've been seeing—the devil with the silver claws. She's nothing more than a facet of your overactive mind. The image itself is what we refer to as an external tormentor, a persistent vision causing terror and paranoia, usually taking the form of something the person fears most—say, clowns, black cats, or even devils. It is all a construct of the mind, Jennifer. Once you realize that, you will see there is nothing to be afraid of."

Jennifer took another deep breath and nodded gratefully.

"Now," Mei said, "have you seen any of the ravens yet today?"

Jennifer looked at the raven sitting on her nightstand. The raven looked back and cocked its head to the side curiously. "I've seen a couple so far." She pointed to the nightstand where the raven still sat. Mei and Saki looked where she pointed, but their faces told her that all they could see was a battery clock, a lamp, and a Rubik's cube.

Mei turned back to Saki and gave her a nod, and Saki began to prepare the syringe.

"Do you remember the medicine we talked about?" Mei asked.

"Yes!" Jennifer grew excited. "The medicine that's supposed to help me, right? But I'm afraid. What if it doesn't work?"

Saki handed Mei the syringe.

"Everything will be all right," Mei reassured her as she thwacked the syringe to free the bubbles and squirted them from the tip. "I need you to be strong for me now, and I need you to trust me. Can you do that for me?"

Jennifer hesitated for a moment. Then she took a deep breath and held her head high. "I don't want to be afraid anymore. I do trust you, Miss Mei, and I'll be strong for you."

The raven grew agitated. It started flapping its wings wildly and cawing loudly. All Jennifer could do was close her eyes and try to ignore it. As Mei swabbed her arm with disinfectant, the cawing grew louder, more urgent. When she felt the needle pierce her skin, the cawing became shrieking, filling Jennifer's ears. The fluid felt cool under her skin as it slowly ran into her arm.

Her anticipation in the moment following was almost unbearable. Would it work or not? It seemed an eternity passed as she waited to find out. Then, steadily, the cawing grew quieter and quieter. Finally she opened her eyes and looked at the nightstand.

The loud, obnoxious raven was no longer there.

"He's gone," Jennifer said, unbelieving. "He's gone!" She folded her hands and prayed. "Oh thank you, God!"

Bright smiles came over the two women as Jennifer jumped up from her bed and danced around the room. "I can think clearly!" she exclaimed. "No more fear, no more visions. It's a miracle!"

Mei gently caught her and tried to settle her down. "I'm so happy for you, Jennifer." She quickly took out a penlight and shined it in Jennifer's eyes. "Pupils look good, breathing is normal." Mei took Jennifer's wrist. "And pulse feels good too. I think you're going to be just fine, Jennifer."

Jennifer looked into Mei's eyes with a happy calm. After all the chaos she'd experienced, she felt she could finally feel true peace once more.

"Thank God for you, Miss Mei!" Jennifer exclaimed. "You're my angel!"

"Congratulations, Jennifer." Mei gave her shoulders a loving squeeze. "You've taken a big step on the road to a normal life."

"I just can't wait." Jennifer's excitement grew with each passing second. "I'll be with my sister again. We'll do gymnastics together. And I'll get to see her school. Oh, and I'll enroll there too and we'll be in all the same classes."

Then Jennifer felt a change coming on. Her intense emotions seemed to drain away, and her attention started to drift. "And… and we'll… go to class…"

When she saw Jennifer's eyes begin to wander about the room, Mei tried to bring her attention back. "Jennifer? Is everything all right?"

Jennifer looked back at Mei as if roused from a daydream. "Oh, I'm sorry, I just can't seem to focus all of a sudden." Her attention drifted again, her eyes slowly running along the floor.

"Jennifer, look at me." Mei gave her a gentle shake. Jennifer looked back at her, but all Mei got was a blank stare. "Jennifer? Jennifer, can you hear me?"

There was no response. Her eyes just drifted back to the floor, and she stood there motionless. Mei shook her lightly several times, but it was no use. Sadness came over Mei as she realized what had happened. With a tragic smile, she held Jennifer close.

"It's all right, Jennifer. Everything is going to be fine." Then she gently laid Jennifer down on the bed and pulled the covers over her. "You're going to be just fine, okay?"

Mei gave Jennifer's shoulder a light squeeze. Then she and Saki left the room. Saki closed the door behind them and locked it with her set of keys.

Chapter Twenty-Five

Back in their office, Mei paced back and forth, while Saki frantically looked over her notes.

"My calculations…" Saki's eyes raced from one column of mathematical formulas to the next. "They couldn't have been—"

"Your calculations were off!" Mei interrupted, anger flowing hot in her voice like lava. "You gave her too much and pushed her into the negative symptom range."

"I—I'm sorry, Mei." Saki's voice was filled with remorse. "I know it's my fault. I was so certain my calculations were correct. I just can't figure where I went wrong."

Mei took control of herself and continued in a calmer tone. "No, Saki, I'm sorry. I didn't mean to yell. You didn't deserve that. Your work has been crucial to this project, and I couldn't have gotten this far without you." Mei sat down at her desk and took out her own notes. "I'm going to double-check a few things. Why don't you run the numbers one more time? We have to get this right. Jennifer can be normal again, and our work is what will make that happen."

"Absolutely." Saki sat down with her calculator and started going over her formulas.

Mei had the sudden feeling that something was off. She was lighter somehow. She felt around her person and noticed that her keys were missing from her lab coat pocket.

"Saki, have you seen my keys?" Mei asked as she looked around her desk.

"No, I haven't." Saki looked around as well. "Would you like me to call security and have them search the building?"

"Yes, please. Thank you, Saki." Mei continued to hunt through the office. She checked the shelves, drawers, and even the floor. "That's really strange. I never leave my keys anywhere. Not only does that set have my car keys, but it has keys for every door in the institute. We have to find them. Where could I have left them?"

At 9:10 a.m., second period was just letting out at Kingsley Academy. The hallways filled with students pouring from their classrooms. Endless chatter and countless footsteps flooded the school.

Down the first-floor main hallway walked three boys with the light of trouble in their eyes. Tyler, Conner, and Brad were three freshmen known for stirring up trouble wherever they went. Posturing and strutting as they sized up the other students passing by, they shared crude jokes among themselves.

Tyler stopped his two lackeys when he caught sight of a certain brunette struggling with her locker combination. Seeming frustrated, she was trying combo after combo with no success. Every few seconds she adjusted the turtleneck of her uniform, keeping it as high on her neck as possible.

"Yo, Stephanie!" Tyler looked up and down the hallway and walked up to her. "I don't see your knight in shining armor around. What say we have a little fun, huh?"

She remained focused on the lock, as if ignoring them.

"Hellooooo?" Tyler crowed as his cohorts laughed. "Stephanie Sebastiano, I'm talking to you."

She let go of the lock, turned around, and looked at the three boys with an unimpressed glance. "Is there something I can help you with?"

Tyler smiled deviously. "Now that you mention it—"

"No, wait." She smiled back. "I got it. You're lost, right? The Special Ed classrooms are down the next hallway. See ya." She turned to walk away, but Tyler grabbed her by the shoulder.

"Whoa, whoa!" He turned her around to face him. "What's this? I think our little Stephanie here has grown a backbone, boys."

She looked at Tyler's hand gripping her shoulder. Then her eyes slowly met his with a chilling gaze. "Remove your hand or I'll remove it for you." The darkness in her tone took Tyler aback for a moment. But the feeling quickly wore off, and he resumed his swagger.

"Oh yeah? Or you'll do what?"

Her eyes narrowed. "Last chance, Chuckles. What'll it be?"

Tyler simply laughed and kept his hand right where it was. He was about to make another snide remark, but before he could utter another syllable, Stephanie grasped his hand firmly, wrenching it from her shoulder and twisting his wrist inward. This caused Tyler so much pain that he yelped and bent over. Taking advantage of this opportunity, using his arm for leverage, Stephanie grabbed the back of his neck with her free hand, swung him around, and slammed him face first into a locker.

Tyler fell to his knees holding his face, dizzy and in shock from the impact.

Joey came around the corner to see Conner and Brad standing in awe as their leader, Tyler, knelt helplessly on the floor. Joey caught sight of a security guard heading toward the scene, but stopped him half way seeing who was involved. Joey persuaded him to back off and that he would handle it. The guard was reluctant, but realized Joey had a gift for resolving these types of situations. The guard nodded, but said at the first sign of trouble he'd intervene. So the guard faded back, while still staying close enough to observe.

Conner and Brad looked at the apparently not-so-harmless girl standing before them. Her arms folded, she gave them the icy-eyed stare-down, as if to ask, "Who's next?"

The two boys raised their hands in surrender and slowly backed away. She took one step forward, and they immediately darted off like frightened deer. Completely ignoring Tyler still on the floor at her feet, she went back to fiddling with the combination lock.

"Stephanie?" Joey said from behind her.

"Great!" She seemed irritated. "What is it?" She turned to see Joey standing there. "Yes? You need help too?"

Joey shook his head, confused for a moment. "Need help? What are you—what the heck happened here?"

She looked down at Tyler. "Oh, him? He had trouble finding his locker." She pointed to the locker beside her with the greasy face print ruining its polished finish. "So I showed it to him."

"You—you mean you did this?" Joey looked closer at Tyler. "Hey, wait. Isn't that one of the kids who was giving you problems?"

"Oh, so those were the three idiots. I see. Good to know. Although I'm sure they'll think twice from now on before approaching this face."

Joey stepped carefully over Tyler who was still a little confused and took a concerned tone. "Stephanie, what's going on with you? Are you feeling okay?"

She gazed into his eyes and a mischievous smile came over her face as she moved closer. "You know something? You're pretty cute. What's your name again?"

"My name?" Joey moved back. "What's wrong with you? You're like a completely different person."

"That's because she is a different person," a familiar voice said.

They turned to see Stephanie with her arms folded disapprovingly. Pat stood next to her, looking in amazement at Tyler, who was bewildered that there was now two of the girl that just attacked him.

Joey's confusion reached a whole new level as he looked back and forth between the two identical girls. Once the opportunity presented itself, Tyler made a run for it and disappeared into the crowd.

"I think this charade has gone on long enough," Stephanie said. "Don't you agree, Jennifer?"

Jennifer's smile grew wider. "Okay, Sis. I give up. You got me."

"Wait." Joey turned to Jennifer. "You're Stephanie's twin sister?"

Jennifer shrugged. "Guilty as charged." She sent a sideways glance toward Stephanie. "Dear sister, shame on you, keeping a big hunk like this all to yourself." She looked back at Joey. "You never said anything about Patrick being so tall and muscular, Stephie."

Pat let out an awkward laugh and raised his hand to get her attention. "Actually, Jennifer, I'm Pat. That guy is Joey Scorpione."

"Scorpione?" Jennifer's whole demeanor changed at the mention of his name. "You're Vincent's grandson?"

"Yeah, that's me." Joey smiled as he held up one hand in a salute. "It's nice to meet you, Jennifer."

Jennifer took a step back as she studied him suspiciously for a moment. "Nice to meet you too, Joey."

"I'm sorry, Joey," Stephanie interrupted. "Could I talk to my sister for a moment?" She pulled Jennifer aside and spoke to her quietly. "Jennifer, you're supposed to be at the institute. How did you even get here?"

Jennifer pulled out a set of keys. "I drove here in Miss Mei's Beemer."

"Mei let you drive? Where is she? Is she here?"

"Oh, she's back at the institute." Jennifer twirled the set of keys around her finger. "I doubt she even knows her car's gone."

"Wait. Rewind. How did you get out?"

"Well, that was the easy part. Remember the new medicine I told you about? It works! It's incredible how clearly you can think when you're not distracted by hallucinations and feelings of dread."

"But there's a camera in your room. How did you get out without someone noticing?"

"The red light wasn't on, so I took a chance."

"All right, so tell me how you escaped the institute."

"Basically these keys were all I needed. I saw an opportunity, and I took it. After Mei gave me the dose and my mind cleared up, I came up with a plan and faked a catatonic episode. When she got close enough, I swiped her keys from her pocket and hid them."

"That's horrible, Jennifer! How could you do such a thing?"

"It's not that big a deal—I just got so excited, I wanted to start my new life right away."

"I can understand that, but what you did was still wrong. How did you even get past institute security?"

"I went into the janitorial locker room, took some coveralls and a hat, and walked right out the front door. The guard even waved at me. I'm guessing he's never looked too closely at any of the patients there. Otherwise he would have recognized me."

Stephanie looked down at Jennifer's school uniform. "And where did you get that school uniform you're wearing right now?"

"A while ago, Mom told me where you guys were currently living. I just went there and got one of yours." Jennifer straightened the skirt and brushed some lint from her shoulder. "Fits me perfectly, don't you think?"

Stephanie seemed about to continue her inquiry when Jennifer interrupted her. "And you're about to ask, how did I get into the house? I found the key inside the hollow rock next to the back door, just like at the old house."

"Of course Mom is working or she would have caught you." Stephanie narrowed her eyes at her. "And how did you get into the school?"

"I told the guard at the front gate I was you and I was just running late because of a doctor's appointment. He let me right in."

Stephanie heaved a sigh and slowly shook her head. "Of course he did."

"What is it?"

"You always were too smart for your own good, Jenny."

"Hate to burst your bubble, twin sis, but you have the same capacity."

"Please don't remind me." Stephanie straightened up and put her hand on Jennifer's arm. "We need to get you back to the institute."

"Aww, but I'm having so much fun being you."

"Shut it, Sis. It's time to go."

"All right, all right," Jennifer surrendered. She whispered to her sister, "Can we keep this between the two of us, though?"

"You seriously want me to act like this never happened? Are you cra—I mean, are you out of your—oh, never mind. Fine! I'll forget about this little incident, but you'd better return my clothes and get back to the institute as soon as you can. You got it?"

Jennifer gave a mocking salute. "Yes, ma'am!" She hugged her sister and whispered in her ear again, "You've gotten bolder, dear sister. Hanging out with Pat has done wonders for you."

Stephanie's face grew bright red. "That's none of—"

But before she could finish, Jennifer ran over to Pat. "It was nice to meet you, Pat."

"You too, Jennifer." Pat smiled as she gave him a quick hug. "Hope everything turns out all right on your way back."

"Thanks, and you'd better take good care of my sister, or else I'll—" She glanced back at the locker she used against Tyler. "Well, you get the picture."

Then Jennifer trotted over to Joey and gave him a sweet smile. "It was nice meeting you too, Joey."

Joey laughed. "Yeah, 'nice.' That's one word for it. 'Unforgettable' might be another one. Hey, when you finally get out, you and me should get a coffee together, eh?"

"I'd like that. You know, when I heard your last name, I had my doubts, but you seem pretty cool."

Joey smiled. "If that's supposed to be a compliment, I'll take it."

Jennifer reached out to touch his arm. But as soon as her fingers made contact, black feathers tumbled through the air around her. She got a flash of something in her mind. She was silent for a moment. A tear formed in her eye and ran down her cheek. "I see." Her voice was shaky. "You and I… we…" She broke contact and the vision, along with her memory of it, was gone.

"You see?" Joey looked at her curiously. "What do you mean? What do you see?"

"It's strange. I can't remember what I was doing just now." She wiped the wetness from her cheek and looked at it for a moment. "Why am I crying?"

"Did you think of something sad, maybe?" Joey asked.

Jennifer smiled again, "Nah, must have been something in my eye." She turned and looked at all of them. "I really had a lot of fun, but I gotta get going. See ya, everyone!"

She took off toward the entrance.

Joey's eyes followed Jennifer admiringly as she quickly walked away. He was astonished and fascinated by the strong spirit of this girl, whom he'd only just met.

"She's amazing."

"Yeah, she's amazing all right," Stephanie said sarcastically as they watched Jennifer together.

"You did cut her some slack." Pat wrapped his arm affectionately around her waist. "I'm sure she's grateful."

"I'm sure she is too," Stephanie agreed, as she leaned into him. "You know, if she hadn't worn that turtleneck to hide her scar, her whole plan would've gone belly-up."

"Say, Stephanie." Joey said, his eyes still on Jennifer. "One of these days, can I go with you to visit Jenny?"

Back at the institute, it was just after ten in the morning. Mei opened Jennifer's door to see her lying quietly in her bed, staring into nothingness. There on the nightstand were Mei's keys, as if they'd been there all along.

"There they are," Mei said with a smile.

"Security checked most of the building," Saki said. "This should have been the first place they looked."

Mei looked Jennifer over for a moment. "She should come out of it in about six hours when the medicine finally wears off. Have the kitchen prepare something special for her. She should be hungry by then. As I recall, she's a big fan of spicy food."

"Certainly," Saki confirmed.

They stepped out into the hallway, and Saki locked the door behind them. As they walked toward their office, Saki spoke to Mei in a quiet voice. "She's a clever one, isn't she?"

"Yes, she is, but not clever enough. When I tucked her in two hours ago, the covers were up to her neck. When we checked on her just now, they were only up to her chest. In a catatonic state she should have been completely motionless."

"She was the one the guard saw leaving—disguised as a janitor. Should she be punished? Her privileges taken away?"

"No. I'll let this one slide for now. She did come back, after all. If she did take my car, she probably went to see her sister. She genuinely misses her and their time together. I can certainly understand that." She sighed and spread her hands. "I should've known right from the start, though."

"What do you mean, Mei?"

"Because your calculations are never off," she said with a smile.

Chapter Twenty-Six

At 7:50 p.m., a small cargo carrier crept down the Hudson River, slowly making its way toward a certain dock. The temperature had just dropped below freezing as a strong wind constantly blew over the water. The afterglow of the reflected city lights gently descended from the clouds above, illuminating the otherwise dark waters between New York and New Jersey.

The boat's name stood in tall black letters against the white hull: *Demetrius*. It was carrying four large metal cargo containers. One in particular had the serial number 89425G on its side. Standing on the deck looking over the edges of the boat were twenty guards carrying AK-74 submachine guns. All of them looked rough and capable; many had stocky builds and scruffy beards. A few were missing some teeth, a couple had neck tattoos, and some even had long facial scars.

The captain of the ship, a tall, husky man with a bald head, stepped out onto the deck. In a deep baritone voice, he spoke loudly in Romanian to the guards. "Listen up, men. Scorpione said to be on the lookout for a ninja girl who may try to destroy the cargo. Chances are she will come up from the water. So if you see anyone crawling up the hull, shoot them. Understand?"

"Yes, sir!" the men shouted before going back to carefully watching the waters.

One guard watched the coastline through a pair of night vision binoculars. As he gazed over a small white boathouse near the river's shore, he could barely make out someone standing on its roof—someone in the shape of a girl wearing a white mask.

"Hey, Nicolae!" he called to the guard nearest to him. "Come here a moment."

The other guard let out an annoyed sigh. "What is it, Emil? I'm supposed to be watching the hull."

"Yes, yes, I know, but look at this. Take these and look at the white boathouse over there. Tell me what you see."

Nicolae grabbed the proffered binoculars and looked at the boathouse. "I don't see anything. What am I supposed to be looking at?"

"You don't see a girl in a white mask?"

"No, I don't see a girl in a white mask." Nicolae handed the binoculars back. "I think your perverted mind is playing tricks on you."

Eagerly, Emil looked at the boathouse again. "Where did she go? She was right there. I saw her—I know I did."

"Yeah, yeah. Get back to work."

A sudden deafening metal clang shook the entire boat. The guards looked toward the cargo. There, on top of container 89425G, standing in a deep depression, was the wolf assassin. She had come from the one direction they hadn't anticipated: above.

A black katana sword was strapped to the assassin's back and several kunai knives were fastened on the outside of her thighs. A gray duffle bag hung from her shoulder. The serum level on her forearm readout was at 100%. When the guards raised their weapons and opened fire, Wolf took cover in the deep depression. Wasting no time, she removed a large block of C4 explosives from the bag and attached it to the container.

The men rushed up the side of the container, trying to reach her. She quickly attached the charge and prepped the remote detonator. Then she heard several weapons click around her. She looked up and saw twenty submachine gun barrels pointed directly at her head.

"Don't move! Drop the device!" one of the guards yelled in English.

The captain of the ship stepped out from behind the intruder carrying a 10-gauge pump-action shotgun. He cocked it and pressed the barrel against her back. The other men lowered their weapons and backed away. A smile crept over the captain's face, revealing his crooked yellow teeth.

"There is nowhere to run, little girl. Get down on your knees and hand me that device in your hand. Do it slowly now. I have an itchy trigger finger." He gave her a push with the barrel of the shotgun. She crouched low, but not on her knees. He aimed the shotgun barrel at her head.

"Now hand over that device. Is there anything you want to say before you die, little girl? Come on, I haven't got all night."

She looked back at him and said, "No, you don't." Then without warning the assassin shot straight up into the air, startling the captain so much that he fired his weapon randomly. The slug he discharged hit the chest of one of his men, sending him out into the water.

Now five hundred feet above them, Wolf pressed the red button on the detonator. What followed was a bright flash and a deafening boom. The shockwaves of the explosion sent ripples out across the water. Wolf spun, tumbled through the air, and landed hard on the asphalt dock area on shore, causing cracks to spider-web around her in all directions. The boat on the water behind her was engulfed in flames. Thick black smoke rose into the sky.

The roaring wind slowed to a weak breeze. The skies above were aglow from the noisy fire on the water, a fire that was still setting off explosions from the ammunition but slowly going out as the boat sank.

Spotlights went on all around and centered on the assassin. She found herself surrounded by twenty-five armed goons in dark suits.

Wolf let out a short laugh as she stood up slowly. "Out of the frying pan…"

Johnny's right-hand man, Donnie, stepped forward and took aim at her heart with his .357 magnum revolver. "We got you," He said with a cruel laugh. "It's just that simple. We got you, 'cause there's nowhere left to run, sweetheart."

"That's what the last person who threatened me said." She pointed to the burning boat wreck, half afloat on the river. "And look what happened to him."

"You blew up our shipment!" Donnie yelled. "You owe us for each and every gun you just sank. Now, if you don't mind, we'll take our payment in blood."

Wolf started to laugh quietly, and Donnie's anger intensified with each light-hearted chuckle. "Oh, you think something's funny? What're you laughin' about, huh?"

She drew the sword from behind her back, gripped it in both hands, and took a low stance.

"Girlie, you gotta be some kinda crazy." Donnie shook his head. "You're surrounded by twenty-five armed men. Do you understand that? We got you."

"Got me?" Wolf mused. "You can't even handle me."

Donnie was about to give the order to attack when he felt something cold quickly run through his midsection. Then he noticed that Wolf was now right beside him, her knees deeply bent and her head down. He hadn't even seen her move. One second she was standing twenty feet from them and the next, there she was. The sword she now held so still in front of her shone in the bright spotlights. Dark red blood clung to the blade and slowly fell to the asphalt, drop by drop.

All feeling left Donnie's legs, and he collapsed with a deep groan. The men gasped as they realized what had happened. Donnie's top half had been cleanly separated from his bottom half. No words left Donnie's mouth as he lay there quivering, on the ground; just one or two quiet whimpers before death finally claimed him.

Her head still lowered, Wolf stood up, raised her sword high, and swung it downward, swiping the remaining blood from the blade. Then she raised her eyes to the men. "All of you mafia lapdogs, run away now—or die!"

The men looked at their fallen lieutenant, then at each other, and as one they ran off. Wolf could hear mutterings of "Forget this!" "I'm outta here!" and "I don't get paid enough for this crap, I quit!" coming from the men as they cleared the area.

Once they were gone, she sheathed her sword behind her back with a huff of disappointment. "Damn cowards, they didn't even put up a fight."

Then she heard the sound of clapping coming from somewhere above her. She looked up and saw a tall, well-built man in military fatigues and white Kevlar body armor standing atop a tall storage container. He stopped clapping, and a wide smile stretched across his face. "Wow!" he proclaimed. "Now that was impressive."

Wolf remained silent as she carefully studied this man. His long, dark hair hung down to his jaw line, framing his darkly tanned Native American features. An air of confidence surrounded him as he gave her a half smile, but there was something else there as well. Caution could be derived from the way he rested his hands on the two silver-plated 12.7 mm semi-automatic pistols holstered at his hips. A US M3 military dagger, a very sharp and durable blade trusted by American soldiers for generations, was sheathed at his right boot. It was a proper tool of last resort when backed into a corner, which led Wolf to believe this mysterious man always had a backup plan.

"You know," the man continued, "there's an old Chinese proverb: 'Execute one to warn one hundred.' Now that philosophy may work against twenty-five common thugs, but not me."

"Maybe they were the smart ones then," Wolf said, taking a relaxed posture, her hands on her hips. "So tell me, is there a name that goes with all that confidence?"

"You can call me Timber Wolf."

"Timber Wolf, huh?" She laughed. "I'm afraid there's room for only one wolf in this town, and I'm it. So unless you want to leave these docks in a body bag, I suggest you take off with the rest of the strays."

"Let's not be hasty now. We've only just got here." He waved his hand in the air. Behind him, four other soldiers appeared—three men and one woman. They each had their own unique armor and weapons. "It would be a shame to leave before things get interesting." Timber Wolf began to pace leisurely from side to side. "You see, I brought some friends along, and we're all very eager to meet the girl who took down half the Scorpione family without a single scratch to show for it. Yet."

Wolf scanned them through the starlight zoom lenses equipped in her mask.

"Hmm… custom armor, custom weapons. No military patches. Your hair is way too long for you to be enlisted soldiers. I'd say you're all mercenaries. Did Johnny hire you?"

"Quite the observant one, aren't you?" Timber Wolf said. "Yes, Johnny hired us. He even offered us a bonus to bring you in alive."

Wolf folded her arms in fascination. "What makes you different from any other soldier willing to shoot a gun for money?"

"We take the jobs the other guys are too afraid to take. And we do it with style. Starting at my right is Bear, seven feet and five hundred pounds of hell on wheels."

The black muscle-bound man beside him stood tall, with a proud smile. He was massive: legs like tree trunks, arms like pythons, and a chest like a stone wall. Heavy metal armor covered his forearms, torso, and lower legs. He didn't seem to be carrying more than a few daggers and a simple pistol. Judging by his appearance, it was a safe bet he didn't need them.

Timber Wolf continued, "Beside him is Cobra—as deadly as she is beautiful."

Cobra was a shapely woman with deep green eyes and long, flowing red hair. Light scale-mail armor covered her perfect physique in white, gold, and black, imitating the scale patterns of her namesake. Two short swords were crossed on her back. She sized Wolf up with a skeptical scowl.

"Next is Chameleon, expert in electro-magnetic camouflage."

Lightly armored from head to toe, Chameleon's suit was covered with millions of tiny metal discs interconnected by a tightly knit network of electrical wires. The discs also ran up the hood pulled over his head. The round lenses of his night vision goggles glowed an eerie red. Numerous pistols and daggers hung at his sides.

"And finally, the man whose skill and cunning is surpassed only by his madness: Jackal."

Jackal was slender, yet very defined in his ropy musculature. His wavy black hair gave great contrast to his piercing blue eyes and pale skin. His armor was basic: black Kevlar around the torso and jungle camouflage fatigues. Many knives of all types were fastened across his chest, up his forearms, and at his hips. Three different kinds of grenades hung around his waist—incendiary, concussive, and fragmentary. A creepy smile stretched across his face as he caressed the handles of his blades with a burning gaze.

Timber Wolf raised his hands dramatically in grand conclusion. "Together, we are the Magnificent Five!"

Wolf was silent for a moment. Then she let out a snicker. "The Magnificent Five? What is this, a sixties Western?"

"You'll be changing your tune once you end up like the villain at high noon."

"I fight for justice," Wolf snapped back, "while you kill for money. Who's the real villain here?"

Timber Wolf formed a sly smile. "Nice mask, by the way. I'm a big fan of wolves myself, as you can probably guess by the name. The thing about wolves is, there can be only one Alpha. When an Alpha is challenged by another wolf, he must fight to the death. Why? It's simple: he must prove to his fellow wolves that he and he alone is worthy of leading. And if he doesn't, doubt will spread and he will eventually be devoured by his own pack. So, assassin, are you strong enough to be the Alpha?"

Wolf drew her sword in anger. "Why don't you come down here and find out?"

It was then that Wolf heard Den Mother's voice come through her earpiece. "He's working your emotions, Wolf, trying to throw you off your game. Don't let him get to you. Keep your feelings buried. As long as you're upset, he has the power."

"There are five of them," Wolf said quietly. "They all look pretty capable. Retreat is not an option. How should I handle this?"

"They're not part of the plan, but they must be dealt with now, or else they will surely interfere with our agenda. How should you handle this? Wise ninja use what is at hand and exploit their enemy's weaknesses. Don't let them surround you, and keep on the move. Wolf, I gave you the healing serum in the hospital because I was confident of your skills. You're good at thinking on your feet and are an excellent tactician. I gave you a second chance. Don't make me regret my decision."

"Understood. I won't let you down."

Timber Wolf, who was still standing by, grew impatient. "If you're finished talking to whoever's on the other end of your conversation there, I was hoping we could discuss your surrender."

Wolf remained silent and simply readied her sword.

"So be it." Timber Wolf cracked his knuckles as he prepared to jump down. "If you're that eager to fight, I'll indulge you. I suppose we can forego the bonus for bringing you in alive. It'll be more fun this way."

"No!" Bear's deep rumbling voice sounded. He stepped forward and touched his boss's shoulder. "Let me fight her first."

"Me too." Chameleon advanced as well. "I want to see just how strong this Mafia killer really is."

Timber Wolf rubbed his stubbly chin as he contemplated their requests. Then he looked back at his remaining soldiers. "Cobra? Jackal? How about you?"

Cobra's smile was devious as she looked down at Wolf. "There are so many ways to kill her, I can hardly decide."

Jackal had a mad look in his icy blue eyes as he pulled out a twelve-inch bowie knife and slowly licked the blade. "I want to taste her blood."

Timber Wolf raised an eyebrow. "Okay, Jackal, that was a little too creepy. But that's fine; you be you. Lord knows nobody else wants to be."

Jackal gave Wolf the evil eye as he reversed the grip on his knife and slapped it back into its sheath.

"It's decided then," Timber Wolf announced. "I must keep my employees pleased, after all. Bear and Chameleon will have the first crack, then Cobra and Jackal. After that, if you're still alive, you'll get the pleasure of facing me. How does that sound, little wolf?"

Wolf took the sheath from her back and slid it through her belt at her left side. She raised her blade close to her right shoulder and held it upright as she slowly slid her left foot outward in the shape of a half moon. Then she performed several fancy moves, almost too fast for the eye to see. The trails the blade's shine gave off formed circles and swirls all around her in a magnificent demonstration of Japanese swordsmanship. She finally ended her mesmerizing movements in an aggressive forward thrust. Then Wolf reversed the grip on her sword and slowly slid the blade back into its sheath at her side. Wolf gave a beckoning gesture with her right hand, as if to say "Just bring it."

Wasting no time, Bear leapt from his spot as Chameleon disappeared. Wolf quickly rolled out of the way before Bear could crush her under his incredible weight. He slammed onto the concrete hard as Wolf regained her footing several feet away.

But as she did this, she heard a low electric hum behind her. Her instincts kicked in, and she immediately dodged to one side. Chameleon appeared right behind her, combat knife in hand, missing her throat by mere inches.

As Bear started barreling toward her, she noticed Chameleon touch something on his belt before disappearing again. A weakness?

Bear lowered his head and became a battering ram, intending to slam Wolf into the metal container behind her. Intensely focused as he rushed forward, Wolf ran at him, placed her hands on his shoulders, and leap-frogged over him—allowing him to crash headfirst into the container.

She heard the electric hum behind her again, but this time she was ready. As Chameleon reappeared with his blade, she ducked forward, planted her hands on the ground, and performed a donkey kick, sending Chameleon flying helplessly into Bear's broad back. Taking advantage of their momentary confusion, she quickly grabbed Chameleon by the back of his armor. With her incredible strength, she lifted him up and performed a dead-weight German suplex, slamming him down hard onto the concrete behind her.

With Chameleon in a daze, she kicked her legs and hopped back to her feet. But before she could fully recover, her left leg was caught in the iron grip of Bear's large hand. He swung her whole body right into the side of a container with a loud clang. The pain in Wolf's head was crushing, but she still had enough sense to toss a flash pellet into Bear's face, temporarily blinding him. Growing more furious by the second, Bear swung his arms about wildly, trying to grab her.

As Wolf kept her distance, she noticed Chameleon had recovered and was starting to rise to his feet. Though still a little wobbly on her feet, Wolf rushed toward Chameleon, grabbed his belt, and ripped it off. She found the electrical device controlling his auto-camouflage and crushed it in her gauntlet.

"No!" Chameleon protested as he lunged forward with his knife.

She quickly dodged to the outside of the attack, grabbed his right wrist with one hand, and got behind him. With her left hand she applied all of her strength in a downward slam on his right shoulder, mashing him face-first into the ground. He slumped unconscious, and Wolf kicked his blade clear.

She then focused her attention on Bear, whose vision seemed to be clearing. Within seconds, Wolf had formed a plan. He was heavily armored, had plenty of weight to throw around, and used that to his advantage. Bear was a walking fortress, but he didn't seem to move too quickly. She glanced at the metal guards surrounding his knees. If she could destroy the foundation holding up all that weight, the fortress would come crashing down.

She checked her serum level, which was at 89 percent. She would have to take him down quickly, but if she used too much of her speed this soon in the fight, her serum level would plummet to nothing before she could even reach the boss. She'd have to rely on brute strength and finesse for now. *All right, let's do this!* She told herself.

His vision now clear, Bear zeroed in on Wolf. Anticipating his next move, she punched two holes in the concrete to give her feet leverage against the oncoming attack. Bear ran right for her, balling up one gigantic fist and reaching way back, ready to pummel her with one blow. Wolf positioned her feet in the holes and leaned forward. She had to get the timing just right.

Bear's heavy right fist came down on her just as she raised her right hand, stopping his attack cold with a deafening boom. Deep cracks formed in the concrete behind her feet. Bear's right knee was now within reach. She grabbed the metal guard protecting it and ripped it off.

As she tossed the hunk of metal aside, Bear hopped back and covered his exposed knee, surprised at what had just happened.

"You think you're so clever, don't ya?" he roared, pounding his fists together. "When I'm done with you, you'll be just a red smear on the ground." He was on guard now, and he wouldn't fall for the same trick twice. She would have to change tactics.

Wolf looked quickly at her surroundings. Metal containers formed walls to her right, left, and behind. Directly above was a large wooden crate hanging by rope. She carefully studied the angles of the walls. Then Wolf's attention fell on Bear, who was getting ready to charge again.

"There's nowhere to run." Bear's grin was cruel. "I'm gonna turn you into a bloody flapjack."

As Bear barreled toward her once more, Wolf took one big step back and pulled out a *shuriken* from her belt. She waited for just the right moment before throwing it hard at the wall next to her.

"Hah!" Bear let out as he got closer. "What was the point of that?"

The shuriken ricocheted from one wall to the next until it reached the perfect angle to cleanly cut the rope holding the crate above. Oblivious to the impending danger, Bear charged on until a 1,000-pound crate landed right on his head, stopping him dead. The crate broke open, and over two hundred tire irons tumbled everywhere.

Once the dust had cleared, Wolf moved some of the broken wood and tire irons away from the unconscious Bear. She knelt over him.

"First rule of a ninja: You must always pay attention to your surroundings." She patted him lightly on the head. "Sweet dreams, Yogi."

Chapter Twenty-Seven

At the Benton City Police Department, Jimmy stood in a conference room with five police sergeants and twenty SWAT Team members, reviewing his plans for the operation at the docks.

Jimmy rolled out a map of the docks and the surrounding area on the large table in the center of the room, as all the men gathered around.

"All right, like I said before: operation starts at 2300 hours. We quietly show up at the pier around 2130 and begin setting up our net. The assignments will be as follows: Officers Garret, Matthews, Thomson, Humphrey, and Jones are Blue Team and will be posted here to the north. Garret will be Blue Team Leader. Officers Kowalski, Jackson, Meyer, Crowley, and Tull are Red Team posted here to the south. Kowalski will be Red Team leader. The SWAT Team will be posted here to the west. In case Johnny's men try to run, the Red and Blue teams can funnel them toward the SWAT Team. Out on the water, I want police boats here to the east, northeast and southeast. Now as for firepower—"

Jimmy was interrupted by the phone ringing next to him. He immediately picked up the receiver. "Yes?"

"This is Officer Goldberg. We just received word of a small cargo boat exploding near Pier 15. There are also reports coming in of fighting going on between several armed soldiers and one girl in a white mask."

"What?" Jimmy glanced at the clock, which showed ten after eight. "Damn it, it's too soon!" Jimmy hung up the phone and spoke to the men surrounding him. "Change of plans, boys. Johnny must have changed the time. It's going down at the pier right now, which means we gotta be there ASAP."

At that moment, Officer Taylor ran into the room holding a printout.

"Jimmy, it's the transmission again! One's coming from the docks, and I'm still tracking the other."

"Keep at it, and let me know as soon as you pinpoint that other signal." Jimmy grabbed his coat, and shouted, "All hell's breaking loose at the docks, and we gotta stop it!"

Everyone in the room followed him out.

Wolf jumped from one storage container to the next, avoiding the countless incendiary grenades Jackal lobbed at her. His incessant laughter was beginning to get on her nerves. At the same time, she was dodging the hit-and-run tactics of Cobra, who had spectacular agility that almost rivaled her own. Jackal demonstrated a certain acrobatic prowess as well in his quick leaps and flips.

The temptation to move her body at super-sonic speeds was almost too sweet for Wolf to resist—almost. She had to save it. Wolf had made the same mistake Fox had: She had packed only an extra booster shot for the serum and not a full spare vial. She thought it would be a quick job, in and out. She couldn't have been more wrong.

Moments before leaping onto the Romanian cargo boat, she'd shot herself up with the full dose. At peak performance, the serum would burn up in her bloodstream within fifteen minutes. If she limited herself, she might get an extra fifteen or twenty minutes. With the booster shot, maybe longer, but not by much.

The serum level showed 78 percent on her readout. It was too soon to use the booster—way too soon. She was going to save it for him, the leader, just so she could smash that smug look right off his face.

She didn't even consider just running off and escaping. Although she could have done so at any time, she wouldn't. Even though she had assumed the role of ninja—stealthy information gatherers and assassins who flee when the odds are no longer in their favor—in her heart, Wolf had always believed in the ways of the Samurai. Honor and duty bound, Samurai never turn their backs on their enemies, even in the face of certain defeat.

Wolf jumped onto a wall and clung to it by digging her claws into the metal. She looked in the direction of her pursuers and saw only Jackal as he readied another incendiary grenade. Feeling that this was the perfect opportunity, Wolf pulled out a kunai knife and threw it directly at the grenade still in his hand.

Jackal's reflexes were something of a marvel themselves. Not only did he move the grenade from the kunai's path, but he actually caught the kunai with his teeth. While doing so, he didn't even break pace but continued lobbing his fiery little presents. Before Wolf could let out a sound of amazement, she heard movement above her and dodged just in time to avoid Cobra's twin blades coming down on her.

The two mercenaries kept Wolf on the move, barely giving her time to think up a strategy. Just ahead she could see a warehouse. If she could get inside, she might have an advantage. She headed there, and once she got far enough ahead of them, she dropped a smoke pellet to conceal her movements.

The two mercs, however, had a countermeasure.

"Heat vision!" Cobra called out, and both she and Jackal donned special visors that allowed them to see Wolf's heat signature through the smoke.

The wall of the warehouse was just within her reach. Tall windows ran the length of the building. An access door lay twenty feet from her, and Wolf made a run for it. Jackal hurled several incendiaries into her path and one right at her. She jumped to avoid the grenade, but was powerless to avoid Cobra's lightning-fast airborne assault, which sent both of them through the glass window and into the dimly lit warehouse.

Wolf rolled along the floor as Cobra jumped to her feet, her blades ready. Jackal came in behind Cobra; he pulled out several throwing knives and positioned them between his fingers. As Wolf climbed carefully to her feet, she minded Cobra and her blades, but also kept an attentive eye on Jackal.

Jackal jumped, took a fast foothold on a wooden crate, and did a side flip while throwing a handful of knives at Wolf. While Wolf was occupied deflecting the knives with her sword, Cobra came in from behind and made a thrust for her neck. Hearing the sound of Cobra's footsteps through the clanging of Jackal's knives against her sword, Wolf dodged Cobra's blade just in time to receive only a shallow cut across her left upper arm.

As she instinctively grabbed at her fresh wound, Jackal came in with a forward somersault and kicked Wolf right into the wooden crate behind her, breaking it on impact. Cobra quickly moved in, grabbed Wolf by the front of her suit, and threw her into another crate. Then, laughing insanely, Jackal grabbed Wolf's arm and slammed her into a support beam hard enough to make her see stars. Wolf noticed that her sword was no longer in her hand, but she didn't know where it had gone.

"Hah!" Cobra grinned at Wolf as she tried desperately to pull herself together. "Comc on, girl—what's wrong? You're supposed to be a wolf, but look at you; you're nothing more than a defenseless puppy."

"Let's kill her now!" Jackal yelled. "She's down, let's do it."

"Patience." Cobra gestured at Jackal to be calm. "I want to enjoy this. We'll cut her up slowly." Cobra bent close to Wolf and caressed the skin of her neck. "How does that sound, little puppy?"

Wolf's head cleared to the point where she could focus. She glanced at her wrist readout: 68 percent. "Enough," Wolf murmured.

"What's that, girlie?" Cobra raised her blades high and pointed them at Wolf, ready to get on with her gruesome plans. "Giving up already?"

"I said," Wolf spoke louder now, with more strength, "I've had enough!"

Time slowed to a halt. Cobra and Jackal became like statues. The two mercs grinned smugly, as if already enjoying a victory. Wolf reached up and grabbed both of Cobra's blades with her gauntlets and broke them off. Tiny shards of metal slowly floated through space as Wolf stood up. Still they grinned, not reacting yet to what had just happened. How could they? Wolf was now moving two thousand times faster than any normal human being.

Seemingly taking her time, Wolf ran the blades though both their hearts. *I really am sorry,* Wolf thought, as if speaking to them. *I was hoping to beat you both fairly and with honor, but I'm running out of time. Forgive me.*

Time finally returned to its normal flow. Simultaneously, Cobra and Jackal clutched their chests where Wolf had stabbed them, then they collapsed. And died.

"Forgive me," Wolf whispered, feeling a twinge of guilt for what she'd just done. She felt as if she'd cheated, played dirty. The guilty twinge became a pain she felt briefly in her heart. Then the pain quickly subsided as her attention was drawn to Timber Wolf, who was applauding loudly as he walked toward her with a swagger.

"Bravo, my dear Wolf." Timber Wolf smiled at her. "Bravo!"

"Your teammates are dead, and you're smiling and clapping?" Wolf said, horrified. "Don't you care?"

"Of course I care. They were the best hired hands I've had the pleasure of working with. But that's all they were: hired hands. No more, no less. Losing them is no different from losing a knife or a gun. I can always buy more."

"You heartless bastard!" Wolf screamed. "You're lower than scum."

"Me?" Timber Wolf said. "You forget—you're the one who killed them, not me."

"No, that was—I had no choice, I—"

"You murdered them, Wolf," he said, taking a tender but condemning tone. "I saw you do it. The way you moved, they were defenseless. There's no possible way they could've fought back against that kind of speed. You called me a villain, but from what I've just seen, you're more a villain than I could hope to be."

"No, I'm not a—" Wolf's resolve was beginning to waver.

"Yes, you are. You killed innocent, defenseless people without a second thought. My team and I came here to stop an assassin who's killed at least fifteen people in cold blood. You are that assassin. That guy out there, Donnie—could he have really stood up to you in a fight? I mean really? No, he couldn't. Of course he couldn't, not against your power."

"But, it was justice…" Wolf's voice was shaky now.

"This isn't justice. It's slaughter, merciless and brutal. If a judge were to look at you right now, he would call you a deranged serial killer. "

"No!" Wolf cried. "I'm a hero, I'm a—"

"Come now." Timber Wolf's voice became soft and sympathetic. "Are you, really?"

"I'm… a villain?" She almost couldn't believe her own words.

"Yes, you are a villain. And I'm a good guy, here to take you to justice."

Wolf dropped the broken, bloodied blades from her hands as doubt flowed through her soul like a plague. All this time, while Timber Wolf had been talking, he was reaching for his knife, a knife he kept carefully out of view by turning to the side as he slowly crept closer.

"Don't listen to him, Wolf," she heard over her earpiece.

"No, just… wait a second," Wolf whispered back.

"He's trying to work your emotions again."

"I signed on for justice," Wolf said softly. "Am I just another criminal?"

"You are a Sword of Justice, Wolf, just like you've always wanted to be."

"But he's right. I've killed people who never stood a chance against me. Where's the fairness in that? Where's the justice?"

Timber Wolf came closer still.

"Wolf, I know he sounds reasonable, but he's just setting you up. You have to believe me."

"I—I don't know what to believe anymore." Wolf realized something then. "But wait a minute."

With one quick motion, Timber Wolf pulled out his knife and thrust it at Wolf's chest. But before it hit its target, he felt an iron grip clamp down on his wrist, making him drop the knife.

Wolf looked up at him. "I am Justice." Her voice was cold and dark. Timber Wolf struggled uselessly to get free. "And you are guilty, Timber Wolf. The blood of countless victims stains your hands. I hereby sentence you to death." Wolf could smell a nervous sweat coming off the mercenary.

"Are you nuts?" he said. "Have you been listening to a word I've said?"

"I don't listen to dead men." A strong dizziness came over Wolf, and she released her enemy suddenly. Timber Wolf fell back against the hard concrete floor. He grabbed a crowbar lying nearby.

Wolf's eyes began to lose focus as the lights outside seemed to become brighter. "Wolf!" she heard in her ear. "Listen, your vitals are reading abnormal. I think you've been poisoned."

Wolf raised her hand to the cut on her arm as she suddenly realized…

Timber Wolf let out a laugh. "You're starting to feel it, aren't you? Cobra's little surprise? She coats her blades with actual cobra venom. Even if her prey should escape, they won't survive. Feel those pins and needles around the cut? Starting to sweat? Is your heart beginning to race? The neurotoxin should be working its way through your bloodstream by now."

Wolf began to feel weak. Deep pain stabbed her abdomen. Her mouth was dry, and it was hard to breathe. She had to get away, but her legs weren't acting like they should. They were wobbly, uncoordinated. Timber Wolf grabbed this chance to take a free swing at her face with the crowbar. Not only did the heavy hit knock her flat on her back, but it also cracked away the lower part of her mask, exposing her mouth. Blood trickled down her lip. The dizziness was getting worse. Timber Wolf slowly closed in, ready to take another hard swing.

"Wolf? Wolf!" came a shout in her ear. "If you can hear me, reach into your left belt pocket and throw the flash pellet at him."

With weak, clumsy hands, she struggled to find the pocket and open it. Timber Wolf raised the crowbar. She found the flash pellet and tossed it at him as best she could with her blurred vision. She closed her eyes as the bright flash filled the room. Then, while Timber Wolf was blinded, Wolf quickly crawled away and found cover behind some crates near the far wall. She leaned back against the cold brick wall as an intense drowsiness came over her.

"Wolf, there should be some anti-venom in your right leg pocket. I'm not sure if it's strong enough for cobra venom, but it's worth a try."

"So tired." Wolf's voice was weak. "I just want to sleep."

"If you fall asleep, you will die, do you understand? If the venom doesn't kill you, Timber Wolf will."

"It's too late. It's over." Wolf's eyes drifted shut. "Just… let me sleep."

"Pull yourself together, damn it! You call yourself a hero?"

Wolf's eyes opened. "I…" Her fists clenched and she gritted her teeth. "I am…" She took a deep breath and forced herself to sit up. "I am a hero!" With shaky hands, she reached into her right leg pocket, pulled out a green vial, and snapped it into her injector gun. She pressed it to her neck and pulled the trigger. As the cold fluid flowed through her veins, the symptoms started to disappear. Slowly she began to regain her strength and focus.

"Vitals are stabilizing," the voice in her ear said, sounding relieved. "You should be back to full strength in a few minutes."

Chapter Twenty-Eight

Timber Wolf found the assassin's sword among some shattered boxes. He dropped the crowbar and took the katana sword by its skillfully woven leather hilt. Despite its heavy use, it showed not a ding or a scratch.

"What's this thing made of?" he asked himself while admiring the flawless shine of the blade. He reached into the left pouch of his Kevlar vest and took out a heartbeat sensor. The small, handheld device, designed to detect the rhythmic sound waves of a beating heart, had a three-inch LCD screen, a tiny parabolic microphone and an effective range of about fifty feet. On the screen, a heartbeat would show up as a pulsing red dot that would become larger as it moves closer to the target. He swept it from left to right until he got a reading about twenty feet ahead of him against the far wall.

Timber Wolf hurried to the location and, sure enough, there she was—resting against the brick wall, apparently unconscious. With a devious grin, he pulled the sword back, ready to deliver the death stroke. Then he swung it at her with all he had. The blade hit nothing but wall.

Timber Wolf blinked several times and looked around. He couldn't believe it. She'd disappeared without a trace. Confused, he shouted, "Where are you?"

He heard something drop right behind him. Turning, he saw Wolf standing there, cracking her knuckles and loosening her neck. At her feet was an injector gun. "That's my sword you're holding," she growled, her voice dark and menacing.

Red and blue flashing lights shone through the windows, but she didn't seem to notice. Timber Wolf had gained her complete and undivided attention. A nervous sweat formed on his brow, and in desperation he swung the sword madly at her over and over again. All he sliced was air. Then she caught him mid-swing, and Timber Wolf screamed in pain as she crushed every bone in his wrist. The sword dropped from his fingers, and she caught it in her other hand.

With his good hand, he pulled out his pistol and, with an angry roar, began firing where he thought she was. Again, he hit nothing but air. She'd disappeared into the darkness of the warehouse. He looked all around, trying to catch sight of her.

"You and your goon squad tried to kill me, Timber Wolf." Her voice echoed throughout the warehouse. "Tell me, can you fight the darkness?"

For the first time since childhood, Timber Wolf felt terror run through him. He pulled out a grenade.

She laughed. "That's really not going to help you."

"Oh, yeah?" Timber Wolf cried. "Watch this!" He pulled the pin and threw the grenade at the far wall. The resulting explosion blew open a hole wide enough for him to escape. About to make a dash for the outside, he felt a strong hand grab him by the collar.

"It's time to put this dog out in the yard," she said, her voice ringing in his ear. She tossed him hard into the cold air outside, where dozens of police cars were waiting with their flashing lights and sirens. Then, in midair, she grabbed his ankle and pulled him back. "I'm not done with you yet, mutt!" she screamed. "Time to put you to sleep."

With a single blow of her fist, she pounded him down into the pavement, creating a three-foot-deep crater in the concrete. A few moments later, after the dust had cleared, Wolf hopped out of the hole and drew her sword. Around her stood dozens of policemen; their weapons were raised and aimed at her.

Jimmy Ziminski took a step forward and spoke through a bullhorn. "You are surrounded. Drop your weapon and put your hands behind your head now."

"Orders, ma'am?" Wolf asked quietly.

"Your serum level is still good. The mission is complete. You may return to base. An army of police shouldn't be able to stop you."

"Understood." Wolf was about to carve a bloody path through the army of policemen when she felt a sharp, agonizing pain in her chest. It was her heart. Sword in hand, she raised her hilt to her heart and gasped deep for breath.

One of the officers, a rookie with less than a year on the force, was sweating nervously, his finger twitching on the trigger. As the assassin clutched her chest, he pulled the trigger and fired a .45 caliber round into her shoulder, knocking her to the ground.

"Hold your fire!" Jimmy yelled. "I said hold your fire!" He threw down the bullhorn and ran to Wolf. Dropping to his knees beside her, he put his hand on her shoulder and applied pressure to the bullet wound, trying to slow the bleeding. "Get me a medic, damn it!" Jimmy called back to the officers. "I need a medic right now."

Jimmy had a quick flashback to the Gulf War, when he'd done the exact same thing for a fallen soldier who'd been knocked down by a sniper bullet. Jimmy could taste the desert dust in his mouth, feel the scorching Middle-eastern sun on his back and the hot dry air in his lungs. Then he felt a weak hand on his forearm. Just like that, he was back in the here and now, looking at this dying teenager with a grimace of pain on her face. Slowly, she took off her mask and looked up at him.

"It's you," Jimmy said. "Kira Shirou, right?"

"Yeah," she said weakly. "I need help."

"Paramedic's on the way, Kira. Stay with me, okay?"

"My heart." She groaned. "It hurts."

"Just hold on and try not to talk."

"You want to know why I did it, don't you?" She gave a wan smile. "I'll tell you. That's why you want me to live, isn't it? To solve the case?"

"That's not it. We're here to help you."

"It's okay. I know you're lying. The Scorpiones ruined my father's business, destroyed his reputation. He lost everything. With the last of his money he sent me here. I wanted justice for what they did to him, but I didn't have the means. Then she came along and answered all my prayers. 'Den Mother' she calls herself. She wears the red face of an obsessed female demon: the Han'nya mask. The Scorpiones destroyed my father's business, so I vowed to destroy theirs. And she's the one who gave me the means to do it. Well… there you have it… your case is solved." Her voice was getting weaker.

"Where's that medic?" Jimmy called out. He spoke softly to Kira. "Tell me about Den Mother, Kira. Who is she?"

"I don't know her real name. All I know is she hates the Scorpiones as much as I do. And that's it. I… I guess my time is up."

"No, we're gonna get you fixed up, so don't you worry."

She gave him a tragic smile. "You don't understand. Now that you've caught me, do you honestly think she'll let me live?"

Jimmy heard a beeping coming from her wrist. He turned it over to see a countdown on the digital readout: 20, 19, 18, 17…

"Oh my God," Jimmy whispered. Then he noticed a blinking red light on her belt. At that moment, the paramedics finally showed up. Jimmy grabbed one of them by the shirt. "Give me a knife, something sharp, anything—hurry!"

One of them took a scalpel out of her medical bag and handed it to him. Jimmy ripped it from the package and started working on the belt, trying desperately to get it off her in the precious seconds remaining. "You're not dying today, Kira. Do you hear me?"

Finally he cut through the belt, pulled it off her, and threw it as hard as he could toward the river. He dropped to the ground, shielding Kira with his body. There was a flash and a loud boom as an explosion ripped up the edge of the pier. The resulting shockwave knocked the paramedics to the ground.

Jimmy rose to his knees as the ringing in his ears started to fade. He looked down at Kira, and she gave him a smile as the paramedics scrambled to their feet and started to work on her. Jimmy took her hand.

"Find her," she whispered.

"Yes?" Jimmy bent close as she raised her lips to his ear.

"Find her up high, facing our homeland." Then her eyes slowly closed as tears slid down her cheeks.

"I've lost her heartbeat and breathing's stopped," one of the paramedics called out. "Starting CPR—get the paddles ready." He took out a pair of medical scissors and cut away her suit to expose her chest for defibrillation. Then he gave her rescue breaths and chest compressions while the other paramedic charged up the defibrillator. After thirty seconds, the paramedic giving CPR checked for signs of life. When he found none, he grabbed the paddles and placed one on the upper right side of her chest and the other on the lower left.

"Clear!"

He gave her a jolt. Kira's chest rose as her back arched, then she dropped again. The medic checked for life signs. There was nothing. He jolted her again. Still there was nothing. He repeated the protocol for another ten minutes until finally he said, "All right, I'm calling it." The paramedic looked at his watch. "Time of death: eight twenty-four p.m." He looked up at Jimmy. "Who was she?"

Jimmy gave him a grim look.

"Kira Shirou. Another poor girl led to ruin by the sweet-sounding promises of a demon."

Joey and Pat were sitting in the center row of the ABC Movie Theater in Midtown, New York. They had chosen this particular theater because of the Rocky movie marathon that had started at 4 p.m. and would be running until after midnight. So far they'd seen Parts I and II. Part III would be starting shortly. Joey was finishing off his second bag of popcorn, and Pat was working on his third box of chocolate covered-raisins.

"So what do you think, Pat?" Joey asked, handing him a fresh bottle of cola. "Is Rocky gonna win this one again?"

Pat laughed. "No, Clubber's gonna beat him. Of course he's gonna win, man! It's not like we haven't seen these movies a hundred times before."

"I know." Joey smiled. "It's like they just never get old. When I see Rocky fightin' in that ring, it gets my blood pumping every time."

"Tell me about it. I can't wait 'til he fights the Russian. That one was by far the best."

"No, no, no." Joey shook his head. "The best one was the second one, when he had the rematch with Apollo Creed. It was like the Battle of the Titans. It was a clash of egos, man."

"Listen, you wanna talk epic fights, let's talk Rocky versus Drago. America's best against Russia's best. It wasn't just two men fighting in that ring, it was two nations. How can it possibly get better than that?"

"Hey, at least Apollo had style, man. What did Drago have? He looked like Lurch from *The Addams Family* and had the personality of a tree stump."

"A tree stump? Drago was like a Russian bear, and bears don't need personality. They're vicious and don't stop fighting until their enemy is down for good. That was Drago."

"Yeah, I see what you're sayin'. And Rocky was the Tiger, right? He was all fire and passion and never backed down."

"All right, you got it." Pat gave a pleased nod.

"I still think Part II is better."

"Dude, you're completely hopeless!" Pat heaved an annoyed sigh.

"By the way, Pat, where's Stephanie tonight?"

"She said she had a ton of homework to finish. Besides, I don't think she's into boxing movies."

"Do you think Jenny likes these movies?"

"Hmm, I'm not sure. Why don't you visit her with Steph tomorrow? She's over there every day. You can ask her then."

"Yeah, I think I'll do that." Joey smiled as he remembered their meeting from earlier that day.

"Don't tell me you're falling for her already?" Pat teased. "You just met her."

Joey put on a cool exterior to hide his embarrassment. "I just wanted to know what kind of movies she likes, that's all."

"Yeah, yeah, whatever."

Joey pointed to the screen. "Hey, the movie's startin'!"

The screen lit up, and the MGM lion gave his trademark roar. The two boys could already feel the excitement building, for they knew Rocky would have to defend his pride against yet another seemingly unbeatable foe.

Chapter Twenty-Nine

Just after the paramedics covered Kira's body, Jimmy got a call on his cell phone. The ID said Phil Taylor. Jimmy pressed the answer button. "I need some good news, Phil. Tell me you have some."

"Yes, I do. I got a trace on both signals."

"All right, let's hear it."

"The first one came from the docks where you're at. The second signal came from Low Town around the area of Gibbons Avenue and Adams Street."

"Gibbons and Adams? There's nothing over there but empty lots." Then the wheels started turning in his head. There was also an old business building in that vicinity that hadn't been used for fifty years, St. Martin Tower. They called it the Tombstone because it was an ugly, gray, twelve-story tower surrounded by acres of tall grass and cracked pavement. Isolated and out of the way. That was their best bet right there. Jimmy ended the call and got on his radio. "Ziminski to Teams Red and Blue. Report immediately to the Tombstone in Low Town. Keep flashers and sirens off. I don't want any noise, and nobody enters the building until I get there. Got it?"

"Red Team leader, Ten-Four."

"Blue Team leader, copy that."

"Ziminski to Sergeant Davis."

"Go ahead, Jimmy."

"Pier 15 is now officially a crime scene. I want it closed off and forensics on location in twenty minutes."

Ten minutes later, Jimmy pulled up to the Tombstone, where Red and Blue Teams were waiting for him. He got out of his car and motioned to all of the officers to gather around. "We have reason to believe a second suspect named 'Den Mother' has set up her base of operations somewhere inside this building," he told them. "We're gonna do a sweep, quick and quiet. We'll start on the first floor and work our way up. Any observations so far?"

Garret, the Blue Team leader, spoke up. "We spotted an antenna on the edge of the roof through the night vision scope. It looks brand new and high tech."

"That's probably what Den Mother is using to communicate. Okay, people, leave no stone unturned. In the meantime, I want all exits blocked off. No one gets in or out of the building." Then Jimmy remembered Kira's last words: *Find her up high, facing our homeland.* "Wait," he said.

The teams stopped and looked back at him, awaiting further orders.

"Garret and Kowalski, you're on me. We're going to the top floor, east side. The rest of you get started on the sweep."

The two men joined Jimmy as the rest quietly entered the building ahead of them. While the others scattered, Jimmy and his two-man team turned on their flashlights and climbed what seemed like an endless number of dusty, cobweb-ridden stairs all the way up to the top floor. They found the doorway leading from the stairs to the twelfth floor wide open.

As they slowly advanced into the large, open room, Jimmy signaled them to kill their lights. All the windows were either broken or missing, and an icy cold wind moved through the floor. The only source of light came from downtown off in the distance. Fresh snow and old refuse had gathered along the edges and corners of the room. Old wooden office desks, half rotted and warped, lay strewn about, along with rusted metal chair frames and what was left of glass-block cubicles.

A single closed door with a tiny slice of light across its bottom edge lay ahead of them at the east end of the floor. Jimmy drew his gun, as did the other men, and they quietly made their way to it. Garret took his position to the left of the door as Kowalski grasped the door knob. Jimmy stood in front of the door, his weapon ready.

Kowalski silently counted down with his fingers: three—two—one. Then he pulled the door open, and Jimmy stormed into the dimly lit room. Seeing no one inside, Jimmy called out "Clear." He gave the hold-your-positions sign, and the two men remained outside, guarding the doorway.

It looked to be an old manager's office. The manager, apparently one Justin L. Roderick, had left his name plate on his desk in the center of the room. Dusty bookcases and rusted metal filing cabinets were situated along the walls. The carpet at Jimmy's feet was molded and in tatters. However, atop the old desk were three brand new LCD computer monitors, their screens streaming some kind of digital code. The shiny keyboard in front of them was illuminated by a modern LED desk lamp. Cutting-edge radio communications equipment covered the rest of the desk, wires from which led out a window and up toward the roof.

All of this equipment was apparently powered by a compact high-tech generator the likes of which Jimmy had never seen before. It didn't appear to run on any fossil fuel, judging from the lack of exhaust pipes or fuel tanks. The circuits of the generator gave off a pulsing blue glow, and the generator produced a low hum.

Jimmy sat down in the soft leather chair, which also seemed new. He had to see what information he could get from the computer. Just as he was stretching his fingers over the keyboard, he heard cries of pain outside the door, then two heavy thumps.

He quickly pulled out his Beretta 92 FS and flashlight and aimed them through the doorway. There was nothing but darkness out there. Cautiously Jimmy eased out the door and shone his flashlight on the floor. Both Garret and Kowalski lay motionless, facedown at his feet, with kunai knives sticking out of their backs. Keeping his eyes on the room surrounding him, he lowered his fingers to their throats. Both were dead. He pulled out his radio and was about to report two officers down and request backup when it was struck from his hand by something unseen and went flying into the darkness.

Now frantic, Jimmy directed his flashlight to the stairway exit, the windows, and even the snowy corners. No sign of the killer anywhere. Jimmy finally lost his patience and called out into the darkness, "Two more people are dead, Den Mother. How many more until you're satisfied?"

"As many as it takes," a warped voice said from behind him.

Jimmy turned to face this mysterious person, but suddenly he felt himself being thrown into the air. He landed clear across the room, pinned helplessly against the wall next to the exit door. Two incredibly strong hands gripped his neck and gun hand tightly, and metal claws started to cut into his skin. Staring him right in the face was the person he could only assume was Den Mother—mask, sword, utility belt, everything he associated with these ninja, but she had a stronger, more adult build. And unlike the others, this one had short dark hair.

"You, James Ziminski," she continued in a deep, distorted voice, "won't be one of them. At least not yet, you won't."

She loosened her grip on his throat, just enough for him to talk.

"Why's that?" he choked out.

"You found the empty serum vial, you uncovered the connection between the rash of assassinations and the Scorpione family's past, and you were even able to track me down through the radio frequency I hijacked from your police system. You've impressed me enough that I'll let you live."

"I will stop you," he said between bouts of coughing.

She laughed. "You are no threat to me."

"Not so long as you have the serum flowing through you, right?"

"Oh, please. I've been trained in the secret ninja arts since birth. I don't need the serum."

"What's your endgame, Den Mother?" Jimmy struggled in her grip. "What are you after?"

"We only want what is rightfully ours."

"And what's that?"

"Come now. Use that brain of yours."

"I'm guessing it's that old mirror that Johnny caught you two trying to take from his father's living room. One of you was shot."

"My sister." A hint of sadness colored her voice. "She did not survive."

"So all this, just for a mirror?" Jimmy asked. "What's so special about it?"

"The Mirror of Princess Mayumi belonged to my family long ago, but then it was lost. We searched for it for centuries until we finally found it in the hands of the Scorpiones."

"But this isn't about just the mirror anymore is it?" he asked. He wanted to keep her talking, hear more of the story, and live through this long enough to use it against her. "Now you want revenge for the death of your sister too."

"Don't presume to analyze me. You have no idea how deep my plans go."

"Your assassins are dead. Your plan is finished."

She let out a loud laugh. "My plan was completed about fifteen minutes ago."

"What? The docks? Kira never got the mirror. She was nowhere near Johnny's house."

"Kira fulfilled her role. She got her justice, yes, but at the same time she wreaked enough havoc not only to gather every officer in the city to the docks, but all of Johnny's men as well."

Jimmy broke out in a cold sweat as he suddenly realized what Kira's true purpose had been. And how coldly she had been sacrificed.

"Yes, Kira was merely a diversion. Johnny was my real goal. After all, he was the one who put the bullet in my sister. You see, I've carefully planned this for years. I've watched the Scorpiones closely, studied them. With time and patience I eventually discovered every last one of their dirty little secrets. And I used those secrets against them. I used Lisa Smith to kill Vincent and Tony. Vincent's drugs killed her brother through an overdose."

"And Tony raped her mother," Jimmy added.

She gave a nod. "You're catching on."

"Kira wanted justice for her father. But she and Lisa were your only assassins, right? If you've been here the whole time… no, there's another one, isn't there?"

"Bingo!" she said cheerily. "I sent my final little fox on her one and only mission."

"Who? Who is she?"

"Ah, ah, ah. No spoilers. Besides, I'm sure you'll find out soon enough." She squeezed him by the throat again, and he struggled to release himself from her grip. Then abruptly she dropped him to the floor. As he coughed and hacked, she lowered her face to his. "But for now, you'll need to sleep while I make my getaway."

"Wait! You—"

She sprayed Jimmy with a white gas from a device on her wrist. He felt himself overwhelmed by drowsiness, even though he fought it. His vision narrowed, and he could hear the demon's words begin to fade into darkness.

"It's been fun. By the time you wake up, I'll be long gone. It's a shame we couldn't get to know each other better. Sayonara—I doubt we'll meet again."

Before Jimmy finally lost consciousness, he muttered. "Don't… count on it."

Chapter Thirty

Flames crackled and sparked in the fireplace that evening at the Scorpione estate as Johnny paced back and forth by the window. Over and over he dialed Donnie's number, and every time there was no answer. Then he called the numbers of the men who were supposed to be with him. They weren't answering either.

"Idiots!" he roared. "What am I paying you all for?"

He stormed over to the small bar by the fireplace and poured himself three fingers of scotch. Once he'd downed that, he poured out some more. As the alcohol warmed his throat, he stared into the rolling flames. He had a bad feeling about all these unanswered calls. Donnie might not be bright, but he was loyal. He wouldn't ignore Johnny's calls.

He dialed another number on his cell phone, thinking, *He'd better answer, considering how much I'm paying him.* It rang twice before a man picked up on the other end. "Yeah it's me," Johnny said. "Do you know if the police got involved with my shipment at the docks? Pier 15. All right, but make it quick. I don't like waiting." A short moment passed before the man came back on the line. "What? How many cops? What about my shipment? Are you kidding me? I'll get whoever's responsible—so she's dead, huh? That's the best news I've heard all week. What about my men? No—Donnie too? Oh, my God, did they get his cell phone? Damn it, my number's in that cell phone. Now you listen to me: As soon as that phone hits the evidence room, I want it to disappear. Do you understand? Good. Keep me posted."

Johnny hung up. Despite the bad news regarding his gun shipment, he found some pleasure in the thought of the assassin turning up dead. But that feeling was fleeting. The assassin they'd found tonight was a seventeen-year-old girl, much too young to be one of the thieves from that night several years ago. Anxiety over when that particular ninja might return began to creep into his mind.

While Johnny had sent the majority of his men to the docks, he'd kept four of them behind to patrol the grounds of the estate. Johnny was thankful Joey was out seeing a movie. He figured his son would at least be safer there, in case something bad happened at the house.

Then he noticed that something was amiss. None of his men had passed by outside the window for a while now. He went to the window and cautiously peered out into the night. The grounds appeared to be completely empty, his men, gone. He was alone in the house.

"Where the hell is everyone?" Johnny had never felt so vulnerable. He stepped closer to the fireplace and set his glass on the mantle, then he pulled out his Colt .45 revolver and checked that it was loaded. He was wary of the window, considering what had happened to his father in this very room. Johnny went to the glass and looked outside again. Narrowing his eyes, he couldn't see much in the darkness encircling the property. Shadows seemed to move, but didn't. Was paranoia taking hold of him, or was someone really out there?

An ember popped in the fireplace, startling him enough that he aimed his gun in that direction. There was just the roaring fire, the elegant silver mirror displayed above it, and shadows dancing on the walls around him.

Johnny took in a deep breath and let it out slowly. "I gotta calm down," he said out loud. He laughed despite himself. "This is ridiculous. I got nothing to worry about. One assassin's dead over at the docks, and if the main girl shows up, there are four strong, capable men guarding this place. Maybe their phones batteries are dead or they accidently left them on silent."

"Strong and capable they were," a soft, yet darkly confident voice said.

His heart leaping, Johnny quickly turned to the open doorway on the other end of the room, swinging his pistol around to point at the door. There, standing against the darkness of the hallway was an assassin wearing a white kitsune fox mask. Hanging across her back was a crimson katana sword. Her long dark hair was tied into a flowing ponytail with a red leather strip. Silver-clawed gauntlets covered her slender hands. In her right hand, she was carrying something Johnny couldn't see.

He took aim, his eyes wide, his heart pounding like a piston in his chest. But he hesitated to pull the trigger, though he wasn't sure why. She took slow certain steps, closing the distance between them.

"However, their phones were not on silent nor did they run out of charge." She tossed four blood-covered cell phones at his feet.

Johnny's hands were shaking, but he did his best to steady the gun. "It's you, isn't it—the one I didn't kill. Don't come any closer!" She stopped about seven paces from him, and Johnny nodded toward the mirror above the fireplace. "Still after that damn mirror, huh? What's so special about it? Why go this far?"

"She wanted the mirror. I want something different: revenge. Revenge for the life you took, Johnny."

Johnny grinned. "Heh, you're gonna have to be a little more specific, sweetheart."

He unloaded all six shots at her. The speed of her sword deflected all of them. The final bullet she aimed right into the muscle of his left thigh, and Johnny fell to his knees with an agonized scream. He grabbed for the spare ammo in his jacket pocket, but she was much faster, snatching the gun from his hand and slamming him in the head with it. Then she crushed the revolver like it was tin foil and tossed it aside.

His skull felt like it had been hit by a freight train, and his vision blurred. Before he knew what was happening, she grabbed him by the front of his shirt and threw him into Vincent's chair by the fireplace.

"Have a seat, Mr. Scorpione," she said with a certain satisfaction. "I promise this won't take long."

Blood from his head trickled down Johnny's cheek. He felt of his head with a shaky hand and winced when he touched the wound. "What do you want?" he asked. "Money? I'll give you anything. You have my word."

"Your word is worth as much as your life right now," she said, wagging her head. "Besides, I don't want your blood money. All I want is for you to look upon my face before you die." She slowly removed her mask and dropped it to the floor.

Johnny's eyes took in her features, and he immediately recognized her. "It—it's you! Now I realize the mistake I made." Then, as she tightened her grip on the sword's hilt, a fiery anger ignited inside Johnny. "I should've killed you first, you miserable b—"

His words were cut short as she darted behind him. Then the upper part of the chair's backrest fell away, and Johnny's head, detached from his neck, fell forward into his lap.

The assassin sheathed the blade after cleaning it and secured it across her back. Then, with a small smile of satisfaction, she walked to the fireplace, taking a moment to look at her reflection in the silver mirror. Her smile grew wider as she removed the mirror from its display, carefully slid it into a small, padded black bag, and tied it to her belt.

She donned her mask again and made her way to the door. Before she left, however, she paused and looked back at Johnny's corpse. "What do you think, Johnny?" she said softly. "Was that business, or personal?"

Then she disappeared into the vast darkness of the hallway beyond.

Jimmy swam in a vast, dark abyss. He could hear a voice calling to him, but it seemed so far away. Then a bright light shone in his eyes and the voice became crystal clear.

"Jimmy!" He could feel someone shaking him. "Come on, man, wake up."

Jimmy gradually came back to his senses. The last thing he remembered was falling unconscious on the top floor of the Tombstone. He looked around: still there, and Officer Tull was standing over him, urging him awake. The room was filled with officers looking over the scene.

"Tull, get that flashlight out of my face, will you?" Jimmy said, pushing the light away.

"Thank God." Tull breathed a sigh of relief. "We thought we'd lost you too."

"What happened?"

Tull helped Jimmy to his feet. "We spotted a Black Hawk helicopter landing on the roof. We called your radio, but there was no answer. By the time we got up here, the Black Hawk had lifted off and headed north like a bat outta hell." Tull looked at the bodies of Garret and Kowalski. "That's when we found their bodies and you unconscious. Now it's your turn. What happened to you up here?"

"We found the main suspect. Den Mother." Jimmy walked over to the windows and looked northward. "She admitted to organizing the whole thing, all the Scorpione killings. The docks were meant to be a distraction while her final assassin took out Johnny Scorpione. We may still have time—I want four squad cars and an ambulance at the Scorpione estate right now. If his son Joseph isn't there, I want him contacted ASAP, got it?"

As Tull rallied the available men, Jimmy pulled aside another officer. "I want to know as soon as any evidence from the docks is collected that could connect the Scorpiones to the dock incident."

"We already have some," the officer replied. "A cell phone belonging to Donnie Cappella. Poor guy was cut clean in half. Johnny's number was in his phone's address book. It's been bagged and tagged and is currently on its way to the evidence room."

"What about the five armed soldiers we found?"

"Still investigating. Three are dead and the others are still unconscious. We'll interrogate those two when they wake up."

"It shouldn't take too long find out who they are. If they're mercenaries, they're probably registered with a private military corporation. By the way, what time is it?"

"Quarter to ten."

"A whole hour? Jeez, no wonder I missed so much."

Jimmy ran to the office at the end of the floor and looked inside. All the equipment was gone, as if it had never been there. He pounded his fist on the door in frustration. She was a ninja all right; she hadn't left a single trace of herself behind. Capturing her was going to be a lot harder than he'd thought. But right now, there was something else he needed to check on.

Ten minutes later Jimmy was pulling into the police headquarters parking lot. As soon as he entered the building he checked his cell phone. He had a text from Pete, the young officer assigned to the evidence room.

Donnie's cell arrived in Evidence. Nobody's shown up to take it yet. Williams is with me.

With a sigh of relief, Jimmy nodded. *Good boy, Pete,* he said to himself. He walked down the hall to a storeroom a few doors from Evidence. Pete and Lt. Freddy Williams were there waiting for him, sitting in front of a closed-circuit TV monitor. Freddy handed Jimmy a fresh cup of coffee as he took a seat next to them.

"Got some bad news, Jimmy."

"Please don't tell me..." Jimmy hung his head.

"They found Johnny. It wasn't pretty. He was decapitated in his own living room. Gruesome scene, I heard. They also found four of his men scattered about the property—well, they think they found four of 'em. They're still counting the body parts."

"Damn it!" Jimmy pounded his fist into the palm of his other hand. "If only he'd come clean, he'd still be alive."

"Guess you won't be getting that confession, huh?" Freddy mused.

"Yeah, looks that way." Jimmy narrowed his eyes at the screen in front of him. "So this is the feed from the miniature camera we placed in the Evidence room?"

"As you can see, the picture's crystal clear." Freddy said. "We're just waitin' for the main star."

"How long's it been since they brought in Donnie's phone?"

"Forty minutes, give or take," Pete replied.

Jimmy rubbed the back of his neck in irritation. "Come on, he's gotta bite sooner or later."

After several minutes, someone entered the evidence room. It was Robert Hawes, clear as day.

"This is it," Jimmy said quietly. "Get ready, everyone."

Hawes was looking back and forth between a piece of paper in his hand and the shelves. When he found the box he was looking for, he opened it up, took out Donnie's cell phone, and placed it in his jacket pocket. Then he closed the box and walked back out.

Jimmy rushed out into the hall, with Freddy following close behind. Pete stayed in the storeroom per Jimmy's orders. He didn't want this coming back on Pete in any way.

"Hawes!" Jimmy called out as he caught up to him.

Hawes turned back to Jimmy with a curious look. "Yeah, what is it?"

"You and I need to have a conversation." Jimmy gripped his arm. "Let's go."

Hawes raised his hands in seeming confusion. "I don't know what this is about, but I'm sure we can discuss it in my office tomorrow. I don't have time right now."

Jimmy grabbed Hawes by the front of his jacket and slammed him back against the wall. "You're gonna make time, Hawes. Tell me how long you been on the take."

"You've lost your flamin' mind!" Hawes struggled, but Jimmy held him. "What the hell you talkin' about?"

"Don't play stupid!" Jimmy barked. "You've been removing evidence and not signing it out for months, maybe even longer. Now start talking." Jimmy lifted him off the ground. "How long have you been on the Scorpione take?"

"Jimmy, you gotta believe me." Hawes was shaking, and beads of sweat broke out on his forehead. "I don't know nothin' about that, I was just following orders. He tells me to get something from the Evidence room without signing it out and I bring it to him. That's all."

"Who?"

"The chief."

Jimmy couldn't believe what he'd just heard. But it all made sense now. The reason the Scorpiones were never convicted, and in some cases never even charged for the crimes they'd committed; the reason Tommy's backup had never shown up the night he died. The Scorpiones had bought someone all the way at the top.

Jimmy released Hawes, withdrew Donnie's cell from Hawes's pocket, and looked back at Lt. Williams. "Freddy, cuff him and keep him here until I get back. The big man and I are gonna have a word."

Freddy slapped a pair of cuffs on Hawes's wrists. "Take your time, Jimmy. We got all night." Freddy smiled at his suspect. "Don't we, Hawes?"

Jimmy climbed the stairs to the third floor, walked past Internal Affairs and the secretary's office, and stopped in front of the door at the end of the hallway. The black letters on the door's frosted glass window read:

Chief of Police

Edward J. Stonebreaker

Jimmy didn't knock, just opened the door and walked in. The chief, a middle-aged man with a strong build, dark hair, and a graying beard, sat in his chair with his back to Jimmy as he looked out over the city. Jimmy shut the door behind him.

"Did you get it, Robert?" the chief asked. "Just leave it on the desk."

Jimmy dropped the cell phone on the desk, folded his arms, and waited. When the chief didn't hear him leave, he turned around in his seat. "That's all, Robert. You can go— Jimmy?" The chief stared at Jimmy, momentarily speechless, then stumbled over his words. "Jimmy, what brings you up here?"

"I'm afraid Robert Hawes is indisposed at the moment, Chief. Mind telling me why you needed Donnie Cappella's cell phone removed from evidence without it being signed out?"

"That's classified, Jimmy," Stonebreaker said, narrowing his eyes. "An internal matter. You shouldn't concern yourself with it."

Jimmy slammed his hands down on the desk. "Don't give me that. Hawes admitted to being your errand boy. Now tell me what's really going on."

Edward got up from his chair, all fire and brimstone. "You're out of line, Ziminski!"

"How long, Ed? How long have you been on the Scorpione take?"

"That's a wild, unsubstantiated accusation, and one that could get you thrown out of this department."

"All I need is Hawes's written report of all his visits to the Evidence room that coincide with the Scorpione evidence disappearing. And then it's a one-way trip to prison for you."

Stonebreaker gritted his teeth and his body shook with anger. His eyes became wild. "You won't make it through the night, and neither will Hawes. Johnny will make sure of that, and no way will any of it get hung on me."

Jimmy pulled a tape recorder from his pocket and pressed the stop button. "Well, thank you for that." He stuffed the recorder back into his pocket. "Just so you know, Chief, Johnny was found dead in his home tonight. The house of Scorpione has fallen. Hawes will testify against you. And you will be held accountable for your actions."

"I won't go down for this, Jimmy. You're dead!" Stonebreaker reached for something inside his desk drawer, where Jimmy knew the chief kept his personal weapon. Jimmy reached for his own gun and shot Stonebreaker's pistol right out of his hand. Stonebreaker cried out and grasped his hand in pain. Jimmy jumped over the desk and slammed a fist against the chief's jaw, knocking him unconscious. Then he kicked away Stonebreaker's gun.

"That was for Tommy," he spat at the unconscious Stonebreaker. "He died on the cold, hard floor of that warehouse just so you could line your pockets with Scorpione blood money. I hope you like the color orange, Chief—you're gonna be wearing it for a long time."

Chapter Thirty-One

Pat and Joey were watching Rocky train for his big fight with the Russian when Joey felt his cell phone vibrate in his pocket. He hit the answer button and covered his other ear to block out the movie's loud '80s music.

"Yeah, hello? You're who? Okay. Uh-huh. Wait, what was that? I can't even hear you. Hold on a sec." Joey turned to Pat. "I'm gonna step out for a second. I can barely hear what this guy is sayin'."

Pat nodded and went back to watching the action on the big screen while Joey walked out into the theater lobby and sat down on a bench by the wall.

"Sorry about that," Joey said as he glanced across the lobby to the snack bar, suddenly feeling a little hungry. "Now what were you sayin', Officer Tull? No, I'm in Midtown at the ABC Cinema 8. What? My—my dad? He's… Oh, God! All right, I'll be right there."

Joey ended the call and ran back into the theater. He found Pat and shook his arm to get his attention away from the screen. "Pat, we gotta go. It's my dad."

"What? What about him?"

"I'll explain on the way. Come on, we gotta go now!"

Pat jumped up from his seat and ran out of the building with Joey to the parking lot. They hopped into Joey's black Mercedes and burned asphalt as they took off onto West 42nd Street. As they flew down the Lincoln Tunnel toward New Jersey, Pat was becoming more and more uneasy. "Come on, Joey. Talk to me, man! What happened with your dad?"

"They found him tonight in our living room." Joey said, his voice full of pain. "He's—oh, God, he got killed."

Pat was speechless. Then again, what could he say to that? "I'm sorry to hear that" didn't really cut it in a situation like this. Pat sank down in his seat with a long sigh, and said the only thing he could think of. "Oh, man…"

Twenty-five minutes later, they pulled up to the Scorpione estate. A heavy snowfall had begun as soon as they'd cleared the tunnel, and it had already blanketed the New Jersey area with a fresh inch of fluffy white by the time they arrived.

The front gates were wide open. Parked along the driveway leading up to the house were five police cruisers, an ambulance, and a paramedic vehicle. The whole house was lit up like Yankee Stadium. Joey parked the car near the front door. He and Pat got out and dashed through the snow up the stone steps.

To Joey, everything seemed to be going in slow motion. The red and blue flashing lights shining in his eyes made the world around him seem surreal. Countless officers moved to and fro and around them. The toasty warmth once they entered the house did nothing to allay the icy chill of shock clutching at Joey's heart. He knew what he was in for, and there was no way he could ever be ready for it.

The living room was packed with police gathering evidence and taking notes. Joey and Pat were about to go in when an officer stepped forward and gestured for the boys to hold on for a moment. "I'm Officer Tull. Is one of you Joseph Scorpione?"

Joey nodded. "Yeah, that's me."

"Before you go in, son, I'm gonna have to warn you—it's pretty bad. I'd like to ask you some questions first, and Detective Ziminski will be here any minute to go in with you."

Joey frowned darkly. "I'm the son of the man who's lying dead in that room, Officer. The questions can wait." He walked past Tull and into the living room; Tull motioned to the other officers to let them through. Pat followed close behind. Joey's eyes immediately locked on the sheet-covered body in the chair by the fireplace. The flickering light caused shadows to dance on the folds of the white sheet. A deep red had seeped through here and there, creating a horrid contrast.

Several officers were standing around the chair, filling out reports and taking photos of the scene. For some reason, the sight of them around his father made Joey furious. He called out to them in growing anger. "Get away from him. I said get the hell away! Now!"

The officers looked to Tull, and he simply gave them a nod and gestured to them to clear out for a moment. Once they were alone, Joey made his way to the blood stain on the wall. He felt a chill as his eyes traced the long, bright red, speckled line running down the dark maroon wall to the hardwood floor. Then he turned and stared at the white sheet. For a moment, he was paralyzed, yet his mind raced at the possible sight that lay beneath it. Finally, Joey mustered the courage to reach out his shaking hand and grab hold of the fabric. Then, slowly, he pulled the whole sheet away.

There it was: the decapitated body of his father. When Joey had gotten Tull's call at the theater, deep in his heart he hadn't wanted to believe it. *My dad ain't dead. He can't be,* he had kept telling himself. But there it was, right in front of him: the terrible truth removing all doubt. As he looked at his father's severed head lying in his own lap, Joey began to shudder uncontrollably. An icy cold flowed through his body. He lost the strength in his legs and fell to his knees. Clutching the sheet tightly in his hands, he silently lowered his head, pressing it hard to the floor. He felt his face contort. He wanted to scream so badly, but his voice was caught in his throat. He took in a couple of shallow, hoarse breaths, until he could finally get enough air in his lungs to speak again.

"Gonna pay," Joey said quietly.

"Joey?" Pat looked back at him, trying to avoid the sight of Johnny Scorpione's body.

Joey's head came up. The yellow flames in the fireplace reflected deep in his eyes. He raised his head as if to shout to the heavens above. "I swear on my life, the one who did this is gonna pay!" He roared like a wild beast as he dropped down again and beat his heavy fists on the hardwood floor. Finally he stopped and looked at his shaking hands, which were now bruised and bloody at the knuckles. Pat gently laid a hand on his shoulder. Joey took Pat's wrist in one hand and grabbed his shirt with the other. He gave Pat a wild look, like a man possessed, as if he didn't see him at all.

"Joey!" Pat pleaded. "It's me. Relax, man."

Apparently coming back to his senses, Joey released him. "I'm sorry. I'm just… I don't know what came over me. I've never been this angry before."

"It's okay. Don't worry about it." Pat looked toward the hallway outside the door. "Listen, maybe we should let the police do their jobs, huh? They've got a lot of work ahead of them investigating what happened here tonight."

"Investigate? These police couldn't investigate their way out of a paper bag. The family will take care of this."

"Family? What family, Joey? There's no one in your family left."

Joey gave Pat an intense look. "So long as I breathe, the Scorpione family lives on. You got that?"

Fearful of Joey's glare, Pat simply nodded.

"All right." Joey seemed to regain his composure. "Might as well let these bozos finish up here. Thanks for comin' here with me, Pat. You're a true friend."

"Any time, Joey. You need me, I'm there."

Joey gave Pat's shoulder a grateful squeeze. "Listen, why don't you head on home? This could take awhile. With all the questions they're gonna ask me, I'll probably be up all night. Stop by tomorrow after school. We'll talk more then, eh? Again, thanks, buddy."

Pat gave his friend a quick hug and saw tears in his eyes. Knowing there was nothing more he could do, he headed out into the cold, walking down the long Scorpione driveway toward his house across the street.

Jimmy rubbed at his aching shoulder where Den Mother had slammed him against the wall back at the Tombstone. As he entered the Scorpione home, he saw several officers heading back into the living room. Joey was standing by the staircase with a melancholy expression. He stared at

Jimmy from across the room—may as well have been an endless void. Jimmy wasn't willing to say the first word, be it one of condolence or contempt, and it seemed that Joey felt the same way.

In the early afternoon of the following day, Joey sat quietly on the long couch in his family's living room. He hasn't slept since yesterday. Exhaustion pulled at his body, but he didn't feel like sleeping. The shock of last night's incident was still too strong, and he could feel his heart pounding in his chest. The sight of his father's decapitated body burned in his mind like a brand, leaving a mark that would surely haunt him until the end of his days. They had carried Johnny's body away on a stretcher just after midnight. Detective Ziminski had left shortly after, but not before giving Joey his condolences, which seemed hollow at best.

All night long after that, the house was filled with the sounds of stomping police boots, chirping radios, and loud voices. There were also the seemingly endless questions that repeated themselves from one officer to the next:

"Did your father have any enemies?"

"Yeah, plenty. And I'm sure they're all gathered together doing happy dances right now at the local bar."

"Have you noticed anything unusual over the past week or so?"

"You mean besides my grandpa, uncle, and Pops getting killed by a ninja girl? No, not much."

"Have you noticed any suspicious individuals on or around your property?"

"Well, you guys seem pretty suspicious. What with all your clean, pressed uniforms and shiny badges, you gotta be up to no good."

"When was the last time you saw your father?"

"About six hours before his head got chopped off. How's that work for ya, Columbo?"

"Where were you during the time of the murder?"

"I was at a gambling den in Mexico. Where do you think I was, genius? At the ABC Cinema in Midtown, like I told the last couple cops who asked me that."

Now the silence filling the house was deafening. The emptiness echoed in the deepest reaches of Joey's soul, pressing him down, yet ripping him apart at the same time. Joey had never felt so utterly alone. For the first time in his life, he had no one… no one at all.

Since Joey was still a minor, Social Services was supposed to send someone to his house that morning, but they still hadn't arrived. He hoped they would stay away as long as possible. One less headache at this point would be bliss. He let out a deep, hopeless sigh as he laid his head back on the couch. He noticed several cobwebs hanging from the white ceiling tiles above him. Ambient light poured in through the windows from the overcast skies outside. Dark gray clouds added the perfect finishing touch to an already miserable day.

As he rolled his head to the left, he noticed a tiny hidden camera in one upper corner of the room. That was when he remembered: after his grandfather had been killed, Joey's father had had a home surveillance system installed. Hundreds of camera angles covered every square foot of the property. No expense had been spared.

He ran upstairs to his father's room, grabbed the set of keys from his desk drawer, and then hightailed it down to the basement. At the bottom of the musty wooden staircase, he flipped on the light. A white door lay ahead of him; he tried the knob, but it was locked. It was no surprise that the police hadn't noticed the locked room or the cameras, since they had mainly concentrated not only on the crime scene itself, but also the floors, windows, and doors of the main house. Joey recalled one officer going down to the basement and then coming back up two minutes later, saying he noticed nothing unusual.

Joey took out the keys and tried each one in the lock. After five keys, he finally found the right one. He opened the door to see twenty flat-screen monitors covering the wall. To his right were eight digital hard drive recorders connected to each and every camera on the property.

Closing the door behind him, Joey sat down in the swivel chair in front of the main computer screen. He went down the list of cameras on the screen and selected the living room. He typed in the date, and then the time in which the murder was most likely to have occurred. The database prepared the video and readied it on monitor #1. All he had to do was press a button to play the video.

He hesitated at first, certain he would see the moment his father was killed. He took a deep breath and slowly let it out. Then he hit the button and the video started. The picture was in vibrant color and crystal-clear HD. There he was: Joey's father standing by the fire talking on his phone. For a brief moment, Joey thought it was all just a bad dream. His father couldn't be dead. He was alive and well, right there on the screen. A few minutes went by, and all seemed normal. Johnny was pacing back and forth in his usual manner when he was upset.

Then she came into the frame, the masked woman. Joey felt his heart begin to quicken. Words were exchanged, but there was no audio. Joey wasn't a lip reader, so he could only guess at the conversation. Johnny pulled out his gun and fired. There were bright flashes as the bullets ricocheted off her lightning-fast blade. Next came the injury to Johnny's leg, the heavy hit to his head, and the crushed gun.

Then the moment Joey had been waiting for. She slowly reached for her mask. Joey zoomed in and cleared up the image. Once the mask was off, he hit the pause button. He could see her face in great detail. He couldn't believe it. His whole world had just shattered.

"No, it can't be." He shook his head, unbelieving. "It can't be her!" He got up from the chair and stumbled backward into the door. "It was her. All along it was... her."

Chapter Thirty-Two

At Kingsley Academy, Pat was walking down the hallway toward his last class of the day. Usually he caught Stephanie on this walk, and today was no exception. There she was, standing by her locker. Through Pat's eyes, she seemed more beautiful than ever. Since they'd started going out, he'd been on cloud nine; each passing moment, he looked forward to seeing her bright smile again, just one more time.

Today, however, she wasn't smiling. Her eyes were downcast, and she looked grim. Pat laid a gentle hand on her shoulder. "Steph, is everything okay?"

She looked up as if he'd stirred her from a daydream. "Oh, Pat." She nuzzled into his chest, and they embraced tenderly. "I, um… heard about Joey's dad. I'm so sorry."

"Wow, news travels fast. I thought I was the only one who knew so far."

"I haven't seen Joey today. He probably stayed home, didn't he? It's understandable."

"I got a call from my mom. She said Joey asked if he could stay at our house for a couple days. She said it was okay and that he could stay as long as he likes. The police gave him some time to himself in the house today long enough to grab some things so he could stay somewhere while they closed his house for the investigation. Where else did he have to go, you know?"

"That's so nice of her. I'm sure Joey was very grateful."

"Yeah, he's going through a tough time right now. His whole family's gone. Steph, you should've seen him last night. I've never seen him so angry."

"I should stop by your house after I visit Jennifer. He'll definitely need some cheering up."

"Yeah, he's got me worried, you know?" Pat shuddered as the image of the covered body appeared in his mind. "No one should be alone for too long after something like that."

"Okay, I'll catch you there later then?"

They embraced once more as the bell rang.

"I'll miss you," Pat said as they parted.

Stephanie cracked a smile. "I'll miss you more." She blew him a kiss.

At Benton City Police Department, Jimmy leaned back in his chair, contemplating what had happened over the past twenty-four hours. His thoughts kept coming back to his encounter with Den Mother. That warped voice of hers was most likely the result of a voice changer. And she'd whipped him against the wall pretty hard. If her strength didn't come from the serum, he'd like whatever training she'd had. In all his time in the Persian Gulf, he'd never met an enemy that formidable, that unstoppable—that ruthless. How could he take down someone like that?

Then his mind flashed back to Vincent's prized antique. The mirror! If he could find out why she wanted the mirror so badly, maybe that would give him more clues. He picked up his desk phone and dialed Lin. "Hey Lin, it's Jimmy. I need your help."

"When don't you?" she said with a laugh. "All right, lay it on me. Ask and ye shall receive, as they say."

"I need you to do some research on a small antique mirror that belonged to the Scorpiones. It's called 'The Mirror of Princess Mayumi.' I have a picture of it on my phone. Hold on. I'm sending it to you now."

"Got it. This is the mirror? It looks fancy—and ancient. I'll see what I can dig up and get back to you as soon as I can."

"Thanks, Lin. I owe you."

"Your tab's running a little high there, soldier. Pretty soon I'll start asking for collateral."

"How about I leave you my unending gratitude?"

"Well, it's a start."

Jimmy hung up, brought back the photo of the mirror on his phone, and stared at it. *What are your secrets?* He thought as his eyes traced the details of the image. *And why did that demon want you so badly?*

Fifteen minutes after school let out, Pat walked into his house and threw his coat on the hook by the door. He couldn't help but worry about Stephanie's odd mood. It was understandable she'd be sad at the news of Joey's situation, but the look on her face was beyond that. It was like something had happened to her personally.

Then Pat's mind came back to the here and now. As he passed his mother, she told him Joey was in the guest room upstairs.

Within moments, he was standing outside the closed guestroom door. He stared at the door, wondering how he could possibly console his friend during this terrible ordeal, suffering three losses in such a short time. Pat couldn't even imagine what Joey was going through. Finally, he reached out and gave a few short knocks. A long moment passed before Joey opened the door. He stood tall, his hair slicked back, clean shaven, and wearing one of his father's three-piece suits, which fit him surprisingly well. His expression wasn't one of anger or sadness. He seemed oddly well adjusted, given his current family situation.

"Hey, Joey," Pat said. "I see you're sporting some of your dad's wardrobe, huh? Looking sharp, man."

"Thanks." Joey brushed a bit of lint from his shoulder. "Yeah, it fits good, eh? Come on in."

The walk into the large decadent room was awkward and silent. As he sat down on the couch by the window, Pat could still picture Johnny's body sitting motionless in that chair by the fireplace. "If you ask me," Pat said, unable to relax, "I'm not sure I could live there after what's happened. Feels kind of like the place is haunted, you know?"

"Nope." Joey sank into the recliner seat across from him. "That place is my family's home. No way I'm givin' it up. I spoke to the family lawyers about an hour ago. Dad had a lot of money. Some was stashed away for a rainy day, and the rest he inherited from Grandpa. With that money, I could live there indefinitely. You see, the whole house was paid off years ago by my grandpa. All I gotta worry about is property taxes, maintenance, and utilities. Once I get that cash in hand, I can cover those expenses for the next ten years at least."

"That sounds cool and all, but aren't you afraid?"

"Afraid of what?"

"Afraid of what?" Pat stood up. "Joey, they killed your whole family. What makes you think they're going to stop? You've got to get out of town."

"I ain't afraid of no one." Joey stood too and got in Pat's face. "I'll go after them first."

"What are you talking about? Do you know something I don't?"

Joey walked over to the window and looked outside over Pat's back courtyard as he straightened his suit. "The less you know, the better. I got a plan. Let's leave it at that."

This new side of Joey completely boggled Pat. A long silence passed before he spoke again. "Well, if you aren't planning to tell me anything, all I can say is, let me know if you need me, man. You know I'm there for you."

"Thanks." Joey turned with a sincere expression. "You've never let me down. You know if I need you, I'll call you. You can count on that."

Pat felt the air grow even more uncomfortable. He had to get out as soon as possible. "I'd better get going. I got homework to finish up. I'll just be in my room down the hall."

Pat was stopped by Joey's voice. "Hey, Pat? How's Stephanie doing? Have you seen her today?"

"She was looking a little down earlier after she heard about what happened to your dad, but I think she's okay. She was actually hoping to stop over here later, after she sees Jennifer."

"I guess I'll see her then." Joey turned back toward the window and muttered something to himself, something barely audible.

"What was that, Joey?"

"It's nothin'." Joey continued to look out the window. "I'll see you later, eh?"

A moment later, as Pat entered his room, he couldn't help but feel a chill run through him. What was up with Joey? Pat knew his dad's death would affect him, but not like this. It gave him the creeps.

Joey stood staring out the window. A smile ran across his face as he pressed his hand to the cold glass. "I know who you are, assassin," he said out loud. He squeezed his fist. Vengeance was now surely within his grasp. All he needed was a means to exact it. What could he use?

Then it occurred to him: his father had been able to retrieve his uncle's gun from the police. He kept it in a lockbox under his bed upstairs in their house, the key to which was in Joey's pocket.

Joey ran out of the room, down the stairs, and briefly told Pat's mother that he was stepping out to get some fresh air and would be back soon.

Avoiding the several investigators gathered out in front of his house apparently taking a break, Joey walked around behind his property and snuck in through a small gate at the edge of the back courtyard.

Tearing away the police tape from his back door, he peeked his head inside. The coast was clear. He carefully glanced out the front window and saw the investigation team still there, smoking cigarettes and talking about the basketball game from the night before.

Joey hopped up the stairs, entered his father's room and reached under the bed. He pulled out the metal box. It took him a few seconds to find the right key, and he got it open. There it was: his uncle's M1911 Colt semi-automatic. The shining instrument of revenge was exactly what he needed right now.

He took the gun in hand and grabbed the loaded magazine that went with it. Carefully, he pushed the magazine into the stock until it clicked. Then he pulled back on the slide and let it snap back, charging the barrel. With both hands, Joey raised the gun and looked down the sights as a dark grin stretched across his face.

"You're mine."

Jennifer sat quietly in her room at the institute. Because she'd been responding so well to the new medication, they had allowed her several comforts, such as the book she was currently reading. The title read, *To Cherish Forever.* It was the final book in The Young and the Hopeful series.

A contented smile crossed her face as she turned the page. She couldn't wait to see what would happen next. Then suddenly she dropped the book in her lap. A terrible pain ran through her head. The black feathers returned and swirled around her.

"No, not now!" She grabbed her head. "I'm cured. I'm cured." But her words made no difference. A vivid vision came to her, clearer than ever before. As her mind's eye watched the events yet to unfold, she shook her head as if to deny them. She didn't want to see these things anymore. Then her eyes widened when she saw two familiar faces.

"Wait. Stephie? And him? What is he...? Oh, no! Don't trust him, Stephie—don't trust him!"

Stephanie left gymnastics practice and made her way to the Institute. She straightened the duffle bag strap over her shoulder, grateful it wasn't any heavier. Inside the bag were her gymnastics clothes and the first book in a new teen reading series called Blue Horizon. She figured Jennifer might enjoy it.

As she walked along, an eerie feeling came over her—a strong sense that she was being followed. Stephanie stopped and looked back for a moment. There was no one there, just an empty street. She continued walking, but the feeling refused to go away. She looked back again. Still, there was no one.

Fear and anxiety started to take hold of her, and she sped up her pace, hoping to quickly reach the main road. There would be plenty of people around once she got there.

A hand touched her shoulder, and she screamed.

"Whoa, whoa!" she heard a familiar voice say.

She turned. "Joey!" she yelled disapprovingly when she recognized his smiling mug. She slapped him on the arm. "Don't do that—you scared me half to death."

"Sorry, I didn't mean to make you jump."

Stephanie took a deep breath to calm down. "It's okay. Just don't do that again, all right?"

"No problem. I'll make sure you know it's me next time. Anyway, I thought I'd join you on your way to see Jenny."

"Oh, okay. I was planning on seeing you later anyway, and I'm sure Jenny will be happy to see you."

As they started walking together, Stephanie noticed his new attire. "So tell me, what's with the suit?"

"Oh, you like it? It belonged to my dad."

"I'm really sorry about what happened to him." She took out her cell phone to check the time. "My heart goes out to you. If there's anything you need…" She looked around, but it seemed Joey had disappeared. "Joey? Where did you go?"

In the next instant she felt a rag being pressed hard over her nose and mouth. A strong, sweet smell came from the thick cloth that blocked her airways, making her dizzy. At the same time a powerful arm held her body tight. She tried to struggle, but she just wasn't strong enough, and she was getting weaker by the second. The cell phone slipped from her hand and hit the sidewalk at her feet. Her body went limp, and her vision blurred.

Patrick! She called out desperately in her mind before she finally fell into the dark abyss of unconsciousness.

Pat sat at the desk in his room, in the middle of his math homework. For some reason, he thought of Stephanie and a feeling of worry came over him. He dialed her cell phone; his call went right to voicemail, which meant she either had the phone turned off or was in a bad area for cell phone reception. He called again and got the same result.

She should be visiting her sister right now, and after that, his house. She always kept her phone on in case of emergency, and she always kept it charged. He dialed her number one more time and got voicemail again. Something wasn't right. Maybe if he tried her house phone…

He dialed and got her mother.

"Patrick, it's good to hear from you," she said. "Is everything okay?"

"I hope so. I haven't been able to reach Stephanie at all. My calls keep going right to voicemail."

"That's strange. She never turns her phone off."

"Yeah, tell me about it."

"Have you tried the institute yet? That's where she should be right now."

"I'm going to try them next."

He heard her let out a nervous sigh. "Now you've got me worried, Patrick. As soon as you reach her, have her call me right away, okay?"

"You got it, Mrs. Sebastiano."

Pat ran a search on his phone for the Borgestedt Institute and quickly found the number. His foot tapped impatiently as he dialed it and listened to it ring. Finally someone picked up and told him that Stephanie hadn't shown up for her usual visit with Jennifer. Pat hung up, a feeling of fear seeping into him along with a sense of urgency. He just had to get out there and find her.

He grabbed his coat and the keys to his mom's Cadillac CTS Coupe and took off.

First he went to Stephanie's gymnastics building downtown. By the time he got there, it was already getting dark outside. He talked with several people he encountered in the building, and all of them said Stephanie had left right after practice ended. Pat tried to think rationally for a moment. He knew that Stephanie was a creature of habit. Every day her routine was like clockwork: school, gymnastics, and the institute. If she'd never made it to the institute, something must have happened somewhere in between.

He decided to trace her steps, see if he could find something.

He followed the route she usually took to the institute. As he drove slowly down the dark street leading to the main road, he saw something small ahead of him on the sidewalk, reflecting his headlights. Pat stopped and got out. He felt a tug in his heart when he saw it was Stephanie's cell phone. He picked it up and looked at it. The phone was badly damaged, as if someone had stomped on it several times. He couldn't even get it to turn on.

All right, he had her phone. Now where the heck was she?

He looked around and noticed what appeared to be fresh tire tracks in the snow ahead of him, leading from an alley out to the street. From what he could tell, the car had turned and gone east, away from the institute. He tried to imagine the scenario. Stephanie had been walking down this sidewalk, someone had threatened her, grabbed her, and she had dropped her cell phone, maybe while trying to make a call for help. They had stashed her in a car and driven east.

But something didn't seem right. Stephanie was in great physical shape. She might not be a fighter, but she could outrun almost anyone. If there was one thug or even five of them threatening her, she would still have run as fast as she could to safety. So why didn't she? Then something occurred to him.

She wouldn't run if it was someone she knew. That was the only way they could get close enough to grab her. He had to find out who had done this, why, and where they had taken her. He decided to head to Stephanie's house and update her mother on what he'd found so far.

Within minutes, he was at the Sebastiano home, telling an already shaken Linda that her daughter may have been kidnapped. Linda immediately called Jimmy's cell phone. While she spoke with him, Pat asked if he could use the bathroom. Linda pointed down the hallway to his right.

Pat went in and washed his face. He took a moment to look in the mirror. His worried expression reflecting back at him only made him feel worse. All sorts of terrible scenarios regarding Stephanie's possible fate ran through his head. *No,* he thought abruptly, *I have to think positive. I can't give up hope!*

As he walked back down the hallway from the bathroom, he noticed what must have been Stephanie's room on the left. The door was wide open. From where he stood he was able to see a crumpled-up newspaper on the floor, and it piqued his curiosity. He felt uneasy about entering her room, as if he were invading her privacy—which he was to an extent—so he quickly grabbed the paper and returned to the hallway. Opening it up, he saw that it was dated one year ago. He remembered the headline, as he'd read it before. It was about Stephanie's father being found dead in the warehouse.

Then a thought occurred to Pat: the warehouse district was in the direction the tire tracks had pointed to. But who would take her there? And why?

Then for some reason, Pat remembered his conversation with Joey and how odd he'd been acting, given the circumstances. Joey had wanted revenge on the assassin. He swore he'd find her. But today he had seemed right as rain, as if he were relieved. Pat recalled his and Joey's conversation in greater detail. After Joey had asked about Stephanie, he'd said he was looking forward to her visit. Then he'd muttered something Pat could barely hear. He saw Joey's lips move, but what did his friend actually say?

Pat thought about it long and hard—then it clicked in his mind. What Joey had said sounded like, *Looking forward to killing that ninja witch.* With this realization, everything fell into place. For some reason Joey must have had it in his head that Stephanie was the assassin.

Pat was pretty sure the Scorpiones owned an old warehouse on the docks. He guessed that Joey had left his house, met up with Stephanie, somehow kidnapped her, and taken her to the warehouse, which was in the direction the tire tracks pointed. It all made sense. Pat called his house, and his mother confirmed Joey had left earlier. He also got an ear full about taking the car without permission. Regardless, he'll surely deal with that later. Right now he had no time to lose.

He ran to the front door, past Linda, who was still on the phone.

"Pat?" Linda called out as she turned away from the phone. "Where are you going?"

"I think I got something, but I need to check it out first. I'll call you if I find anything."

"Patrick, wait!" Linda stopped him at the door. "I'm talking to Jimmy Ziminski. He has officers out looking for her now. If there's something you can tell us that could help, now's the time."

"I don't know, Mrs. Sebastiano. It's just a hunch."

"You call me if you find anything, do you understand?"

"Yes, ma'am," Pat reassured her.

He jumped into his car and left. He'd lied, but he had no choice. His best friend and the love of his life were in trouble. He didn't want to see Joey get arrested over something like this, not if he could talk him out of it first. And if the police did get involved, who was to say that Joey wouldn't use Stephanie as a human shield.

Pat knew Joey wasn't himself right now. Blinded by feelings of rage and vengeance, he wasn't thinking clearly. And Pat might be the only one who could reach him before it was too late—for Joey and for Stephanie.

Chapter Thirty-Three

At the Scorpione warehouse, a black Mercedes S-Class sedan was parked just outside the main door with its trunk open. The night sky was completely clear and the air bitter cold.

Inside the warehouse, it was dark. The air was thick, musty. Several industrial fan heaters hanging from the rafters kicked on now and again to maintain a hospitable temperature. Most of the concrete floor was wet with puddles from the leaky, snow-covered roof. In the middle of the room, one overhead light was on. Below it sat an unconscious Stephanie in an old wooden chair, her wrists and ankles bound to the arms and legs of the chair, her mouth gagged with a rag knotted behind her neck.

Slowly but steadily, she awoke. Her head was pounding and her hands and feet ached. She opened her eyes, but everything was a dark blur. She could hear footsteps, but she couldn't tell where they were coming from. Then someone said her name.

"Oh, Stephanie! Wakey wakey, Stephanie."

She turned her head and saw the shape of someone behind her, but her vision was still blurry. It was the voice of a boy or a young man, and it was a familiar one—but whose? Her mind was so foggy. She just couldn't figure it out.

"Wake up, ninja girl!" Stephanie felt a hard slap to the back of her head. She let out a muffled scream of pain. It was a rude awakening. The sudden adrenaline rush from the hit served to kick-start her brain, and she realized who it was.

"Joey!" she yelled, her voice muffled by the gag. As her vision cleared, she saw Joey's face in front of her. He untied the gag and removed it. She loosened the cramp in her jaw, and then raised her voice. "Joey, why are you doing this?"

"Oh, you know why." Joey grabbed her by the chin. "You know exactly why, ninja girl."

Stephanie jerked her chin away from his hand. "Why do you keep calling me that? Let me go!"

Joey just grinned and shook his head.

Stephanie looked around and shuddered as she realized where she was. It was the warehouse of her visions—the place where her father had died. There were still bullet holes in the old wooden crates to her right and left. She looked down. There at her feet was a dark stain in the shape of a puddle. Could this be the exact place where Tommy Sebastiano had drawn his last breath?

With much effort, Stephanie quieted her emotions enough to speak calmly to Joey. "Listen, I don't know what this is about, but if you untie me, we can talk about it. You can tell me what's wrong, Joey."

Joey pulled out his uncle's M1911 Colt. The gun was loaded and the barrel charged. All he had to do was pull the trigger. Stephanie fixed her eyes on it, and a chilling fear gripped her. She wondered what had happened to the Joey she knew, that cheerful, charming jock with the great sense of humor who would do anything for her. Who was this raving madman who had taken his place?

She chose her words carefully. "Please talk to me, Joey. Why did you tie me up?"

Joey pointed the gun at her. "You know what you did."

"I have no idea what you're talking about."

"Stop lying!" Joey's voice echoed through the warehouse and rang in Stephanie's ears. "You murdered my father." Joey pressed the gun barrel to her forehead. "It was you, Stephanie; I saw you."

"Joey, please, you have to believe me—"

Her words were cut short when Joey pistol-whipped her in the face. The sharp pain was so intense, tears fell from her eyes. A few drops of blood ran down her lower lip.

"Please, Joey, stop!" she cried. "I didn't do it. I didn't kill him. You're hurting me, it hurts so much. Please stop!"

"Stop the crocodile tears, Stephanie." He stood before her with his hands on his hips, the gun stuck in his belt. "You're supposed to be a cold-blooded killer, remember? I know what this is all about, too. It's about those rumors that went around when your dad died. You wanted revenge because you think my family killed him, right? Well, my family didn't do it, damn it!"

Stephanie was afraid to look up at him for fear she might get hit again, so she simply hung her head and took a deep breath before speaking again. "Joey, look down at the floor."

He followed her gaze. "It's an old oil stain, probably from a forklift. So what?"

"Not oil," Stephanie said sadly, "but blood. This is the spot where my father died. Your father is the one who did it, and he used a revolver. When it was over, they took my dad's body and moved it to another warehouse so they wouldn't be implicated."

"My father didn't kill nobody! And how did you know he owned a revolver?" He lifted her head up by her hair. "Listen to me: he might've been a ruthless businessman, but he wasn't no murderer."

"How can you be so naïve?" Stephanie looked into his eyes with warm sympathy. "All these years, you must have suspected something wasn't right with your family. Why did they have so many guns if they didn't use them? Think about it. Ever notice how troublesome people seem to disappear around the Scorpiones? How about all the money your family has. Do you honestly think all that cash came from a simple distribution company?"

Joey hesitated. "The guns are just for protection, you know? And we've just been really lucky over the years in our business. That's why we're so rich." Then doubt seemed to creep over his face. "My family ain't killers… they can't be."

"Joey, I'm so sorry, but your father killed my father right here on this spot. You're standing on his blood stain."

Joey looked skeptical, as if he was considering whether what she was saying could be true. Then his resolve seemed to return, and he pressed the gun to her head again.

"You almost had me there, witch. The only killer here is you, and I will make this right." Joey started to pace back and forth. "My Pops and Grandpa—I've been searching for their killer. All the while, she's been right there in front of me, day after day." He stopped and took her by the chin again. "Now I have her and I got the video footage to prove it."

"Footage? What footage?"

"Didn't think someone was recording, huh? You took your mask off, and I saw your face. You're guilty, Stephanie—a villain! And I'm the good guy, here to take you out." He stepped back and took aim, his finger slowly squeezing the trigger. Stephanie closed her eyes, shedding silent tears.

Then there were footsteps, coming from the darkness behind Joey. He turned and pointed the gun in that direction. "Who's there? Come out here, right now."

Pat stepped slowly into the light, his hands raised in a peaceful gesture. "It's okay, Joey. It's only me."

"Pat!" Joey let his breath out in a sigh. "Am I glad to see you. I found her, man." He moved back and grabbed Stephanie by the shoulder. She flinched with fear. "Your sweet Stephanie is the assassin."

Stephanie was sure Pat could see the terror in her eyes as she looked at him for help.

"Is anybody with you, Pat?" Joey turned away for a second to look for others. Pat took this opportunity to show Stephanie a tiny smile, as if to tell her that everything would be all right.

"No," Pat told him, "I'm alone."

"Good." Joey turned his attention back to Stephanie. "I gotta tell ya, man, I was shocked when I discovered the truth. My father set up cameras all over our property after Grandpa died. And guess what the camera in the living room recorded last night?" Joey grabbed Stephanie by the hair and ran the barrel of the gun along her cheek, making her cry out in fear. "This girl right here, in HD and full color. She never looked better. Isn't that right, Stephanie?"

Stephanie shook uncontrollably in Joey's grip. She was too frightened to speak.

Pat was horrified by what he saw, but no matter what, Joey had to think they were on the same side. He had to talk Joey down somehow. "Joey, wait," he said, inching his way closer to Stephanie and Joey. "Even if she did kill those people—"

"She did kill them." Joey insisted.

"Okay." Pat paused, carefully considering his words. "Be that as it may, is it really right to shoot her? That would make you a killer yourself."

"You make it sound like it's wrong, but it ain't." Joey shot him an intense glare. "This is Scorpione justice."

"Joey, please. We can stop this right now." Pat edged closer, but he was still at least a dozen steps away. "Nobody has to know about this. We can all walk away from it. Just put down the gun."

"Just put down the gun, huh?" Joey repeated in a tone of suspicion. "You're in love with her, aren't you? You just want me to let her go so you two can live happily ever after. Well, what about me? What do I have to look forward to? I have nothing. Nothing!" Joey pressed the gun to her temple. "She took everything from me."

"Damn it, Joey!" Pat said, struggling not to lose it. "Stop pointing that gun at her."

Joey just smiled defiantly. "This ends now. And I don't care how you feel about her. This witch is finally gonna pay for what she's done."

Joey took a step back and aimed at Stephanie's heart. Pat thought he heard thunder outside, but he wasn't concerned about that right now. Now was the time for action. He dashed toward them just as Joey began to pull the trigger, but before he could reach them, a blur rushed past him, faster than anything he'd ever seen.

Joey fired one shot, and the loud bang echoed from one end of the building to the other. Joey's eyes widened in disbelief; beads of sweat formed on his brow. There, standing between him and Stephanie, was the fox-faced assassin. The bullet had bounced right off her body armor, leaving a dusty mark on the impenetrable surface over her abdomen. The black armor was sleek, shaped to her physique, protecting her arms, legs, and torso, and embossed with several Japanese symbols.

Fox drew her katana sword and raised it to Joey's throat; at the same time, he trained his gun at her heart.

"How—how is this possible?" Joey stuttered.

"You stay away from Stephie," Fox's warped voice said.

"Stephie?" Pat repeated. "Wait a minute—Jenny, is that you?"

Fox removed her mask and dropped it to the floor. Indeed, it was Jenny. Fire flared in her eyes as she stared at Joey with murderous intent.

"Jennifer!" Stephanie yelled. "Get out of here—he'll kill you."

"Relax, sis," Jenny reassured her. "I got this."

"It was you, Jenny?" Joey said. "You did it? But how?"

"I'll tell you, Joey." Jenny narrowed her eyes at him, never moving the edge of her blade from his Adam's apple. "The night before my father was killed, I had a dream. I saw your father, Johnny Scorpione kill my father, Thomas Sebastiano, with a .45 caliber revolver. Imagine the horror I felt when I realized the dream had come true. I was so angry. I wanted revenge, but it was just out of my reach. That's when Den Mother found me. She gave me the means to do it. Do you understand now, Joey? *I* killed your father."

Joey now realized his mistake. The camera footage had recorded the assassin from her right side. Jennifer's scar was on the left side of her neck, out of the camera's view. "Oh, God," he said, "I'm so sorry, Stephanie—I thought it was you."

"It's okay, Joey," Stephanie said. "Both of you please put your weapons down and stop all of this."

Joey lowered his gun slightly when he saw the pleading in Stephanie's eyes. Then he looked at Jennifer's eyes, which were filled with dark hate, and he was reminded of his need for vengeance. "I'm sorry, Stephanie." Joey aimed his gun at Jennifer once more. "I can't forgive her for what she's done."

Jennifer gave a derisive laugh. "You can try to kill me, Joey. But I bet I can kill you first, you filthy mob scum." She moved at lightning speed, appearing and disappearing here and there all around Joey. "Catch me if you can, hotshot," she said playfully as she moved from one random place to the next. She appeared in front of him. "Am I here?" Then to his left. "Or here?" And right behind him, she whispered into his ear. "Or here?"

Joey quickly turned, firing three shots, but all he hit was air. Then she appeared at the foot of a metal staircase leading up to a catwalk, beckoning him to follow her. Angered, Joey gave chase.

While Joey was distracted with Jennifer, Pat untied Stephanie and dialed 9-1-1. He gave the dispatcher a quick rundown as to what had happened and where they were. Then, with his phone still on the call, Pat helped Stephanie out of the chair. She was weak and shaky on her feet, so Pat wrapped her arm behind his neck and aided her as she walked. The exit was still far away, and they moved as quietly as possible to avoid catching Joey's attention.

Behind them, the warehouse echoed with Jennifer's taunting laughter and the sound of gunshots as Joey fired at every shadow and trick of the light. Then the magazine ran empty.

"Look, gangster boy!" Jennifer mocked him. "You're out of bullets, hahaha!"

"Shut up, damn you!" Joey yelled as he switched to a full magazine. "Stop being a coward and face me."

"Coward?" Jennifer's voice was full of anger. "I'll show you a coward when I have you running for dear life." Then she appeared on the ground floor below him, taunting him. "Here I am. Come get me, pretty boy."

Joey dashed to his right and stormed down to the steps. Once he hit the main floor, he started shooting round after round at Jennifer. Her blade deflected every shot, and she laughed after each one. But then Jennifer heard her sister scream in pain, and she instantly understood what had happened. She dashed to her sister's side near the exit, pushing Pat out of the way.

Stephanie was on the floor where Pat had gently laid her, bleeding from a bullet wound. One of Joey's rounds had ricocheted off Jennifer's sword and struck her sister. Jennifer dropped her sword and took Stephanie in her arms. "Stephie, are you okay?"

Stephanie couldn't speak; she cried out in pain at Jennifer's touch. Under the light of the exit sign, Jennifer could see that the bullet had gone cleanly through her back and out her stomach on her right side. The blood pouring out was almost black, and there was so much of it. She had to do something fast to staunch it.

"Pat, give me your jacket now!"

Pat removed his jacket, and Jennifer pressed it to Stephanie's stomach. "You're not dying, Stephie." Jennifer's voice shook with fear. "Just hang on."

Pat pulled out his phone; the 911 dispatcher had heard nearly everything and already had an ambulance on the way. Then Pat knelt beside Stephanie too as the dispatcher walked him through emergency procedures. Pat took over for Jennifer by keeping pressure on the wound.

Joey kept his gun raised. He wanted to kill Jennifer while she was distracted, but didn't want to shoot Stephanie by mistake. The two being so close together, he just couldn't risk the shot.

As Stephanie began to lose consciousness, she reached up and gently touched her sister's shoulder. "Please, Jenny," she said, her voice growing weaker, "don't fight anymore. It always scares me when you fight. Please... no more." Stephanie's eyes closed, and she went quiet.

"Stephie?" Jennifer shook her sister. "Stephie, wake up!"

But Stephanie didn't respond. Jennifer held her close as tears fell down her cheeks. Then she looked up and saw Joey standing there.

"You…" The darkness returned to her voice as she felt hatred flow through her once more. "You did this!" Jennifer grabbed her sword, and Joey leveled his weapon at her as they locked eyes in a deadly stare-down. She stood up slowly and started walking toward Joey, her sword gripped tightly in her hands. Jennifer bent her knees and stepped carefully, like a predator closing in on its prey.

"Don't move, you crazy witch," Joey warned her. "I'll put you down—I swear I will."

"I'll kill you!" Jennifer screamed the words with such power that Joey could actually feel the sound waves hit his body. She aimed her sword at his heart as she moved closer.

"Don't do it, Jenny!" Joey yelled. "I'll shoot!"

"You killed Stephie," she snarled, "and when I'm done with you, there'll be nothing left but chopped bones and bloody entrails."

"Your sword deflected that bullet," Joey argued, taking a step back as she advanced on him. "So *you* killed her."

"You fired it," Jennifer shot back.

"All right, you want a piece of me?" Joey beckoned. "Come on!"

Jennifer let out a battle cry as she barreled toward him with her sword. Joey fired off as many shots as he could, but each one bounced off her armor. A tremendous force hit him, and he felt something cold run through him. He looked down and saw her blade in his chest, all the way up to the guard.

"You… you got me," Joey said weakly, coughing up blood.

"It's over, Joey," Jennifer said quietly in his ear.

Joey gave out a feeble laugh as he struggled to stay on his feet for a few more seconds. That's all he needed.

"What's so funny?" Jennifer asked calmly.

"I found… a weak spot." He pressed the barrel of his gun to a soft area under her left arm and fired one shot. Jennifer gasped for breath as the bullet ripped through her.

The two leaned into each other as death drew closer.

With as much breath as he could muster, Joey whispered in her ear, "You know what the messed up part is? When you and I shared that moment in the hallway… I think it was love."

"Yeah…" Jennifer smiled. "It was for me too."

No longer able to stand, the two fell to their knees in an awkward embrace.

Pat performed CPR under the instruction of the dispatcher. He was so afraid that if he became too exhausted and could no longer carry on the chest compressions and rescue breaths before help arrived, she'd be gone forever. He prayed hard from the deepest part of his soul that she'd live. He begged God to grant him just this one request.

Sirens sounded outside. He looked up at the windows and saw red and blue flashing lights. The exit door to his right flew open, and several police officers came in, their weapons ready.

"Here!" Pat yelled desperately. "We're right here!"

Seeing Pat and Stephanie on the floor, the police immediately waved in the paramedics. Two paramedics rushed over to Pat and Stephanie, while two more ran over to Jennifer and Joey. One officer found a switch box and flipped on all the lights, illuminating the warehouse like it was the middle of the day.

Pat was shaking as he grabbed the paramedic's arm. "I'm begging you—please save her!"

"We'll do everything we can," one of them assured him.

Pat felt a hand on his shoulder and looked up. It was Jimmy, a horrified expression on his face as he looked between Stephanie and Jennifer. "Come on, Pat," Jimmy said. "How about we let them do their jobs." He led Pat over to the far wall, away from the controlled chaos of the paramedics.

"All right, Pat," Jimmy said, "let's start from the top, huh? I want you to tell me everything that happened here, okay?"

"It… it was… I don't know." Pat choked over his words. "I'm trying to figure out where to start, but all I keep seeing is Stephanie falling to the floor and all the blood. Oh God, I just want her to be all right."

"It's okay. They're doing everything they can for all three of them."

One of the EMTs suddenly called out, "I got a pulse here!"

Chapter Thirty-Four

Stephanie found herself walking down a long, dark tunnel. She was wearing a long dress as white as freshly fallen snow. The bricks of the tunnel walls shimmered like copper and bronze in the dim light. The path beneath her feet was yellow cobblestone. The air smelled of wildflowers and sunny meadows, giving her a sense of comfort.

Ahead of her she saw a light, and from beyond the light she could hear the sounds of a melody more beautiful than anything she'd ever heard. There was even a festive feeling surrounding her. As she got closer, she could feel the pleasant warmth of the light on her skin.

Stephanie quickened her pace, wanting to get closer to this phenomenon. Then she was able to make out a figure in the light. As she got closer, she was able to see the figure clearly. It was a man, but not just any man. It was her father. He smiled at her with open arms, and she ran into his embrace.

"Dad!" She squeezed him tight. "Oh, Dad, I've missed you so much."

Thomas Sebastiano gently kissed the top of her head. "I've missed you too, sweetie. You've done so well since I've been gone. You've helped your mother and your sister, got good grades. And you've grown as a person, opening up to those around you, and learning to express yourself more. You've accomplished so much, and I'm proud of you."

"I'm so glad to see you again," Stephanie cried. "I just want to be here with you forever."

"I know." Her father released her and took a step back. "But you still have so much more to accomplish."

Stephanie looked up at him questioningly. "Can't I stay here with you?"

"I'm sorry, sweetie—it's not your time yet. You have to go back."

"No, I want to stay here," Stephanie said longingly. "Please, just a little longer?" She reached for him, but she felt a powerful force pulling her away, and they began to separate.

"I love you, Stephanie." Thomas gave her a bright, loving smile. "I will always be with you. Take care of yourself, and look after your mother."

"What about Jenny?" Stephanie called out as the distance between them grew. "Is she all right?"

Her father's pleasant smile changed to sadness. Then he turned and started walking back into the light.

Stephanie raised her voice and yelled as loud as she could. "No, wait!" The force increased a thousandfold, and she was rushed away at incredible speed. "What about Jenny?"

It was dark again, and complete silence surrounded her. Then she heard beeping sounds behind her. They were very faint at first, and muffled, as if she were underwater. As she moved in their direction, the sounds became clearer, and the closer she got, the louder they became. Stephanie opened her eyes. Everything was bright and blurry for a few moments until she was able to focus on her surroundings. She finally zeroed in on the beeping sound, which was coming from a heart monitor beside her.

She looked around at the white room and realized she was lying in a hospital bed. Outside it was daytime, sunny. As her eyes took in the snow sparkling in the light, she became aware of an aching pain in the center of her body. She ran her hand along her stomach and felt bandages and an ice pack there.

Her attention was drawn to a TV mounted to the wall at the other end of the room. A local news station was on, and the reporter was commenting on the events of the night before. "There is still no word as to what caused last night's sonic boom heard from downtown Benton all the way to the docks. Countless windows were shattered, and hundreds of car alarms were set off throughout the city. Still, no one has been able to shed any light on the mysterious incident. We contacted Bolling Air Force Base in Washington, D.C., but they deny flying any aircraft in the local area during that time. Several reports of a dark blur moving down the city streets at high speed are as yet unconfirmed."

Then the door to her room opened. She looked over, and the person she saw brought a smile to her face. "Patrick!"

The source of her happiness matched her smile as he laid a bouquet of flowers on the table next to her. He sat down in the chair beside the bed, took her hand, and held it gently in his. "Hi there, beautiful." He looked in her eyes as his smile deepened. "You gave us all quite a scare there. Your poor mom has worn a track in the floor with all the pacing she's done."

"Sorry to worry everyone." She gave his hand a squeeze. "What happened?"

"Well, you took a bullet in the abdomen, which went through your liver. You were lucky, though—if the paramedics had arrived five minutes later, it would have been too late. Your heart actually stopped on the way to the hospital. Thank God they were able to revive you. What makes you even luckier is, if the bullet had been two inches to the left, it would've severed your spinal cord. Two hours of surgery, a blood transfusion, sixteen hours of unconsciousness, and here you are."

She laid an affectionate hand on his cheek. "You must be my good luck charm then." A tear formed in her eye. "Patrick, thank you so much for finding me. If you hadn't been there, I don't know what would have happened. You untied me and tried to help me out of there. That was brave. Plus you called the ambulance that saved my life."

Pat reached out and caressed the soft skin of her cheek with his fingers. "I would've turned this whole world upside down to find you. After all, I need you and… I love you, Stephanie."

Stephanie had never felt so much happiness at the sound of three simple words. Tears of joy ran down her cheeks. Pat leaned down, and the two met in a long-awaited kiss. After what seemed an eternity of bliss, they slowly parted and gazed into each other's eyes. Then she remembered, and a feeling of horror came over her.

"What's wrong?" Pat asked, looking deep into her eyes.

"Where's my sister?"

Pat's expression saddened, and he fell silent.

"Is she here in this hospital? Please tell me."

"Stephanie…" Pat couldn't seem to find the words. Then he took a deep breath and plunged in. "I'm so sorry, but Jenny and Joey both died. They—they killed each other."

His words shocked Stephanie. There was a cold aching in her heart, as if the bullet had passed through it instead. She could no longer contain her overwhelming sorrow. Pat held her close, and she finally broke down and sobbed. She buried her face in his shoulder, shedding her tears into the fabric of his coat. Stephanie called out her twin's name, begging God to bring Jenny back. Pat just held her close and told her it was going to be okay.

Without her sister, Stephanie felt like half a person—incomplete. There had been a deep connection between her and Jennifer, a connection only identical twins share. Now, with that connection severed, there was only a frigid emptiness inside her soul. But somehow, with Pat here, she didn't feel so alone. She felt another kind of connection with him; maybe not like the one she had shared with her sister, but one of romantic love, trust, and warmth, feelings she'd never experienced before she'd become involved with him.

In realizing that, she knew everything was going to be all right.

Jimmy sat silently in his office, facing the window, as the warm light of sunset hit his face. He was staring at the unopened manila folder on his desk. Inside were the coroner's autopsy reports for Jennifer and Joey. Their bodies were currently resting on cold slabs just a few floors below him.

This pain inside him—it felt as if he'd lost his own daughter. He'd known Jennifer and her twin sister since the day they were born. Soon after they'd learned to speak, they'd started calling him Uncle Jimmy. And from that moment on, his role in their lives had been solidified. Jimmy was and would always be their family, and that made these feelings of loss and grief all the more unbearable.

He took a deep breath, opened the folder, and began to read the report on Jennifer. Lab tests confirmed the presence of serum in her blood. Hairline bone fractures and microscopic muscle tears were also present. These things, along with the suit, the mask she wore, and the weapon she used, all pointed to one thing: she was Den Mother's final assassin, her ace in the hole.

It chilled Jimmy to think that Den Mother's influence could reach even a young mental patient whose only dream was to return to a normal life. And Den Mother had twisted that dream to manipulate Jennifer into doing her bidding. Just like Kira. Just like Lisa. The thought of Jennifer being used in that way made Jimmy furious.

He set the files aside and leaned back in his chair. The sun was disappearing behind the city rooftops. The case seemed to have run cold, with many pieces still missing from the puzzle. It frustrated Jimmy that Den Mother might actually get away with these unspeakable crimes. Jimmy was about the close the folder when his desk phone rang. He picked up the receiver and heard Lin's urgent voice on the other end.

"Jimmy? Thank goodness I got a hold of you. First I want to say how sorry I am about Jennifer. Are you okay?"

"I'm taking it pretty hard, Lin. But let's not talk about that right now. I need to get my mind off it, if only for a little while. How's the research? Find anything?"

"You won't believe what I found on that mirror."

"Give me every detail," he said, his interest piqued. "Whatever you can tell me at this point would be helpful."

"All right then." Lin cleared her throat. "The Mirror of Princess Mayumi, or Mayumi-Hime no Kagami, has quite a history attached to it. Legend has it that the mirror was enchanted, and every five-hundredth summer, when the full

July moon is at its apex, whoever stares at their reflection in the moon's light shall become immortal. Legend also says that the mirror belonged to a Japanese princess named Mayumi Tanaka in the early 1500s. It was a gift from her father, the warlord Kagerou Tanaka."

"Immortality, huh?" Jimmy chuckled. "Okay, go on."

"In June of 1515, before she could take part in the mirror's ritual that would have taken place that following July, Princess Mayumi was killed during a siege on Tanaka castle. Then the mirror was lost. Centuries later, in 1955, the mirror was found in an archeological dig just outside Kyoto, Japan. The archeologist who found it, Toriyasu Seto, confirmed it was indeed the lost mirror of Princess Mayumi.

"The incredible find soon made Seto famous throughout Japan. However, two months after the mirror was found, it mysteriously disappeared from the archeologist's office in Tokyo. The local authorities attributed the disappearance to burglary. The mirror was lost again for almost eleven years, until in 1966 it arrived at an old man's antiques shop in Benton, New Jersey. The seller refused to put his name on the paperwork and accepted very little cash in exchange. It was almost as if he wanted to get rid of it."

"Weird," Jimmy said. "Interesting, but weird."

"Wait, there's more," Lin said. "One night, the shop was robbed and the owner killed by a gang of local criminals. One of the things taken was the mirror. Though Vincent claimed he purchased the mirror from an antiques gallery in New York several years later, I think it may have been Vincent's men who robbed the shop all those years ago."

"I wouldn't doubt it," Jimmy said.

"Now this is where it gets even better: according to my research, soon after the rediscovery of the mirror in '55, there were two families voicing their claim to the mirror. First was the Tanaka family, obviously, and second was the family who claimed the mirror was stolen from them by the warlord Tanaka during a raid on their village. This family also said the mirror went under a different name: Mirror of the Silver Dragons. Now, do you remember the woman doctor who treated Jenny at the institute? Well, you're never going to believe this, but the name of the other family claiming ownership of the mirror was…"

When Jimmy heard the name, he knew she was right, although he found it hard to believe. He thanked Lin for the info and started making some calls.

A day later, Mei Tachibana was heading for her homeland of Japan, crossing the Pacific Ocean in a Boeing 747 jet. The many passengers sitting on the plane around her went about their business, laughing, talking, coughing, and sleeping—a typical long, monotonous flight through the friendly skies. She sat alone in her row, staring quietly out the small window to her left as the fluffy white clouds passed by below. On her lap sat a silver briefcase.

Mei reached into her black leather jacket and took out a photograph. A slight smile crossed her features as she looked at it. The photo showed a sunny day in Okinawa, Japan, about five years before. Mei and her triplet sister Mari were smiling together on a street corner after a long day of having fun at the beach.

They had been so young and carefree on that April day in the southern heat. It was a week before a very important trip that would take them to New Jersey, USA. Both of them would go there, but only one would return alive.

Mei put the photo away and opened the briefcase. Inside was a red Han'nya mask with its fine, polished surface shining in the sunlight that poured through the window. She took out the mask and set it aside for a moment. Underneath was the mirror once known as Mayumi-Hime no Kagami.

She held up the mirror and gazed into it intently. Seeing her smile reflected back at her, she said quietly, "Ninja do not forgive nor forget. The Scorpiones were formidable, yes..." She paused as she placed both items back into the briefcase and closed it. "But we Tachibana are just a bit more clever."

"Clever, huh?" a voice said from the aisle to her right.

She looked up, and her eyes widened with surprise at the sight of the man sitting down next to her. "Detective Ziminski?" She placed both hands protectively on the briefcase.

Jimmy gave her a charming smile. "It's funny you should know my name, Doctor Tachibana, seeing as we've never met before."

"Oh, but I've heard so much about you from Jennifer, I feel like I know you. She also showed me a picture or two."

"Hmm, I see." Jimmy nodded grimly. "You know she's dead, right?"

"Yes, it's such a shame. My condolences—I know you were like family to her. I never would have thought she could be one of the assassins."

"Now that's funny as well, since we haven't released that information to the public yet. How did you know?"

Mei looked slightly away, as if to hesitate, but then she met his eyes once more and gave him a devious smile.

"Planning to arrest me, James? That will be difficult, since we're out of Benton's jurisdiction."

"That's exactly why I brought my friend along," he said, motioning to someone behind them. An older man with a narrow, pronounced nose and dark, slicked-back hair, walked up and sat down next to Jimmy in the aisle seat. "Mei, I'd like you to meet Jean-Pierre Bardot, International Police."

"Bonjour, Mademoiselle." Jean-Pierre gave her a wide smile.

"When we contacted his agency and gave them the information we had," Jimmy continued, "a few red flags popped up in their database. It seems that fourteen months ago there was a series of murders in a town called Adrano in Sicily. An entire family was wiped out, starting with a Mr. Federico Falzone. The next to be killed was his son, Micheli. Then Micheli's two sons, Angilu and Ginu. The interesting part is, they all just happened to be close relatives to Vincent Scorpione. The mysterious assassin, according to one eye witness, was wearing a gray suit and white animal mask. Sound familiar?"

Mei maintained her composure, staring hard at her manicured fingernails. Jean-Pierre handed Jimmy a case file, and the American detective flipped through a few pages before going on.

"Now, according to an investigation by local police, you were tutoring three teenage girls in algebra in the same town during the same time the killings took place. All of the girls, by the way, turned up dead within a couple of days of the killings. One died of a heart attack, another of a severe brain hemorrhage, and the third died from possible severe anemia or an otherwise unknown blood abnormality. That last one is still being written about in medical journals to this day."

Jimmy studied Mei carefully, but she refused to react.

"From accounts of their families and peers, during the week leading up to their deaths, these three girls demonstrated extreme irritability, aggression, and unnatural strength. Of course, your connection to the three girls made you a person of interest in the case, but before the local authorities could question you, you had already fled back to Tokyo."

Jean-Pierre handed Jimmy several other files as he continued. "As you can see, this pattern of killings repeats itself several times within the past five years. The Mazzini family in Rome, the Botticelli family in Florence, the Modena family in Venice, and the Verga family in Milan are among the most notable. In each case, you were there at the same time the killings took place. First you were a high school math teacher, then a college professor of psychology, then a Japanese language teacher, and even a guidance counselor. Every role you assumed gave you the opportunity to recruit teenage girls to commit serial murder."

"You have no proof," Mei said quietly, not meeting his gaze.

"As for the Benton incident, we were lucky you waited a couple of days to avoid suspicion. Apparently learning from your mistakes didn't help you in this case, as it gave us enough time to hop on the same flight as you. Now, setting aside all the connections in Sicily and Italy, the sight of the mirror in your hands just now pretty much makes this a closed case. It's the Mirror of Princess Mayumi, correct?"

Her hands tightened on the silver case, and Jimmy grinned. "According to Japanese historical records, the one other family claiming ownership over the mirror, besides the Tanaka, were the Tachibana."

Chapter Thirty-Five

Mei turned to look directly into Jimmy's eyes. "Well done, James. I am very impressed. Of course you couldn't have figured it all out without the help of… what was her name? Ah, yes, Lin Misaki, your little investigative journalist."

Jimmy felt a tug of fear on his heart at her mention of Lin's name.

"Surprised?" Mei said. "You must remember—ninja are masters at information gathering as well. Don't worry, though. We have no interest in killing her. Rest assured she is safe, for now."

James felt his heart relax. Yet his curiosity grew. "There's one more thing I need to know, Den Mother."

She didn't flinch at the name he called her. "Which is?"

"Jennifer. How did you recruit her? I spoke to the institute staff; they confirmed that she was monitored twenty-four hours a day."

"Simple. I hacked the security camera system. I was able to stop the feed and put it on a loop any time I wanted. You should have seen her, James. So intelligent, agile, and ruthless: the ideal embodiment of vengeance. She just needed to be cured of her mental illness. After I succeeded in doing that, I told her the truth about who killed her father, and everything else fell into place. Plus the beauty of the serum I give my girls is that it bypasses ninja skills and prowess with pure speed and brute strength—perfect if I need to recruit in a pinch."

"You're a monster," Jimmy said in disgust.

She ignored his comment. "Jennifer was my greatest accomplishment. I am so proud of what she did. Not only did she avenge her father's murder, she avenged my sister's as well."

"Then it really was you who broke into Vincent's home. Your sister was the one who was shot."

"Yes, we wanted to take back what rightfully belonged to us. I didn't see Jonathan's gun in time. My sister, Mari, jumped in front of me and took the bullet. I ditched the mirror on the couch, dropped a smoke grenade and got her the hell out of there. She was bleeding badly from her chest. I tried so hard to get her back to our base in time to save her with our advanced medical equipment, but it was too late. She died in my arms less than a mile from Vincent's mansion. It was then I swore that Jonathan Scorpione would die, along with all his blood relatives."

"Be that as it may, you're still a murderer, and I'm taking you in."

She opened her briefcase again. As Jimmy looked upon the red Han'nya mask, anxiety rose in him.

"What's wrong, James?" Mei asked in a mocking tone. "Are you remembering the last time we met, that cold night on the top floor of the Tombstone? My hand around your throat as a feeling of helplessness gripped your soul? Not easy to forget, is it?"

"There are innocent people on this flight," Jimmy reasoned. "I ask you to please come with us quietly. No one needs to get hurt. We already have a plane waiting at Narita International Airport. From there, you'll be taken to Lyon, France, where your case will be heard and, if you are found guilty of these crimes, you will be given the appropriate sentence."

"Mm-hm." She nodded. "You mentioned innocent people, James. Where are they?"

"They're all around us. Look—" Jimmy realized, to his surprise, that the three of them were surrounded by empty seats. "What the—there were over one hundred passengers on this plane!" Baffled, Jimmy rose from his seat and looked up and down the aisle. "I saw them. Where are they?"

Mei let out an amused laugh. "They were never here. Understand, James, you see only what I want you to see." She called out toward the flight attendant's lounge. "Isn't that right, Illyana?"

A woman emerged from behind the closed curtain. As she walked slowly toward them down the aisle, the elusive passengers appeared and disappeared, over and over again.

While Jimmy was distracted, Mei moved to the center seat next to Jean-Pierre. He seemed suspicious of this, but Mei showed him a friendly smile and gently patted his hand, causing him to lower his guard once more. The Frenchman soon turned his attention back to Jimmy and Illyana.

"What the hell is going on?" Jimmy drew his Beretta. "Illyana, or whatever your name is, stay right where you are."

Before Jean-Pierre could reach for his own weapon, Mei grabbed hold of his head and quickly snapped his neck.

"No!" Jimmy yelled. He pointed his gun at Mei.

Illyana materialized next to Jimmy, ripped the gun from his fingers, and crushed it in her hand.

"How did you do that?" Jimmy slowly backed away. "Did you get the serum from Mei as well?"

"Actually, it is the other way around." Illyana grabbed him with one hand and lifted him up by the front of his coat. "She got the serum from me. More specifically, she derived it from my blood. You see, I have lived a very long time; my kind often do."

"Huh? What the hell are you talking about?"

That was when Jimmy caught sight of two sharp points gleaming in her smile: fangs. "Oh, you've got to be kidding me," Jimmy shouted. "This is insane!"

Mei stood up and got close to Jimmy as he struggled to free himself from Illyana's grip. "Seeing is believing, James. Isn't that what they say in your country?"

"You know what else they say in my country, Mei?" As he spoke, Jimmy quickly reached into his coat pocket and took out a flash bang grenade. Then he pulled the pin and dropped it several feet away. "Yippie ki-yay!"

Jimmy closed his eyes and turned his head from the impending flash. The grenade exploded, and Jimmy was immediately dropped to the floor. He opened his eyes to see Mei stumbling back, blinded, but otherwise unharmed. Illyana however, let out screams of intense pain, as second degree burns became visible on her exposed skin.

While they were distracted, Jimmy grabbed the SP 2022 pistol from inside Jean-Pierre's coat and set his sights on Mei. "Don't move!" he commanded. "I'm taking you both in, one way or the other."

Mei recovered her vision quickly and glared at Jimmy. Illyana's burns were already starting to disappear. Jimmy had to be careful where he aimed. He didn't want to blow out a window and lose cabin pressure.

Seemingly losing her patience, Mei dashed forward in an attempt to grab the gun, but before she could reach him, Jimmy fired off three shots, each of which Mei dodged easily in an amazing display of speed and agility. She grabbed the gun from him, hit the safety and slipped it into her coat pocket.

When Jimmy saw Mei reach her free hand for his neck, he ducked, rolled to his right and dashed to the neighboring aisle. Jimmy had flown in this type of aircraft before. Ahead of him, past the curtain and at the end of the next section was the staircase leading up to the second level business class and the cockpit. If he could dodge the two women long enough to reach the captain, they could radio for help.

Mei and Illyana soon moved behind him, blocking his retreat. No turning back, Jimmy ran forward. He threw the curtain aside and pushed on into the next section which was also devoid of passengers.

As he made it a couple rows up, something dark appeared in the corner of his eye to his left. It was Illyana running toward him fast with her fist raised ready to pummel him. Jimmy did a forward summersault just in time. Her fist missed him and ripped right through an aisle seat.

He looked forward only to see Mei standing before him. She quickly spun with a roundhouse kick for his head, which he also narrowly avoided by bending down to the floor. As Mei recovered, Jimmy tipped her over with a forward push. She barely was able to catch herself. Meanwhile, Jimmy reached into her pocket, grabbed Jean-Pierre's pistol and slipped past her.

Jimmy ran up the spiral stairs. His reflexes were still pretty sharp. His body however was starting to feel the strain of age. He was no longer that nineteen year old kid fighting the ground war in the Persian Gulf. Now he had to fight smarter, not harder.

He looked over at the business class seats. No one there either. Ahead was the cockpit. The door of course would be locked for security as well as bulletproof. His best chance would be to bang on the door and get the pilot's attention through the camera above. But the women were fast and strong. He may have to try something more desperate.

Illyana floated up the steps seemingly on a cushion of air as Mei followed close behind. Arriving at the cockpit door, Jimmy looked at the gun in his hand, disengaged the safety and checked the magazine, which was three cartridges shy of full. He looked to his right and left and saw he had plenty of room to maneuver.

Illyana centered her sights on Jimmy who stood ready directly in front of the cockpit door.

"This has gone on long enough." Mei called to Illyana. "Kill him!"

Jimmy showed no fear, beckoning her to come at him. Illyana grinned as sharp black claws grew from her fingers. Reaching her hand back, she shot right at Jimmy.

But Jimmy was crafty. He pulled out a second flash grenade, removed the pin, jumped to the side to avoid Illyana and tossed the grenade right at Mei.

Illyana crashed through the door as Mei was temporarily distracted by the flash. The pilots were shocked and confused by this strange woman tearing into their cockpit. Illyana's hand was stuck in the door and she tried to get it out. Seeing Jimmy appear in the doorway with his gun raised, she thought quickly and used the door to block his following two shots at her.

Becoming frustrated with the door, she went into a rage. Swinging her arms desperately this way and that, she finally freed herself of the door. Unfortunately the pilot and copilot were ripped to shreds by the twisted metal of the door in the process. Most of the console had been torn up as well.

Jimmy noticed Mei suddenly come from behind, and his military reflexes went into action. He grabbed the wrist of Mei's hand reaching for his neck, repositioned himself and threw her over his shoulder into Illyana.

Jimmy felt a sudden sense of weightlessness. They were losing altitude. From the looks on their faces, the other two must have also realized what had happened. Illyana's rage must have damaged the navigation computer and the autopilot.

The plane took a nose dive. Illyana disappeared. Uneasily setting their differences aside, Mei and Jimmy knew the greater danger at hand had to be dealt with. They had to right the plane's angle of descent, and fast. A crash into the Pacific Ocean would not end well.

Mei kicked the pilot's body aside, hopped into his seat, and grabbed the plane's yoke. Jimmy stood in the doorway, trying to hold on as best he could. Mei struggled hard with the yoke, but to no avail.

"The controls aren't responding!"

Jimmy pointed at the long deep slash marks across the control panel. "Look!"

"Yes I know—everything must have shorted out!" she screamed. Through the windows they could see the ocean coming up fast. "There's no way we can right this thing."

"There must be something we can do," Jimmy yelled over the loud rumbling of the plane.

A sad expression came over her face, and she looked back at Jimmy. "There is something I can do. Illyana—take him out of here!"

Illyana appeared behind Jimmy and grabbed him by the shoulders.

Mei gave him a tragic smile. "I can do at least one good thing in my rotten life." Mei looked at Illyana. "Illyana, you may not have given birth to me, but you still showed me a mother's love. And for that I will always be grateful. Give Father my love."

Illyana simply gave her a silent nod.

"Wait!" Jimmy shouted. He could feel himself moving backwards as Illyana began to carry him. "No, Mei! She can save you too."

Mei just shook her head. "No, I don't want her to. Goodbye, James."

Illyana pulled Jimmy away from Mei. He struggled as best he could against her strength, but it was useless. His surroundings moved by so quickly, and then the emergency exit blew open and he was floating high in the open sky in Illyana's arms.

What the hell? We're not falling and she's not wearing a parachute, Jimmy thought, noticing he hadn't felt a sharp descent yet. *Are we floating? How is this possible? What is this woman—a demon? A vampire? Wait, she said the serum came from her blood and it's obvious she can fly. That's how the assassins were able to jump so far and so high! They were defying gravity.*

The sun had already set in the west, painting the horizon in brilliant yellows, reds, and purples. The air was cold as the wind blew hard against them. Below, Jimmy could see the jet quickly descending toward the water. Down and down it went, until inevitably it crashed hard into the ocean.

Jimmy felt painful anguish as he watched the wreckage slowly spread out across the choppy waters.

"Why didn't you save her?" he shouted against the wind.

"It was her wish. I suppose it was her way of atoning for all she has done."

"She said you were like a mother to her. Didn't you even give a damn about her?"

"Of course I did. You must understand, I was never able to have children of my own. Mei and her two sisters were the closest I ever could have come to having daughters of my own. And I loved them as dearly as if they were truly mine. Mei had endured so much in her life, and though it deeply pained me to do so, I granted her dying wish—because I loved her. So don't you dare lecture me on the subject of parenthood, James Ziminski!"

Jimmy remained silent. A long moment passed as they watched the scene below. Then Jimmy felt Illyana's hand cover his eyes.

"What are you doing?" he asked.

"Forgive me, Detective Ziminski, but you must sleep now. I promise, once you awake, everything will be fine."

"Hold on—" Jimmy called out, but it was already too late. He could feel himself going back to that deep, dark abyss of unconsciousness.

Jimmy awoke to the sound of his cell phone ringing. He sat up and realized he had been lying on one of the benches in a terminal at JFK airport. The sight of the Medalist Bar directly across from him was a dead giveaway. He looked around and saw that he was at Gate 5. He took out his phone and hit the answer button.

"Jimmy!" It was Freddy Williams's voice on the other end. "I've been trying to get a hold of you for hours. What happened?"

"Freddy, you wouldn't believe me if I told you. What's going on?"

"It's about that Interpol guy you met with earlier, the guy who was supposed to be with you on the plane."

Jimmy remembered how Mei had snapped Jean-Pierre's neck like a twig.

"Yeah, about him—"

"I figured you'd want to know we found him dead."

"What? So soon? But he went down with the plane. How could he—"

"Plane? Jimmy, we found him hanging from the WNJA radio tower downtown at around midnight. He had two puncture wounds in his neck and what looked like claw marks on his arms. The body was completely drained of blood. I figured since you two were supposed to get on the plane together, and he turned up dead, you were too busy chasin' after his killer to answer your phone."

"But that's impossible..." Jimmy felt a spinning swirl of confusion come over him. Outside the windows, he could see the eastern sky getting brighter. Soon it would be dawn. How long had he been out? Besides that, the amazing things he'd experienced on the jet—he had witnessed them, hadn't he? Then he noticed a gate agent at Gate 5, checking people onto their departing flight.

"Freddy, I'll call you back." He hung up the phone and rushed to the gate agent, cutting ahead of several people waiting in line, and flashed his badge to her. "Excuse me, ma'am. My name is Detective James Ziminski. I'm hoping you can help me."

The agent raised her eyebrows disapprovingly when she saw that he'd shoved ahead of several people. But after she'd inspected his badge, she said, "What can I help you with, Detective?"

"I need you to trace a flight that left here yesterday morning. It was flight 2947, direct to Narita International Airport, Tokyo, Japan."

"Give me one moment please." She stepped behind the information desk, punched the numbers into the database, and within seconds the information came up. "Got it. It landed at Narita about six hours ago."

"What? That's impossible."

She showed him the screen. "There it is, clear as crystal."

Jimmy read the information. Sure enough, the plane had arrived at 8:05 p.m. Tokyo time. He took a few uncertain steps back. "Um, thank you for your time."

He walked slowly back toward the benches. Suddenly he felt someone bump into him. He looked down and saw a young Japanese woman in business attire, wearing large round glasses. Her hair was done up in a neat, fashionable twist. "Oh, please excuse me, sir!" She bowed apologetically.

"Don't worry about it. I should've been watching where I was going."

The woman nodded with a kind smile before disappearing into the crowd. Jimmy sat back down on the bench, trying to wrap his head around what had happened. None of it made sense. He'd seen the plane go down with his own two eyes. He'd felt the cold air over the Pacific, smelled the ocean.

Jimmy slid his phone back into his pocket. But at the bottom of the pocket, he could feel something else—a folded piece of paper. He pulled it out, opened it, and read: *You only see what I want you to see. Sayonara, James.* The bottom was signed "M," and next to it was a small drawing of a Han'nya mask, winking at him. He jumped up and ran over to where the Japanese woman had bumped into him. Looking in all directions over the crowd, he couldn't see her anywhere. *Damn it! Where did she go?* He thought. *She must've planted the note when I bumped into her.*

After accepting the fact that he'd lost the strange woman, Jimmy dialed Lin's number.

"Jimmy? Are you in Japan?" was her first question.

"No, I think I missed my flight." Jimmy fell silent for a moment. "She's gone—Mei somehow slipped right through my fingers. She also got away with all the evidence connecting her to the case—the demon mask and the mirror."

"She may have gotten away this time, but sooner or later you'll catch her. And I'll be right there to help you."

He smiled. "I know you will. Say, Lin, how about we discuss the details of the case over dinner tonight? Seven sound good?"

There was a brief pause on her end. Then he heard a tone of pleasant surprise in her voice. "Dinner, huh? It's been a while. Sure, I'd like that. I'll see you then."

Epilogue

Two weeks had passed since Jennifer's death. It was December, and the days were colder than ever. Overcast skies blotted out the warm sun on this icy cold afternoon. Fine powdery snow had fallen steadily since morning, resulting in almost half a foot so far.

In St. Francis Cemetery on the far edge of town, the snow crunched beneath their feet as Pat and Stephanie walked slowly between the gravestones. Stephanie was relieved to have finally gotten out of the hospital two days before. Recovery after the surgery would be long and hard for her.

But nothing could be harder than what she had to do now: saying her final goodbyes to her sister. She carried with her a fresh bouquet of bellflowers.

They arrived at Jennifer's gravestone. Stephanie was shaken by the sight of it—such a beautiful stone dedicated to the memory of her sister. Her uncle Jimmy had pitched in quite a lot of money to have it made. The staff at the institute had made several generous donations as well.

The craftsmanship was well worth it. The stone was black marble with a polished finish in which she could see her refection. Etched in the upper right and left corners were elegant designs of angel wings. The epitaph read:

Jennifer Lynn Sebastiano

May 15th, 1996

November 28th, 2013

Loving Daughter

Dearest Sister

May She Finally Find Peace

Stephanie laid the bouquet at the foot of the stone. She took a deep breath as she tried to hold back her tears. Pat gently wrapped his arm around her shoulders to help give her strength.

She closed her eyes and remembered all those happy times with her sister. Building a sand castle on the beach with their father, a fun day at a baseball game, and even the time she'd won the trophy at the gymnastics tournament. Her sister had been right there next to her, always smiling, laughing, or comforting Stephanie.

When they were young children, both their appearance and their personalities were almost indistinguishable, identical in every way. But as they grew older, they had slowly changed. By the time they were teenagers, though they were still the same in appearance, their personalities had become completely opposite. Jennifer was bold, whereas Stephanie was reserved. Jennifer was quick to anger, while Stephanie was mild-mannered and peaceful.

Stephanie still wondered why, though. Why had she pursued forgiveness while her sister Jennifer had become obsessed with vengeance? Where had things gone wrong? She might never know. All she knew was that the one person who'd been closest to her all her life was gone forever.

She knelt down carefully, favoring her midsection, which still ached from the surgery. She was silent for a long time, uncertain what to say. Then she found the words and began to speak softly.

"Jennifer, I miss you." A tear rolled down her cheek. "You didn't deserve this, sis. You didn't deserve any of it—our father's death, the car crash, your psychotic break. It was all just thrown at you, one thing after another. It just wasn't fair. And you took our father's death the hardest of all of us. Maybe that's why you wanted revenge so badly. You thought it was the only way to ease the pain of loss in your heart. I just wish there was something I could've done to prevent this, some way I could've helped you."

She felt Pat's tender touch on her shoulder.

"You did everything you could, Steph." Pat said solemnly. "Don't blame yourself."

"But I do!" she looked at him, full of pain. "We were sisters, alike in so many ways. Why couldn't I see into her heart better? Why couldn't I see a way to save her?"

"You already know the answer, don't you?" Pat knelt down beside her. "Even though you were twins, you were still individuals, too, walking your own unique paths. Unfortunately, those paths went in opposite directions."

His words comforted Stephanie. She smiled and let out a short laugh. "So when did you become all philosophical?"

"Hey, there's more to me than just my striking good looks, you know."

She laughed a little louder, and her smile grew brighter. Pat moved closer, and they embraced lovingly.

"There's that beautiful laugh I've missed so much," Pat said. "Everything is going to be all right, Steph. I promise."

"Thank you, Pat." She held him closer than ever, and her voice became a whisper. "Don't ever leave me. Stay with me forever."

Pat moved back and gently wiped the tears from her cheeks. "I will never, ever leave you, Steph. I'll always be right here by your side, now and forever."

They shared a long moment together as the gentle snow silently fell around them. Then Stephanie broke the silence. "I have to confess… ever since my father's death, I've been harboring feelings of revenge. But those feelings have weighed heavy on my soul. I don't like violence, and I'm strongly against killing. I don't agree with what the Scorpiones did to my father, but I forgive them. It's the only way I can finally let go and move on with my life. So I forgive them."

Pat moved back, showed her a gentle smile, and nodded in understanding.

Then they stood and said their goodbyes to the departed.

"Take care, Jennifer," Pat said. "I wish I could've known you a little better. Maybe we would have become good friends."

Stephanie reached down and ran her fingers along the surface of the stone. "My dear sister Jennifer, I love you so much, and—"

Suddenly, the world around Stephanie became a whirlwind of white feathers, and her surroundings changed. She found herself in the Scorpione mansion's main hallway. The ceiling, the floor, everything seemed to have an unearthly shimmer. All around her, the feathers fell. Only now they were joined with feathers the color of ravens. As she stared at the main entrance, she heard a familiar voice come from behind her.

"Hello, sis."

Stephanie turned, and the sight brought a tear to her eye. "Jennifer?"

There before her stood her sister, dressed in the assassin's outfit. She could see several blood stains on Jennifer's suit, as well as a few specks across her cheek. Still, Jennifer gave her sister a warm and grateful smile. "It's me, Stephie."

"But how is this possible? Where are we? It looks like the Scorpione mansion, but it feels different."

Jennifer looked around them. "This is a realm beyond time and space. A place only people like you and me can visit. Right now I'm still in the past, but you're in the future. The only reason we can talk like this is because of our abilities. I can see the future, while you can see the past."

"Then you know what's going to happen. You know that…"

"Those who see their own future can become trapped by it. Yes, I know exactly where and how my story ends. But yours is just beginning, Stephie. You and Pat—you both have bright and happy lives ahead of you. I've seen it."

Stephanie ran to her sister and hugged her tight.

"Jennifer, I saw him!"

"What? Who?"

"Dad! When I almost died, I saw him at the end of the tunnel. He smiled and reassured me everything would be all right, but when I asked him about you, he looked so sad."

"I see." Jennifer smiled sorrowfully. "When you do the things I've done, I suppose there's only one place you can go, huh?"

"No!" Stephanie shook her head. "You deserve better. You didn't ask for any of this."

Jennifer slowly rubbed her sister's back to comfort her. "It's okay. I have no regrets, Stephie. I've made my choices, just as you have. The thing is, when you choose revenge, you sacrifice any chance at reaching true happiness. So don't cry for me, sis. Live your life. Don't remember how I died. Remember how I lived. Remember all the happy times we spent together. That way, whenever you think of me, you'll always smile."

They slowly moved back and stared at one another, Stephanie with a look of painful longing, and Jennifer with a warm and reassuring smile.

"Our time is getting short, I can feel it," Jennifer said.

Stephanie took her sister's hands in hers. "No, just a little longer."

"I'm sorry, Stephie. We have to say our goodbyes now. I love you so much, my sister. Be good to yourself and…" Jennifer bent close and spoke more quietly, "I already know you're gonna take good care of Patrick." She gave her sister a wink.

The warmth rising in her cheeks, Stephanie let out a laugh despite herself. "Oh, Jenny, I love you so much, and I'll miss you always." They came together in one last embrace. "Goodbye."

The feathers swirled around them once more. Jennifer disappeared from her arms, and she returned to the cold cemetery where Pat was standing beside her. He moved close and gave her shoulders a loving squeeze. "Is everything okay? You drifted off there for a minute."

Stephanie nodded as she took his hands. "Yeah, everything is going to be just fine." A gust of wind came. The snow stopped, the clouds cleared away, and the bright sun came out. Stephanie looked up at the blue sky and smiled. "Wherever you are, Sis, I pray it's a place filled with warmth, peace, and happiness. Goodbye, Jenny."

She and Pat turned and walked hand in hand down the snowy path towards the cemetery gates. What lay ahead of them was a future of endless possibilities. And that future was as bright as the light shining down from heaven above.

THE END

About the Author

Timothy O'Brien was born in Amherst, New York and raised in North Tonawanda. In his early teens he discovered his passion for artwork and sketching, bringing his imagination to paper. In his late teens, he became interested in writing. Starting out small with several short stories, he soon moved to writing full novels.

In 2001, he graduated from Niagara County Community College with a degree in Criminal Justice having studied Criminology, Abnormal Psychology and Investigation Techniques as well as Anatomy, Physiology and Forensic Anthropology.

Timothy enjoys traveling. His favorite places to visit are: Chicago for its excellent food, musical culture, and history and art museums. Toronto, Ontario for its science museum, vibrant night life, and fantastic restaurants. And finally, New Hampshire for its mountains, fresh air and great hiking.

A few of his favorite physical activities are archery, fencing, hiking, and running. He is a brown belt in Karate and stays in good shape through physical training.

Timothy has a deep appreciation of art, particularly the works of Yoshiyuki Sadamoto, H.R. Giger, Rembrandt and Alex Ross. He is interested in foreign languages, such as Spanish, Polish and Japanese, and foreign cultures, especially those of China and Japan. He also enjoys a wide variety of music genres.

On his off time, Timothy likes to watch basketball, both professional and college. His favorite teams are the Syracuse Orangemen and the Chicago Bulls. He is also a fan of professional wrestling and keeps up regularly with the WWE.

He currently lives in North Tonawanda, New York with his wife.

CPSIA information can be obtained
at www.ICGtesting.com
Printed in the USA
FFOW02n1806140616
24969FF